AF227520

TERRI LYNN THOMPSON

THE SHADOW SIDE

by Terri Lynn Thompson

Sorchae - *Gaelic for brightness.*
He represents the one true Light. His is a gentle light, full of color and nuance. His voice is quiet and soothing but sounds like the mighty rushing waters of many voices. He never shouts or demands attention. He speaks truth, and offers love, hope, direction, peace, freedom and wisdom.

"O God, by the leading of a star you manifested your only Son to the peoples of the earth: Lead us, who know you now by faith, to your presence where we may see your glory face to face, through Jesus Christ our Lord." ~from the Book of Common Prayer (ACNA 2019) Epiphany: Manifestation of Christ to the Gentiles.

PROLOGUE

Heart pounding like a drum, dark had never felt so dark, so heavy. Why couldn't Marie get up? She couldn't even open her eyes. They were heavy—stuck closed, like she was sick or something. Alone. Afraid. And so scared.

Was she going to throw up?

It wasn't that kind of sick.

Where was she? It didn't feel like her own bed.

Where was Mommy?

Scary feelings flew around in that room, alive like an evil beast.

Marie tried to call out, tried to open her eyes again. Something covered her right eye. She reached up.

Ouch. A bandage. Even touching the stuff on her eye made it hurt.

Memories came like a fast, flooded river to Marie's mind now.

She must be in the hospital.

"Mommy," she tried to call out, but her voice cracked and she couldn't swallow.

A squeak sounded from across the room.

"Hello Marie, how are we feeling?" She heard the man's footsteps come closer. The eye not under the bandage opened, and she saw a stranger in a white, long robe.

Marie tried to ask him why she was here and where Mommy was, but it didn't come out. He pushed a button, and her bed raised to make her sit. Picking up a cup of water with a bendy straw in it, he put it to Marie's lips. She took a long sip and watched how the sun came in through the blinds, slowly making light and dark stripes across the floor.

"Thank you," she whispered. "My eye hurts. Where's Mommy?"

"Just a minute." He put up one finger and glanced toward the door. When it opened, a woman wearing a badge on a ribbon around her neck came in.

"Hello Marie, I'm Miss Laura and I'm a social worker at the hospital. That just means you can talk to me about anything you don't understand or are worried about. Okay?"

Marie nodded.

"We had to remove your eye, Marie, honey. I'm sorry. It was broken badly," the doctor's voice sounded nice.

It didn't make sense.

"Where did you move it?" She touched her face.

"We had to take it out, sweetie." His eyes looked shiny. Miss Laura's eyes looked a little shiny too and she looked away.

The muscles in her body kind of shook, and her stomach felt weird. He put his fingers in her hand and squeezed. Their hands together felt strange but good. Mommy had done that before—squeezed her hand.

Marie didn't know eyes could come out. Did she have a hole in her face? "When can you put it back?"

"Oh, no, dear. We can't put it back." The doctor's face scrunched and looked sad, maybe Marie should be sad too. She felt like crying.

"Does Mommy know? Where is she?" Her eye that wasn't bandaged stung and water filled it. And the one under the bandage hurt more.

The doctor looked at Miss Laura.

"She's not here, Marie," she answered instead of the doctor.

"When will she be back?"

"Uh…" The doctor looked at the door, then back to Marie. "I'll let Miss Laura talk to you about that. I need to visit some other patients."

Miss Laura moved closer to Marie's bed and sat in the chair beside it. "When your mother brought you in, I think she was afraid she might get in trouble. She left after signing you in. We haven't been able to get in touch with her."

Miss Laura stayed with Marie a little longer. They didn't say anything. When she left, the room felt cold and big and empty again. Marie shivered and pulled the blanket up to her chin.

Soon, her left eyelid wouldn't stay open anymore, so she closed it.

When she woke up, Marie thought about not having an eye on one side. About not seeing on that side. What would it be like? A knot caught in her throat.

Now she couldn't see with her other eye either. Why?

Maybe they moved that one too, when she fell asleep. Her heart pounded again, and she cried.

The dark was big. So dark. Icky feelings filled the air around Marie. Sometimes they sat on her chest, making it hard to breathe.

It felt like the dark would break her heart and she would die.

You will die in this hospital bed, and your Mommy will never see you again, the dark said. It said other stuff too, like, *You're blind. You'll never see anything again.* The dark said that stuff into her ear.

Marie lay awake as the dark got bigger in her room. It filled the room so there was no more space, not even enough to move around in the bed. She couldn't move. But she could blink.

So, she did.

Marie stared into the black, scary sky above her head, beyond the ceiling. She stared, but she couldn't see.

So black.

So dark.

So scary.

So alone.

Then, looking way up, she saw something… a teeny spot of light. Like a firefly outside on a dark night. It came closer and seemed friendly—one little starlight coming down to Marie to make her feel better. And it winked at her like stars do.

I'll be with you always, the little star told her in her heart. She hoped it was true.

Feeling a little better, she tried to move her head. It worked, so she turned toward the door.

A small light from the hall, not much more than a night light, shone through a tiny crack between the door and the floor.

She sucked in a breath. Would she have been able to see that if they had taken her other eye out? It felt better to know she still had one. Better, but…

Where was Mommy? Marie felt so lonely without her.

Maybe she'd be alone forever? She gulped and swallowed.

Mr. Johnson's face flashed in her mind. She didn't need any eyes to see him in her head. Why had he been so mad?

Mommy had looked happy. She said Mr. Johnson wanted to marry her, that they were going to have a beautiful wedding, and Marie would get to be the flower girl and walk down the aisle with her.

Marie couldn't wait to wear a special dress and carry flowers in a pretty church. She'd only been in church two times. Both times she felt safe and happy.

"I can't go out with you tonight. I don't have a babysitter," Marie heard Mommy say to Mr. Johnson.

Marie remembered how sad he looked and she felt bad.

"We need to get used to her being with us," Mr. Johnson had told Mommy. "Let's take her with us."

"To the drive-in?" Mommy seemed like she didn't want Marie to go. But Marie wanted to go. She was a big girl now, cuz she turned three on her last birthday. She wanted to go with Mommy.

Mommy agreed.

Marie had skipped to the car. She'd get to see a movie outside. Mommy said most towns didn't have those places anymore.

Pain shot through Marie's right eye again. She reached her hand up and laid it like a cup over the bandage. Pressing down soft-like, she felt the empty space…

And empty in her heart, remembering the rest of that night. Scared in the backseat all alone, Marie tried to get in the front with Mommy. Mr. Johnson wanted her to stay in the back. When she tried again, he grabbed her and threw her in the back seat. Then he got out of the car, opened her back door, and dragged her out of the car. He hit her in the face. She couldn't remember how many times. Mommy screamed. One punch got her in the eye.

After that, Marie only remembered screaming and laying her head on Mommy's lap. "It's okay, Marie, baby." Mommy held a towel to Marie's face. "It's going to be okay."

The car went very fast. Then she saw the super bright lights of the hospital, and blood on her favorite bunny shirt.

"Her mother hasn't even been here," a woman's voice out in the hall broke into Marie's thinking. "She just brought her in, then disappeared after filling out the forms, minus her own information."

"Probably afraid she'd go to jail," a man's voice said. They talked soft, but the night was so quiet that Marie heard them.

"We had to report it," the woman's voice said. "Social Services will take her case now." Then shuffling feet sounded in the hall.

She learned tears could still come from the eye they moved cuz the nurses had to come change her bandage when she cried.

They tried to calm her, saying nice things. Sometimes it helped.

"Marie, I know you're scared," a nurse woman, older than Mommy, said. "But did you know God loves you?" Marie heard that at Sunday school once when she went to the big, pretty church with a neighbor.

"Uh-huh."

"It's true." The nurse's eyes were big like blue moons, and her arms lay across her large belly in front. "And no matter what happens, God will never leave you or forsake you."

Marie didn't know what "sake" meant, but she liked that God would not leave her alone. She felt so alone here.

"Even if you think it's the worst thing that could ever happen to you, your loving Heavenly Father will be there right with you."

"I don't have a father." Marie knew that.

"I'm talking about God." The nurse smiled. "He's the Father of everyone in the world. He made everyone, and he loves every person that he made."

Marie liked the words the nurse said. "What's your name?"

"I'm Mrs. Buttons. Yes, ma'am, just like the buttons on a shirt."

Marie smiled, but when Mrs. Buttons left the room, she felt lonely and scared again. Miss Laura had come to talk with Marie several times, but Marie liked Mrs. Buttons better. She knew how to make her smile, and when she talked about God, Marie felt safe.

A bunch of days went by, and Mommy never came. Marie missed her so much that it made her eye hurt more.

The nurses must've felt sorry for Marie being in that room all alone all the time because they took her out of her room and let her walk around and see some other kids in the hospital. She liked talking to them and tried to cheer them up if they looked sad. Sometimes she let them hold the soft bunny Mrs. Buttons bought her at the gift shop.

"You have visitors coming today," Mrs. Buttons announced to Marie one morning as she opened the curtains to let the sunshine in.

"Mommy?" Marie couldn't wait to see her. She'd be able to tell Mommy everything that happened to her and to her eye. Maybe Mommy would take her home. Excitement filled Marie, then suddenly not-excitement came and she got a yucky feeling in her stomach. She didn't want to see Mr. Johnson.

"No, dearie." The nurse looked sad then and sat next to Marie on her bed. "Didn't Miss Laura talk to you about this?"

Marie nodded. Miss Laura said something about the legals, a judge and Mommy, but Marie didn't understand it.

"Your Mommy can't come see you, sweetheart. She let you get hurt, so they won't let her take care of you anymore."

She wasn't going to see Mommy anymore. Why? "Mommy didn't hurt me." Tears felt hot on her cheeks.

"I know, dear. But if she is with the man who hurt you, you could get hurt again. They can't let that happen."

Would Marie live in the hospital forever now? It seemed like she'd been there so long already. Would Nurse Buttons be her mommy? The sun still came through the sheer curtains, but the room seemed darker.

"A new mommy and daddy are coming to meet you today." The nurse brightened into a smile, like it was the best news ever.

"A new mommy and a *daddy*?" Would they be nice? What if they were mean? What would it be like to have a daddy? Would he be like Mr. Johnson? "Will they like me?"

"They will love you, Dear." Mrs. Buttons seemed sure.

"Will the daddy hurt me like Mr. Johnson?"

"Absolutely not. You will be his precious little princess."

She was going to be a princess?

"And never forget that your Heavenly Father will be with you, too. Wherever you go."

Marie smiled. Mrs. Buttons meant God would be with her. A lump formed in her throat. But what about her own mommy?

That afternoon, after lunch, Marie drew crayon circles on paper. A noise made her look up.

"Marie?" A woman with long dark hair spoke her name. She was pretty and smiley.

"Hi, I'm Arie, and this is Bud. But you can call us Mommy and Daddy if you want."

"We're so happy you'll be part of our family." Bud had dark hair, too. He was a lot taller than Arie. His face was nice, and he had eyes that looked like love—not like Mr. Johnson's.

"I'm broken." They should know before they took her home. "My eye broke, and they moved it."

"We know, sweetheart." Arie came over and put her arm around Marie's shoulders. "We're sorry about your eye, but we love you just the way you are."

They loved her?

God, her Heavenly Father, loved her too. Maybe it would be enough love. But she'd still miss Mommy.

"You're my Momma and Daddy now?" Marie thought this mommy should have a different name from her mommy.

"That's right, Marie." Her new daddy held her hand. "You're going to be a Summerfield."

Marie Summerfield.

———— • ● • ————

The Summerfields had a big, white house. It looked like a mansion. Marie had her own room, but she liked to sleep on blankets on the floor in Momma and Daddy's room at first.

Nonna lived with them, too. Nonna looked like Momma but had some gray hairs in her black ones, and her skin had some crinkles, but she smiled just as big and hugged just as hard.

Nonna told Marie stories every night. Some she read, and some she made up.

"Have you ever heard the story of the wren?" She asked Marie one day.

"No."

"Wrens are small birds. They remind me of you."

"Me?" Did Marie look like a bird?

"Yes, you are like a wren."

"How?" Marie held her bunny close and snuggled up to Nonna on the couch with a cozy blanket over them.

"Wren's roost together. They like to be with their families, and they take care of each other. Wrens are adaptable to different habitats—"

"Habits?" She wrinkled her nose.

Nonna laughed. "Many birds have only one place where they build their nests and live. Eagles build their nests high in the trees. Sandpipers build their nests on the ground. But wrens can build anywhere they find a little space. Places like little holes in a tree or wall, in bushes, in hanging plant baskets, or even a mailbox."

"That's funny."

"And whereas some birds only have one or two sounds that they sing, wrens have rich complex songs. They can chatter, whistle, or trill." Nonna imitated their sounds.

"I like wrens." Marie smiled and hugged her bunny.

"Me too."

"I want to be a wren."

"You already are, my dear. You're brave, and you love to help your family. You draw and color as beautifully as a wren sings. You've also lived in different places, even hard places, and survived."

It made Marie a little sad to think about that, but proud too.

"I'm going to call you 'Wren' from now on," Nonna said.

And she did.

CHAPTER ONE

Sixteen Years Later

Tree limbs bobbed, their leaves dancing on the fall breeze beyond the divided-lite windows of Wren Marie Summerfield's college classroom. Sunbeams poured over the trees, creating varying shades of green with highlights of yellow, and shadows defining each leaf and limb.

She would probably need to use oil crayons, watercolors, or at the very least, colored pencils, to do justice to those trees on a page or canvas. Though she might capture the feel of their richness using her go-to charcoal pencils. It would only be for herself after all.

"Miss Summerfield, are you with us?"

Wren's thoughts jerked back to where she sat in the classroom, her eye shifting from the window to Ms. Carter, one of her accounting professors, who'd been droning on about individual tax law. When Wren looked her way, the professor cleared her throat. "Can you tell the class what I just said?"

Wren took a slow breath, then jerked at the sound of the computerized alarm Ms. Carter set to indicate the end of class. Literally saved by the bell.

The students jumped up and gathered their things. Ms. Carter wouldn't be able to nail her for daydreaming in front of the class this time.

Why couldn't Wren stay focused in class? It wasn't high school anymore. Her parents were paying for these classes.

Jostling her armload of books, Wren headed out of the classroom. How would she ever get through her first year of college? They'd only just started. Not yet October, and she struggled to pay attention.

She glanced down the long, sunless hallway of Fairhope Alabama's Coastal Community College—just minutes from Daphne where Wren still lived. Pausing at an art display by a former student, Wren noticed the artist had used geometric shapes in the drawing.

If only Wren could study art. But that question had been settled since fourth grade when her art teacher told her that one-eyed people couldn't be artists. "The lack of depth perception keeps them from seeing the subject as it really is," she said. So, really, the matter was settled when she was three years old and lost her right eye.

Wren could draw as a hobby, her parents often reminded her. "As long as it doesn't interfere with your studies." She just couldn't come up with a good excuse to spend $100K to study art at a university.

Accounting—ugh. Boring, but safe, and Wren would always be able to find a job. Momma was right about that. That's what Wren needed, even if it wasn't the funnest thing. She had to grow up, right? She was in college now. The future was now. No more daydreaming about art.

Wren had actively created this plan. Being an artist was out of the question for her, so it didn't matter what she did, as long as it gave her security. Accounting had seemed like a good option. A high school counselor had directed her that way when she said she had decent grades in math and wanted something she could rely on. It didn't have to be exciting, just reliable. She never expected that it would be so unexciting that she wouldn't be able to pay attention in class.

Maybe she'd try painting those incredible trees when she got home, just to relax before homework. She used oils at a friend's house a few weeks ago and loved them, but watercolors were more affordable. It wouldn't hurt to expand her media beyond charcoal, as long as she considered the cost.

"Bye, Wren. See you Monday." A classmate brushed past, startling her and breaking her focus from the framed art.

Wren nodded. "I'll be here."

She hustled down the hallway toward the outer doors leading to the parking lot and fresh air. Just inside the double doors, she stopped to wait for her best friend, Olivia Olsson, Liv for short. While she waited, Wren glanced at the community board filled with papers and business cards pinned this way and that, intended to capture students' attention.

One flyer turned her head. She lifted a paper that partially obscured it. A picture of a man holding a microphone adorned the front of the flyer, advertising him as a guest speaker—a good-looking guest speaker—on the topic of sex trafficking. She dropped that flier and perused some more.

Roommate wanted: Girl, someone who doesn't care about neatness.

Wren laughed, relieved she didn't need to find a room or a roommate. Home was the cheapest place to live. Practical. And it's what Momma and Daddy wanted. Liv had offered the extra bedroom in her apartment more times than Wren could count.

It sounded fun, but there were so many things to consider. What if she got distracted and her grades dropped? Like now? Her thoughts challenged her. What if she and Liv got sick of each other and she lost her best friend? What if her parents ran out of money and couldn't pay for her school anymore? After all, adding housing and meals would quickly cut into the pie.

Unless they couldn't pay for her housing and meals. Then where would she work to make enough money to live? And if she worked, it would be harder to keep up with her grades.

The double, metal doors squeaked as two students pushed them and headed out.

She'd stick to being practical.

Liv still hadn't gotten out of class. Maybe Wren would wait outside in the sunshine. The teacher in Liv's last class always let them out late and people in Fairhope lived for moderate, sunny days like this one.

"Oomph." Who had Wren plowed into this time? Looking up, she saw… "Mr. Cho?" What was her high school English Lit teacher doing at the community college? Easygoing, with a peaceful presence, Mr. Cho had always made Wren feel comfortable.

"Hello Wren. You can call me Bae since I'm not your teacher anymore." He shifted a stack of papers to his left arm and held out his right hand toward her. "Funny I should run into you."

She chuckled. They'd literally run into each other. "Why's that?"

"I was just thinking about you." He smiled, and the creases at the corners of his eyes deepened.

"You were?" Why on earth would a teacher from Daphne High School be thinking about Wren?

He placed the stack of papers on a narrow table against the hall wall, just underneath the community bulletin board, and handed the top page to her.

Setting her books on the table, she took the page and skimmed it. "An art contest?"

The kindness in Mr. Cho's—Bae's—eyes accompanied his genuine encouragement. Her college professors weren't as personable as the high school teachers had been.

"I remember your talent for art," he said. "I saved the shaded drawing you gave me a couple of years ago. It's on the wall of my classroom by the interactive whiteboard."

"Really?" Wren recalled that piece. It had been a chiaroscuro assignment for art class her junior year. They were to pick a subject that had something to do with their own life. She'd chosen a close-up of one eye. Since losing her right eye and getting a prosthetic at the tender age of three, her life had been affected in so many ways. Not to mention gaining new parents in the bargain.

The lack of that one little eye even dictated her field of study in college—accounting—ack! If only she had two eyes.

"Mr. Cho?" Liv's voice lilted upward as it echoed from down the hall behind Wren.

"Hello, Liv. It's nice to see you." Mr. Cho gave her a side hug as she was coming in for one anyway. Liv did that—hugged everyone. She assumed everyone loved her. And she wasn't wrong. Liv was beautiful, blue-eyed, blonde, and people loved her contagious energy. "Like I told Wren, y'all just call me Bae."

"Thanks. What are you doing at Coastal? You're not leaving Daphne High, are you? We sure could use you here, though. Wouldn't that be great, Wren?"

Wren smiled. She could never get a word in when Liv was excited about something.

When she came up for air, he answered, "I was starting to tell Wren, I'm putting these flyers out for my friend whose design company is sponsoring an art scholarship." He caught Wren's attention. "It covers the costs of classes at the winner's choice of schools, as long as they study art."

"Oh, my gosh! Really?" Liv pierced Wren with an ice-blue stare. Wren knew that look. It meant that she'd better do what Liv wanted, since she'd get her way eventually anyway. "Wren, girl, you've got to do this!" Liv turned back to Mr. Cho. "Wren avoids art. She thinks the lack of one eye keeps her from greatness. But honestly, she's the best artist I know, don't you think?"

"I'm an accounting student, Liv. Why would I need an art scholarship?"

Liv rolled her eyes at Wren, then turned her gaze on Mr. Cho. "Can you even believe that Bae? She never even liked math. This girl is an artist, am I right?"

"I was just saying how good that picture was that she gave me a couple of years ago." He turned to Wren. "Do you remember it? The charcoal shading of one eye."

Wren nodded. How could she forget? It was a close-up of one eye—her fake eye. It looked real enough. No one knew the picture was of the fake eye, but she knew. She always knew. Fake. Like her artistic ability.

"I loved how you handled the light. The image was dark," Bae continued. "With what looked like a little light shining on the eye, and down to the lower lid. But more than that, there was a haunting look in the eye, a knowing of sadness in the world."

Wren swallowed. How could someone who never knew her, except as a student in one of his classes, read her art so well?

"Don't look so surprised, Wren." Liv's blonde layers bounced as she flipped her head toward Wren. "That's how good your art is. You draw better than I sing."

"That's just not true." Wren shook her head, then glanced at Mr. Cho again.

Bae locked eyes with Wren. "You only need one eye if your whole soul sees the world."

Wren swallowed the words into her heart. Wow. She needed to ponder that for a while.

Bae tapped the flyer she still held in her hand. "Really, Wren, think it over. Pray about it. This hardly seems like a random meeting. But I won't be offended if your heart is set on being an accountant. There's absolutely nothing wrong with that. We need good ones. Lord knows I do." He laughed at his own joke.

"Nice to see you, Bae," Liv said, giving him another hug.

He leaned in to give Wren one too. The gentle hug felt like hot tea on a rainy day. Remembering his wife was Samantha O'Connor, the author of one of Wren's favorite books, she spoke up.

"Yes. And please tell your wife how much her story, *Mona and the Selkie*, meant to me. It comes to my mind so often." If only he knew how much. Wren needed to believe in a 'Sorchae,' the bright fairy that saved Mona and led her home in the end.

"I will." He smiled his wide smile, eyes almost closed. "That will make her day. And you know, Wren, Sorchae's light is for everyone. We all have dragons we need to fight, don't we?"

She nodded. "We sure do." The accounting test at the end of next week, for example. Doubtful that's what he referred to.

"Hey, did you see this flyer? They're looking for extras in a movie." Liv held the free corner of a flyer on the board. Her attention had drifted.

Wren shook her head, then turned back to Mr. Cho.

"It was nice to see you both." He waved.

"You too." Sometimes, Wren missed high school.

Mr. Cho turned to go, then stopped and turned back around. "I just remembered something else from your drawing, Wren. There's a window of light reflected in the iris of that eye."

"Yes." Why had he pointed it out?

"As if that eye perceived the smallest light in the darkest place." He smiled. "I liked that." Then he turned back toward the door.

Wren gulped down emotion. She folded the scholarship flyer and slid it into her accounting book.

"I always liked him," Liv said. "One of the good ones."

Wren nodded, then quickly turned her head to the right to make sure she wouldn't run into the door frame or anyone else on the way out. Checking had become a habit, but occasionally she still bumped into things. Her face warmed. Or people, like Mr. Cho. How humiliating.

Liv jumped in front of Wren, stopping her short.

"Hey, so, I wanted to let you know that I'm singing with a few musicians at Page and Palette tonight. Can you come?"

"Well, I should get my homework done early this weekend." She hated to think about it, but it was better to get it out of the way.

"You have the entire weekend for that." Liv draped her arm over Wren's shoulder. "Pl-e-e-a-se?"

"You're right." Why not have some fun and support her friend? After all, singing was Liv's dream. "Okay. I'll come." Liv didn't have to force her. Someone should achieve their dreams after all. Wren ducked under Liv's arm and walked outside.

"Yea!" Liv clapped and spun around, her golden hair splaying in her wake. "I'll meet you there since I have to be there early. But can you drive me home? I can ride with Bill, the drummer, but he's going somewhere afterward. Can't wait till I can get a car. I just can't affor—" Liv paused. "Better yet, you can drive me early and just hang out the whole time."

"I better just drive you home. I'll come later. I can make it by seven. My parents will want me to eat dinner with them first."

"Gotcha." Liv winked. "Hey, you should go for that scholarship."

Wren didn't take the bait. Talking about it would just make her sad.

CHAPTER TWO

Busy with their latest project, Aria and Bud Summerfield—Momma and Daddy to Wren—were outside painting the house when Wren drove into the driveway. Daddy's forehead gleamed where his still-black hair had receded. He dipped his brush into the paint can he held by the narrow metal handle and smeared paint on the house. Decked out in his paint clothes—an old pair of jeans and a white undershirt he designated for messy projects—he teased Momma about something.

The scent of pine greeted Wren when she opened the car door.

"I already told you I loved this trim color, Bud." Wren heard her mother before she saw her. "Yes. You're a genius. Okay, I admit it." A bandana held Momma's long dark hair in place. Her brown eyes flashed as she gestured with one hand in Daddy's direction. Nothing unusual about that. Mom wore her Italian heritage on her sleeve. How she stayed on that ladder and gestured with her hands like that was beyond Wren.

Daddy smiled up at her, pausing his trim work on a downstairs window, then he caught sight of Wren. "Hey, Princess." His smile grew.

"Wren Marie, my angel on earth," Momma added. Marie had become Wren Marie not long after Nonna started calling her Wren. They filled out some papers, and when they went to the probate office to make the adoption final, they submitted the papers to change her first and last names officially. She'd felt so special when they allowed her to choose her name all by herself. She'd only been five.

"It's good to see you." Momma opened both arms wide as if to hug Wren from way up on the ladder, making Wren and Daddy jump at her precarious position.

"Get your hands back on that ladder, Aria!" Daddy ordered.

Wren chuckled to herself, slowing only to lean into Daddy's hug. Then she left her parents to their painting and jogged to her room upstairs, taking two steps at a time.

Homework could wait until Saturday. Mr. Cho, or Bae, had stirred up her yearning for art. Dropping the books on her small desk, Wren crouched to her knees and reached under the bed until she felt the edge of the lid on a plastic box—her art box. Some people wrote all their feelings in a journal. Wren drew her feelings.

A little secret, a treasure just for her, though the box didn't really need to be a secret. No one forced her to quit drawing or anything. Momma and Daddy had always complimented her on her drawing skills over the years. But what did it matter if she could never make it a career? Momma encouraged her to focus on something useful. Being older and wiser, her parents knew more about the demands of life.

The rubber box lid popped when she lifted it, and Wren set it to the side. She scooted the box closer and took a cardboard cylinder from inside. She pulled the top until it slid off, then she brushed the charcoal pencils inside with her fingertips. Replacing the top of the charcoals, she set them down and took out a stack of her old drawings.

On top was one of Liv at 13. Her friend had shrieked when she'd seen it. She wanted to frame it, give it to her parents for Christmas, but Wren preferred to hide it away.

Now treasured memories, these pictures sometimes accused Wren, sometimes encouraged her. And they always tormented her, sparking the wayward desire to lose herself in art.

She ran her fingers over a tiger head profile as if she could feel its fur. This one came to her in a dream. When she woke up she sketched it out and one thought came to her, *Jesus is your strength—like a tiger inside you when you are weak and afraid.* Maybe she'd frame this one and put it on her wall. She could use the reminder.

One picture had a row of live oaks with Spanish moss hanging from their limbs. They lined a walking path that ran along Mobile Bay. Typical of coastal Alabama, Wren used trees and moss in many of her landscapes. Several of her drawings featured eyes, or just one eye, as the subject, like the one she'd given to Mr. Cho—Bae—that would be strange to get used to.

She placed one of a single enormous eye with a tear dripping from its lower lid to the back of the pile. At the next drawing, she froze. The right side of a woman's face could be seen with broken glass lines in front of it, as if a broken window distorted the view of the face. Wren would never forget the terrible event at school that inspired that drawing.

Liv had talked her into trying out for the cheerleading squad. "You'll get in for sure. You've got that dark mysterious look and beautiful long brown hair." Liv knew Wren's story, she was the only one that Wren confided in completely, but she still insisted that Wren had some Italian blood. She play-acted jealous of Wren's "natural beauty," as she put it, but Liv was the one the boys and girls wanted to be around—including Wren.

"A fake eye doesn't change who you are," Liv told her. "You're beautiful, strong, talented, and you're my best friend." Liv flashed her a huge, goofy smile.

"I'm not very coordinated," Wren protested.

"You can do anything you set your mind to," Liv repeated that often. At times, Wren was inspired to believe her, against every circumstance proving otherwise and every unspoken signal she got from people. But other times… Well, Liv didn't have a clue what it was like for Wren.

It didn't matter, though. Wren would support her friend to the end of the world. And she'd always support her dreams, such as becoming a cheerleader.

"Even if you don't make it, it'll be a fun day spent together," Liv had argued. They both knew Liv was a shoo-in, and they wouldn't have as much time together once practice started. So, Wren went to the tryouts.

Bad day didn't express the half of it. Disaster was a better word. Wren cringed at the memory. Later, Liv had even apologized for asking her to come, and apologies didn't come easily for her.

The image would never leave Wren's mind. Her turn had come to be assessed for the tryouts. The squad leader demonstrated the moves, then Wren stepped out onto the middle of the gym floor. Not everyone watched her. Many were off in the outer rim of the gym practicing jumps and things to be ready for their turn, but too many stopped to watch.

Wren's lack of depth perception and peripheral vision on the right side must've played a role. She made it through the short routine, all the way to the jump at the end, then misjudged the distance to the floor. She hit the floor so hard, but only realized the full extent of the damage when she heard hard plastic clink on the wood floor. Her prosthetic eye slid across the floor into the crowd.

Screams pierced her ears as girls ran from the gym. The head cheerleader gave her a look of disgust. "You're sick.

I'd never trust you in a pyramid." She flung her head around and her body followed lifting her cheer skirt in the twirl as she marched away.

Liv ran to Wren, helped her up and together they found the prosthesis. The only good thing about that day was Liv.

Her friend stuck with her through everything, even the most embarrassing moment that Liv chose to share when she could've conveniently gone to the bathroom. Wren thought of herself as a loyal friend, and she valued that kind of loyalty.

That evening after tryouts, Wren had retreated up here to her safe space and drawn this picture of the shattered glass over the right side of a face. She touched the cracked face.

The day after tryouts, Momma took Wren to get fitted for a new prosthetic eye. She'd been overdue—they needed to be replaced every few years while growing. Since that time her growing had slowed, and she hadn't needed another new one.

Wren flipped the shattered-eye picture to the back of the stack and glanced at the others. Next, a girl's profile emerged from a sea of charcoal shadows. Obviously, Wren had a thing for eyes. She also had a thing for light and dark. In this one, it gave the feeling that the eyes searched for light.

Rummaging through the box, her fingers ran across a partially torn piece of paper, which she carefully pulled out. A man in an overcoat, the room door behind him. Her surgeon—the one who removed her eye and then came to talk to her. She couldn't have been more than four or five when she drew this. It would be unrecognizable to anyone else. Now, memories of the hospital room and the surgeon who removed her eye played out like a movie in her mind.

She stacked all the drawings and returned them to the box.

Taking a regular number two pencil, Wren did a loose sketch of Mr. Cho holding up a flier for the art contest. She half-smiled, then stuck it into hiding with the others.

Wren would never be good enough to win a contest. Her fourth-grade teacher did her a favor.

"Bud, can you tell if I missed a spot?" Momma's voice came through Wren's open window, where sheer curtains fluttered.

Wren peeked out. Her mother was off the ladder now, working on the window downstairs, outside the kitchen. She noticed the trim on her bedroom window hadn't been painted yet. She could use a distraction.

How hard could it be for someone who loved art to paint the trim on one window of a house?

It would feel good to chip in with the family project and be helpful for a change. They did so much for her. She could contribute to the beauty of their home. Not art exactly, but it was something.

— • ● • —

Rummaging through her closet, Wren found a pair of jeans she no longer wore and an old sweatshirt with a faded picture of Van Gogh's Starry Night.

September had been unusually cool, especially in the shade, so the sweatshirt would be fine. She snuggled into the old favorite, washed to bunny-fur softness. She might wear this to lounge in for the rest of winter.

Outside, she grabbed an unclaimed can of paint and a clean brush. She set them on the ground and took the ladder Momma had been using earlier. Locking it in place beside her window, Wren climbed up with the paint and brush in one hand, holding carefully to the ladder with the other.

At the top, she allowed herself to take in the view. Bushy trees all around, mostly green, but one or two had yellow and orange leaves, another with purplish-red. The breeze caressed her face and lifted the hair from her back. She closed her eyes, inhaled, and listened to the rustling in the trees.

They always inspired Wren, standing strong, arms outstretched, no concern at all about rejection or abandonment.

Wren opened her eyes and set the paint on the ladder's little shelf. She needed the ladder in the middle of the window since she didn't have peripheral vision on the right but she was right-handed. She knew how to keep her head turned a bit to the right so she didn't lose her balance—at least when she was paying attention. And this job demanded her full attention.

Wren dipped the brush into the peachy trim color Dad had picked out and ran it across the left side of the trim piece. Careful in the corners, the way he taught her several years ago when they painted some inside rooms, she didn't let one drip get past her.

She held her head back to admire her work and smiled. Just what she needed today. Satisfaction seeped into her heart.

"My God, Wren!" Momma's voice shrieked. Wren nearly toppled from the ladder at the sound, expecting some killer osprey to swoop down on Wren with its giant talons, or some other such horror. "What on earth are you doing? Get down from that ladder this instant." Mom continued.

"Momma, I'm fine. Look. I even did the corners like Daddy taught me."

"Wren, it's great, honey, but really, I can do this. Or your father can. Come down off that ladder."

"Aria," her dad walked over and spoke Momma's name with his calming, never-overused voice. "She's fine."

"No. No. I need to know she's safe, Bud. She must come down."

"Come on down, Wren. For your mother's peace of mind."

"But Daddy, I just have a little more to finish up."

"It's great, sweetheart. But I can finish it," a hint of sadness in Daddy's voice. Did he know she could do it and feel sad that her mother was making a stink about it? Or did he feel sad that Wren's life was so limited that she couldn't even safely paint the house with her family?

A lump formed in Wren's throat. She backed down the ladder slowly, swallowing hard to stop the tears, though a few escaped.

"Oh, Princess, come here." Daddy reached out to hold her, but she turned away. She needed to get inside before the dam burst.

"I'm sorry, Wren." Momma tried to smooth it over. "I just get so scared ever since…" Her words trailed off.

Wren whirled back around toward her mom, tears and all. "Since I was eight years old and fell off a ladder?" Wren paused. "I broke my arm. Kids break bones." Wasn't that a natural thing? "It's been almost ten years. Haven't I learned something about how to compensate by now?" She was in college after all. In all honesty, she still had collisions with doors and people, just not as often. She stumbled off curbs and tripped occasionally. Didn't everyone?

"I know, but…" Momma hesitated. "I guess it's a reaction to seeing you on a ladder."

"If you know that, then why can't I finish what I started?" Wren swiped at the wayward tears.

"I just don't want to see you get hurt. You know there's a chance you could fall."

"Anyone could, but you get on ladders, and you don't have a problem when Daddy does."

"I know, baby, but—"

"But…" Wren repeated, knowing what her mom meant to say. "I'm the weak one. I'm dis-abled."

"Wren, you know I don't think of you that way." Momma's eyes flared.

"Well, maybe that's what I am." Wren ran inside, leaving the paint and brush at the top of the ladder.

CHAPTER THREE

Wren closed her bedroom door, the window, and the shade. If her parents tried to finish the trim around her window, she didn't want to hear them.

She flopped onto her bed, face-first.

Didn't she think of herself that way? Disabled. Handicapped.

She couldn't pursue art, she couldn't be a cheerleader, she couldn't stand on a ladder to paint a house. The *couldn't* list went on and on.

She rolled onto her back and stared at the ceiling.

Couldn't she at least try?

On the other hand, what if she really injured herself? Parents knew best, right? Maybe Wren needed to be sheltered. She should be thankful they cared about her safety.

A picture of Nonna came to her. Standing in the kitchen with her straight black and gray hair in a long ponytail, adding cloves of garlic to a large pan of boiling water for pasta on the stove. "There is nothing impossible to him, or her, who will try." Turning away from the pan to look at Wren, who sat on a stool at the counter, Nonna had continued, "Do you know who said that, Wren? That was Alexander the Great."

Wren couldn't remember how she had reacted, but not with enough enthusiasm to please Nonna.

"He conquered many lands and was never defeated." Nonna washed her garlic hands under the faucet. "And do you want to know what Thomas Edison said? He said, 'Our greatest weakness lies in giving up.'"

Wren learned in high school that Edison tried to make a working lightbulb many times and failed. He never quit until he achieved his goal.

"And you know what our Lord said?" Nonna didn't wait for Wren to respond this time either. "He said, 'With God all things are possible.' And who are we to argue with our Lord and Savior, bless his holy name?" She lifted the cross on her necklace to her lips and kissed it.

Leaning on both hands in front of Wren, Nonna looked her square in the eye. "So, if at first you don't succeed, try, try again."

She never could remember what had triggered Nonna's now-famous *try* speech, which she reiterated every time Wren thought something was too hard. But it had become Nonna's theme.

At least Nonna had truly believed in Wren's ability, which was more than she could say for Momma. More than she could say for herself. If only she still had Nonna around.

So, why not go to school for an art degree? What would Nonna say to that? Go for it?

In Italian, the words for missing someone literally meant that the person was missing from you. That's how Wren felt about Nonna—she had a big hole in her life where Nonna should be.

Sitting up, Wren wondered… hmm

She stepped over to the desk and opened the laptop. The keys clicked as she tapped out her search. She landed on the website for the Savannah College of Art & Design.

Art programs they offered: graphic design, architecture, and animation. Art History. That last one could be fun, better than accounting, but none of them really appealed to her.

If she had more confidence in her art, she could just start selling her stuff while she went to community college.

Still, that meant hours of studying accounting while working on art projects. Argh!

Scrolling through more schools, she found Auburn's art programs. Wow. Degrees in studio art and art history. They made it possible to major in one and minor in the other. With an art history degree, she'd be able to work in galleries, or it would set her up to continue her education and then work in communications or education.

The idea thrilled her. Even if she didn't continue, that degree would really boost her confidence.

An invisible darkness swooped down over her happy thoughts.

Unless you totally fail and those teachers say the same thing your fourth-grade teacher said.

Wren pushed that out of her mind. "La la la." She physically shook her head.

So, if she got the scholarship, she could attend Auburn, which would get her away from home in a safe way—in a controlled environment—and she could study art.

That could work, right?

"You still wouldn't have anything to fall back on if art didn't pay off after school." Wren heard her mother's voice in her head.

Okay, worst-case scenarios. Wren was good at those.

She might graduate from an art program, leaving her parents with a much larger debt—unless she won the scholarship, which was highly unlikely. Room and board would increase her bill a lot. She could have her degree and be unable to find a job that paid enough to support her. Then she'd have to go back to school, take out loans and get into debt herself in order to find a boring job that gave her a decent income. She'd be back to square one, only she'd have an enormous debt, and so would her parents.

Daddy and Momma didn't have the money to spend on an education that might not lead to a career that would fully support her. They wanted to know she'd be okay financially, even after they were gone.

Wren collapsed back onto her bed. A tear rolled down to her ear.

So… accounting for now.

Once graduated and established as an accountant, she'd slowly begin to draw. She'd like to explore different kinds of paint as well. Maybe she'd get an Etsy page.

Her parents loved her, after all. And Wren needed security. Turning her head, she glanced at the accounting book on her desk.

Could she be satisfied with that day after day for the next several years? And the question she couldn't bring herself to consider, though it lurked in the back of her mind, was what if she wasn't good at accounting?

She tried to pray about it, but felt guilty even bringing it up to the God of the universe. He had more important things to worry about. There were so many poor, mistreated people in this world who needed his help. Her request felt lame in comparison.

She needed to suck it up and do what was best. Swinging her feet off the bed, she sat up, then walked to her desk.

The accounting book stared back at her. She should start her homework.

No, she couldn't face it now.

— • ● • —

Wren shivered. Maybe she should've brought a jacket. A gust of wind entered with her as she opened the door to Page and Palette, the cute New Orleans-style, two-story corner shop. Wren passed through the coffee shop, now closed. Inside the bookstore, the staff were prepared to close that too. The back would be open, though. Complete with a bar, a few tables, and some chairs set up in rows for the concert, it wasn't a big place, but the locals loved it.

Page and Palette supported all kinds of authors and musicians from the region. Wren felt comfortable there though she and her friends joked about it being more of an old-person hangout.

She had spent plenty of time in the coffee shop and the bookstore. It's where she got her signed copy of *Mona and the Selkie* from the author, Samantha O'Connor, Mr. Cho's wife.

Bohemian-style scarves hung behind a small stage, making for a cool, indie backdrop.

Wren took the last seat at the bar and waved at Liv as she and her band got situated. Liv smiled and waved, mouthing, *Thanks for coming.*

"What'll ya have, little lady?" the bartender asked.

"Um..."

"I'll have to see I.D. of course," he added with a friendly wink.

"That's okay, I'll just have a Sprite." Not the fake-ID kind of person, Wren didn't mind Sprite or sweet tea.

Despite her age, the bar made the perfect place for her to sit. The rest of the room was on her left side. The only thing she couldn't see while looking at the stage was the bartender.

Wren hadn't spent too much time choosing her outfit; after all, Liv was performing, not her. She wore jeans and a cream-colored, loose-knit lace sweater with a camisole underneath. The sweater dressed up the jeans a bit, and she felt pretty, but comfortable—the perfect combo.

Liv's outfit, on the other hand, demanded recognition.

How did that girl do it? She had on a long white halter dress with a slit up the front left side, a brown leather belt tied around the waist, rough-looking cowboy boots and a brown cowgirl hat. A turquoise necklace popped just below her collarbone completing the ensemble which complemented the band's country pop genre.

Liv was made for the spotlight. Sitting on a stool on the small stage, Liv picked up her guitar. Several in the audience clapped in anticipation.

Liv's voice sounded like an angel, like someone who'd been singing all her life. Nonna used to say Liv looked like a young Farrah Fawcett—a famous model/actress back in her day. Whoever it was, Wren had to agree, Liv looked like someone famous. One day she'd be famous, for sure.

But Wren never envied Liv. Liv needed all that attention. Sometimes when she didn't get enough, she'd go through bouts of depression. Wren tried to give her all the love and attention she could, but she wasn't always enough. Liv missed her dad, who had run off a few years earlier, leaving no way to contact him. He had doted on her and treated her like an angel until he left.

Devastated, Liv said she felt like she had died inside. Wren had stuck to her like an old sticker on a computer. Little by little, Liv came back to herself, but her need to be adored never left.

Wren wouldn't let Liv down, never. Nothing was worse than being abandoned. She knew that firsthand.

Wren sipped her Sprite, which had appeared on the bar in front of her without her noticing. She relaxed and enjoyed the music, forgetting her worries.

"The band and I are going to take a quick break. Don't y'all go anywhere. We'll be right back," Liv said into the microphone, then bounced over Wren's way. "How do we sound?" She confiscated Wren's glass and sipped half of it through her straw. Good thing she wasn't a germaphobe.

"Your voice is so beautiful! And you look like a star."

Liv turned away, then looked back over her shoulder, raising her eyebrows at Wren like she was flirting. Then she smiled big and did a little twirl. "You like it?"

Wren nodded. "Beautiful. You have such style."

"I picked it up at the thrift store downtown, just on the next block. Fits me too."

"I love it."

"Well, got to get back." Liv whirled around, walked to the other end of the bar, and lifted on her tiptoes so she could whisper something to the bartender. He nodded. Then she got back up on stage and picked up her guitar.

"Hey, miss… Miss…" the guy behind the bar sounded frustrated when Wren turned to see him standing right there. "Your drink?"

"I didn't order another one."

"Olivia said to bring you another one and put it on her tab."

Wren nodded. "Thank you."

The band played again, but this time with a quieter song.

"Hey," The guy two seats down from Wren switched places with the woman who'd been sitting right beside her. "What's your name?" he asked tossing his blond bangs away from his eyes.

"Wren Marie." Sometimes she felt like giving both of her names. Often her parents or other family members used both when speaking to her or introducing her—a southern thing.

"Wren? Like the bird?" This guy had perfect hair, blond like Liv's, and a square jaw. The lack of lighting prevented her from discerning the color of his eyes, but she was sure they were nice. Defined muscles too, like he worked out. Probably close to their age, if Wren had to guess.

A gust of cool air swept across Wren's face as someone came into the bar through the side door. Wren put her hands on her upper arms, her sweater too lacey to be warm. "Yes, spelled just like the bird."

"That's interesting."

"It was my Nonna who picked the name. She told me wrens have rich, complex songs for such a small body. They roost together to keep warm, and th—"

"That's cool." He glanced away from her to the band on stage.

Okay, over-share.

"Hey, do you know her?" His head nodded back in the direction of the stage and Liv.

Now it made sense. Wren nodded.

"I sure would like to meet her." So that was his angle. Not surprising.

"Introduce yourself to her," Wren suggested.

"I was hoping maybe you could introduce me." He winked at her as if he'd been getting his way with that smile and a wink all his life.

"Forget it. I don't know you." Did he think she was naïve? Young, maybe, but too smart to fall for that.

He stuck out his hand for her to shake. "Name's Cade." They shook. "Now you know me."

"I don't know the first thing about you." Creepy creeps could be good looking too.

He gave up pestering Wren for the moment and listened to the music—or, more likely, just stared at Liv.

On her next break, Liv came over and struck up a conversation with the guy. Amazing how chummy two people could get in the course of a fifteen-minute break between sets.

When the band finished for the night, Liv and Cade sat across a small round table from each other. They talked and talked while Wren waited for her at the bar. Finally, Wren had waited long enough.

She cleared her throat and tapped Liv on the shoulder. "Liv, we need to get going."

Cade looked disappointed.

"Oh, yeah. Sorry. We got caught up talking."

"Let me take you home," Cade said. "Then we can have a few more minutes to get to know each other." His tone was casual—forced casual? Wren wondered.

She hated for Liv to fall for the first good-looking guy that paid attention to her after her breakup.

Liv and Randy had dated three out of four years in high school. Their relationship was as cliché as one couple could get. Randy, a football star, was the most popular guy in school. Liv, a cheerleader and was loved by everyone. Who could resist her joyful spirit?

Since graduation, they'd gone to different schools, had separate lives. Randy broke up with her by text two weeks ago. He probably had someone he wanted to go home with over fall break.

Liv hadn't really dated anyone since he left. She thought they'd wait for each other. Not that she hadn't had offers. She'd been pretty broken up after that text and even wrote a couple of songs as therapy. Wren had never seen Liv single for long, but she hoped her friend would give herself time to heal.

Liv held Cade's gaze. "Yeah, we can do that." She turned to Wren. "Is that okay with you, Wren?"

What could she say with both looking at her like that? She wasn't Liv's mother. She had no authority. "I guess." But Wren wanted to make sure Liv got home okay. "Can we talk just a minute?"

"Sure." They stepped just inside the bookstore side. "What's up?"

"You should give yourself more time."

Liv put her hands on her hips.

"We know nothing about this guy." What else could she say? It wasn't like she had a rap sheet on him.

Liv rolled her eyes. "Look, I know you don't trust people. You never have."

"I just want—"

"Sometimes you should give people a chance, Wren. Cade seems like a nice guy. Talking is easy with him. I haven't had that in a long time."

What could she say? "I get it, Liv, but maybe y'all could meet tomorrow, or next week. He doesn't need to drive you home tonight. Then he'll know where you live."

"Would you feel better if I still lived with my parents, like—" Liv stopped mid-sentence and put her hand on her mouth.

"Like me?"

"I'm sorry, Wren. I didn't mean to offend you, but living with them is hindering you."

"How's that?" Wren really didn't want to hear the answer. So, why'd she ask? She glanced at the guy getting an early start on sweeping in the bar.

"You know what I think. I've told you often enough."

"That they don't let me grow and do things on my own?" She thought about the painting incident earlier that afternoon. She'd been just fine on the ladder. Was Liv right? Or did Wren still need their wisdom? Wasn't it safer to obey the authorities in your life? Maybe Wren couldn't do life alone.

"They don't believe you can."

"Maybe I can't."

"Of course you can. You're a wren." Liv winked. "Remember what Nonna used to say about wrens?" Nonna had loved Liv too. And Liv spent a lot of time at Wren's house when Nonna lived with them.

Of course, she remembered.

"Wrens are small but adaptable to all kinds of environments," Liv said anyway. "They can thrive in difficult situations." She squeezed Wren's arm, like an encouraging grandparent would do.

How had this conversation become about Wren's lack of bravery rather than Liv's safety? "You can do anything you set your mind to," Liv added. "There are stories all over the internet about people with much worse problems than yours who accomplish amazing things.”

Whether or not Wren needed her parents’ protection, maybe Liv didn’t need Wren’s.

A throat cleared back inside the bar.

“I don’t know, Liv. Maybe you’re right about some things. But let me drive you home like we planned.”

“I’m not ready to go yet, and Cade wants to go down to the pier to see the lights and talk.”

Liv must’ve read her facial expression.

“I’ll be fine,” she said. “Cade has been telling me about a job opportunity. I’d like to hear the details.” She raised both palms. “Honest. I won’t go home with him or invite him up. I’m not that easy, you know?” She winked.

Wren smiled. Liv wasn’t a dumb blonde. Her intelligence exceeded Wren’s. Still, Wren’s gut tightened as she walked out the door.

CHAPTER FOUR

The flirty girl at the front desk of the Hampton Inn in downtown Fairhope, Alabama might have been cute, who knew? James Fielding just wanted to get up to his room and rest before dinner. He needed a good night's sleep before his lecture tomorrow. He'd been on the road too much lately.

Yesterday's interview with a survivor had gone well. That, coupled with some other research, was going to make a good in-depth article he'd pitched on spec: *Signs That You're Being Groomed.* Or maybe he'd come up with a catchier title later.

After dinner, he'd edit his article for The Atlantic. Tomorrow's deadline had snuck up on him. He'd be up late again.

Jim tossed his laptop onto the queen-size bed. Who would have dreamed two years ago that he'd become an expert on all things trafficking? An honor he never wanted… still didn't.

Tired from the flight to Pensacola, and the subsequent hour-long Uber to Fairhope, he stumbled over his duffel on the floor, moved it to the platform for suitcases, then stretched out on the bed next to his computer.

After a power nap, Jim found a little seafood place near his hotel. He relished the flavors in the stuffed flounder, remembering how Stacy had loved that dish. She ordered it every time they went to the coast.

Eating alone again, Jimmy? His mother's voice sounded in his mind. Not that she'd ever say it like that, but he knew how she felt. Mom didn't want him wasting his life looking for the guys who killed his sister. Her concern centered on Jim rather than on the new would-be victims.

But justice demanded it… Stacy deserved it. The innocent victims needed it.

Had it already been a year? Maybe he should say, had it only been a year?

He sipped a Pinot Gris. Since the funeral, he had investigated, researched, written articles, spoken anywhere that would open the door to him, and traveled in his used Cadillac SUV over much of the United States. But it hadn't helped him discover the key people who had a role in Stacy's kidnapping, abuse and death. And he could not stop until they were all behind bars. No other girl should have to experience the things Stacy had.

Bread pudding and an espresso made it back to the hotel with him. A treat while he worked. Minutes later, he punched the talk button on his ringing phone.

"Hey, Mom."

"You sound tired."

"Mm-hm."

"Why don't you cancel this one and come home? I'll make shepherd's pie and apple pie. We'll eat comfort food, talk and rest. We won't think about anything horrible. Just for a day or two."

"That sounds perfect, Mom, but you know I can't cancel. I'm speaking at a college tomorrow. I think the administrators are making the lecture mandatory for first-year students."

"They aren't kids, Jimmy."

"Yes, but most of them aren't much older than Stacy was. They're young enough to be ignorant of the dangers of the world."

"You should let yourself stay in one place for a while. How will you ever meet a girl when you're on the road all the time?"

Always the same with her.

"Is that really important?" He left the desk to sit on the bed while they spoke, stacking three pillows behind his back. Why couldn't she see the urgency of stopping this insidious evil? He rubbed his eyes. "There has to be justice, Mom."

"I loved her too, you know. So much, it hurts." He heard the catch in her voice. "Some days I allow myself to give the day to grief. I cry and pray, then I give it to the Lord, and he gives me the strength to go on. But I also love you."

"I'm so glad you have peace, Mom. Really. But I believe this is what God has given me to do."

"Okay, but I hope you don't try to find these guys yourself. Let the police handle it. Have you heard any more from Officer Windly?"

"No. I was going to call him in a few minutes."

"I'll let you go then." Her sigh gave away just how much she worried about him. "Please get some rest." They clicked off.

Fully awake now, he dialed the memorized number for the investigator on Stacy's case.

"I'm sorry, Jim," Officer Windly said through the phone. "We've come to a standstill. We have no more clues, and I have to focus on other cases now." Jim heard the disappointment in the detective's voice. He hated for the traffickers to get away with it as much as Jim did. Well, maybe not that much.

After the call, Jim went over the notes for his lecture tomorrow. He prayed for the Lord to lead him. Even though his basic speech didn't change, it came out slightly differently each time. He had to believe that was the leading of the Lord. The Creator knew the details of each student's and each community's situation.

The first section dealt with prevention. If the young people knew what to look for and would pay attention, it would keep some of them safe. "Too good to be true opportunities." Young people with their futures in front of them could easily be sucked in by these promises of gaining something for virtually nothing. It seemed obvious to Jim that one must question those things, but life experience had aged him more than his twenty-four years.

After his article in the high school journalism contest got so much attention, he had offers from big-name magazines and newspapers to write for them. He started writing for a couple of them before graduation. Living on his own in Washington DC at nineteen had made him grow up quickly and made him question everything. If only he could impart wisdom from his own life experience. And from Stacy's.

Number two under prevention: Tell a trusted adult where you're going. They never wanted to listen to this one. Just discovering their independence, older teens wanted to check in with adults about as much as they wanted to catch a fly baseball in the head. He got it. He wasn't much older than them now, but the hard knocks—losing a sister—taught him. What do older people say about hindsight?

Number five was trusting their gut. Man, if only young people would do this one rather than reasoning their gut feelings away.

Statistics told Jim that of all the college students who'd be at his lecture tomorrow at least a few of them would get caught in a trafficking situation at some point. His advice might help them too. Dear God, let them hear. Let them remember to guard their mind, to remember who they are, and to pay attention to everything. May they never give up. And may you show them a way of escape.

He often prayed as he reviewed his notes. It had become a habit. After all, only God could really make a difference no matter how good his advice might be.

A growing number of survivor interviews informed the points Jim put in his speech. He'd continue tweaking it with each one.

Jim finished up his dessert, then turned to the article he still needed to edit. He'd have a few minutes after his workshop in the morning to finish up and send it to the magazine. He crashed just before one in the morning.

• ● •

Watching dust float through morning sunbeams floating through the living room windows, Wren held the phone to her ear and hoped she wouldn't wake Liv; she'd likely sleep in on a Saturday.

"Hello?" Liv sounded groggy.

"Sorry to wake you. Just wanted to make sure you got home okay." Wren sounded foolish, even to herself—just one of the small sacrifices of being a true friend.

"He was a perfect gentleman," Liv assured her. "The night was so clear we could see all the lights of Mobile. We sat on the wall with our feet hanging down toward the water and talked about a modeling opportunity that pays very well. Cade says I'd be perfect."

"Did he see where you live?" Wren couldn't help asking.

"Yes, but he doesn't know which apartment is mine. He didn't come up." She let out a small laugh. "He kissed me on the cheek before he said good night. That's it!"

"How sweet." Wren said, happy to be surprised. She sat back in a more comfortable position on the couch and twirled a section of her long hair. "I'm glad, Liv."

Momma came down the stairs. On her way to the kitchen, she blew Wren a kiss. Wren waved a finger at her so as not to disturb her conversation.

"Hey, did you see the notice about Monday's lecture on trafficking?" Liv changed the subject. "All the freshmen are required to go. I guess it's like a school assembly in high school, at least for freshmen. James somebody is speaking. I just hate thinking about downer stuff like that. Don't you?"

"Actually—"

"I know. You like to learn all you can, so you're prepared." Liv's voice mocked, but Wren knew she loved her.

"I like to be ready for the *worst-case scenarios*." They said the last three words in unison. "Have I said that before?"

They both laughed.

"I saw a flyer about the lecture," Wren remembered seeing the speaker's picture on the bulletin board when Mr. Cho came. "The speaker is not hard on the eye." Did she just say that out loud?

"Oh, really?" Liv's tone turned devious.

"No, Liv. Don't." Wren begged. "Good looks are not enough to be interested in someone."

"Wah-wah-wah…" Liv droned. "Anyway, we all have to go, so I'll save you a seat—or you save me one."

"Okay. I'm glad everything went well with Cade." Wren circled back. "And I'm glad you had an enjoyable time. I know it's been a while."

"Thanks. Hey, I've got to get ready." Liv's voice, now fully awake sounded like she'd already moved onto the next thing in her day. The rest of Wren's questions would have to wait.

—•●•—

Father, open the ears of any who need to hear this message. Bring key points back to their minds in critical moments. And please protect them, Jim prayed Monday morning before his speech in Fairhope. God knew and loved these kids. He cared far more than he did. Looking out over the crowd of students, he wondered how God did it. How could he care so much without his heart being broken?

I choose to let my heart break.

Wow. God was so unlike humans, who never stopped trying to protect their heart from pain.

Please give me the words to say, Jim asked silently while a student introduced him.

"Hello. Like he said, I'm James Fielding. You're welcome to call me Jim." He began with Stacy's story. The punch of a button and her picture appeared on the large screen over his head. The room went quiet other than a few shuffles and whispers. His heart broke every time he looked at it. Her first party dress for her first date. "My mom told me how excited Stacy had been that night. Here on her first official date, she had her whole life in front of her."

"So did each of these before they were trafficked." Jim clicked through a series of pictures, each one of a survivor he'd had the privilege to interview. "These brave women, and a couple of men, shared their stories with me in the hopes that others might avoid what they endured." He remembered each one and never wanted to forget their faces—these pictures were for him as much as they were for the students. "These are the survivors. They are free and working toward healthy, contented lives. Others, like my sister, were not so lucky."

"I hope you understand, these were just regular people. They each had dreams and talents just like you. Most of them had families. None of them sought out the abuse and trauma they found. Not one ever expected to end up as a victim." Looking at their faces, his words paused a moment. "Today, due to their endurance and bravery, they are no longer victims but survivors."

Jim took a sip from the water glass provided.

"Looking back, they can sometimes see where they made mistakes. Just a small thing at the time, but now they see how, with a few changes, they might have prevented all the pain they went through. I bring their advice to you today."

Jim sensed Stacy looking down on him, smiling. He smiled back.

Whispers from several conversations throughout the audience echoed around the auditorium. Hopefully they'd take this lecture seriously. How he prayed they'd listen and remember. "I've heard this first point many times. Be skeptical of opportunities that seem too good to be true. Temptation here is real, and these guys know how to play on people's dreams and fears."

Jim's mind settled into the familiar speech. "Now I know you won't like number two but hear me out. Always tell a trusted adult where you're going, and preferably who you're with." He paused for the groans and chuckled along with them. This one always got that reaction. What teen wanted an adult to know their every move?

Jim finished the Prevention portion of his speech with warnings about social media and signs of someone grooming you for an unhealthy, possibly dangerous relationship. "The last of my points on prevention is connected to the first in a way. It's to trust your gut." Jim took the mic in hand and stepped away from the podium at this point. He wanted to connect with them, look them in the eye, so to speak. "I'm not kidding about this. You know that little voice that says, 'something's not right about this?' Or it says, 'Hey, this seems almost too good to be true.' Or maybe it says, 'Why would someone I just met want to bail me out of a financial jam?' These are actual thoughts people brushed aside. Why? They didn't want to offend a new friend." Jim stopped pacing and faced the audience. He didn't speak until the room had become silent.

"I tell you now, take the time to explore the worry in your gut. Don't make any decisions until you do. Go ahead and risk offending the person in front of you. Most true friends wouldn't be offended by your hesitation. But a trafficker doesn't want you to stop and think. They rely on you *not* listening to that voice."

He walked back to the podium. "Now I'd like to address what you can do if you are trapped and being trafficked. I know," he paused for effect, like he was having a comfortable conversation with a friend. At least that's the effect he was going for. "Nobody wants to imagine themselves in that situation. But we must face the fact that it is a possibility, not just for *those* people, for anyone. Wouldn't you rather know how to protect your mind and heart from the kind of manipulations these guys have planned for you?"

— • ● • —

Centennial Hall overflowed with more than just the freshmen. Some teachers probably recommended it. Wren's Humanities teacher, for example, offered extra credit for notes from the lecture.

Wren got the feeling they might've opened it up to the community as well when she saw several groupings of people her parents' age and older.

"Let's sit here, Wren." Liv pulled her arm leading her to two seats on the aisle a little closer than halfway to the stage.

Notebook and pen ready, Wren hoped she could get some good notes out of it. Any extra credit would be good at this point. Too bad it wouldn't help her accounting grades. That's where she really needed it.

Liv leaned toward Wren. "Cade called again. He's so nice to talk to. He's so encouraging and can talk about more than just college football, you know?"

"You talked again since we talked on the phone yesterday?"

"I told you he's a gentleman, no need to worry."

But Wren was good at it. "Does he live close? In town?"

Mark, the student body president, stood at the mic and gave the speaker's name and credentials.

"I think he lives close, but not in town. That's the sense I got."

Wren caught a glimpse of the speaker standing to the side waiting to come up.

"Hello. Like Mark said, I'm James Fielding. You're welcome to call me Jim."

"And we will, Jim," Liv's eyes flashed, and she elbowed Wren.

"Why's a guy like me going around the country talking about sex trafficking? Yeah, it's strange, but I have a story to tell you..."

"You're right, Wren, he's not bad. I could see you two together."

"Shhhh." Wren felt her cheeks warm, then Liv's words earlier floated back to her She needed to ask. "Cade didn't say where he lives?"

"We were so busy talking about life, our families, and this job opportunity, that we didn't get around to that. Did you know he lost both of his parents?"

"No," Wren wanted to hear all about Cade, but she needed to hear the lecture too. "I don't know him at all."

"Family is important to him."

"You already discussed family?" Quick, Wren thought. She'd like to know the guy better before Liv jumped in with both feet. "Just be careful."

"Okay, Little Miss Mom." Liv gave her another playful elbow to the ribs. Her words ceased momentarily, then she whistled in Wren's ear. "You should totally go for it."

"Go for what?" Wren whispered.

"Him," Liv's eyes darted toward the platform where the man from the flyer stood speaking at the podium.

Wren rolled her eye, but not before she got an eyeful. Dark jeans with loafers, a camel-colored wool blazer over a striped dress shirt. Simple, tasteful, not flashy. "He's just here for the lecture." She smiled and elbowed Liv back. "Now stop talking and listen. We get extra credit for notes."

"You mean you do. My teachers didn't offer that."

"Sorry." Wren missed hearing the introduction.

"Hello." James adjusted his mic. "Like he said, I'm James Fielding. You're welcome to call me Jim."

"And we will, Jim," Liv's eyes flashed, and she elbowed Wren.

"Why's a guy like me going around the country talking about sex trafficking?" he said. "Yeah, it's strange, but I have a story to tell you…"

"How long do you think this will go?" Liv whispered in Wren's ear. "I told Cade I'd meet him at Page and Palette since I have a free period after the lecture."

Wren shrugged but didn't respond. What had the man said?

"Or I could text Cade and say I'll be a bit late so you and I can go down there and meet *Jim* after the lecture." Liv's voice droned into the background.

"What?" Wren really wanted to hear this. So many dangers in the world.

"I'll take you down and introduce you when he finishes."

"You don't know him, Liv," Wren whispered again.

Liv widened her eyes, and she mouthed, So?

"I'd have done anything to keep my sister alive and safe," Jim said. "If only I had known then what I know now. If only she did."

How horrible.

Liv quieted during most of the lecture after that, keeping her interruptions to a minimum.

Some of Jim's points seemed like common sense, but it was always good to be reminded. Trusting your gut, she jotted that down. If she could get the main points, maybe that would be enough.

She wrote "Remember who you are." And "Keep a positive outlook that you will get away." How awful to have someone plotting to harm you, manipulating and planning how they might destroy your mind. Evil, pure and simple.

The next point seemed obvious: "Don't believe their lies." If you know someone wants to harm you and you know they're lying to you, why would you believe them? But she wrote it down anyway.

"Force yourself to be aware." She jotted that in her notes. Jim took a sip of water. "Notice small details, routines, anything that you might be able to draw on later when planning your escape. Keep your mind active and sharp. Count things, make mental maps, recite your favorite books or poems, or even memorized scriptures or prayers. Draw images in your head." He paused. "Do anything you can that strengthens your mind and builds resistance to their efforts."

A good speaker, Jim knew how to capture his audience's attention.

"And watch for windows of escape. They want you to believe it's impossible, but it's not. In situations like this, you have to be smart. You might even have to do things you don't want to do until a good time presents itself to escape, but when it does, be ready and take the opportunity."

He finished by admonishing them to never accept hopelessness.

When he finished, Wren looked over her notes. Seemed like she was missing something… In the beginning when Liv was talking to her. What had he said?

Liv grabbed her wrist and pulled. "Come on." She looked determined. For what? Then it dawned on Wren.

"Oh, no… I'm not going down there."

"Yes, you are, Wren Marie," Liv sounded like an old aunt commanding her compliance. "And there's already a line, so hurry." Liv pulled her into the aisle, where she bumped into a few upperclassmen.

People crammed the aisle, some going toward the exit, others going forward toward the speaker. Wren had to stretch to reach back and retrieve her notebook and pen.

Soon they waited in the line to meet James Fielding. He had a cute way of tossing his long bangs back away from his eyes. He seemed sincere and so concerned for the students as well as for the victims, including his own sister—such a tragedy.

"Hi Jim. I'm Liv, and this is my friend, Wren. We really enjoyed your lecture." Liv talked so much, relief washed over Wren. She wouldn't have to say a word. "Wren here is a worrywart, so she took notes and will remember every word you said."

"What about you—Liv, is it?" James asked, his face kind and nicely tanned.

"Yes, that's right. I will totally remember everything too. It's very important and helpful."

Wren smirked. Had Liv heard anything he'd said?

"What did you think?" Jim directed his question to Wren, and Liv held her tongue, unfortunately.

Wren's face warmed. "I'm very sorry to hear about your sister. How is your family doing?"

Jim sucked in a breath as if startled by her question.

"Um, it's not easy, you know. It's been almost a year. And I still can't believe she's gone. She was only fourteen." Moisture in his eyes caught the light, and he glanced away, clearing his throat.

"I should probably talk to the others." He looked past her at the line behind them.

"Right, we'll let you go." Liv grabbed Wren's arm again and pulled her toward the side door at the front of the lecture hall.

"Thank you for sharing your sto—" Wren tried to say, but it was too late. James had moved on, and Liv had pulled Wren too far away. But his vulnerable eyes would stay with her.

CHAPTER FIVE

Slamming the cover of her *Principles of Accounting* book, Wren spun in her desk chair, a weight lifted. Wheeeee!

Weekend homework—check! And it only took five hours. Good thing she got up at 5:00 a.m. Now she had the rest of the day to…

To what?

She called Liv to make sure she'd gotten home okay from her second date with Cade.

"Thanks for not calling sooner, Mother Hen," Liv teased. "Maybe I'll call you Hen instead of Wren." Liv laughed at her own joke. "It's still a bird."

"Don't you dare," Wren warned, but held back a laugh. She wouldn't admit it, but it was kind of funny. "So, the date went well?"

"It wasn't really a date, like I said, just…" her voice trailed. "You know I've done some modeling, and I was an extra on that Hallmark movie they filmed in Fairhope last year."

"I remember."

"Modeling pays way more than singing, and if I could get a decent role on screen, so would acting."

"But I thought singing was your passion." Wren spun herself in the chair again. The room sped by in circular lines of dark and light. How might she draw the spinning lines she saw?

"It is, but aren't you the one always focusing on the practical side? I have an apartment to pay for. My mom won't pay for it. She doesn't have the money, and I'm going to school in town. Technically I could live at home and save money, so why should she?"

"That's tru—"

"Anyway, Hen…" Liv emphasized the *h* sound.

Wren took the hint.

"Anyway, I need the money. I mean, I want the money. And besides, I enjoy modeling and acting too."

"So, what's the opportunity?"

"Cade knows a guy holding an audition for a modeling gig, but this guy also recruits for Indie movies."

"Like an agent?"

"I think so. And if he likes me, he'll put me up for a role in a movie!"

"That's amazing, Liv. You'd be great." Wren really meant it, but her stomach tightened. "You'll check it out and everything before you audition, right?"

"Sure, I'll Google the company. But Cade says it's legit."

"What about Cade?" Wren heard Liv sigh before she finished the sentence. "Okay, sorry. He seems nice. I just get this feeling… I don't know."

Wren stared out the bedroom window at the flock of geese on the lawn, coming to winter in the south.

"Why don't you come with me?" By the sound of it, Liv was clapping at the idea. "You could easily be a model."

"Oh, right," Wren laughed. "One of those one-eyed models. I hear they get paid the most." Sarcasm seemed appropriate.

"Knock it off. In a photo, no one could tell you have a fake eye."

"Not true, but thanks for saying so." Wren flipped her hair as if Liv could see it through the phone. They should switch to FaceTime.

"Gotta go, Wren. Talk to you soon." Liv hung up before Wren had the chance to give her an answer. No way would she audition to be a model or an actress. Maybe a role behind the camera, but not in front of it.

But it was Liv. And if Liv needed something from Wren, she'd be there. Maybe this was the steppingstone Liv needed to boost her career.

Wren jogged down the stairs. A deafening screech pierced her ears, stopping her dead on the bottom step. Both hands flew to her ears to block the sound.

Melanie, Wren's youngest cousin, was having one of her meltdowns. Being in a new environment, or not getting her way, could be more than enough to set her off.

At eleven, Melanie was beautiful, with long black wavy hair, deep brown eyes and that bronze Italian skin. Liv said Wren had it too. Maybe a little, but no one in the family knew her heritage. Her birth mother had been white and fair-skinned. Wren never knew the true color of the woman's hair. She didn't remember ever having seen her real father. The man who punched her eye had been a live-in boyfriend.

Due to some severe form of autism, Melanie didn't speak. Ever. She could make noise though, and boy, how she could scream. But she understood at least some conversation and responded by pointing and making facial expressions.

This time, her anger must have flared when her mother stepped out the door for a seminar, leaving Melanie behind.

Wren got a late breakfast for herself—a toasted bagel with cream cheese, avocado, and a slice of tomato.

Melanie had quieted by the time Wren returned to the living room and sat on the stuffed couch. Melanie ran over to her, grabbed her hand, and pulled. She wanted to make a puzzle with Wren.

"Great. Y'all do the puzzle while I throw in a load of wash." If that was a question, Momma didn't wait around for Wren to respond. She carried her full basket toward the laundry room.

Wren loved Melanie, and it seemed the feeling was mutual. Something inside Wren understood the fears Melanie must feel as she navigated her world without all the cues most other people had. Or maybe it was just empathy. Adults at school and church over the years had told Momma and Daddy that Wren had great empathy. That always made her feel good.

"Wrens live in groups," Nonna would say. "They know the safety of living in a community. People are that way, too, if we'd just get our heads out of our… well, you know what I mean, my dear." Nonna never finished that sentence. She'd just smile and wink. "We need each other. No one was meant to be alone."

Maybe that's why Wren wanted Melanie to have someone she felt connected to.

Wren helped Melanie find the corners and edges. Melanie concentrated, turning each piece around. Momma's cell whistled from the other room.

She poked her head into the living room. "I have to run this wallet up to your father at church. He's taking the youth kids on a field trip today and he's the driver."

Wren nodded. She remembered the annual weekend youth trip to a campground on Oyster Bay. It had been a beautiful place just up from the Gulf Coast—no camp for her this year. A college student now, Wren had responsibilities. Coastal would have their fall break in a few weeks.

"I'll have to take Melanie," Momma said. "Can you help her with her shoes while I get mine?"

"Mom, just leave her here with me," Wren suggested. "It'll only take you twenty minutes, and we'll play. Changing her environment again will only upset her." She glanced down as Melanie fit a puzzle piece into place, a picture of calm and sweetness.

"I don't know. What if she has another meltdown?"

"I can stay calm."

"What if she starts hitting you? She does that sometimes."

"I know, but she's never hit me." Wren stroked Melanie's head.

"I have to go."

"Then go." Wren would be nineteen soon. Most kids got to babysit by the time they were twelve or thirteen. "We'll see you in a few minutes. Right, Mellie?"

"Okay," Momma consented. "This will be a good test. Thanks, Wren." She waved and ran out the door.

The door clicked.

Melanie looked up and realized Momma had left.

Her eyes widened. She looked from the door to Wren. Then back to the door again.

She ran to the door. The scream started like a siren in the far distance. Then it grew…

Wren's eardrums threatened to burst, and her thoughts scrambled with the sound. What should she do?

She took a deep breath, trying to remain calm and ignore the eardrum-piercing sound.

"Melanie, sweetie, I'm here. It's okay." Wren tiptoed up behind the girl with a soothing voice. At least that's what she was going for.

Melanie turned, a raged look in her eyes. Fear shot through Wren. What if she attacked her?

No, Wren couldn't go there.

"Mellie, we almost finished the puzzle. There's only one more piece." She reached her arm out toward the girl.

Melanie slapped at Wren's hand, faced the door, and let out another scream.

Momma would never trust her again. Wren had to think of something. How could she refocus Melanie's attention?

Drawing always calmed Wren's own crazy emotions. Maybe it would work for Melanie. She'd have to risk leaving her cousin alone for a second.

Wren sprinted upstairs, grabbed her drawing pad and a simple pencil. She got back to Melanie in fifteen seconds, according to her counting.

She sat on the tile floor, two feet behind Melanie, who lay sprawled by the front door. Wren opened the pad and hummed "Jesus Loves Me" as she shaded an outline of a simple teddy bear. She hoped it would remind Melanie of her favorite stuffed animal and calm her down.

The girl screamed until the shape made more sense. Suddenly, Melanie stopped and stared at the drawing. Then she made an interested sound.

"Yeah. It's your teddy. See?" Wren turned the drawing pad to face Melanie. She reached for it but didn't take it. She made the sound again.

Wren stretched out her arms toward Melanie, hoping she'd come sit on her lap so she could soothe them both.

Melanie moved toward her, face smeared and long hair sticking to her cheek. Wren opened her arms wide. Melanie stopped short of the embrace. She flopped back to the floor like a rag doll and curled up in the corner of the wall by the front door. But she looked around for the picture. Wren held it down and cockeyed so Melanie could look at it straight. At least she was quiet.

"Do you want to see how I can make him look a little better?" Wren didn't wait for her to answer. She took the side of the pencil lead and rubbed it back and forth around the bear, shading the shadow side, so it looked like sunlight was shining from the opposite direction.

Melanie sat up and began rocking back and forth in the corner, her self-calming movement. Wren breathed a sigh of relief.

Suddenly animated again, Melanie leaned forward on one hand toward the drawing and tapped Wren's arm, pointing to the page. Wren didn't understand.

Melanie picked up Wren's arm and shook it up and down over the picture.

"Yes, it's Teddy."

The girl grew more agitated. What was she trying to say?

"Do you want a drink?"

Melanie slammed her fists onto the picture.

"A snack? Let's get a snack." Melanie loved Goldfish. "How about Goldfish crackers? Auntie Aria got a big box from Costco the other day." Wren stood and hesitantly reached for Melanie's arm in case she tried to bolt.

Melanie followed her into the kitchen without a problem and ate a small bowl full of Goldfish. Hopefully, she'd be quiet when Momma got home.

Returning to the living room, Wren handed Melanie a puzzle piece. She put it right in place, like she'd known where it fit all along.

Then Melanie picked up the drawing again. Wren's stomach cinched. Would it start again?

Melanie made a guttural sound and shook the pad of paper in front of Wren's face. Suddenly Wren got a flash of something like light in the picture. She took the pad from Melanie and stared at it.

Opposite the teddy bear—the space Wren hadn't paid attention to—a star shape appeared within the haphazard shading.

It reminded Wren of Sorchae, the light fairy, from the book *Mona and the Selkie*. An Irish fairy of sorts, Sorchae brought light into darkness, defeated the dragon trying to consume Mona, the main character, and led her to the safety of home and her family, who loved her. To Wren, Sorchae represented wisdom, truth, and safety.

But what did Melanie see? Wren had read Melanie the story several times, but never knew if she understood it.

Wren realized Melanie wasn't screaming, hitting, or making that guttural sound anymore. Wren glanced up at her face to find the girl staring right at her. Melanie never looked people in the face, much less stared. But here she was, staring hard into Wren's face.

"Melanie, do you see Sorchae in there?"

The girl's eyes lit up, as if she knew exactly what Wren said, like that's what she wanted Wren to see.

The front door opened with a squeak.

"How'd y'all do without me?" Momma said. Melanie ran to her and wrapped her arms around Momma's thighs. "Sweet girl." Momma patted her back. "Seems like it went well."

Wren nodded, still staring at the drawing. She tore it out of her pad and left it on top of the puzzle, then went upstairs to put her drawing things away. And to think.

Once Wren thought she saw a light like Sorchae in real life. Closing the door to her room, she sat cross-legged in her desk chair, elbows on the desk. *Mona and the Selkie* fascinated her, maybe because Sorchae reminded her so much of that previous experience when she'd been in the hospital after her eye surgery.

After the first few days, the couple—who were strangers to her, but whom she quickly came to know as Momma and Daddy—came to the hospital and stayed by her side every day and most every night. Nonna had come too.

Wren had felt loved and safe for the first time in her brief life. She remembered feeling something like relief. When she wondered about her Mommy from before, she got a sad feeling. Was Mommy all alone? Did her boyfriend hit her? But mostly Wren felt safe and happy.

In those first few lonely days at the hospital, before Momma and Daddy came, wondering where her Mommy was and what it meant that she didn't have one eye anymore, Wren had been scared, scared of being alone. Scared of the dark. She had called the nurse every few minutes. Finally, they told her not to use the call button anymore. "We have other patients that really need help," one nurse explained.

That long, scary night, Marie—as she was known back then— had lain awake staring into the darkness of the room. The dark came to life, evil and threatening, like it would swallow her whole. And she knew it could.

Fear had filled the room. She couldn't help but breathe it in—swallow it down. Her heart raced, and she thought she might throw up. She tried to reach the button for the nurse, but her muscles wouldn't move. Paralyzed, she couldn't even lift her hand, which scared her even more. Nothing else had been wrong except for her eye. She'd been able to move everything perfectly fine during the day. During the night, paralysis held her body. She had wondered what was going on.

She remembered seeing an evil presence, like a dragon, flying around inside her room. Imagination?

You're going to die in here, she heard   or thought.

She tried again to reach the nurse's button.

Nothing. She couldn't lift her finger, much less her arm.

She tried to scream.

Not a single sound came out of her throat.

Heart pounding, her breathing became hard and fast. Marie hadn't wanted to die all alone in the hospital.

The darkness felt so thick, like she was drowning in it. She believed if she closed her eyes—well, her good eye— she would die.

Staring up at the dark ceiling, unable to move, wanting to scream but incapable, she saw it.

A tiny light like a star shone far, far away, like she could see through the ceiling, out into the night sky. She stared at the tiny pinprick of starlight—a small goodness in the sea of evil.

Her left eye locked onto it as if it were her only hope. If she kept looking at that spark, maybe she'd be okay.

The twinkling light grew as if coming closer to her. Light oozed out from its core like a tiny sun, and around it the darkness backed away.

After a while, Marie tried to whisper, testing her voice.

"Help" came out when she forced the word through. It was quiet, but a whisper was better than nothing.

The light grew a bit more. The fear quieted. Maybe she'd live through the night.

Using her voice encouraged her to try to move her arms again. She did. It worked. She pushed the button to call the nurse.

The nurse appeared in her doorway looking a little angry. "I told you not to press that button again. At least you waited a few minutes more this time."

What was she talking about? Marie had been drowning in that darkness for hours, hadn't she? Of course she couldn't explain any of it to the nurse, but the woman came in with a gentle touch, fluffed Marie's pillow, and gave her an extra blanket. Then, somehow, she fell asleep.

Funny how the mind works. Wren had forgotten all about that night until she read about Sorchae in O'Connor's book. Now she thought about it from time to time. Had it been her three-year-old imagination? Or had there been some kind of real evil in that room, and an actual light more powerful than fear?

Wren attended church with Momma and Daddy. She believed in God. But no one at church ever talked about God coming to someone like a star to cheer them up and chase away evil. Wren liked to think God was the kind of God to do something like that for a scared little girl. He was love, after all.

Had Melanie seen something like that?

Wren wondered… and her insides quivered at the mystery.

CHAPTER SIX

Wren hummed. *"Come to me, come to me when you are weary. I will give you, I will give you My rest."* The song from Sunday's service played over in her mind.

She parked on the school side of the road. She and Liv were meeting before their early class at the Refuge, one of their favorite coffee shops. Favorite because it was across the street from the school, because they offered a latté with cardamom in it, and because they employed a cute barista who smiled at Wren when she came in. Of course, he smiled at everyone, but that was beside the point.

Humidity hung heavy in the autumn air. They'd had some cool days, but this one was much more common for September in Fairhope. She tied her hair back in a ponytail with a scrunchie and jogged across the street.

The door's jingle caught her off guard, and she hoped it wouldn't offend any late-night partiers who had to get up early this morning.

Liv sat on the L-shaped cushioned bench in the back. Wren waved to her on the way to order. Liv waved half-heartedly, already sipping her coffee. She was one of those who didn't know the sun was up until she'd had at least two cups of caffeine.

No handsome barista today. Just a student with cropped hair and a sleeveless shirt revealing tats on each shoulder, working the early shift. She gave Wren an emotionless greeting. Wren took no offense and gave her order. Later in the day, the same barista would be more chipper.

"Hey, you awake, lady?" She teased Liv as she walked over. Liv rubbed her eyes and yawned.

"No problem," Liv waved a hand in front of Wren. "It's a glorious day." But her puffy eyes said something else.

"Did you have another gig last night? I would've come."

"No. I met Cade to talk about the details of this modeling thing."

Wren would support Liv in whatever she wanted to do, as long as she could keep up with what that was.

"Really, Wren." Liv must've noticed her less-than-enthusiastic expression. "It's legit."

"Cardamom Latté!" The barista sounded more alive already.

"That's me." Wren jogged the few feet to the counter. "Thank you."

The girl nodded.

The cold-coffee-brewing system behind the counter caught Wren's attention. Coffee flowed slowly down through thin glass, spirally tubes with all the twists and turns of life.

She turned back to Liv. "Did you see the coffee going down through that glass thing by the wall over there?"

"Yeah, cool." Liv didn't look up.

"Cade must've been attracted to you?" Wren nudged Liv with her elbow.

Liv blushed, then rolled her eyes. "Silly. He just thought I'd be great for this opportunity his uncle has."

"You mean to tell me y'all have met two or three times and he hasn't tried to kiss you, besides that peck on the cheek?"

Liv blushed again. Her fair skin could never hide the truth. "Well, there was that one kiss." She rolled her eyes up and to the right.

Wren sucked in air. "I knew it!"

"I kind of like him," Liv admitted.

"His looks don't hurt either." Wren winked her good eye.

"Okay yeah, but he's a truly nice guy."

"I hope so, Liv. You deserve the best." Wren sipped her latte.

Liv gave Wren a little shove, nearly spilling her drink.

"What's the opportunity?" She needed details.

"You know I've done some modeling?"

Wren nodded. "And some acting, not to mention singing."

"Right, but those don't pay."

Wren nodded. She'd already heard this.

"I need money, Wren. It's awful. Ever since Dad left, Mom works all the time, and we still don't have money for anything extra. I mean it. No clothes, no shoes, no make-up—"

"No makeup?" Wren figured Liv just wanted new clothes, but for those who wore makeup, that was a consumable product and needed to be replenished regularly.

"Well, I can't afford the one I want. If Daddy were around, he'd give me the money even if I lived in my own place." She glanced down, then back up at Wren. "I sound like a spoiled brat, don't I?"

"No. It makes sense. You want at least some things you were used to."

Liv flashed her a hopeful look.

Wren smirked. "Okay. You're spoiled rotten."

Liv flipped her hair back. "Why, thank you very much." They both laughed then, hearing the jingle they glanced up at a thirty-something coming in for his morning brew.

"But seriously, Liv, why don't you move home? You could save on rent and use your money for whatever." It seemed the practical solution to Wren.

"Mom wants me to. She says she has a home to offer, not much else." Liv sighed. "I know she means well, but I need to be on my own. It's hard to make your way in the world when you still live with Mommy," her voice trailed. "Sorry, Wren."

"No, it's okay. I understand. And maybe my parents do hold me back sometimes."

"Maybe?" Liv had that shocked look on her face.

"I guess I let them," Wren admitted.

"True, but why?" Liv pressed her. "You could do so much. You're super smart and talented… the best artist I've ever met, and that's saying something in this artsy town. Why don't you step out?" Before Wren could answer, Liv added, "You could live with me. It would help me save money and help you become more independent."

"How many times have you offered?" Should Wren consider it? It seemed so risky. "I don't know, maybe you're right, Liv. But I would need some money coming in if I did that." What if she couldn't make it without her parents? What if she were too weak or too dumb? "And then I'd have to work as well as do accounting homework." The thought made her gag.

"Not if you dropped accounting." Liv sat like a victorious cat who had just caught a cricket.

Wren couldn't do that. She pinned Liv with a stare, to no effect whatsoever.

You'll never be good enough. You can't perceive depth.

Wren had been over it a thousand times. She needed something safe and profitable. She needed security.

But didn't all the effort she put into accounting, which she didn't even like, keep her from giving art a fair shot?

"What if you studied to be an art teacher?" Liv piped into Wren's thoughts. "You could fall back on that, and you'd be studying art."

The dark thoughts gave way to a glimmer. Why hadn't Wren thought to bring that up with Momma and Daddy?

"Hey, how'd we get off on my problems? I thought we were talking about you. You and Cade?"

"Yeah, can we get back to *moi* now?" Liv pointed both thumbs toward her chest. They laughed again. "It's so exciting, Wren. An audition for a real modeling gig. It's a magazine—"

"Which one?"

"Cade's not allowed to tell yet. They like to keep it secret and then only tell the ones who make it, but he said I'd recognize the name."

"Like Vogue or something?"

Liv shrugged. "Why not? It's big, whatever it is. They have openings for five new modeling positions. And if those work out well, there might be opportunities to do a movie!"

"Have you checked it all out?" *Too good to be true,* Wren thought, remembering James Fielding's lecture. She kept the comment to herself… for now.

"Yes, Cade has brochures, and he sent me to their website. It's all there. And I looked them up on the Better Business Bureau. The company isn't listed there at all, so no complaints have been filed."

When Wren didn't reply, Liv continued, "He showed me their ad on TikTok too. It looked very professional."

"Hmm."

"I'm ignoring that less-than-excited attitude for now." Liv sipped her double-shot latté. "But Wren, come with me."

"You know you're crazy, right?" Wren had no intention—

"It pays a lot and could get us both ahead. Maybe just a few gigs and we could quit to sing and draw. At least it would give us time to focus on what we love and see if we could make a career of it. And we'd be in it together. If one month was down for one of us financially, the other could cover."

It almost made sense. But no. No way would Wren pose in front of a camera. "You have a point. If only we had a way to really focus on what we love long enough for it to take off. What we need to learn is marketing."

"But if we become even a little famous, we'd have enough followers to have a good start on that as well." Liv's reasoning might be sound, but what if…

Momma and Daddy would never allow Wren to—"Have you told your mom about the audition?"

"No way! She'd say no for sure. She doesn't understand show business. And I'm no longer a child. I need to learn to make my own decisions. How are we going to do that if we don't make some? Sure, we'll make some mistakes, but that's how we learn, right?"

"That's what I always hear." It didn't seem like a safe plan to Wren. Her parents had been her safety net, her support. "Liv, don't you think—"

Liv's expression stopped her mid-sentence.

"What if Cade's some psycho?"

"Okay, just drop it, Wren. Have you met Cade? Have you talked to him?" Liv paused and looked around. "And when you become an adult, living on your own, it's not really practical to call and tell your parents everywhere you're going, is it?"

True, but getting advice from people who'd proven their wisdom and care for her over the years was Wren's go-to for decision-making. Even if they drove her crazy sometimes, after all, she had these great parents, so why not use them?

"You have to take some risks." Liv was determined. "So do I."

"It is risky, so just let your mom know where you're going. She might be mad, but, like you said, you're an adult making your own decisions."

"Absolutely not." Liv raised her voice, not angry, but resolute. "And you can't tell her either. And you can't tell your parents either, or they'll tell mine."

"Liv, come on."

"Not another word." Liv closed her eyes and held up one palm. Her mind was set.

"So, you're determined to go no matter what I say. And you're going by yourself whether I come or not. And you refuse to tell our parents." Wren nut-shelled the situation.

"You've got it, friend." Liv had that cat look again.

Wren glanced at the time on her cell phone. "Dang it, we have to get to class."

They stood and grabbed their book bags.

"Promise, Wren. Not a word."

"I promise, but if that's the case, I'm coming with you. You can't go alone."

Liv shrieked, waking up the sleepy customers, and threw her arms around Wren's neck. Her book bag hit the floor with a thud. "I knew there was a reason I loved you. Besties forever, right?"

"Of course." Wren smiled and put an arm around Liv's back even as her stomach chilled.

———•●•———

After she finished her homework, Wren came downstairs with a rumbly tummy. Six o'clock already? Good thing she didn't have to make dinner—perks of living at home.

"Hey Wren, how was school today?" Daddy placed silverware on top of napkins to the left of each of the three plates.

"Eh."

"Come on, you can do better than that. Make your mother proud." They both laughed. No secret that Wren's disposition had more in common with her father than her mother. Neither of them could keep up with Momma's WPD, as they called it, Words Per Day. "Momma will be home in a few minutes. She's getting pizza from Section Street on the way."

"She was in Fairhope today?" Usually, Momma worked as a travel agent from home, but sometimes she agreed to meet a client in Daphne or Fairhope. Occasionally she met someone in Foley, Mobile, or Pensacola.

"I'll drive anywhere for a wealthy client who might rack up the overseas miles," Momma had been known to say.

"Just got a text." Daddy lifted his phone. "She has pizza in hand and is on her way." He set plates on the table.

"Great, I'm starving." Wren went to get the wooden pizza peel and a spatula. Momma liked to re-cut the slices. "I'll fill some water glasses."

"Greetings and pizza." Momma somehow flung the door wide open while holding the pizza box and two bags of unidentified groceries in one hand and gesturing with the other.

"Aria, my love." Daddy kissed her cheek as he relieved her of the pizza box.

"You say that to all the girls who bring you pizza."

"You're right." He winked.

Momma pinched his backside. Wren turned her head, thinking more seriously about Liv's offer to move in with her. She'd be glad to avoid these embarrassing moments.

"What kind did you get?" Wren shifted the focus back to the pizza.

"Capone." It was Mom and Dad's favorite. Wren loved it too—tomato cream sauce, mozzarella, garlic, Italian sausage—who wouldn't love it? But then again, what pizza didn't she love?

"Yum." Wren lifted the top of the box. Standing by the table, Momma pushed it back down.

"Let's eat together," she said.

When they all sat down, Momma told them about the clients she met earlier in the day, where they were going and what tours she'd been able to set up for them. When she slowed her words long enough to get a bite of pizza, Wren jumped in.

"Hey, I've been thinking about that art scholarship more. It covers a good part of the tuition for two years. After this year, I'll only need two more years to get a bachelor's degree. And that would be perfect."

"It covers two years for the winner?" Momma asked.

"Exactly." Wren could win, at least Liv thought she could. Maybe she had a shot? "Don't you think I should at least try?"

A little groan from Daddy's side. Wren couldn't tell if he was simply tired of the same old discussion or if he disagreed with her trying.

"Wrennie, we've talked about this over and over." Momma set her slice of pizza down. "You're just starting your associate's degree in accounting. When you get that in place, then you can work a job and do some drawing on the side."

"What if it's not enough? What if I really hate accounting, or worse, what if I'm terrible at it?"

Dad looked up from his pizza. "You've always done well in math."

"I did okay in math, but it was never my favorite. And accounting is so boring." How could she make them understand? It's not that she wanted to be entertained, but… "Even if I understand it, my mind isn't engaged and I make mistakes."

"Well, get it engaged, Wren," Momma said, reaching for her slice again. "You can tough it out, can't you? Two years isn't that long." She folded the piece and took a bite.

"I don't think I'd like the work of an accountant." How could she make them understand?

"There are plenty of things grown-ups have to do that they don't like," Momma reminded her. "Time to grow up."

Wren dropped her head to stare at the sausage on her pizza, but not before she caught Daddy glaring at Momma.

"Don't look at me like that, Bud," Momma told him. "You both know the reasons. How many times do we need to go over them?"

"Maybe I could finish a general associate's degree at Coastal, then transfer to a university offering Art History. I could work in a museum or gallery."

"Those jobs are rare and make little money," Momma said. "Unless you're the key person who has loads of experience."

"I could get a master's degree and become an art teacher."

"Teaching would be great for you, sweetie," Daddy encouraged. But they both knew, even though she was technically an adult now, it came down to her mother's opinion. He wiped his mouth on the everyday cloth napkin.

"Your art teacher said you weren't qualified to do art in any professional way," Momma reminded her. "Even if you got a job as an art teacher somewhere, would it be fair to your students? You couldn't show them anything relating to depth perception." Momma rubbed her eyes, then put her glasses back on. "I love you, Wrennie. Of course, I want you to be happy. I also want you to be independent." She paused. "You could even be a liability in the school around so many little kids."

"Aria!" Daddy's voice wasn't loud, just shocked, exactly how Wren felt.

"Well, it's true, Bud. Wren could walk into a child she doesn't see squarely, and they could get hurt."

Could Momma be right? Would Wren be a risk to the children's wellbeing? Doctors used to tell her that having only one eye would hardly affect her life at all. How wrong they were. She'd hate to go to work each day worried that she might harm a child.

"But the biggest risk," Momma continued. "Is that a principal may not want to hire you for art knowing your disability, and it wouldn't be right not to reveal that."

"Disability," Wren whispered under her breath. She took another bite of her pizza, but the flavor was gone.

A bitter revelation popped into her mind. "Actually, they'd have to hire me. Ever heard of the Americans with Disabilities Act?"

"What?" Momma asked.

"The ADA. It would be discrimination if they didn't." Wren would hate to work in a place where they didn't want her, but she didn't say that out loud.

"How would the parents feel?" Her mother continued.

This just kept getting worse. "What do you mean?" Wren's expression must've shown the hurt she felt.

Daddy got up, came over by her, and kneeled, stretching out his hand as a peace offering. "Now, Princess, your mother doesn't mean anything against you."

"Of course not, I just want you to have something secure. My daddy went for two years without work in Italy. The family suffered until they finally moved to the United States on a work visa. It was very stressful. I don't want that for you."

Wren's stomach burned. Daddy's hand was still suspended. She closed her eyes, a few tears escaping down her cheeks.

"Wren. Do you understand your mother's fear?" Daddy broached. She sensed his compassion even in the question, but she wanted them to understand her fears.

Words escaped her. This conversation had to stop. She couldn't take it anymore. Standing, she decided to stop it right now. This was not how she imagined this conversation going.

She lifted a hand, palm out, tears in her eyes, and ran up the stairs.

Closing her door, she sat on the bed and cried into the pillow she scooped onto her lap.

After a while, the tears subsided.

You are handicapped.

No one even used that word anymore, but that's what so often resounded in her mind.

You are disabled.

Used or not, that word spoke the truth. She was unable to do the things she loved.

She wished she could be more like Liv. At least she was giving her dreams a shot. One day, at the very least, she'd be able to say that she tried. But Liv wasn't impaired like Wren.

She shouldn't discourage her friend from chasing her dreams. And she shouldn't put her own fears on Liv. Maybe it was time she listened to Liv rather than the other way around.

But didn't her youth leader say that they should listen to the still, quiet voice in their head? As long as that voice wasn't outside God's laws. Kind of like that James Fielding guy who spoke at the college. He told them to trust their gut.

What did Wren's gut know? Her fears had always led her, and look where it got her. Nowhere... stuck in an accounting program, living with her parents.

Did the creepy chill inside whenever Liv talked about the modeling audition qualify as a gut feeling?

Naw. Like Liv said, Wren had fears all the time. She allowed those fears way too much freedom. If Wren couldn't chase her dreams, at least Liv could.

CHAPTER SEVEN

For the past year, it had been a struggle to go home to Opelika, though Jim just lived a few miles away in Auburn. He kept busy writing, traveling, and speaking, hoping to make a difference.

At least that's what he told everyone. If he were honest, the empty feeling in his childhood home without Stacy's presence played a part as well.

This time Mom convinced him to come for dinner. His next speaking engagement was at Auburn University, less than ten miles from Opelika. Mom and Dad were hurting and needed to see him.

He'd been able to ignore his parents' pain and keep himself busy until that girl at Coastal, the community college in Fairhope, asked about his family. How insightful. Since then, he'd been thinking more about them.

Facing the emotions in that house wouldn't be easy. He needed to be out doing something to catch Stacy's killers or at least raising awareness so other young people wouldn't get sucked into the traffickers' traps.

Being quiet with Mom and Dad, in their house, seeing the pictures of him and Stacy… that wouldn't fix anything.

But they needed him. He needed them too.

After dinner, they sat in the living room. Jim had a slice of Mom's apple-pear cobbler with vanilla ice cream and a cup of coffee. He relaxed into the other side of the couch from Mom. Dad sat to their right in his well-worn recliner.

"Remember how Stacy loved this time of year?" Mom's eyes looked moist, a dreamy expression on her face.

"She loved everything about harvest time," Dad added.

Jim swallowed hard and set his plate on the coffee table. Stacy had been eight years younger than him. She'd be sixteen by now. Watched leaves flutter around outside through the window. His parents had lost two babies between Jim and Stacy; now Stacy was gone too.

She'd been full of joy. Jim had always been more serious about life, with a take-the-bull-by-the-horns kind of philosophy. Stacy enjoyed life and made sure other people did too. She entertained them all from the moment she could walk and talk. He could still see her dancing in front of the TV, singing into her hairbrush.

He wiped moisture from the corner of his eyes. Why had he been so far away when it happened? His big, important journalism job in Washington. Success had seemed so important. If he'd been in Alabama, maybe he could've done something.

"It's okay to remember and be sad, Jim," Mom said.

"I know." Did he?

"Has Officer Windly made any progress?" Dad asked. Jim had become the contact between the police department and the family.

He shook his head. "They're running out of clues. I wish we had something more to give him. The captain is closing the case. They're calling it a cold case now."

It burned inside him. He'd have to find a way to investigate this himself. The men who took Stacy, used and abused her, and then tossed her out on the ground to die when all she needed was a simple inhaler… those men should burn in Hades. At the very least, rot in jail.

"Jim?"

He looked up. Dad had been asking him something.

"I asked what things might help the investigation further?" Dad repeated his question.

"I don't know. Maybe if we had her phone, but they asked for that early on and it was not with the body."

"Anything else?" Dad asked.

Jim shrugged. He stared at his dessert, which he now held without really seeing it, thoughts turning over in his head. "Maybe if we knew what she was looking at online before she went missing." Why hadn't he thought of it before? There could be a clue in there.

"How would that help?" Mom asked.

"I'm not sure if it would."

"We have her computer. In fact, her room is pretty much how she left it." Mom's face flushed. "I know, I know… But sometimes I go in there and just lie on her bed imagining she's just at school and she'll be home in a few hours." Tears dripped down her face.

Jim reached across the couch and grabbed his mother's hand. She squeezed back.

"It might help." Jim sat forward, ready to stand up. "Do you mind if I take the computer? I can look through it when I'm home or in a hotel."

"You're so busy, Jim." Dad reached for his pipe. "I don't want this to consume you."

"I think it's a little late for that, Henry," Mom said.

— • ◉ • —

Back at his apartment, Jim opened Stacy's computer. She never set up a password as he'd advised. Too bad he couldn't give her a hard time about that. He went to her history and started scrolling through it. Amazon, TikTok… lots of those two. A makeup company, a couple of fashion design schools. He'd forgotten how much she loved fashion.

She used to draw new outfits and talk about how she might get them made one day.

Her YouTube history was entertaining—a few dance videos and several bands that she liked. Her TikTok friends included people she knew from school and many others who shared her interests.

Wait. What was this? An ad for a modeling audition. Had she been interested in modeling? He never knew that, though it was fashion-related. Stacy would have made a beautiful model.

He found a few direct messages about the modeling audition. It looked like a few of her friends had been interested as well.

Those were the last messages he'd seen except for one talking about the guy she liked at school with one of her friends. Could the guy have been a plant in the school? Maybe he was undercover for the traffickers and just had a young-looking face.

Are you writing fiction or investigating? He chastised himself.

Maybe he should take a course in investigating. He knew investigative reporting, but he could be more effective if he studied police investigation.

Yeah, right. When would he do that?

The work he did now made a difference. He needed to believe that. At least he had a voice with a wider audience. The articles in The Atlantic had the potential to reach over a million subscribers. And speaking to students on college campuses helped raise awareness. Though college students weren't the most vulnerable, nor the most common target.

He should be speaking to the junior high and high schoolers. Evil creeps targeted the younger kids since they were more naïve and easier to fool.

He needed to get the message to them, or at least to the parents of young teens. But how?

You can't do everything, Jim. Just do what you can, and it will be enough.

God's voice?

Mom and Dad would certainly agree.

But… Stacy… His throat tightened. He swallowed.

So, what could he do? Whatever it was, he had to do it.

He went back to Stacy's social media, searching until his head started to drop.

— • ● • —

Wren stood in front of the mirror, her head turned to the right, not completely disappointed with her appearance. Not gorgeous, but pretty, like Liv said, in a natural way. If she had to pick her favorite feature, it would be her hair, dark brown reaching her elbows, not straight but not curly either. She straightened her terra-cotta sweater, hoping the color brightened her face for the audition after school.

Had she made the right decision?

Liv and Cade had been together every minute she wasn't in class or sleeping for the past two weeks. And Wren wasn't sure about the sleeping part.

She hadn't seen Liv but once in the last week. Even then, they'd hung out at Page and Palette with Cade.

They spoke on the phone, though. Liv was falling in love, Wren could tell. Cade seemed to do everything right. Thoughtful and sweet, he didn't rush things in Liv's eyes. And he had money to spend on her.

Cade would be with Liv at the audition, but Wren still wanted to go. She wouldn't miss Liv's big moment. One day they'd each be married, and all the special occasions would be reserved for their husbands. At this rate, Liv could be married before they finished their freshman year of college. So, it wasn't only Wren's worst-case fears that made her want to drive Liv to the audition.

Wren ran her hands over the sweater again. Not only was it an excellent color, but it was also lightweight enough to be comfortable in the warmer afternoon weather. Enough glaring at herself in the mirror. She had to get to class.

After class, Wren waited by the bulletin board, where she'd run into Mr. Cho a few weeks ago.

Liv burst out of the hallway and flashed her pearly whites. "We could be highly paid models before the end of this day." She grabbed Wren's arm and pulled as if she'd been the one waiting for Wren all this time.

"Yeah, sure." Wren tossed her head, imitating someone famous, hair rippling like a flag in the wind.

"Cade said he'd meet us in the parking lot behind The Refuge." Liv hopped into the passenger side of Wren's car. "I'm nervous." She pretend-bit her freshly painted nails, sparkles on her thumb and pinky.

"You're a shoo-in, Liv. You're made for the stage. And you look great in a bikini." Wren tossed her book bag into the backseat.

"You too!" Liv shot back. "Who could turn you down?"

"Well, I'm not here for me, b-u-u-t…" Wren shrugged one shoulder, like she might consider the chance if it came her way. She knew better.

"If it works out, you won't mind, right?" Liv winked.

"You know me, always clamoring for the stage." They both laughed. It was fun to do something daring and to do it with Liv. Wren started the car, then her mood turned serious.

"What's wrong?" Liv asked.

"I hate lying to my parents." Wren pulled at the collar of her cropped jean jacket and adjusted her rearview mirror, then pulled out. Cade would be waiting be just around the block.

Liv slipped her phone into her gem-studded clutch purse. "Me too, but it will be worth it when we get the job and tell them how much we'll be making."

Wren nodded, but she couldn't shake the cold tightening in her stomach.

"And we'll remind them that we can choose the jobs we want to do so it won't interfere with homework like a regular job."

"Really?" That seemed fair to Wren. "That's a plus."

"Cade said that was the case."

So why did Wren wish she could go home and work on some accounting analysis forms?

They pulled into the parking lot where a silver Kia waited. Liv opened the door and got out. She leaned back in and looked at Wren. "This is Cade." Liv was ready to get in the car with him.

"Uh, Liv," Wren yelled through the open passenger window. She had no intention of going without her car. "I thought Cade would ride with us in my car."

"No, he said we can all fit comfortably in his."

"We can follow Cade in my car." She put on her I'm-not-budging-on-this face, hoping her left eye could portray enough resolve to convince Liv.

"But it would save gas—" Liv stopped. "Okay."

Liv leaned near Cade's window. "I guess we're going to follow you, Cade. Sorry about that."

Turning back to Wren's car, Liv got in. Wren caught a whiff of something floral, gentle. She'd have to find out what perfume Liv wore. "I told him we'd follow."

They crossed the Bay in quiet excitement, nervousness in Wren's case. It would be so embarrassing to be in front of modeling scouts who would analyze everything about her.

They'll just love how your right eye has such minimal movement. She kept the sarcasm to herself.

Hopefully, they'd just let her hang out with Liv and watch.

In downtown Mobile, a horn blared against the backdrop of general traffic noises. Wren tensed. She had to watch everything due to the abundance of pedestrians.

Wren checked her GPS. "All I see are a bunch of warehouses." Something didn't feel right. Was it normal to hold modeling auditions in a warehouse? Maybe.

"Our audition must be inside one of them," Liv said. "Look for a sign for The Lumina Talent Group. Cade said that's the company holding the auditions."

"I hope Cade knows where to go. I don't see a public entrance." Wren glared ahead.

"He's turning into that parking garage over there." Liv pointed and Wren followed.

They pulled into a space right next to Cade's car and got out.

"Hey ladies, we'll have to walk around to the side." Cade twirled a key ring around his index finger.

"Strange spot for a modeling audition for a major magazine." Wren's voice echoed into the musty parking garage. She didn't mind sounding skeptical despite Liv's sideways glance. A breeze brought a sudden chill to the air. Wren closed the front of her jean jacket with one button.

"I don't think they own the building." Cade flipped his bangs back. "They hold pop-up auditions in large cities all across the U.S."

Liv grabbed his hand. "That makes sense. Now where's the entrance to this place?"

He tucked Liv's hand under his arm, and Wren jogged a few steps to catch up to them.

"Here it is." Liv pointed. A license-plate-sized sign read: Lumina Talent Group—Live Auditions Today Only.

Cade opened the heavy door and held it for them.

"They didn't put much money into this." Wren chewed the inside of her cheek.

"Naw, they probably put the money into paying the models," Cade said with great cheer.

Did Cade even know what he was talking about? How well did he know this uncle?

"Sounds good to me," Liv piped in. She ducked under Cade's arm as he held the door. Wren followed her, holding the door for herself.

"Hello, ladies, and sir," a man dressed in a bow-tieless tux greeted them with a heavy accent. He sat behind a desk in one corner of a large, otherwise bare, room. The man stood. "Come right this way." He led them with one arm outstretched.

The warehouse was empty except for his wooden desk, a standing lamp with a stained-glass umbrella lampshade next to the desk, and a camera on a tripod a few feet away. He had a laptop on the desk and a mug, presumably for coffee. A bare stage stood off to the side, surrounded by folding chairs at the far end of the warehouse. The man picked up a basket as they passed his desk.

Probably in his thirties, but still very good looking, the man's olive skin and brown eyes added warmth to his welcome. He should be one of the models, Wren thought.

"Drop your phones in here," he said holding the basket in their direction.

Sirens sounded in Wren's head. He must've seen the look on her face.

"You can pick them up at my desk as soon as you've finished. We can't have lights flashing or sounds going off during the auditions." His smile comforted her.

She noticed three other phones already in there. So Wren, Liv, and Cade tossed their phones in. The knots in Wren's stomach tightened.

"I need to get a headshot of each of you for your files." He motioned for Liv to stand on a masking-tape X on the floor, perfectly distanced from the camera on the tripod. Wren hadn't noticed it until the man pointed it out. He snapped her photo and then motioned for Wren.

"I don't know that I'm auditioning, I just came for my frie—"

"We need your picture just in case." So, she complied. Then he motioned for them to follow him. "This way," he said.

They followed him to a smaller room off the big open room where his desk had been. Five other girls and two boys sat lining the walls in folding chairs awaiting their auditions. Liv sat down and Wren sat next to her, Cade on her other side. No one talked.

The silence rubbed Wren like a burr in her shoe. That plus the irritating scent of mildew in the old building.

"Someone will be in soon to take you to wardrobe," the man explained. "There you'll pick an ensemble of your choice. This is about your sense of style as much as it is about how you look, so get creative."

Liv bounced in her seat a little. More than a pretty face, Liv had a natural sense of style. Wren gave her a thumbs-up signal. She tried to breathe into her stomach to help it relax while they waited.

A different man, near forty, stepped into the open doorway of the room. "You can go back to wardrobe now," he said, pushing one side of his shoulder-length blond hair behind his ear.

"Oh, hey, Romeo!" Cade knew the guy. "I didn't know you'd be here. How's it—?"

The man nodded in his direction, his expression cutting Cade off. He pointed at Liv and Wren.

"But..." Wren tried to protest.

"What?" The Romeo guy pointed more insistently down the hallway. "Do as you're told, now."

"I'm not here to audition. I just came with my friend." Wren squeezed her jean jacket between her hands.

"You're here, so you'll audition. Now go pick an outfit." He pointed down the hall, leaving no room for discussion.

A shock of nerves seared through Wren's body. How could they force her to audition? Of course, they could make her leave if she didn't audition, and she wanted to stay for Liv.

"Come on, Wren," Liv pulled at her elbow. "This will be an experience you can tell your grandkids about."

Cade, Wren, and Liv walked together down the long white hallway. Fluorescent lighting and a drop ceiling led their way in lieu of actual sunshine. Romeo quick-walked to get ahead of them and show them where to go.

He stopped and turned his head. "Where are you going?" He pinned Cade with a glare.

"I invited these two. I thought I could watch their audition." Cade looked hopeful.

The man shook his head and pointed like the Ghost-of-Christmas-Yet-to-Come back toward the waiting room.

"I'll see you ladies after the audition," Cade said. "You'll have to fill me in on all the details."

"We will." Liv blew him a kiss and waved.

They followed Romeo farther down the hallway. Wren jumped at the sound of a heavy door slamming. Sounds in the warehouse echoed, and she couldn't tell where they came from. Then the sound of a bolt sliding into place.

"What was that?"

"Sounded like a door locking," Liv whispered, a question on her face. She shrugged, then leaned toward Wren. "If this works out, the next thing we do together is something to promote your drawings," she whispered.

Wren winked at her friend, but if they started modeling, in addition to classes, there'd be no time for art.

The man indicated a room and they went in.

"Let's see what we can find." Liv walked to the rack of clothes at the far end of the small room opposite the hallway door they had entered from. "It should be a little suggestive, but subtle. Bold, but slightly feminine." Liv was talking to herself.

The door to the wardrobe room must've been heavy. It closed with a bang and Wren jumped, its sound echoing in the room.

They stood near the hanging racks with a few other people. Tasked with choosing an outfit for their audition, Wren didn't have a clue. She heard a bolt slide and click into place. Were they locked in?

Wren pierced Liv with a look. Asking without asking, *what was going on?*

"They'll come get us when they're ready for us," she assured Wren.

"But…" Wren studied the back wall. Her gaze moved up to the corners where the ceiling met the wall. Something didn't look right. "Why does that wall curve where it meets the ceiling?" Wren pointed.

"This shag vest is amazing." Liv lifted the hanger from a rack.

Ignoring her, Wren scanned the walls of the room and then the floor. "Something smells funny."

Liv held up the vest for Wren to see. "What do you th—" Her gaze shifted upward.

Wren followed Liv's eyes and noticed some kind of smoke coming through a vent in the ceiling. "What in the world?"

CHAPTER EIGHT

Wren couldn't see a thing. She searched the blackness for any speck of light. Something flashed. A tiny flutter of light, like a lightning bug, flew around. She watched its circling path as it grew smaller and farther away. Then no light at all.

Ouch. Her hip and head had bumped into a hard surface. Bouncing again, she rubbed her head just above her ear. She blinked and touched the right eye with her fingers. Luckily, the prosthetic hadn't fallen out when she hit her head. But she could barely see anything out of her good eye. Where was she?

The floor underneath her vibrated.

What was going on? Where had she been? Thoughts started to form. She and Liv had gone to the modeling audition. There had been a waiting room, then a hallway to… Oh right, they were supposed to pick out some clothes to wear for the audition. Liv had picked out something to show Wren. She was standing in front of the rack of clothes when—nothing.

Wait… something else. The walls had been strange, then smoke seeped down into the room through a vent. O God, they'd been drugged. Her heart pounded in her chest.

A big bump tossed her against the wall of… a moving vehicle—of some kind of truck with no windows. Eyes open, all she saw was a thin sliver of light coming in from underneath the truck's back door. She braced herself for the next bump, pressing her hands down onto a plastic clothes hanger.

In fact, she felt hangers strewn all around her. The truck must've been pulled up to a loading dock of some kind and disguised as part of the room in the building. The whole thing had been a setup. What kind of sick people would do this? Why?

Jesus, help. She just wanted to be home with Momma and Daddy as she heard a car zip past their truck on the road.

Where was Liv?

"Liv, are you here?" she whispered.

No answer.

"Hey, Liv…?" Her voice came out louder this time.

Wren maneuvered up onto her knees, spreading them to stabilize herself. The truck swerved, shifting her knees. Ouch. Pain shot through her kneecap. She sat cross-legged instead, reaching out to feel what might be around her.

"Lord Jesus, Son of God, have mercy on us," she whispered the words of the memorized prayer. Her hand brushed into what felt like a body and she shrieked falling back onto her hip.

"Watch out!"

At least the body wasn't dead.

"Where are we?" Wren asked.

"I don't know." The male voice replied.

"Me neither." Liv's voice was groggy but alive. "I'm afraid to move."

"Liv?" Wren needed to be sure.

"It's me." Liv's voice cracked, but Wren breathed a sigh of relief. She was alive, and they were together.

"I'm glad you're okay," Wren said.

"I feel some clothes and hangers," Liv said. "We must still be in the wardrobe room with all the clothes."

"I think so, or part of it," Wren said, coming to the same conclusion. "It must have been a truck backed up to a building." That was her theory so far.

"What?" Liv sounded shocked. "Is this one of your worst-case theories, Wren?"

"How many people are in here?" The male voice spoke before Wren could answer.

Good question. Trapped with strangers… and where were they being taken? Wren gulped hard against the rising panic. She couldn't imagine any good scenario.

"I've counted four voices," an accented female voice said.

"They must've drugged us," the male voice said.

"I saw smoke coming through a vent in the ceiling," Liv said. "That was the last thing I remember."

"That's messed up," he said. "Everybody say their name, then we'll know how many are in here and kind of where you are in the truck. I'm Damiano."

"Liv," her voice shaky.

"I'm Wren."

"My name's Mei." Wren couldn't tell where she might be from by her accent.

"I'm so sorry, Wren," Liv's hand found hers. "Is that you?"

"Yes." Wren squeezed Liv's hand. "We're going to be okay though."

"How do you know?" Mei asked.

Wren shrugged, then realized no one could see her. "I-I don't know." But she needed to say it.

"Aren't you afraid, Wren?" Liv asked. "You're always terrified of something."

"I am." But she had to hold it together… to think positively. If she gave in to worst-case thinking now, fear would swallow her whole. "I don't know. I just feel like we're going to be okay." She had to focus on that faint feeling, possibly only delusion, but she clung to it like a life preserver.

"Ridiculous," Mei, responded.

Liv cried quietly. "Not only did I get myself in trouble, but I've put you in danger too, Wren. You tried to tell me you didn't feel good about it. I just thought you were a worrywart, like always."

"You're usually right about me." Wren squeezed her friend's hand. "We're going to get out of this, Liv. You'll see."

"What do you know that we don't?" Damiano asked.

"I just feel it. I mean, we have to." Wren paused. "And like Liv said, I'm not one to be overly positive."

Liv laughed between sniffles.

"What do you mean, you feel it?" Damiano questioned.

"I don't know." How could she explain it? She felt terror constrained behind a wall of peace. An unexplainable peace. It had to be the Lord, but terror sneered at her from the other side of that wall.

"I wish I had that feeling," Mei whispered, like she spoke more to herself than anyone else.

"Me too," said Damiano. "But I'm ready to fight if I need to."

The truck slowed and the bumps jarred them even harder. Wren probably bruised her tailbone on that last one. She tried to brace herself, feeling the seams in the truck floor. Then the truck came to a stop.

Fear surged inside Wren. Where was that peace she felt seconds ago? What would happen next? She got a flash image of a slave auction. She'd seen a reenactment on a field trip to a plantation in high school. She pushed the image from her mind.

The double doors at the back of the truck swung open. Wren squinted and shaded her eye against the bright sunlight. A guy in a black ski mask holding a shotgun stood between them and freedom. Turning to the right, she saw a second guard, also gripping a shotgun. One stood at each open door, a bulky, black rifle pointed to the ground. A third man—unmasked—jumped up into the truck with them. They all stepped back. Bald, with bushy eyebrows and an even bushier mustache, probably in his fifties. He took out a knife and stepped right up to Wren.

Had she been wrong to trust that peace? Could this be the end of her life? Of all their lives? She held her breath.

He watched her, maybe enjoying the fear he saw on her face. Ice filled her stomach. This guy didn't even care if she knew what he looked like. He held the blade an inch or so from her nose, then pulled her to her feet and shoved her ahead.

"You'll call me Daddy, cuz that's my name." He grinned with a twisted smile. No way would she use that sacred term for a person like him.

The truck bed's ramp now led right to the open delivery door at the back of a run-down pink motel. Wren glanced around at the surrounding buildings. Most looked old, like you'd see in history books. Similar to downtown Mobile, some buildings were tall, French-style, and others low and spread out like a town from the seventies. This motel fell into the second category.

They'd been driving for at least an hour since she woke up. How much more before that, she couldn't tell. But she doubted they were still in Mobile.

"Look straight ahead, girl." A gruff voice commanded as something hard jabbed her in the center of her back. Wren flung forward and fell to the ground, scraping her hands and her knees through the jeans.

The unmasked guy standing just in front of her turned to glare at the others behind her, still in the truck. "You will all follow me or I'll make an example out of this one." He motioned with his head to Wren, and fear surged through her again. "And these two." He pointed his thumbs backward over his shoulders, indicating the masked guards with guns. "They aren't afraid to make an example out of any one of you."

Wren heard rustling behind her and knew the others would follow without a fight. One of the guards guided her into the building. After a couple of minutes, a door slammed, and Wren heard metal sliding across metal. She assumed it had been a bolt sealing the door. Turning her head to see if it was something she might be able to open by herself, the butt of a rifle connected to the same spot in her back. Pain seared up her spine and into her head.

Being pushed from behind, Wren stumbled across the big, gray room where they probably stored deliveries. Then they walked down a back hallway, past some offices—definitely not the check-in desk or front office. Motel management offices, she assumed. Hearing voices, she glanced inside one of the offices.

She caught sight of the blond man from the warehouse. Romeo. He sat at a large wooden desk, and across from his desk sat… Cade.

Wren sucked in a breath. Cade? A kidnapper?

Wren had had a bad feeling about him at first, but kidnapping? How could she have misjudged someone so badly?

"Get them out of here. I don't want them looking around too much," the bald man in charge said, standing inside the same office.

Cade caught her eye and quickly dropped his gaze to the desk, his face flaring red. The weasel. If only she could focus on her anger for Cade rather than the fear piercing her brain with pain.

What did the kidnappers want with them? She didn't want to think about it.

Even God can't help you here. Hopelessness threatened and circled around in her head. The sense of peace had vanished.

Masked guards—one gunman in front of the small group, one presumably behind—led them down a hallway, up some steps, through a doorway, and into a hallway of hotel rooms. Shuffling feet and sudden exhalations sounded from behind Wren, then Liv stumbled into Wren's back. In front, the guard stopped at a door and unlocked it, his rifle pointing to the floor. Wren glanced to either side, hoping for an escape.

Just then, the guard lifted his gun, pierced her with a gaze through the eyeholes in his ski mask and yelled, "Move," pointing his gun into the room.

She stepped inside, then turned to see Liv and Mei enter the room behind her. At least she'd be with Liv. Next Damiano came flying into the motel room, arms flailing from a violent shove.

"Now don't y'all get any bright ideas," one gunman said. "We got this whole place wired. You'll get a powerful shock, and we'll get an alarm if you try to get out of any door or window." He sounded almost giddy. Probably not too bright. "This technology even tells us which door or window has the breach." He laughed, airy and high-pitched, then closed the door, locking it behind him.

Facing the interior of the room, two other people already occupied the space, their faces devoid of emotion.

———•●•———

Cold, unwelcoming stares greeted them. Neither girl stood from the couch where they sat to introduce themselves. Wren couldn't imagine what they might have been through. They looked younger than she and Liv but aged in some ways… and mean. Would they try to hurt her and the others? After all, they were coming into their world, taking space in their room.

"Did y'all get kidnapped too?" Damiano asked, not over analyzing the situation like Wren. How did he remain so easy-going?

No answer, just stony stares. Maybe she'd been wrong, one girl didn't look hard at all—hopeless maybe—like she'd given up on life. Long blonde hair with an oval face and brown eyes. She couldn't have been over twelve or thirteen.

The other girl looked mean or just angry. Copper-colored hair, which could only have come from a bottle, and a petite face. Her mouth was small and pursed, her eyes sunken. Pretty, except for the vapid, icy stare and the way she clenched her jaw. What had the kidnappers done to her?

What would they do to Wren and the others? A sob caught in her throat. She needed to get the focus off herself, and think about something besides her fear.

Every life is a story... Mr. Cho's wife, Samantha O'Connor's words came back to Wren. She'd heard her speak at Daphne High, her senior year. The other part of that quote escaped Wren, but she understood that each person in that small motel apartment had a life before. They had family, good or bad, and they had had dreams.

A picture formed in her mind of a drawing including each face represented there. Maybe she'd draw it someday.

"Don't just stand at the door looking like deer in headlights." The words might have been a welcome, but the redhead's tone sounded anything but friendly. The four of them took a few steps away from the bolted front door at their back.

More than a motel room but less than an apartment, the large room in which they stood had two long, thin couch-like seats with no backs. More like covered foam rectangles, which sat right on the floor, they formed an L-shape with a small table at the corner. The wall on the far left supported a kitchenette—a sink, a couple of dingy cabinets, and a half fridge. A table and six chairs took up most of the kitchen area. An open door to the left of the kitchenette revealed a bathroom. A thin wall separated the kitchen and living room, with openings on both sides, just big enough to support a TV screen on the wall facing the couch.

Noting their surroundings kept Wren's mind occupied and could be useful later. Her worst-case thinking might serve her well. She'd continue making mental notes as the others filtered into the space around her. To her right, Wren noticed a coat closet and, between the coat closet and the end of the couch, another door into a bedroom.

Wren took one step toward that room to see how big it was and if there were more—no more rooms. Four single mattresses lay on the floor in the bedroom. No dressers, no tables or chairs.

"Yeah, it's not much." The mean girl glared in Wren's direction. "And I'm not sharing a bed." She placed both hands on her hips. "I'm DeeAnn, and I'm in charge."

In charge of what? Wren wondered. What was this? What were they involved in? But she held her tongue.

"How long are we going to be here?" Liv asked. "Will we be able to go home soon?"

At that, the younger girl looked up from a book she'd been reading, or pretending to, as if she hadn't noticed them barging in on her and DeeAnn.

"What?" Mei challenged the young blonde girl. "Can you help us?"

"Shut up, Amy," DeeAnn said to the girl, who hadn't spoken a word. The girl looked back at her book, stealing wayward glances at them from time to time.

"I'll give you the rundown," DeeAnn spoke again. "There are basic undergarments, socks, and robes in the bedroom closet. There are various sizes and colors. It really doesn't matter; just grab what you need while you're in the apartment. You'll be outfitted downstairs where they keep the nice stuff before going out," DeeAnn said, as if that made sense.

"When do we get to go out?" Damiano asked.

"When you have a job," DeeAnn said, as if it should've been obvious.

"How can we find a job if we can't leave?" he pressed.

"The jobs come here to us."

At DeeAnn's words, the younger girl's face turned bright red, and she studied the crease in the middle of her book.

A sense of horror sank into the center of Wren's chest. What did they want them to do?

"What the—?" Damiano used some colorful language. "I know what kind of sick thing this is."

"Look, it's not as bad as it seems at first. We do our job. They clothe us, feed us, give us housing—"

Damiano cursed. "No way!" He punched the wall. "I'm not about to stay here!"

"I really don't see that you have a choice." DeeAnn was matter-of-fact. The horror must've left her long ago, which by itself was enough to make Wren fear. "Those guys out there have big guns. Did you see them?"

"Yes, we saw them," Damiano mimicked her tone.

"Well then. You see my point." DeeAnn stood and stretched. "You might not stay here long, anyway. They like to move people around. But your needs are taken care of. Like housing." She opened her hands and looked around the room, showing how well they'd been provided for.

Liv dropped to the couch between Mei and Wren, whose knees had already given way and forced her to sit as understanding of their situation dawned. Wren saw the tears glistening in Liv's eyes and felt the same in her own. The young girl sat on the other couch. Damiano and DeeAnn faced off in the middle of the room near the TV wall.

"You call this housing?" His voice rose. "A one-bedroom studio thing for six of us in a run-down motel?"

"Look, man, I'm not the one who put you here." DeeAnn held up both hands. "I'm just saying, make the best of it, cuz they will not let you leave. Believe me, I know."

"What's the job they want us to do?" Wren wished he hadn't asked. But they'd know sooner or later.

"Really?" DeeAnn rolled her eyes. "Are you stupid? Sex, you idiot." She threw her arms in the air.

She and Liv sucked in at the same time. Oh God. Their lives were over.

"Figures." Damiano lacked the shock Wren felt.

Wren turned her attention to the girl DeeAnn had called Amy. Her head bent so far down that it almost touched the top of the book in her lap now. Who would use that sweet young girl for sex? She couldn't even be in high school yet.

The evil of the whole thing settled into Wren's gut. This was serious.

Liv grabbed her hand and squeezed the life out of her fingers.

Wren glanced at Mei, who looked resigned. *Why not horrified?* she wondered.

Her story. The words resonated inside Wren.

And why hadn't Damiano been surprised?

His story, Wren.

Sometimes, Wren felt this voice inside. She attributed it to God. Sometimes she even had a conversation with it. Was she just talking to herself? Was it God? She couldn't be sure.

If it were God, why didn't it tell her how to get out of there safely?

Wren's birth mother's boyfriend had abused her as a toddler. He'd hit her, given her bruises and ultimately punched her in the eye so hard that she had to have it removed. But she'd never been sexually abused. She'd made it through high school as a virgin and hoped to maintain that until her wedding night.

She gulped. *God, this is awful.* What an understatement.

"So, who here is a virgin?" DeeAnn asked, raising one hand in example. Wren looked around. No one raised their hand. Neither did Wren.

She swallowed hard. In this environment, questions like that must be normal.

"Right, well, we can discuss that later." DeeAnn walked over to the kitchenette. "They'll probably bring us some more food, since they brought all of y'all." She rolled her eyes. "For now, we have chips, crackers, cereal, boxed milk, orange juice in the fridge—it's not much—also some eggs and white bread for toast. If anyone is hungry."

Wren's stomach churned. She could've gagged. How could they think about food? Though eventually, she'd need to. "Are you hungry, Liv?"

Liv locked eyes with Wren. Her face pale, she shook her head.

"I know," Wren whispered.

The young blonde, who was yet to speak, reached a hand across the corner table toward Liv, took a lock of her hair and held it between her fingers for a moment before dropping it. Wren thought she might speak to Liv, but she never did. Maybe she admired Liv's hairstyle. When she noticed them looking at her, she dropped her gaze back to her book.

After all they'd been through, Liv's hair still looked good. She'd curled back the layers around her face. It looked a little messy, but still pretty. The young girl's hair hung straight and long. She had sweet, large, brown eyes that revealed her youth, but also her pain. "I'm Liv, short for Olivia."

Amy glanced up at Liv. Wren thought she might smile.

"If we're going to do the introductions, let's do them out loud for everyone," DeeAnn demanded.

"Oh, um. I'm Liv."

"Live?" DeeAnn rolled her eyes. "What kind of name is that?"

Liv dropped her gaze. "It's short for Olivia." Wren wasn't used to seeing Liv intimidated.

DeeAnn rolled her eyes and looked at Wren next.

"Wren," she said quickly to get out of the girl's spotlight.

"I'm Mei."

"Damiano."

"You know me, DeeAnn. And that's Amy," she said pointing to the younger girl. "Now that we all know each other, we don't need any more talk about ourselves. Just keep it to yourself. Nobody cares." She grabbed the remote and clicked to an episode of *The Office*, then flopped on the couch beside Amy, who scooted closer to the corner table to allow DeeAnn more space. "And don't get any ideas about the TV. It's not connected to anything, so we don't get news, or time, or anything but a few old series that got saved like *Monk* and *The Office*."

Great. And would they not be allowed to get to know each other? At least it would take their minds off things. And they would need to focus on the situation and discuss how they might escape.

Escape sounded scary. The kidnappers were determined to keep them, but they couldn't just sit around and do nothing.

Damiano sat on the floor. Wren tossed him a cushion from the couch.

"Thanks." He scooted it under him.

Silently, Wren prayed, *please, God. Please God. Please get us out of here. Help our parents find us. Please help us.*

No one's listening, Wren, the cruel voice in her head threatened. Who could come? The room felt darker than it had a moment before. *Your parents have no idea where you are, and you don't have your cell phones. You never told them about the audition. You kept your promise to Liv, but you knew better. How stupid could you be? Breaking that promise would have been better loyalty to your friend than walking into this.*

Putting her hands to her ears, Wren shook her head and squeezed the tears out of her eyes.

CHAPTER NINE

Damiano punched the floor. "I can't even believe this is happening."

Wren really looked at him for the first time. His skin was brown—mixed race, probably Black and White. His black hair was very short at the sides, a little longer on top and very curly. He had large brown, kind eyes and his ears stuck out a little. Handsome overall, Wren understood why he believed he could be a model.

Next, she studied Mei more closely. Pretty and Asian, Mei had a unique look. Her very short hair had been dyed a platinum gray. It was layered and lay flat against her face and head—kind of a sassy look. She wore a small silver ring in the septum of her nose. Her nails looked like a professional had done them for a party—painted a deep teal color with tiny diamond studs on the forefingers.

Everyone here was beautiful. As the plain one of the bunch, Wren wondered if they might let her go. Immediately horrified by her own selfish thought, she asked God to forgive her.

"Wren?" Damiano was trying to get her attention but quietly. "What are you thinking?"

"Sorry," she said. Spacing out after he spoke to her the first time wasn't the best way to build trust, and they needed to trust each other. "I don't know." Words caught in Wren's throat. She swallowed as tears warmed the corners of her eyes. "What are we going to do?"

"Y'all are going to be quiet so I can watch this show." DeeAnn acted as if she were one of the kidnappers rather than a hostage like the rest of them. What was her problem?

Damiano scooted across the floor closer to Wren and the others on the couch. Sitting cross-legged, he leaned in toward them and looked up at Wren's face. "Are you in shock or something? It looks like something's wrong with your eye."

"She has a prosthetic eye," Liv explained in her place. "Can you just leave her alone?"

"Sorry, I didn't mean to be like… I mean, I just wanted to ask—" He shifted on the pillow.

"It's okay. I'm used to it." Wren managed a weak smile. She glanced at DeeAnn to see if she had heard. How might that girl use it against Wren when she had the chance?

"Hey, what are y'all whispering about?" DeeAnn turned the volume of her show down and looked their way.

"Nothing," Damiano replied. "You told us to keep it down so you could watch the show."

"Um, we could, uh…" Wren couldn't spit the words out. Why did this girl have such an effect on her? "We could go into the bedroom and talk so we don't disturb your show."

"Oh, right," DeeAnn nailed her with a look. "So I can't hear you? I don't think so." She paused. "You stutter. And what's wrong with your eye? It doesn't move right."

Heat rushed into Wren's face. "I—" She touched her fingers to her prosthetic eye.

"Wren has a fake eye," Liv spoke for her, but now DeeAnn knew.

"Really? I wonder how they'll deal with that," was all she said and rolled her eyes before looking back at her show.

The others stared at Wren's eyes. Her face burned.

"Doesn't it get dry if you can't blink it?" Damiano asked.

"It's not like a real eye. And it does blink."

"But you have tears, don't you?" Mei looked interested in something for the first time since Wren had met her. At least Wren could be a distraction.

"Yes, plenty of tears." Which caused build-up that then needed to be cleaned… but she wouldn't bore them with the yucky details.

"Can you pop the whole ball out like the guy with the glass eye in the movies?" DeeAnn really had no sense of decorum. And Wren didn't have any idea what movie she referred to.

"No, it's not a ball, and it's not glass. It's plastic."

"Whoa, it looks so real," Mei said, staring into Wren's eyes, first left, then right.

"Uh… thanks."

"Do you take it out every night?" Mei pressed for more information. "I want to see it." Wren started wishing she could crawl into a hole and hide.

"No. It usually stays in until I go to the ocularist."

"Ocula—what?" Damiano asked.

"The guy who makes and cleans prosthetic eyes is called an ocularist."

"Sounds like the occult." DeeAnn tossed her input at them without even looking their way.

"Can you see out of it?" Mei asked.

"Can't y'all just leave her alone?" Liv's volume increased a few notches. "It's bad enough we're all stuck in this situation. Now you have to pepper her with embarrassing questions?"

Wren squeezed Liv's fingers in thanks.

"I guess it's a distraction for everyone," Wren whispered to Liv. "I can't see out of it at all," she explained to everyone else. "But I see fine out of my left eye."

When Wren caught Amy staring at her eyes, the girl quickly looked away.

They settled into their own thoughts after that. It was a relief until Wren's thoughts filled with imaginings about what her life was about to become.

She shot up another prayer. *Lord Jesus, Son of God, have mercy on us. Father, help us, please.*

She crisscrossed her legs on the couch and closed her eyes, trying to focus on God. Would he speak to her? Could he send a light fairy like Sorchae in Ms. O'Connor's book?

In the book, Sorchae brought messages of truth, offered understanding and wisdom—light, in the midst of darkness. That's exactly what they needed.

Father God, if you hear me, please send Sorchae, or make some other way, and show us how to get out of here quickly and safely.

At youth group they talked about how God was with them through everything, the good and the bad. The youth pastor said that God would never leave or forsake them.

Was it true? Could God be with her now? Here?

Did she believe it now, in the worst circumstances of her life?

Was this really the worst?

Yes, this was the worst thing that had ever happened to her, including losing her eye.

Her thoughts shifted from her prayer to the blonde girl on the couch by DeeAnn. Amy had looked her way when everyone else was asking about her eye. Her face looked almost concerned for Wren, but she never asked a question. Now she stared at her book again. Wren didn't even know if the girl had turned a page the whole time they'd been there.

Pray for Amy. The thought seemed like direction coming from a source other than herself, since fear had been all she could muster on her own.

God?

Wow, maybe he did talk to her. Or she was making things up. Well, prayer never hurt.

God, please help Amy. It seemed like she'd been terribly hurt and like she was super scared. *I pray for her and for the rest of us. Please get us out of here.*

Wait, now she accidentally jumped back to praying for herself. Was that enough prayer for Amy?

Was it, Lord?

Nothing.

After trying to listen for a while, Wren closed her eyes, and her thoughts faded.

Time passed, but Wren didn't know how much. Rarely sure whether it was day or night, she'd been napping often. All four of them seemed to sleep a lot. Maybe they were sleeping off the effects of the drug that originally knocked them out.

"Wren… Wren, they left pizzas outside the door for us." Liv shook her arm. "We should eat. Who knows when the next opportunity will come."

Wren's stomach growled. How long had it been since she'd had a meal? Liv was right. They needed to eat something.

Wren opened her eyes and sat forward. It seemed dark at the window, though something had been smeared over the glass so no one could see in from the outside, and no one could see out from the inside. She took a deep breath, trying to ease the claustrophobia. Were all the windows painted like that? "What time is it?"

"Nighttime." Liv grabbed her hand and helped her get moving. They stumbled over to the marble-looking table with metal trim. The "marble" was some kind of synthetic material, maybe vinyl. The chairs were metal with plastic-covered seats.

"There's pepperoni, cheese and sausage." DeeAnn opened the boxes at the table and gave instructions. "What kind do you want, Amy?"

The girl stood beside DeeAnn and pointed to the pepperoni.

Was she just afraid of DeeAnn? Or was it a deeper trauma that held her tongue silent? Or was she afraid of Wren and the others?

Father, please give Amy peace. Wren prayed silently without even thinking about it. Now, she prayed again with intention, *Give us all peace.*

They sat at the table to eat their pizza, which was cold and had little flavor. They drank water from the tap in plastic cups and spoke very little.

DeeAnn seemed agitated. Wren couldn't put her finger on it. The girl's eyes looked red around the rims. She probably hadn't had enough sleep.

The bolt sounded on the door to the apartment. Everyone froze, even DeeAnn.

"Let's get going." The accented words came from the man who took them from the van when they arrived. The one who wasn't worried about them seeing his face—Daddy. He must've believed they'd never make it out of this place alive to identify him. Bald, in his 50s, the guy wore a muscle undershirt with jeans. A bushy mustache covered his whole upper lip. He didn't sound Mexican. She had a friend at school whose dad was Mexican. He might've been from some other country in Latin America though.

What he was was cold, unfeeling. Even DeeAnn didn't talk back. She dropped everything and went to him.

"Romeo has your clothes ready. It'll be very special tonight." He spoke directly to DeeAnn.

"Yes, sir."

"You too, Amy."

Amy scooted in line behind DeeAnn as quickly as she could, still chewing and swallowing as she went.

"What, no greeting for your daddy?" He grinned at the younger girl and leaned toward her for a kiss. She kissed the side of his face. Daddy's weathered face filled with anger in a millisecond. "What do you call that?" He must not have been happy with Amy's less-than-enthusiastic greeting.

Wren swallowed hard. How could he expect more?

"No gratitude? I bring you these pizzas, and what do I get?"

"She's extra quiet today, Daddy." DeeAnn filled in the space with words. Maybe it was dangerous not to answer Daddy. Maybe DeeAnn was trying to help.

Then DeeAnn kissed Daddy full on the mouth.

"That's better." He smiled at DeeAnn, then turned back to Amy. "Amy?"

Amy hesitated, then put her face near his, and he kissed her on the mouth too. Wren had to look away when his big old tongue slipped inside the girl's mouth. She gagged and tried to hide the sound.

Daddy turned to address the room. "You can all show your appreciation now. Come on." He motioned with a bony finger for each of them to come give him a kiss.

This could not be happening. Wren's stomach twisted and she held back a gag reflex.

No one moved.

Daddy pulled his shirttail up in front to reveal the butt of a handgun sticking out of his jeans' pocket. We can treat you well, giving you food and nice clothes for your outings." He paused, his wicked grin adding to the ice in his eyes. "Or we can make it rough on you."

The whole situation was unbelievable.

"Move!" Daddy's fired the words like a drill sergeant but with the added threat of pain behind it.

They lined up in front of him.

"That's better. From now on, when me or Romeo gives you an order, you obey or pay the consequences."

They each had to kiss him. And not just a peck on the cheek or lips—a full-on French kiss. She'd only kissed one other boy like that, and it was on a dare. Daddy even kissed

Damiano. Ugh. Wren's stomach churned again. She had never felt so scared.

"You four will have chances to pay for your keep. And you'll learn to be grateful." A definite threat. Daddy smiled bigger this time, revealing one gray tooth in front. "For tonight, just relax. Enjoy the TV and the pizza. I'll send Romeo or Cade up to keep an eye on you." He waited for DeeAnn and Amy to step into the hallway in front of him They wore only their bathrobes. Wren heard the bolt lock behind them.

— • ● • —

Jim inhaled. The smell of coffee shops, especially in the morning, had a way of relaxing and invigorating at the same time.

"Cappuccino!" The barista called.

"Thanks, man." Jim waved and grabbed the ceramic mug. He preferred a real cup when he had enough time to sit down.

The barista behind the counter didn't reply, but the tattoo to the right of his Adam's apple jumped with a muscle twitch in his neck before he headed back to the frother for the next drink.

Jim had started the day's work at the coffee shop. He didn't know anyone there, had never been to this shop, and wasn't even sure what town he was in.

He sat back down, opened his computer and sipped his coffee. Oh yeah, he'd spoken at University of North Carolina at Charlotte yesterday. He had the day off—no travel—so he could catch up on correspondence and hopefully get an article written.

People sent him local news stories from their hometowns when something tragic happened involving sex trafficking. It broke his heart over and over, but it helped him understand what was going on around the country. He hoped one day to get a clue important enough to restart the investigation into his sister's kidnapping and death.

Most of all, he wanted to stop the traffickers who took his sister and others like them from doing the same thing to other girls and boys, men and women.

He took another sip. The floral and citrus notes of the light roast pleased his taste buds and cleared his mind. He was becoming a coffee snob… or connoisseur, as he preferred. So many coffee shops under his belt, so many more to go.

But thank God for them.

He clicked on his inbox. *Local girls missing.*

Not again. He clicked on the article. Fairhope, Alabama? He'd just been there a week ago.

Parents of Wren Summerfield and Olivia Olsson issued a missing person's report two days ago, the article said. A local newspaper investigator reported that a bartender overheard them talking to a young man about a modeling opportunity. No one had seen the young man since that time either.

Jim opened the attached picture, and his heart dropped. Two young ladies together on a beach in the photo… he'd seen them before. Hadn't he met these two? It came back to him. They'd come up to meet him after his lecture at their school.

Which one? Oh, right, Coastal Community.

The blonde had been a striking beauty, but her friend was the one who revisited his thoughts. She'd asked about his family. No one ever asked him questions about himself or his family. No one wanted to know his story, though he told people anyway—at least the parts he thought might help them avoid the pitfalls Stacy had fallen into.

There had been something about her… Maybe something about her eyes that he couldn't forget. He hadn't had time to figure it out.

But the memory rushed back, and deep sadness caught him off guard as he stared at the photo in the article. Maybe the Lord had been trying to get him to pray for her. If so, he totally missed the cue.

A breeze brushed his face and lifted his hair. He looked up to see a new customer walking to the counter. His gaze dropped back to the article. Something about the bartender's comment derailed his thoughts. A modeling audition, he'd said.

Jim pulled up his copy of last year's Trafficking in Persons Report. He'd downloaded the TIP from the government website to access it for research. The entire section about the role of technology in trafficking interested him. Obviously, traffickers targeted young people on social media, pretending to be someone else. They were getting more creative with their tactics every year.

Jim knew the stats. The great majority of young people in trafficking situations had been forced into it by a family member or someone they knew well. Horrifying! But the traffickers who took Stacy were different. They targeted strangers through social media and big promises.

His insides burned with anger. If Jim were God, he'd just blast them all to Hades. No need to wait for judgment day. But he wasn't God. And God had patience even with low-life sludge like that.

Jim took a deep breath. Held it a moment. Then slowly let it out. He sipped his cappuccino again.

He couldn't let anger get the better of him. He needed to think clearly. Something in his gut told him the ones who took these girls might be the same ones who took—and ultimately killed—Stacy.

Her small laptop fit nicely into his backpack briefcase, so he'd been carrying hers and his on his back since his parents gave it to him. He kept hoping he'd see something in a new light, something he could offer the police to trigger the reopening of the investigation.

With this information about the Fairhope girls, he needed to look at Stacy's laptop again. He scooted the backpack closer, pulled it out, and started scrolling her email history.

Modeling… modeling… Where was that email? He also remembered it being in her history on social media, but the website had been taken down when he tried it. He rolled his eyes, glancing out the shop's front window. Leaves were beginning to change color on the trees across the street. His eyes dropped back to the laptop.

Searching online, he found an ad for a modeling audition that looked similar in content to the one he remembered seeing. "School-age welcome," it said. This ad promised that those selected could choose their own schedules and assignments—a job that didn't interfere with their school obligations. It also boasted high pay. The company went by the name Lumina Talent Group.

Did the police have hackers able to find the person who posted this ad like they did on TV? He doubted it, but this was an undeniable clue.

Jim glanced at the couple at the booth across from his. He'd need more privacy for his conversation with the police. He quickly swallowed the rest of his coffee and placed the mug in a rubber tub near the counter.

Back at the hotel, Jim sat at the little desk in front of the window and picked up his phone.

"Can I speak to Detective Windly, please? It's about a case he was working on."

The receptionist asked his name, which he gave, and she put him on hold.

"Jim?"

"Hello Detective Windly. I think I found some new information that could get the investigation going again."

Did Jim hear a sigh? Was he annoying the detective? He gazed out the window, seeing only his own frustration.

"Jim, you there?"

"Uh, yes, sorry." He cleared his throat.

"Let's have it. What have you got?"

Jim told him about the modeling connection between the cases and said that maybe investigating this fresh case would put them onto the same traffickers as Stacy's case.

"Is that right?" The detective paused. Maybe he was jotting the information down as Jim heard pencil scratches. "This could be something."

"I sure hope so." Detective Windly said. "Too much time has passed already."

"So true. I've got a lot of files on my desk right now. Trying to keep the boss happy, you know? But if this lead adds up, I have no doubt he'll pass these files along to someone else and let me join a task force to go after this."

"Please do what you can. I'm looking into it too."

"Don't take these matters into your own hands, son. It's dangerous."

"It was dangerous for Stacy too. I can't just sit back and—"

"Jim, come on, you know how evil these guys are. They won't think twice about killing you."

"If your task force gets to them before I do, everything will be fine." Maybe that would put some fire under the police.

The detective made a throaty sound but didn't argue the point anymore.

Jim clicked off the line.

He had access to a few research sites and news databases for writers. He could start investigating there.

He learned about several cartels the government had been investigating over the years. Sometimes high-level criminals in non-extradition countries headed up these rings. They didn't deal just in human flesh. Drugs, pornography, and sex trafficking went together most of the time. Some even smuggled antiquities.

The high-level criminals never even entered the U.S. They had cronies all over the country moving girls and boys around to keep them and the authorities guessing.

Stacy was found in Ohio. They must've moved her so the police couldn't find her.

He continued reading. His insides clenched. He slammed the laptop closed, then punched his fist onto the small desk.

Ouch. He let a curse word slip and shook out his hand.

"Sorry, God," he prayed aloud in his room. "I just feel so helpless. These guys must be stopped. Don't you agree? If so, let me or the police catch them."

Jim moved over to the tightly made bed, feeling convicted. It wasn't the curse word. God wouldn't take the time to reprimand him about a word he used when angry over the sinfulness of the world.

It was more personal, and he knew it.

Lord, I'm sorry for trying to control this, for getting angry when I can't control it. I know… that's unbelief. If I truly believed you could take care of it without me, I wouldn't be so stressed.

But… It's Stacy! How am I supposed to get over this and just go on?

Please let me be part of your solution. But if that's not your will, then please stop these guys without me. Just please stop them.

Was it okay to beg God?

In Jim's theology, God was gracious. He didn't care about a list of rules as much as he cared about the heart.

Peace sprinkled into his spirit like gentle rain into dry ground. He took a cleansing breath, closed his eyes and lay back on the bed. Looking out the open window, he watched the stars in the night sky.

"You made them all. And you know them by name." Another breath. God's majesty and beauty and goodness washed over him again. Why did he try to control the situation when God was so big?

Did he even know how to give up that control?

A tone sounded from his laptop. A new email. He opened it—a message from a survivor of trafficking who wanted to tell him her story.

CHAPTER TEN

Daddy's presence lingered in their apartment even after they had gone. Wren felt nauseous and tried not to think about what was happening to DeeAnn and Amy.

"Did he say, Cade?" Liv directed her question to Wren after the door locked behind Romeo, Daddy and the two girls.

"Yeah." Wren searched her friend's face. She thought Liv had seen him in the office downstairs when they arrived as Wren had. "Didn't you know he was in on it?"

"Of course not." Liv jerked around, her hair flying out in her wake till she faced the window, as if she could see something outside. "It can't be. He's just too nice." Liv turned back around more slowly, her eyes begging, desperate to be right about him.

"I'm sorry, Liv." Wren held out her arms.

"Wait, who are we talking about?" Mei asked in the middle of their emotional moment.

"Cade," Liv told her. "He's the one who told me about the audition, but I assumed he believed it to be real as much as we did. He just couldn't have been in on it."

"I saw him in the office with the kidnappers when they brought us into the hotel." Wren ached for her friend.

"No! Why didn't you tell me?" Liv dropped onto the couch. "I am so stupid!" She put her head in her hands.

"Yeah, that's for sure." Mei took a piece of sausage pizza.

"That is not helpful." Wren pinned her with a look.

Standing near Mei, Damiano bumped her shoulder with his arm. "Come on, we have enough to worry about."

"Sorry, Liv," Mei said, but she didn't sound like she meant it.

"It's okay. I am stupid," Liv said into her hands.

They had too much time to think. Too much time together in tight quarters.

Wren sat beside Liv again and pushed back the hair that had fallen into her face so she could see Liv better. "You're not stupid, Liv. Even I was being persuaded that Cade wasn't so bad."

"You?" Liv looked up.

Wren nodded. "Yeah." He seemed sincere, and she was usually an excellent judge of character.

"Should we leave two of the beds in the bedroom for DeeAnn and—what was that little girl's name?" Mei asked.

"Amy," Wren said. "Good idea. Liv and I can sleep out here on these couches. We've gotten used to it."

Liv nodded her agreement.

"Okay," Damiano agreed. "Maybe we can take turns."

"Hopefully, we won't be here very long," Wren said under her breath. "We've got to get out of here soon."

"I'm going to check all the doors and windows for weaknesses," Damiano said as he started feeling the walls, door frames, and windows.

"Be quiet about it," Liv told him. "Cade or Romeo or someone is probably right outside the door, on guard."

Damiano didn't discover any holes in their cage. What were they going to do?

Dear God, please get us out of here before... before... Oh God... please. Tears threatened Wren's eyes as she mouthed her silent prayer to the Lord, but she couldn't lose it. If she did, she might not stop crying.

Mei dumped the empty pizza box in a large trash bin, then wiped her hands on a paper towel. "I guess we could try one of those bathrobes. Being in the same clothes for days is getting uncomfortable."

No way. It would be like accepting this situation, giving up. "I'll just sleep in my clothes for now." Wren smoothed her jeans, as if it would help anything.

"I'm with you." Damiano ran fingers like a comb through his short curls. "I'm not wearing someone else's underwear and robes worn by who knows who."

They agreed. Even Mei decided not to change.

"Were you praying before, Wren?" Liv asked, and Wren wondered if the others overheard the question. "I know you do that sometimes, and well… it looked like you were."

Wren side-glanced at the others and nodded.

"Can you pray for all of us?" Liv sent a glare toward Damiano and Mei, as if warning them not to tease Wren. DeeAnn and Amy still had not returned.

"Well, if you want me to." A quick concern ran through Wren's mind about what the others might think, but they needed God's intervention. She waited for their approval. Otherwise, she and Liv could pray after the others went to bed.

Damiano shrugged "What the heck? It couldn't hurt." He sat on the couch next to Liv.

"Why not?" Mei rolled her eyes as if she'd never heard of anything more stupid, but she wasn't going to argue about it.

Wren pushed her nerves back. "Well, if you want me to—"

Liv leaned forward. "Don't worry, Wren, just pray for us. Maybe God will hear your prayer and help us."

Wren didn't think of Liv as the praying kind, though she sometimes went to church with her mom, sometimes with Wren.

Taking a deep breath, Wren focused her thoughts on God. She looked down at the vinyl tiles. "Father, we're trapped, and we don't know what to do." When Wren paused long enough to look up, everyone had their heads down. Mei glanced up at her pause as if she didn't know what she was supposed to do. Wren closed her eyes and tried to ignore her audience. "These are bad men," she continued. "With bad intentions for us. We know this is not your will. We are sorry for deceiving our parents—well, at least Liv and I did—but please help us now. Keep us safe. And please make a way for us to get out of here… DeeAnn and Amy too... and help us to be able to sleep tonight. Amen."

"Amen," Liv said. She side-hugged Wren, a tear rolling down her cheek. The other two left the room without a word.

Worry would probably keep Wren awake, but she still felt sleepy. Wren cuddled the throw blanket provided like she was three years old, alone in a scary hospital again.

She woke repeatedly and each time, it seemed the dark in the room grew and took on a life of its own. It pulled her down and down into a deep fog of fear, abuse, and hopelessness.

Gazing into the fog, a single star visible in the darkening sky drew her attention. Dusk hung in the park, heavy with fog, streetlights glowing in the moisture. A blonde girl stood near a large live oak, one of its limbs nearly touching the ground. Her hair, caught up in the wind, blew out to the side along with her scarf. Then the wind subsided, and the scarf settled down over her winter coat, waiting for the next gust.

Wren could easily make out the pattern of the girl's scarf: poppies in different shades of red and yellow, a few in sage and forest green, a matching green trim, all on a light creamy background. The girl tried to hide her face in the scarf, as if she were ashamed.

The scarf slipped down the next time the wind picked up, and a glimpse of her face took Wren by surprise—Amy, her expression tormented with some deep, internal pain.

Wren woke with a start. Light from the hallway poured into their space. DeeAnn and Amy stepped in. The door slammed shut, and the bolt slid into place behind them. Both girls wore the robes they'd left in, but now their hair was messy, and they had makeup smeared on their faces. They didn't speak, maybe pretending everyone slept. Wren pretended too, her heart aching for them. Heavy darkness descended on her chest again.

After a moment they disappeared into the bedroom, and the apartment went quiet again. Wren sobbed, trying to muffle the sounds in her blanket. Breathing deeply, she tried to stop herself. She didn't want to wake anyone who might have a few moments of peace.

The dream floated back into Wren's mind, now awake. Why had she dreamed about Amy? Strange. She'd expected to have nightmares—her worst-case imaginings.

This was different. Unusually vivid, it captured her attention, distracting her from her fear... at least for the moment.

She needed to draw it so she could remember it. Then, maybe the meaning of the dream would come to her later. It had happened before.

Of course, this dream could be just her overactive imagination.

She hadn't seen any paper or writing utensils in the apartment. Why would they supply those? It would be of no use to the kidnappers. She could probably earn it as favors.

Gag. Gag. Gag. She couldn't go there.

What time was it? She needed more sleep. Why couldn't they just have a clock?

They want you to be confused.

Fear shot through her at that thought. The darkness in the apartment settled in on her. Heavy on her chest, it constricted her breathing. An evil presence swirled around and swooped down at her. Wren felt it like a giant beast coming after her to destroy or consume her. Like a dragon searching for its next meal.

There's no escape for you or for them.

Wren swallowed and tried to take a breath.

You'll die here, used and old.

The dark thing swooped down around as sleep evaded Wren. She wanted to sit up but couldn't get her body to cooperate.

This is your life.

She tried to repeat something she'd memorized, something from the Bible or from church.

Nothing came to mind.

Then, one line: *Look down, O Lord… illumine this…* no wait. She tried to remember the nighttime prayers. Then the whole thing came to her, a prayer from the *Compline,* which her parents used to read to her before bed—more so when she was younger and couldn't protest—from the *Book of Common Prayer:*

Look down, O Lord, from your heavenly throne, illumine this night with your celestial brightness, and from the children of light banish the deeds of darkness; through Jesus Christ our Lord.

Wren's chest lightened a bit. She took a breath, deep and slow. How they needed God's light and direction in this dark darkness! Then she finished with the Jesus prayer—the one prayer that had often returned to her since she woke up in the moving truck.

Lord Jesus, Son of God, have mercy on us.

———•●•———

Jim walked into Another Broken Egg, a quaint breakfast joint near the Auburn campus. He loved breakfast and had offered to buy. Food, or at least coffee, often made the process much less intimidating. Much messier to take notes though. He'd have the voice recorder on his phone ready to go if she said it was okay.

The waitress led him to a booth in the back. Perfect. It would feel a bit more private, but still very much in a public place. Jim tried to make everyone he interviewed feel safe but especially survivors.

He could never really understand how they felt, but he tried to imagine how Stacy might feel in their place.

Taking the seat facing the door, Jim positioned himself so he could see her enter. He'd found her picture on the site that had her listed as missing from five years ago.

The bell on the door jingled. He stood and waved. Her hair had changed style and color since the picture—now she had a golden-blond shoulder-length weave, and her face had filled in—but it was her.

"Thank you so much for agreeing to meet with me." He shook her hand, and they both sat down.

"Actually, I want to thank you," she said. "Thank you for your work. I read some of your articles to prepare for this interview. Thank you for listening to us, to me, and other victims."

"Survivors."

The golden flecks in her light brown eyes lit up when she smiled. "Yes. Survivors."

She agreed to the recording, and they ordered their food.

"Can you say your name for the record?" he began.

"Sophie Johnson." Sophie's dark, smooth complexion accentuated her eyes. Although her medium build carried slightly more weight than doctors might recommend, her subtle beauty was obvious. From a pimp's perspective, she'd be good for business—Was he beginning to think like them? Oh God. His stomach turned.

"Again, thanks for meeting with me. These things can't be easy." He repeated himself, but he wanted her to know he was a friend.

"Thank you."

"Just tell me your story."

She ran her tongue over her upper lip and let out a nervous laugh. "Where should I start?"

"Where did you grow up? What was it like?"

"Mississippi. A small town, rural-ish. When I was five, my mom was strung out on drugs. I don't even remember when my dad left us. We had little food in the house. I remember being hungry. I remember cooking soup from a can by standing on a chair I had scooted up to the stove. It wasn't uncommon for me to make food for me and my mom and then try to feed her. Usually, she wasn't interested." Sophie sipped her coffee.

Jim couldn't imagine a child of five having that kind of responsibility.

"Not long after those memories, Social Services came and got me. I thought maybe it would be better. I guess it was, but I worried about my mom, and I hoped I'd get to see her often. They told me I would, but it didn't happen." She paused to eat, and Jim kept his mouth closed. He didn't want to throw the story off. "I had plenty to eat and got to go to school. I tried to do well in my classes, but my mind wandered and I often missed what the teacher was saying. Reading fiction took my mind someplace else, so English became my strongest subject in school. Other books took more effort to get through." She licked her upper lip again.

Jim checked her water glass, but she had plenty.

"I thought a lot about my mom and wished I had someone to love me. Loneliness seemed constant. Even at school, I didn't have many friends. I didn't know how to talk to the other kids.

"In junior high, I had an English teacher who took an interest in me. She liked my creative writing. I guess I developed a good imagination with all that reading and daydreaming."

Jim laughed, enjoying the lighthearted way she relayed her less-than-happy story. And as a writer, he related to the daydreaming.

"I lived in three different foster homes over the years. The last one was the worst. The father sexually abused me and threatened to kill the youngest foster kid in the house if I ever spoke about it to anyone." Sophie paused and rubbed lip gloss on her lips. "I believed him. He scared me so much. We were all afraid of him, and I had a special bond with the toddler, who was black like me and a girl. She came to me for comfort. She allowed me to feed her and put her to bed, but she'd scream when the foster parents tried, so they didn't like her. I felt responsible for her. I loved her, and I think she knew it."

Jim nodded. "Uh-huh." He let her know he was listening without interrupting. He wanted to hear her story in her own words. The interviewers he admired did that.

"When I got old enough to be sick to death of the situation, I literally said to myself if I didn't get out of there soon, I'd have to kill myself. I hated to leave Sue—that was the little girl's name—but I didn't have any way to help her. She'd been the only thing keeping me from running or committing suicide for years. Sue was five then. One day, I whispered to her that I had to leave. She said no, but I think she understood. I hope so. I didn't think the foster dad would touch her since she was so young. Now I wonder." Sophie's gaze drifted away from the conversation, tears moistening her eyes.

"What happened after you left?" Jim tried to gently bring her back to the story.

"Sorry. One day after school, I just didn't get on the bus. I didn't know where to go. I just ran around to the back of the school, then I kept running."

"How old were you?"

"Sixteen." She held out a small rectangle, a school picture, like one that had been cut from a yearbook.

"Beautiful." He handed it back.

"I found an alley and hid behind a big trash can, the kind that businesses use. In the morning when the shopkeeper opened the back door to throw something away, he saw me. He brought me some eggs and bacon. I ate out there in the dirty alley. He tried to get me to tell him where I lived. I played mute. He was nice, but I couldn't let on that I could speak. Soon he had to work." She took a few bites and pulled a sweater over her shoulders. The air in the restaurant must've kicked on. "If he called the police, they'd figure it out and take me back, so I left. I just walked, not knowing where I was going. Eventually, I found a park bench to sit on. I looked around to see if anyone was looking for me there, but it seemed quiet enough. Later, a group of guys came out to play basketball on the court that was at the other end of the park. I walked over there to watch. I guess I wanted some company and hoped they'd speak to me. They did. One guy had a car and a karaoke machine in the back seat. He said he was a songwriter and a rapper. I loved creative writing, and writing a song seemed like an amazing talent."

Jim asked the server for more coffee and motioned for Sophie to continue.

"He rapped for me and a few others who stuck around after basketball. I probably gushed about his talent, then he asked if I wanted a ride. I said no. After all, where would I tell him to take me? He asked if I had any place to go. When I admitted I didn't, he said I could come with them. He tossed the karaoke machine in the trunk and we sat in the back of the car together, his friend drove. He told me I was pretty enough to be a model. Then he started kissing my neck, and I didn't even mind. He paid for a hotel room and brought me some food. He didn't stay there with me at first, but soon he moved in. I fell in love. I desperately needed someone to love me and he was so kind. But then, he started asking me for money, saying he'd run out and needed my help to pay for the room. He said he knew of a modeling audition he could take me to. If I became a model, we could live together, and we'd be set.

"It sounded exciting. I started to believe I was pretty, and my picture might be in some chic magazine." Her gaze dropped.

"It was a scam. I still don't know if he knew what it really was. He dropped me off at the audition site, and I never saw him again. They gagged and tied me, then shoved me in a van and drove to a hotel where I was sold to dirty old men who paid for sex. Guys with guns kept me locked in a room until they came to get me, dressed me and took me to a room where some 'client' would be waiting."

"Can I interrupt you for just a minute?" Jim hoped it didn't throw her off. She nodded. "Where did they keep you? At the hotel itself, or someplace else and then bring you there for… uh…" He glanced away.

"Yeah, I know." She took a breath. "There was a hotel where they kept several girls and boys. I went there first. The upstairs part of the hotel had an inside hallway. They kept us in those rooms. The downstairs rooms had doors facing outside. That's where we met clients."

"Do you know what state that was in?"

"Louisiana. New Orleans, I think. I heard a snippet of a weather report on the radio that I wasn't supposed to hear one time. Then it was quickly turned off. When they moved me to another location, I was blindfolded. There, they kept us in a house across the road from a small hotel. That was in Atlanta, where I eventually got away."

"Thanks. That could be helpful."

"I guess I was pretty stupid from the start." She pushed her food around on the plate with her fork.

Jim had heard similar stories before. So often the victims blamed themselves. "You were young, naïve and scared, and too innocent to understand the motives of evil people, that's all."

Sophie glanced up, smiled and took a few bites of her breakfast. Jim ate some more too.

"Should I keep going?"

"Of course. Unless you'd rather finish eating first."

"No, I'm fine." She took a sip of coffee.

"How did you get away?"

Her face changed like some kind of pride came over her. "One time when I had an afternoon client, only one guard escorted me to the room where we were supposed to meet. Just as we got to the door, a hotel customer was leaving a room close by. Out of the corner of my eye, I saw a mother with her daughter—about my age. When they opened the car to get in, I screamed super loud. Everyone was totally distracted, and I jumped into the car with them. It must've surprised the guard because he couldn't get his gun out in time—or maybe he'd gotten too comfortable and didn't bring it with him that time. I begged the mother, 'Please help me. I've been trapped here.' She didn't wait for any other explanation. We all rode off together. I don't think she even paid her bill. She probably figured if the police came after us, that was all the better."

"That's amazing." Jim set his mug back on the table. He'd been holding it mid-air without realizing it as he listened, until it got too heavy. "Often victims are so beaten down mentally, so manipulated, they can't even think about escaping."

"I know. I was, too. But in that moment, it's like I saw a flash of light, maybe just in my mind, then I saw the entire scene playout in my imagination a split second before it even happened."

"That's incredible!"

"I think it was God." Sophie took another sip and swept a stray braid behind her ear. "I had prayed so many times for help. I never even knew if there was a God or if he cared until that moment."

As they finished their breakfasts and coffee, Sophie shared how the modeling audition worked and how they used the hotels or nearby houses to keep the girls and boys locked up but close and available. "They made parts of the hotel into apartment-like clusters on the inside, so they still looked like hotel rooms with doors in the hallway." She folded her napkin and put it on the table. "Clients would come, pay an exorbitant amount for a room by the hour. Then the guards, who carried concealed weapons, would bring the hostage to the client for the hour or more, if they paid for more."

"Do you believe your story is typical of how girls get into this life?" he asked.

"Some girls get involved through paid porn sites, others by seeing an ad on social media for a high-paying modeling or acting job. I was locked up with two who got into it that way."

"After you got away and spoke to the police, were they able to catch the perpetrators?"

"No. Unfortunately, they realized they'd been busted and cleared out of Atlanta so quickly that there wasn't a trace by the time investigators got there."

Jim had the feeling this could be the same ring, or a related one, that took Stacy. Possibly the girls from Fairhope as well.

"Would you be willing to talk to investigators of other cases if it could help find them?"

She nodded. "I'd do anything to get guys like that off the streets and help victims. I want other victims to become survivors."

Sophie's bravery astonished Jim and his heart warmed. With her kind of courage there had to be hope for a better world.

CHAPTER ELEVEN

Darkness lay like a thick blanket over everything. Wren squinted, trying to make something out. Where was she? It all felt wrong.

Fear lived in this dark. It clung to her, pressing down on her limbs. She couldn't tell if her good eye was open or shut.

Desperation tugged at her lungs. She wanted to cry out, but no sound escaped. An evil presence floated around the room, claiming its territory. This was evil's domain, not hers.

Help, Jesus. She couldn't speak the words but thought them hard in her mind. She wrestled against the paralysis again. Still, she couldn't move.

A tiny pinprick of light drew her attention, far, far away and small. She clung to the sight of it like a life preserver out in the open ocean.

The light grew. It looked like a crooked star, alive with light, with some rays shooting out longer than others. The rays reached out then shrank back into themselves. The overall size of the star steadily increased. This starlight felt familiar, like an old friend. It reminded her of something long past. But what?

Soft noises pulled Wren to her body, and her current situation. She opened her eyes.

Damiano and Mei shuffled around the kitchen quietly, while Wren remained on the couch, but not quietly enough to keep from waking her.

She blinked. Images of Amy, the scarf… then the darkness, its deep drowning depths, and the memory of evil sent a chill through her.

How had she slept at all?

The words of her prayers returned to her, then the memory of the star. Even in the ocean of fear that had paralyzed her, that light, somehow familiar, comforted her.

She needed to draw.

She sat up and smoothed out the sweater she had put on the morning she and Liv had left for the audition. How long had it been? A day? Two? Four? Days and nights ran together.

Soon everyone was up except for DeeAnn and Amy. Wren guessed they'd returned around 2 a.m., but she had no way of knowing for sure.

Wren smoothed her hair with her hand and tried to detangle it with her fingers. "What's for breakfast?" She spoke softly, trying to respect those who still slept, as she crossed the room.

"Captain Crunch." Damiano lifted the box.

Her stomach turned at the thought. They needed real food.

Kidnappers don't give a crap about your health. She swallowed the negative thought down like a pill stuck in her throat.

Wren poured some cereal into a bowl, then stopped at a knock.

Who would be knocking at the door? The kidnappers didn't care about being polite. They just barged in.

"Yeah? Who is it?" Damiano shrugged, looking at Wren as he answered the knock.

"It's Cade." The familiar voice came through, but weak, not haughty or mean. "I have some fruit for you."

Wren opened the door. "You've got a lot of nerve." Face to face with Cade, it was the only greeting she could manage. But what if he got her in trouble? They could make her pay.

"I'm sorry, Wren. I didn't know." He walked to the table with a large box of pears and set them down. "I didn't have a choice. I—"

"You!" The shrieking voice came from across the room. Liv jumped up from the couch. "You liar!" She ran to him, and he took a few steps back toward the door. He shut it quickly then turned to Liv.

"Liv, you have to believe me. I didn't know."

She pounded his chest with her fists, and he stood there, arms limp at his sides while she beat on him. Granted, he was well built, muscular and probably felt little pain, but his composure surprised Wren.

Then Liv just dropped to the floor and cried. Wren squatted beside Liv, her own tears dripping off her chin. Seeing Liv in this desperate state crushed her. Liv had always been the bubbly, happy one. She wrapped Liv in both arms.

"Liv, I—" Cade tried again.

"Maybe you should just go, Man," Damiano walked up to him in a threatening manner.

"But I want—"

"Who cares what you want?" Damiano sounded sure of himself. He gave Cade a little shove. Wren might believe he was serious, but she remembered the guys downstairs with guns.

"Damiano, it's not worth it." Wren caught his eye from her position on the floor.

Cade turned to go.

"Wait, Cade," Wren stood. "Can you get things for us?" It was worth a try. If he really felt bad, maybe he'd be willing to help them.

"Probably not much. Like what?"

"Just paper and a pencil, or even crayons."

His forehead drew together.

"I need to draw." She hurried ahead. "It helps me stay sane."

"I'll see what I can do, but I can't promise. I'm not free to do anything I want. Daddy has to approve everything."

Was Cade trapped as well? It seemed like he could come and go.

Liv was still crying when Cade left. Wren sat on the floor beside her again and held her until it subsided.

Liv sniffled. Her crying slowed, and she wiped her eyes with her hand. "I should've kicked that jerk in the teeth."

Wren let a quick laugh escape. "You practically did."

"I hate him."

"Oh, Liv."

"Don't you?" Liv looked up at her.

"Maybe he's trapped too."

Liv shook her head hard. "You've gone soft."

"I'll say," Mei inserted into their conversation.

Wren ignored it and stood, holding onto Liv's hand, pulling to get her up off the floor. "Let's get some breakfast. There are pears and Captain Crunch."

Somehow DeeAnn slept through the whole thing, but Amy stood at the bedroom door watching the ordeal.

After they had finished eating, Amy got herself some food. She ate quietly at the table alone, her head down.

Late morning sometime, Cade returned with some paper from a copy machine and a box of four pencils.

Surprised, Wren asked, "What are—"

"They're drawing pencils. Not good ones." He handed them to Wren.

"But why? How?" Wren opened the box and felt the pencils as if they were made of precious stone.

"My uncle didn't want any sharp objects up here. I convinced him that art pencils were soft and couldn't hurt anyone."

"So, he paid for—"

"No. I used my own money. Like I said, they're not the best ones."

"Thank you. I know you didn't have to. I don't know why you did, but thank you." Cade had to have some compassion.

"Everyone's life is a story." What was his?

Father, set Cade free too, Wren prayed silently.

Later, she went into the bedroom to think and draw the scene she'd envisioned in her dream. Cade had gotten B pencils, which were indeed softer and therefore darker, so she had to use a light touch to begin. She wanted to sketch the outline of the girl and the scarf loosely. The scarf would drape halfway over the girl's face. She wouldn't detail the face, so if the others saw the drawing, they wouldn't know it was Amy. Then she'd shade the scarf in more detail.

Wren didn't receive any meaning from the picture as she drew, but it felt good to get it out of her head and onto paper.

"What are you doing in here?" DeeAnn poked her head in as Wren finished the basic picture. She could do more on it, but at least she'd gotten the image down.

"Just drawing. It helps me relax."

"Get out of there. It's not your room." DeeAnn planted both hands on her hips like a mother scolding her toddler. It struck Wren as ridiculous, but she complied.

———•●•———

The door opened with a crash. Wren squinted at the hall light flooding into their space.

DeeAnn and Amy stumbled in looking dazed. They must've been so tired.

Wren closed her eyes again, hoping they'd close the door so she could get back to sleep.

"DeeAnn, wake the newbies and bring them to me in robes." Wren heard Romeo's command.

"Well, of course, my love, anything for you." DeeAnn's words slurred. She sounded drunk. Was she in love with Romeo? A kidnapper?

Then it dawned on Wren. He had asked for them. *Oh God, no…please. I know this isn't your will. Please keep us from harm.*

A thought stabbed her gut. *He didn't spare DeeAnn or Amy, so why would he spare you?*

A robe dropped onto her body. DeeAnn was passing them out.

"Put it on. Now. Romeo needs you," she said.

Wren listened to DeeAnn waking the others. They didn't move. Neither did she.

"I said, now!" Romeo's voice boomed, like a crazed animal, starved and let loose for the first time.

"My God. Lord Jesus, have mercy on us." Wren gripped the robe.

Damiano and Mei walked into the living room with their robes in hand.

"There is no Jesus here," Damiano whispered as he walked by.

Had she prayed out loud?

This is the end of your sweet little life. The words in her head bit and accused. She'd been privileged and protected and hadn't even realized it.

An evil presence wrapped around her, slithering and constricting. *The end of your dreams… the beginning of your nightmares.*

"Get your clothes off now." Romeo didn't scream this time. His voice came out in a strained whisper, which chilled her to the core.

Damiano opened his mouth, then closed it again.

The hall light streamed into their dark room in such a way that they clearly saw Romeo's gun pointed at them.

A small cry sounded from down the hall. Were there guests at this motel? Or other rooms of hostages?

Romeo didn't turn on the lights, but he didn't close the door either. He expected them to change right there in front of him, in front of the open door.

"Underwear and everything," he ordered.

They obeyed. Wren knew he'd shoot one of them to make an example if they didn't.

He marched the four of them, dressed only in white bathrobes, down the hall, down the stairs, and to the back office. The room they'd passed on the way that first day.

A bookcase on the wall inside the office slid to the side, revealing a hidden doorway. Romeo forced them through it into a room full of racks of clothes and accessories—far more than had been offered in that little wardrobe room for the fake modeling audition.

Romeo selected an outfit for each of them. Again, he forced them to change in front of him and each other. Wren stared at the cement floor and had the feeling that the others did too.

Wren glanced up in time to see Romeo grabbing Damiano by the wrist. He shoved him toward the door. She wished she hadn't looked. Damiano wore a lion-taming costume with a whip.

Romeo stuck the gun in his back. "Move."

"Where should I go?" he said.

"I'll tell you where to turn when we get there."

He locked Mei, Liv, and Wren in the wardrobe room while he was gone. There wasn't a window in the entire room. The only openings were two small vents, neither big enough for a rabbit to fit through. One lightbulb hung from the middle of the ceiling.

Next, he took Mei, dressed like a Japanese doll—a kimono covering lacy underwear.

When Romeo grabbed Liv, dressed like an Indian princess, with teal see-through harem pantlegs, a skimpy top showing her waist, and a turquoise veil, Daddy appeared in the doorway.

"She's not for sale." Daddy had both hands on his hips, a gun in one of them. Anger filled his eyes.

"What the—?" Romeo argued. "She'll go for at least—"

"The boss said no," he cut Romeo off.

When Romeo still didn't let Liv's arm go, Daddy said. "Leave her, or I'll kill you myself. I can't afford to offend him. We'll all be dead by morning."

Their boss must be evil-on-steroids if these immoral, violent kidnappers feared him.

Romeo made a show of dropping Liv's wrist, like a mic drop. "She has a client waiting."

"Then go get Amy," Daddy suggested and turned to go.

Poor Amy. She'd just gotten back to the apartment, now this. Wren's throat squeezed, and she swallowed hard. Crying wouldn't be accepted right now.

Romeo grabbed Wren by the wrist. "Then you're next."

CHAPTER TWELVE

Oh God, Lord Jesus Christ, Son of God, have mercy on me, a sinner. The words flew through Wren's mind in a split second.

Romeo had shoved a Native American costume at her—a short leather skirt with fringe and an orange bra under a cropped leather vest. Her long dark hair must've made them think she could pull off the look.

Were they supposed to act a part? No one had given her any instruction, which was fine by her. She wasn't about to perform. In fact, she wouldn't do anything with anyone…

Brave thoughts, little one. Evil's voice mocked her.

Who was she kidding? She wasn't brave. What was she going to do? Some tears escaped against her will.

Romeo held a syringe up to her left arm. She pulled away, but he had a vice-grip on her. He gave her a shot of something and marched her outside. Damp, cool air hit her face as they walked at Romeo's quick pace around the corner to the front of the building, where she looked ahead at a long row of room doors with numbers.

The ground-floor rooms faced outside toward the parking lot. No need to go down an enclosed hallway, like upstairs.

He led her to Room 17, shoved her inside, and slammed the door. She heard the door lock behind her.

A middle-aged man sat on the double bed smiling up at her.

"I like the outfit, Pocahontas." He winked. Was he trying to flirt with her? Gag. Airplane noises faded in the distance.

Her head felt a little dizzy. She risked another look in the man's direction.

Brown hair, receding hairline, a bit overweight. He could be a father to any of her friends from school. Did he have a daughter somewhere? Would he want her to be here with him, like this?

A small alcohol bottle sat beside him on the bedside table attached to the wall. A larger, empty bottle stuck out of the little trash bin on the floor beside it.

She stood frozen, her back pinned against the door.

"Come over here beside me." He patted the bed next to him.

She didn't move.

"Look, Mr. Blond Muscle Man is right outside. All I have to do is call him. You don't want me to give him a bad review, do you?"

Romeo.

"Just sit with me. We don't have to do anything if you don't want to."

If?

Hoping… praying he was telling her the truth, she walked toward him like some kind of zombie in a nightmare. Her thoughts got fuzzier as she sat beside him on the bed.

He talked a while. She didn't really pay attention. Maybe she should have. Maybe he'd give away some important information. The man was at least a little drunk. She listened to his words, but soon they slurred and she barely understood him.

He began to grope, pulling at her clothes. He stopped long enough to get undressed. She seized the opportunity and quickly rearranged her own clothes.

Pushing her to the mattress, he climbed on top of her, mouth open, handsy. Wren closed her eyes. *Oh God.*

She looked up at the ceiling. Despite the bedside lamp, the room darkened at the edges of her vision, the muscles in her body relaxing against her will.

Darkness encroached more, threatening to choke her, its evil so disgusting, so complete.

The man pulled at her clothes, which must've been made to come off easily.

So much for the feeling of peace she had in the truck that first day.

How stupid to believe you'd be alright—that evil couldn't touch you.

The man licked and sucked her neck. She closed her eyes and gagged.

Look for the light, Wren. A faint faraway voice filtered in amidst the evil.

No light is powerful enough to fight this evil. The dark voice countered as she struggled to hold on to her skimpy clothing.

What light could there be here now?

The starlight.

Light in this darkness? How? Where?

She stared up, looking for that pinprick of light against the dark sky.

Nothing.

She closed her eyes, then opened them again, searching past the man's head and shoulder, beyond the ceiling. Wait…

Just there… A tiny light.

Light always overcomes darkness.

Her clenched heart released a little of its tension.

Something cool and wet dribbled down her face and into her mouth, shocking her out of any fuzziness in her brain.

"Ack!" She shoved hard against the mass on top of her. It rolled, and she ran to the bathroom.

What was that?

She spit into the sink, then quickly wiped his drool from her face and neck and pulled the clothes back in place that had come off her shoulder and straightened her skirt.

Peeking out of the bathroom, she feared the man's reaction. He lay face down on the bed, naked. She looked away. A sight she wished she'd never seen.

He must've passed out and drooled on her.

She gagged again.

Suddenly, she had freedom. God was going to help her escape!

Well, maybe.

Maybe they had cameras in the room. Standing in the middle of the room, she wondered what to do.

She glanced around. Was there anything in this motel room she could take and hide inside her costume, then use it to break out later? Could she sneak out of this room and get away before they noticed?

Fear and excitement coursed through her veins. This could be her chance. She'd go for help and bring the police back here.

Maybe she could scratch a message on the walls with something sharp.

No, they would inspect the room and the walls each time for something like that.

Wren opened the corner of the curtain just enough to see out into the lit parking lot.

She looked at the parked cars, the street beyond the parking lot, and the other side of the motel with one level on top of the ground-floor rooms. The second level, as she knew, had an inside hallway—doors faced inside.

The hotel buildings made a C-shape, with parking in the middle.

Few cars passed on the road this late at night.

Wren moved to the other side of the window and opened the curtain just a tiny crack again. With her good eye on the left, it took more effort. She had to turn her head at a strange angle, partially obscuring her view. Someone moved to the side of the doorway. Romeo.

He smoked a cigarette and paced back and forth in front of several doors, then sat on the curb in front of her door.

Seeing where he sat down, she risked cracking the curtains right in the middle, still just a small opening. She saw the carport-looking part of the motel situated up by the road on one side of the C-shaped building. There was a light over the number.

The hotel address! Of course. If they got the chance to talk to the police, she'd have the address to give.

She didn't know the name of the motel, or even what city or state they were in, much less the road name. So, would it even help?

She had no way of knowing, but she needed to memorize it, anyway, just in case.

9-2-2-1

How would she remember it?

Um…

92, Columbus sailed the ocean blue.

21, Forever 21—one of her and Liv's favorite clothing stores.

92.-21… 92-21… 92-21…

Romeo ground his cigarette into the cement. She jumped back from the window.

Maybe the guy's time was up.

Quick. Think.

Pull the sheet up over the guy, so it looks intentional on his part. She did, then ran back to the bathroom. Maybe Romeo wouldn't question him or try to talk to him.

The door opened.

"Pocahontas, let's go," Romeo called into the room. She came out of the bathroom hoping he thought she'd just now put her clothes back on.

"Buddy, let's go. You only get this room for an hour, and your time's up."

Romeo held tightly to her wrist and closed the door behind them. Wren kept her head down, her hair hiding her face.

———— •●• ————

"Wren, are you okay?" Liv whispered the question. "What happened last night?"

Wren gazed at the floor. "I—I don't want to talk about it."

"God, Wren, I'm so sorry." Face pink, Liv seemed uncomfortable. So unlike her. "Yeah, no… I mean, that's okay. Whatever you want."

She should tell Liv how she'd been spared, but she didn't think she could talk about it at all, and she didn't want the others to hear.

The bolt turned. Wren's stomach cinched. Someone was coming into the apartment. Not again. This soon? Early morning? She'd barely escaped last time. She wouldn't have the same luck twice. The door opened.

Romeo stepped in. Wren's hand clutched her abdomen.

The air stilled.

Talking stopped.

"Come on, DeeAnn, let's go." His upper body muscles filled out his overtight T-shirt. His strawberry-blond beard and mustache were due for a trim. And the look in his blue eyes reflected the ice in his heart.

What must've happened to him to create such rage? Such lack of empathy?

Her heart tightened. Someone like that could do anything to them without a thought, and Daddy was worse.

"Just me?" DeeAnn asked in a casual tone.

"Just you for now. Amy went out twice last night."

"What about her?" DeeAnn pointed to Liv. "She came back not long after you took the others."

"It's not your concern, Dee." The threat in his eyes countered his quiet voice.

"But we'd earn so much more if—"

He grabbed DeeAnn by the hair and pulled her face close to his. "It's not up to you. You're nothing but a ho." Romeo shoved her away from him.

For the flash of a second, Wren saw horror on DeeAnn's face, but it quickly changed to acceptance.

"Orders came from the top. And those orders are never questioned."

DeeAnn scurried to the bedroom, rubbing away a tear as if she didn't want anyone to see. Romeo stood stiff there in the middle of the room.

Wren glanced at Liv, then Mei and Damiano. No one spoke, each studying their hands or the top of the kitchen table.

DeeAnn came out in her robe again and followed Romeo into the hallway.

When the door opened, Wren thought she heard another sound, maybe crying, from down the hallway again, then the door slammed shut and the bolt slid into place.

Father, we must get out of here. She knew God cared, but bad things happened to people he cared for.

"Jesus said there would be trials," the pastor's words came back to her. *"He never promised to get us out of them. He only promised to be with us through them."*

But please, Lord, please get us out of this.

When DeeAnn left with Romeo, Wren wondered what the others had suffered last night. *Stop,* she told herself, *don't think about it,* but she noticed a bruise on Mei's wrist and a scratch on Damiano's face. She tried to focus on something else.

Her stomach growled. Late morning, and they had had no food since some tacos yesterday.

A knock sounded. Wren jumped out of her thoughts, nearly out of her skin.

"Can I come in?" Cade asked from the other side of the door. He didn't need to ask. Romeo didn't. The man called "Daddy" certainly didn't.

"No!" Liv shouted and jumped up off the couch where she'd been. "Don't let him in." She backed toward the bedroom.

"He could just walk in if he wanted to." Damiano clicked off the TV. "We don't have any rights here, if you haven't noticed."

Mei opened the door for him without a greeting. No one had talked much that morning anyway. Mei turned back into the living space with Cade following behind her. Wren glimpsed one guard in the hall. No mask now, and she didn't see his gun, but she knew he had one. The door closed behind Cade.

His eyes searched around.

"She went into the other room," Wren offered. His face registered disappointment. But his hands held a paper grocery sack. Food?

"I brought y'all something to eat." Cade carried a bag into the kitchen. "It took most of the day to convince my uncle—I mean Daddy—he's in a bad mood."

"Why?" Wren asked.

"The bosses threatened him. Told him to do something he obviously didn't want to do."

"Do what?" Mei asked.

Cade shrugged.

"Really? How can you not know?" Wren asked.

"He doesn't tell me what he's doing, how it's done, or what instructions he receives." He set the bag on the table. "All he tells me is what to do and when I should do it."

"And you just do it?" Wren recognized the sarcasm in her voice. Somehow, she felt safe enough with Cade to let her anger slip out. Or maybe after last night she just didn't care.

He dropped his head.

"Better to be an ignorant jerk than a mean one, I guess." Damiano dug into the sack. "Thanks for the food."

Mei stepped closer.

"What's going to happen to us, Cade?" Wren asked.

He hesitated. She narrowed her eyes and pursed her lips. "The cartel will tell Daddy which administrators across the country to send you to." He glanced toward the bedroom, worry in his eyes.

"Administrators?" Mei asked.

"Um, well…"

"Look, Cade, it's our lives." Wren took milk from the fridge and placed it on the table. She faced him. "We need to know the truth."

"They're pimps, organized by some cartel. I don't really know what it all means." He sat in a kitchen chair and rubbed a palm over his eyes. He looked up at Wren. "You must believe me. You have to make Liv believe it. I didn't know about all this." He rubbed his hands over his head. "My uncle, my father's stepbrother, has taken care of me since my parents passed away in an accident two years ago. I was still in high school then. I never knew what he did for work. But after graduation, he said I'd have to run errands for him if I wanted any more help from him."

"How could you not know?" Wren stood over him. Damiano and Mei sat at the table.

"I bought supplies like food, toilet paper, toothbrushes, assuming it was for models or actors who'd be traveling for their gigs, though he never explained. I dropped off mail at the post office, and I—I swear, I didn't know what it was for."

"That's a lie." Liv walked into the room, fire in her blue eyes.

Cade jerked around at the sound of her voice, then stood up. "Liv, I'm telling the truth. Please believe me." His hands reached out for her, but she stayed far enough back that he couldn't reach her.

"You just happened to go looking for some girls to invite to his phony audition?" Sarcasm saturated Liv's question, but it was a good one.

"A couple of months ago he told me he was a talent agent. He said if I knew any pretty and talented girls, I could invite them to his auditions. That was the first time I did." His tortured face begged Liv's forgiveness. "I like you, Liv. Hurting you was the last thing I wanted to do. I even went to bat for you with my uncle."

"What does that mean?" Her voice harsh, Liv wasn't backing down.

"I begged him not to send you away, and I told him he should let you go."

"Without Wren? Without the others?" Her face defied him as well as her words.

"Liv, you don't understand. I have to keep working for him just to keep him from killing you, Wren, and the little ones. My uncle is evil. I know that now."

Little ones? Wren's stomach turned—the noises down the hall.

They had little children here for sick men to use and abuse. *Oh God.* Wren looked around the room. Had the others caught on to what Cade had let slip?

"If it's true, then get us out of here." At Liv's challenge, they all turned and glared at Cade.

Why couldn't he? He knew the building. His uncle allowed him to come and go. Hope threatened to grow, but Wren dared not allow it.

"I can't, Liv. He'll kill me." He rubbed his eyes again. "He'll kill you and the others too, or if he doesn't—I don't even want to imagine what he'd do to you." Piercing Liv with a look of desperation, fear filled his eyes.

"Dying would be better than what we're facing." Her words sounded like the courageous Liv Wren knew and loved. And she was right.

CHAPTER THIRTEEN

"We need a plan," Wren said, forcing calm into her voice. James Fielding's words in the lecture came back to her. *It's better to wait and plan.*

"A plan? My God." Cade's eyes got crazed with fear. He rubbed one hand through his hair. "Are we even talking about this?" the terror was obvious in his tone. They had better take the threat of Cade's uncle seriously.

"Cade," Wren waited until she had his attention. "Have you seen Amy?" He started to nod and say yes, of course, but she interrupted him. "I mean, have you seen her vapid gaze? Or realized that she doesn't speak? Have you thought about what this has done to her? What it'll do to us?"

"DeeAnn seems fine with it all."

Oh, no, Cade did not just say that. Rage tightened Wren's jaw. Was that his excuse for not intervening?

"I don't know her story yet." Wren strained to keep her voice calm but firm. "But there's a reason. Everyone has a story." Wren felt Liv's fingers slip into hers until they held hands like they were kids at a scary movie. She squeezed back.

"We are not like DeeAnn, that's for sure," Liv said.

"Look, I've got to get back, or Uncle Emil will be—"

"Emil? Who's Emil?" Damiano asked.

"That's my uncle. The one you call Daddy." Cade's eyes widened, and his mouth dropped. "I shouldn't have told you his name. Oh shhh… I'm in so much trouble. I've got to go." He was out the door before Wren could take a breath to say another word.

They ate from a large foil pan of cashew chicken, which Mei pulled out of the grocery sack. Maybe it had been food leftover at the end of the day from a shop owner nearby. Whatever, it tasted delicious. She was so hungry, it's possible anything would've tasted good, even Chinese takeout for breakfast.

Liv hadn't touched her food. "Liv, please eat. It's actually not bad, especially when we've had little real food in the last few days—or however long we've been here. Come on. Eat something."

Maybe she was trying to starve herself in protest, like Gandhi.

"How can you be so brave, Wren?" Liv seemed to search her face. "You've always been afraid of everything when there was nothing to be afraid of."

"I don't know." Wren thought about it. She didn't feel brave, but she was talking brave, and that was new. Also, her usual doubt when confronted with decisions seemed to clarify in this terrible situation. "I guess my history of worst-case planning kind of comes in handy now. But I'm terrified, Liv. I can't even allow my thoughts to play out in my mind."

"Yeah, I know what you mean." Liv pushed the food away. "I'm just not hungry."

"Look, if we're going to come up with an escape plan, you need energy."

Liv's head darted up toward Wren. "Do you mean it?"

Wren hadn't realized it, but she really did. Determination surged in her. There had to be a way. Would the others help?

Liv ate with the rest of them, and they saved enough for DeeAnn to eat when she got back, and Amy when she woke up.

Wren didn't tell Liv what happened… or hadn't happened the night before. She'd been lucky. Who knew what Damiano and Mei might have suffered? They didn't talk about it. They needed to help each other stay positive and strong.

Soon, they sat around the table brainstorming ideas for the escape plan.

"We could swipe Romeo's cell phone the next time he comes and dial 911." Damiano wiped his face on a paper towel.

"What if he doesn't bring it with him when he comes up here?" Mei pushed her hair back behind her ear on one side. It had started growing out.

"Even if he brings it, where would we tell them to come?" This was going to be a lot tougher than Wren had hoped. "We don't even know which state we ended up in. In that amount of driving, we could've made it to Mississippi, Louisiana or Florida by now. Or we could still be in Alabama." She pinched the bridge of her nose. "I saw the numbers for the street address at this motel—9221," she said, proud she'd thought to pay attention.

"How's that going to help?" Mei asked.

Her heart sank. It wouldn't be enough.

"Maybe we should just bang on the windows." Damiano's clenched fists proved he couldn't wait to slam them into something, but that would only send the guards running.

By late into the night, they still hadn't come up with anything that wouldn't get them all killed. They gave up for the night and headed to bed, but Wren couldn't sleep.

A dog's insistent bark sounded outside. Agitated, the animal kept at it for a long time. She thought how nice it would be to be out there and comfort that pooch right now.

But it wasn't the barking that kept her awake. It was fear enhanced by dark imagination.

— • ● • —

The next day, late morning or early afternoon, Amy walked into the living room where the rest of them sat watching Jeopardy. She held a paper in her hand.

Wren's stomach clenched.

Her drawing.

Did Amy know it was her? How could she? Wren couldn't help but watch her.

Amy held the paper toward Wren and lifted her gaze from the floor where it usually stayed. "I—Is—" She cleared her unused throat. "Is this me?" She actually spoke, tears pooling in her lower eyelids.

"How…" Wren swallowed. She never intended to tell her. "What makes you think so?"

"It's mine." Her hand fell gently on her neck and collarbone. "My Granny's scarf." The tears crested her eyelids and trickled down her cheeks.

The TV had clicked off. No sound threatened to breach the silence. Liv scooted from Wren's side, allowing room between them on the couch. Damiano and Mei sat on the other couch in silence. They waited. DeeAnn approached and sat next to Damiano, giving him a little push with her hip to make him scoot over. Even she seemed interested in what made Amy speak.

Why couldn't they all go in the other room and let Wren talk to Amy alone?

Amy's tears turned into all-out crying. Liv got some toilet paper from the bathroom for her to wipe her nose. Wren and Liv both patted Amy's back.

"It's okay, Amy," Liv said. Whatever that was supposed to mean.

Nothing was okay about their situation, and they all knew it.

When her crying subsided, Amy looked up at Wren again. "How did you know?"

What could she say? What did she actually know? Nothing, really. "I had a dream the first night."

"Of me?" Amy sounded as if she couldn't believe it.

Wren nodded.

"Tell me."

Wren couldn't refuse. Amy seemed so vulnerable, so lost. Maybe God wanted to help her. Why else would Wren dream about someone she didn't know?

"I saw you standing in a park, near a large live oak with moss hanging down. Your hair blew in the wind, and so did your scarf. The scarf hung down over your winter coat—"

Amy sucked in air. Her hand flew to her open mouth, but she nodded for Wren to continue.

"I noticed the pattern on the scarf, and I felt I needed to pay attention to that." Amy nodded. "It was poppies in different shades of red and orange mostly, with a few yellows," Wren kept going. "The leaves were dark green— like forest green, which matched the trim around the scarf." Wren swallowed. Should she stop? Amy had been nodding through everything she said.

"Keep going," Amy said.

"Your face held so much pain. Then you hid your face in the scarf like you were ashamed of something, maybe something you did wrong." Warmth collected in Wren's eyes. She wiped around her prosthetic with a piece of the toilet paper she tore off Amy's stash. "That's all," Wren assured her.

Amy still nodded.

"Does it mean something to you?" Wren knew in her heart it did and hoped Amy would share.

Thankfully, the others held their tongues. DeeAnn got up and went to the table. Maybe she'd had enough of the story.

"It was my mom's scarf." Amy blew her nose with some toilet paper. Liv got up to get her a cup of water. She handed it to Amy, who took a big drink. "My grandmother owned it first. Made of silk in the 1920s. Granny wore it every day."

"Sorry, I couldn't make the colors, only shades with these drawing pencils."

"I recognized it." Amy scooted forward on the couch and placed her elbows on her knees. "My mom wore it often, then it became mine when she died." Amy lifted her head and stared at the clouded window. She wiped her nose again. "I went to live with my brother, who was eighteen at the time. The scarf was my most precious thing. It reminded me of Momma, of Granny, and of better times." Her eyes were far away, and Wren could tell Amy was back in that better place.

Wren swallowed hard. All this child had been through…

"What happened?" Mei asked.

"Yeah, how'd you end up here? Was it a modeling audition like with us?" Damiano asked.

"Y'all are so stupid." Sitting over at the table, DeeAnn spoke through a full mouth of Captain Crunch. "You're not supposed to ask each other those kinds of questions." DeeAnn's voice came across as the instructor to whom they should all pay attention. "It just makes it harder."

Amy's head dropped again, her hair falling in front of her face.

"No," Liv said with defiance. "Amy doesn't need to feel bad about anything. She's the victim."

"You think so?" DeeAnn's eyebrows lifted. Maybe she knew Amy's story. Maybe it would hurt Amy to tell it.

Wren dismissed her words with a backward wave of her hand. "Psychologists say it's healing to say the things you want to keep hidden."

"How do you know?" DeeAnn said before taking another bite.

Wren shrugged.

"Go on, Amy," Liv whispered in her ear. Wren overheard.

"Bobby—that's my brother," Amy began. "He was so busy trying to work and pay all our bills—he was only a teenager himself. But he was gone a lot. His friends came to the house a lot. I was glad for the company, especially when Bobby was gone. But then…" Her head dropped again. "They… well, they…"

"They took advantage of you?" Liv asked quietly.

Amy nodded. "But one of them was very nice to me. He treated me like his girlfriend."

"How old were you?" Mei seemed sincerely concerned.

"Ten."

Oh God. Wren shut her eyes.

"His name was Patrick," Amy continued. "I thought I was in love." She dropped her head.

"It's okay, Amy. How could you understand at ten years old?" Liv patted her hand on Amy's knee.

"Well, Patrick said we needed money." She almost smiled then. "I thought I was happy. Patrick often reminded me how hard my brother had to work. He said I could help Bobby if I did some work too."

Wren sighed, guessing what came next.

"He said there was this site online where girls could upload pictures of their bodies and get money for it." Not what Wren expected her to say. "It was like having your own business—at least that's what Patrick said. It sounded too easy. He offered to help me with the business side of it. He took the pictures, uploaded them, read the messages and sometimes answered messages back as if he was me. It felt like he really wanted to help me. And he said we'd split the money, and I could give my portion to Bobby."

"What a guy!" Damiano rolled his eyes and flailed his arm.

"Yeah." Amy gave him a side glance, and her face turned pink. "I had lots of followers. Men liked me."

So many men interested in such a ten-year-old? How sick! Wren handed her a few more squares of toilet paper.

"At first I felt pretty," Amy continued. "But when Patrick read some messages to me, I felt nauseous. The men who came to my site a lot started asking for specific kinds of pictures." She closed her eyes and dropped her head into her hands. "I hate myself."

"No." Liv's voice came out a little too loud. It surprised Wren. "You are not to blame, you hear me?" Liv held Amy's wrist, who now looked her right in the face. Amy nodded, eyes wide. "You are precious to God, Amy. You have been a victim."

Wren hadn't heard Liv talk about God very often. But Wren saw a connection in Liv's eyes with Amy's story.

"I've heard enough," DeeAnn rolled her eyes.

"Then go in the other room," Mei said without looking at DeeAnn.

"I could have said no." Amy's voice cracked

"Could you have?" Wren asked. "You were ten."

"Eleven by that time," Amy corrected.

"Okay, well then, eleven, that's no different." Wren prayed silently that Amy could believe in herself. "Patrick took advantage of your vulnerable age, and your vulnerable situation—no parents, no money, and lots of fear about it all." The longer Wren thought about it, the angrier she got.

Amy nodded. "That's true, I guess." She paused. "I was always afraid."

"So, then what happened?" Mei prodded.

"One man wanted to meet with me. Patrick said that he just wanted to have a real date with me, to take me to lunch. I didn't want to, and we told the guy no a bunch of times, but he just kept emailing. Then Patrick told me he offered 500K just to take me to lunch. He said we couldn't refuse that. When I said I didn't know what K was and why 500 of them were so good, he laughed and said I was such a child. He meant 500,000 dollars."

"Whoa," Damiano chimed in.

"Yeah. I didn't understand how much it really was," Amy admitted. "Patrick said we could buy a house for me, Bobby, and Patrick, and fill it with beautiful things if we had 500K. So, I agreed. He promised to take me and pick me up. He said he'd watch us to make sure the guy was okay."

"And did he?" Mei asked.

DeeAnn sighed loudly. "This is stupid. Amy's just trying to make y'all feel sorry for her. It's stupid." She rolled her eyes as she came over to the living room area and flipped on the TV.

"Hey," Damiano said to her. "If you have the TV on, keep it way down. The rest of us want to hear what Amy has to say."

"Don't talk to me like that!" DeeAnn flung her arm toward Damiano, but he caught it mid-air before the back of her hand slapped him. Then he stood and leaned over her, still holding her arm.

"I'll talk to you any way I want." He was bigger, muscular, and obviously stronger. "I don't know why you think you're any better than the rest of us, but I've had it. And by the way, we both know I could take you in a fight if you're considering it."

Wren's heart thrilled. DeeAnn had treated them like dirt since they got there. They were all in this together and should have each other's backs.

Damiano sat back down and faced Amy. DeeAnn turned the volume down.

"Thank you," Amy whispered, looking up at him from under her lashes.

He nodded.

"We were supposed to meet the man in the park by the big tree. Well, I was. Patrick sat in the parked car, watching to make sure I was okay. I wore my mom's scarf. It made me feel safe and loved." She shifted her position on the couch and folded one leg under her, then glanced around at everyone watching her.

"Don't worry, Amy." Wren touched her shoulder and laid the drawing on her lap. "We're all here in the same awful situation. We can at least understand each other's stories, and maybe we can help each other."

Amy nodded, and so did Liv.

"I stood in the park waiting on that windy day. When the man arrived, he told me he had left his wallet in his car, and I should walk with him. It was on the opposite side of the park from Patrick. When we got there, he shoved me into his car and took off. We drove a ways down the road, then pulled over to the side. He told me if I tried to run or scream, or if I thrashed around in the car, he'd kill me."

Wren's heart sank. How scared she must've been?

"He pulled a knife from his pocket." Head down, Amy lifted her eyes shyly. "It was big too. Then we got back on the road, and he drove me here. He took me by the wrist and handed me to Daddy, like he was delivering groceries."

Liv and Wren wrapped their arms around her shoulders, tears on both their cheeks.

"Daddy pressed cash into the man's hand. 'Five thousand, like I promised,' I heard him say."

CHAPTER FOURTEEN

Amy still hesitated to talk, but would sometimes after that. And she started to eat with them.

They all had a couple of days off. No one knew the reason. Maybe there just weren't any clients. Relief filled Wren with each hour they were left alone.

Cade had dropped off sub sandwiches for them earlier without staying to talk. They sat around the table eating.

Amy set her sandwich down and wiped her mouth. "Tell us your story, Liv?" Maybe she had sensed a kindred spirit from Liv. Maybe she needed to know someone else had made mistakes or been hurt.

Liv hesitated.

A memory of the lecture they had heard about trafficking broached Wren's memory. *Remember who you are,* Jim Fielding had said. "Liv, remember the guy who lectured about trafficking?" Wren asked. "He said to remember who you are. Maybe telling your story out loud will give you a voice and make you feel human again."

"That's how I felt when you all listened to my story," Amy said.

Liv scooted her chair back from the table and crossed her legs on the seat. "Well, Wren knows most of it." She glanced up at Wren. "And it's not a long story. I've been thinking about it a lot since we've been here. Especially since you shared yours, Amy." She quick-braided the back of her hair and took a deep breath.

Wren nodded for her to go ahead.

Liv flipped her braid back, something she did when she was stalling. "Okay. Well, at around age eleven or twelve, my father started touching me." She glanced at the floor. "You know like feeling me in all the places… and um, kissing me like a boyfriend." Liv stopped at the air-sucking sounds from her listeners, her face flaring pink. "I guess you could call it inappropriate touch. It didn't happen all the time, but maybe, like when he was stressed or something."

Liv looked around at the others, but when her eyes landed on Amy, she continued. "He told me we could never tell anyone about our special relationship because it would kill my mom to know that he loved me the same as he loved her." Staring down at the table, she took a swallow of water. "I didn't want to hurt my mom. Also, I felt ashamed, so I didn't tell anyone. Not until a few years later when I confided in Wren."

Wren walked around the table, lifted Liv's hand and squeezed it. No one spoke, but DeeAnn rolled her eyes.

"My daddy always treated me special, even before that. He made a lot of money and would buy me anything I wanted."

"Wow," DeeAnn's voice came out as sarcastic as her face looked. "You poor baby."

"Shut up, DeeAnn," Mei said. "Keep talking, Liv."

"Okay. Well, that's how I grew up. After the um touching started—"

"You can call it abuse Liv because it was." Wren wanted her to understand that it wasn't her fault.

"Right. After he started that, in a way I felt special. I know that sounds strange, because I also felt gross and guilty, so that's why I can understand some of your story, Amy."

Amy nodded.

"But when I was fourteen, Daddy left both of us, my mom and me. He disappeared. We didn't know where he went, if he was all right, or what happened to him. Eventually, Mom figured out that he just ran away." Liv's eyes got glassy.

"It devastated me. Our money situation changed overnight. And okay, I admit it, I was spoiled. I wanted all the things he used to buy for me, but more than that, even though it was bad, I wanted the attention." She paused with a faraway look. "Sometimes I still try to find that attention in a guy or an audience."

Wren had never heard her admit that.

"I had a boyfriend in high school. A football star, you know?" Liv gazed off, and her eyes sparkled with moisture. "He broke up with me when he went off to college. I guess I was feeling bad about myself... or maybe I just craved attention when I met Cade. He came to my performance and complimented me. He took me out every night after that, and he talked about a modeling opportunity." She shrugged as if to say, *Yeah, I'm that stupid.*

"Thanks for telling us, Liv," Amy said. Liv tipped her head toward Amy.

Samantha O'Connor was right that everyone had a story. Good feelings seemed to grow whenever one of them shared theirs.

A knock sounded at the door. *Please don't let it be Daddy or Romeo to take someone.* Wren's gut-reaction prayer came to her mind as it did every time the door opened.

Cade cracked the door a bit. "Can I come in?" Liv bolted that way.

"No." She pushed the door against his forearm.

"I don't think we should make him mad." Damiano walked over. "We could use an ally outside this room." He whispered the last part.

Point taken.

Damiano opened the door, and Liv ran to the bedroom. "Come on in, Cade. Hey, thanks for the subs, man." Was he trying to sound like a buddy?

"No prob." A medium-sized mutt followed Cade in. Wired-haired, black and shaggy, tail wagging.

"Who's this?" Amy asked.

Cade stood speechless, staring at Amy. Glancing Wren's way, he mouthed, *she speaks?*

Wren smiled at him. At least one good thing had come of their situation.

"He was barking in the alley at your window last night," he said. Wren remembered hearing it. "Romeo couldn't make him shut up—afraid it might attract unwanted attention—so he brought him inside. He's been by my side all day."

"Why don't you give him a name, Amy?" Cade smiled at her as she petted the dog.

"I think his name should be Bobby," Amy voiced without looking up.

"That's perfect." Wren knelt to pet the dog too. "Hi Bobby. You sure are cute."

"I thought he might cheer y'all up a bit." Cade glanced toward the bedroom where Liv had retreated.

"We'd cheer up if we could get out of this slave cage." Damiano often used jokes or sarcasm to lighten the mood. Or maybe it was to hide his own fear.

Mei walked to the doorway of the bedroom. "Liv, come see this cute dog. Amy named him Bobby." Mei came back without waiting for a response.

Liv came and stood in the doorway watching everyone gather around the dog.

Wren looked up just as Liv and Cade locked eyes. It seemed Cade silently begged her forgiveness. Eventually she came and crouched down to pet Bobby.

"Have y'all finished lunch?" Cade asked.

"No," Damiano said and moved back to the table.

"Do you mind if I join you?"

"I already finished," DeeAnn said from in front of the TV, remote in hand. She hadn't cared much for Liv's story. Somewhere along the line she'd drifted into the living room and finished her sandwich in there. "I don't care what you do."

Damiano pointed to the chair that DeeAnn had been sitting in. The rest moved to the table, except for Amy and Liv, who stayed with the dog.

"Thanks." Cade sat and unwrapped one of the extra subs.

"Liv, come on and finish." Wren twisted backward to see her friend. She slowly returned to the table and picked up her half-eaten sandwich, then sat down next to Wren, across from Cade.

"Cade, are you okay with what your uncle is doing?" Wren hoped some confrontation would motivate Cade.

"Of course not, you know how I feel." He looked a little hurt... good.

"Then you need to help us. Maybe you're here for that purpose. And maybe you are supposed to get your uncle locked up for what he's doing. Did you know he paid a guy $5,000 to kidnap Amy and bring her here?" Wren waited for the horror to settle into his mind. "She was eleven."

"My God," Cade sighed the words more than spoke them.

Amy dropped her head and stopped petting Bobby.

"She's been here three years," Liv said.

Cade closed his eyes, leaving them shut for a long time. When he opened them, they were moist.

"We don't have a choice. We have to escape." Wren pinned him with a stare from her good eye. "And those guys have to be stopped." She paused. "But you don't have to go down with them."

"You sound like a prime-time TV show." Damiano said. "But yeah." He pinned Cade with a stare. "And think about it, man. It's not just girls, it's boys, little kids, whatever… or whoever sick rich clients want. If they run out of flesh, you could be next."

Was it just Wren, or did Cade's color drain, turning a slight shade of green?

"Do you have a plan?" Cade asked.

"We tried to come up with something, but we don't know the building." Damiano cursed. "We don't know anything outside this room." Damiano pushed the sandwich wrappers to the side until they fell on the floor. Amy hurried over to pick them up and throw them away.

Soon DeeAnn joined them for the *private* conversation.

"I thought you didn't care about this," Mei challenged her.

"Well, you've got me curious. I want to hear it too," she said. Maybe she wasn't okay with the situation as much as she'd like them all to believe.

Cade set his half-eaten sandwich on a napkin. "I can't even leave the building unless I'm running an errand, and I only have the exact minutes that task would take before I'm expected back. He moved me into the motel after Liv and Wren came, so he could keep a closer eye on me. I can't leave unless he approves it."

"They'll probably split us up and send us around the country soon, like you said, Cade. We won't be here for long." Wren wanted him to think about that. "Liv too, you know."

Cade's eyes widened. He had to know it was true. He and Liv locked gazes again, Liv's defiant.

"At least you get out, man," Damiano said. "There's got to be something there. You could stop a cop and give him the address."

Cade looked like a deer standing frozen in the headlights of an oncoming car going 75 miles an hour.

"Let's all think about it today and overnight, then bring our ideas together tomorrow," Cade said.

"Good idea," Mei said. "But what if they move us tonight?"

———·●·———

Jim's next stop was to pay a visit to Detective Windly since he was back home in Alabama.

A small brick building housed the Opelika police department. By this time, everyone in the place knew Jim and greeted him when he came in the door.

"Paul's in the back grabbing a coffee, I think." The older lady at the front desk said. "I'll go get him for you."

"Thanks, Mrs. Matthews." She'd always treated him with respect, even after he'd displayed less-than-respectful emotions in her presence in the past.

"Come on in, Jim." Officer Windly waved him over to his desk. Surrounded by stiff uniforms with buttons and pins, Paul—as Jim had been told to call the detective- -resembled a high school teacher more than a cop. His salt-and-pepper hair was always needing a cut, bangs hanging in his face. He wore a beard and mustache, and his bushy eyebrows were the only part of his hair that hadn't grayed.

Though old enough to be his father, Paul had treated Jim like a friend. A friend Jim hadn't always treated well in return, at least not when he let the frustration get to him.

Walking up to Paul's desk, Jim raised both hands. "Don't worry, I come in peace."

Paul laughed. "You know I understand. I get angry too."

"I know." Jim sat in the chair opposite him and pulled out a notebook. "I have some new information for you."

"I hope you have some clues to get us going again." Paul folded his arms in front of his open zipper jacket and leaned back, ready to take it all in.

"It seems this trafficking ring uses modeling auditions to lure girls—"

"Not just girls. Some are boys too," Paul reminded him. Jim shuddered.

"Right… to lure young people in. Then somewhere along the line the kids are drugged and taken to a motel."

The detective looked skeptical.

"Well, not always a motel, and not a place where a lot of nice families would go. But I've gotten a description of a motel in New Orleans where this happens. At least it's one of their locations. I'm sure they'd move it all out if they thought someone was onto them."

"Did you get the name of the motel?"

Jim shook his head. Sophie never saw the name. These guys were good.

"That's okay, Jim. This is good information."

"I was thinking maybe you could get some kind of special skills team together, like you mentioned. Something you could be involved in since you know so much about Stacy's case." Jim pulled his blazer together in front. Why would they blast the air conditioning when the weather had turned cooler in the last week?

"We're way ahead of you, Jim. There are what we call Safe Streets Task Forces. They're located all over the United States."

"And you're already working with one?"

"No," Paul said, and the air went out of Jim's lungs. "However, I've already been talking with the local FBI office about it, and they seem open to taking me on their regional task force."

"So, you'll go work for the FBI instead?" Jim asked.

"No, I'll still be working for this local law enforcement office. They'll keep paying me and everything, but I'll work out of the FBI office—at least while I'm working with them on this. They'll even swear me in." He stood up and put his right hand over his heart as if the swearing-in was happening right now. Then he sat back down.

Jim chuckled. "That sounds cool. Who knows, you may not want to come back." Jim smiled, wondering what it might be like to do what Paul Windly did.

"I'm not sure about that." He looked doubtful. "Do you have any more information I could use?"

"The company that advertised for models was called…" He scrolled through the Notes app on his phone. *Lumina Talent Group,* though I suspect they change their name from time to time. Also, Sophie said you could contact her. Here." He pushed the paper with her contact information across Paul's desk. "She's expecting your call."

Paul typed her information into his computer, and Jim shifted nervously in his seat.

"Anything else?" he asked.

He hesitated. "Could they put me on the task force as well? I mean, I've been researching this since Stacy. I could be useful."

"You could also cause people to get injured, or worse."

"I'm trained with a gun, and I have a license." He grabbed his wallet and pulled out his gun license.

Paul lifted his open hand. "Even worse." He shook his head emphatically. Jim pushed his wallet back into his pocket. Paul continued. "You keep doing what you're good at, Jim, writing and speaking. And if you discover any clues, keep passing them on to me."

Jim's speaking engagements were dwindling now that college freshmen were no longer brand new, and the university staff had more things to do than orient the newbies. Besides, the traffickers often targeted younger kids.

"You could speak in some churches and youth groups, you know," Paul spoke as if he'd heard Jim's thoughts.

"You think so?"

The detective nodded.

He'd need to adjust the pitch to administrators, as well as his speeches to fit the audience. It was doable.

Jim would make some calls and try to schedule events for younger students. Maybe even in cities where these motels were located, starting with New Orleans. At least it would put him in the vicinity.

But first, tonight, he had an article to write. Jim planned to lay it out in black and white. He'd call for anyone who'd seen questionable activity around a motel, or seen young people dressed questionably going in and out of motel rooms. Or, for anyone who might know anything about a trafficking ring involving girls, boys, and modeling, to message Jim directly.

He opted not to tell Paul this part of the plan.

Jim would submit it to any publication that had ever accepted his writing. He couldn't just sit back waiting to hear what others were doing about this. He had to act.

CHAPTER FIFTEEN

Romeo gave Wren the opening she hoped for and escorted her from the costume room down the sidewalk in front of the guest rooms. The sun was setting, and a few early stars appeared. How she wished to sit outside and enjoy the fresh air and sunset. Too soon, they arrived at Room 17.

Dressed in her Pocahontas costume, nervous energy charged through her veins.

They were ready. They'd planned for it. A simple plan, but those were the best, right?

It had to work. It just had to.

Romeo took them all out for jobs at once this time—a perfect opportunity. Hopefully, Cade knew it was going down now so he could provide the distraction. He was to set a fire to a bush, near enough to the building to warrant a call to the fire department. No matter what happened tonight, she would make a run for it, even if she got shot.

Her muscle response began to dull from the drug, and she prayed she could go through with the plan.

As Romeo closed the door behind her, she slipped the piece of duct tape Cade had provided, over the latch. She wasn't sure it went on straight when Romeo closed the door, but it would have to do.

She'd have to play along with the client until he had his clothes off.

Timing had to be perfect.

"How!" The stupid man raised one hand, palm faced out, like in an old western. Did any Native Americans ever say "how"?

"Me Thomas, You Pocahontas."

She turned her head so she could roll her eye without being seen.

"Let's get you out of that uncomfortable leather," he so generously offered. Gag.

"Or I could dance for you," Wren tried to sound flirty. "While you take off… um, get ready." Blood rushed to her cheeks.

"Great idea."

She unbuttoned his shirt and swayed back and forth in what she hoped was a sexy way. Too bad she didn't know any dance moves.

A siren blared, then grew consistently louder. That had to be it.

The man looked toward the window. Wren did too. She made her way to the curtains and glanced between a crack. No Romeo. Normally, he'd be pacing up and down the row of rooms, on guard, smoking, like a motel customer who couldn't sleep.

She spotted him running toward the offices.

Glancing back at her client, she read confusion in his face. Naked on the bed, up on his knees, he moved to the side of the bed to grab his clothes, but she pushed open the door and ran out before he could get to them. The last trail of sunlight streaked the sky with rose and purple.

Damiano and Amy were already in the parking lot, but she didn't see the others. She couldn't wait. They'd determined that the ones who got free would keep running and go for help.

The three of them ran toward the highway as fast as they could. Only a few streetlights lit the parking lot, but they could see the road. They were going to make it… she knew it. This was their chance, their only chance. Daddy, or those he worked for, would make sure of it.

Wren rounded the outside corner of the building by the highway. Damiano had gone just ahead, and Amy ran behind.

She saw the guard a split second before he shoved a cloth into her mouth and tied her hands behind her. No time to scream, no time to warn Amy. Damiano already sat on the sidewalk, gagged, hands tied behind his back.

They didn't make it. Now they'd never get out. A streetlight burned out at that moment, and the road became even darker.

After the guards brought them to the back office, Daddy and Romeo took everyone up to their room, forced them to change into their robes—nothing else—and cuffed their hands.

In the motel, pipes—water, maybe gas—ran, exposed, along the walls. Daddy cuffed Amy to one pipe and Damiano to another beside her in the living room. Then he cuffed Wren to the lower part of the radiator near the window, and Mei on the other side. None of them were in a convenient location to get to a bed or couch. They sat on the floor.

At least, they each only had one hand cuffed, she thought. She'd be able to eat, scratch an itch, or whatever, with her free hand.

"Where's DeeA—?" Before Mei got the entire name out, the girl waltzed in, hanging on to Romeo's arm. He kissed her tenderly, then closed the door behind her.

"What the— DeeAnn!?" Damiano yelled.

"What?" She shrugged, making an innocent face. "Hey, I'm a survivor. I did what I had to."

"You want to stay here?" Wren's good eye must've widened like a saucer. How could anyone want to stay in their current situation?

"Romeo and I are in love," DeeAnn said, flipping her reddish hair out of her eyes. "I've always known I'd be with him forever."

"You know you're crazy, right?" Mei asked the rhetorical question, eyes wide. "You get that he doesn't love you, don't you?"

"He didn't cuff me to the wall, did he?" Smugness captured her face.

"Oh yeah, that's true love." Damiano's sarcasm dripped from his words as he rolled his eyes.

"Y'all wouldn't understand love if it bit you in—"

"Or raped us." Mei's poignant sarcasm hung in the air.

"Be nice to me. I don't have to feed you, you know." DeeAnn lifted her nose. "And I don't have to use the beeper to let Romeo know if you need to use the restroom." Then she headed to the bedroom.

"Where's Liv?" Wren asked the others.

"I didn't see her outside," Amy said. "I didn't see her in the changing room either."

DeeAnn poked her head out of the bedroom. "Oh, and by the way, Wren, because of your little stunt, Daddy is sending Liv away." Her cruel laugh faded as she went back into the bedroom.

Wren's stomach clenched adding strength to the knot already in her stomach. What had she done?

She cried, prayed, begged and prayed and cried some more.

You sentenced your best friend to a fate worse than yours—a fate she'll now have to live out alone.

DeeAnn was right. They'd never get out. She should have left well enough alone.

That wasn't "well enough," Princess.

Princess—the name her real Daddy used for her. Maybe he would've been proud of her for trying. But her trying had been foolish.

The tears subsided, then started again. She leaned against the radiator, prayed and begged God for what exactly, she couldn't say. Some of her crying prayers escaped her lips. She didn't care if the others heard.

—•●•—

The room was foggy, like the window, or like a dozen chain smokers had been there recently. It was dark, probably nighttime. Wren stepped slowly through the smoke. Looking down, she stopped and noticed her legs. The bottom of a white robe hung over her shins and above white slippers. Awareness dawned… she had nothing on under the robe.

She swallowed the knot forming in her throat. She was a captive.

The darkness and fog drew her attention again. There had to be a streetlight outside the painted window because she had just enough light coming in to warm the foggy darkness so she could walk forward one step and then another.

Where?

She stopped in front of the window. The light hadn't come from outside. It was coming from under the sink in the kitchenette. Her gaze fixed on the light spilling through the cracks around the sides and underneath the cabinet doors.

She moved again, step by step, making her way to the cabinet. What could the source of light be? Maybe someone put a night-light in there.

No. It would have to be plugged in, and who would put outlets underneath a sink?

She moved forward, somehow unafraid. She felt warm and safe.

In the kitchen, she knelt and opened the cabinet doors. Brilliant light streamed out. Wren's hand flew up to shade her good eye until she realized it didn't hurt her eye at all. She looked directly at it without the least bit of pain in spite of its brightness.

At the center of the brilliance, she made out the shape of a star. A familiar star, the one that had appeared to her the other night. It had looked familiar that night as well.

Peace spread out inside her body and she relaxed.

Make a plan to escape, Wren.

Those words played in her head over and over. But how? They'd already tried and failed. They were being watched now more closely than ever. What could they do?

Wren sat on the floor in front of the open cabinet with crossed legs. "God, please show me the way," she whispered into the night.

Was this starlight God? Or maybe it was his messenger, like Sorchae, the light fairy.

"What should we do, Sorchae?" She whispered to the light, hoping she didn't offend the light—or God—by using the wrong name.

Was this really happening? Talking to light underneath a sink…? Maybe she'd lost her mind. Man, she hoped it was real and Sorchae had an escape plan for them.

No instructions came.

She sat there thinking for a long time, until the light had gone.

———— • ● • ————

"Wren, you awake?" Mei's voice crept into Wren's hazy, swirling dreams.

Wren glanced around, her sight landing on Mei, propped up on the other side of the radiator. Their eyes met.

"We're never getting out of here, are we?" Mei's face revealed her sorrow, a rare show of emotion.

Wren shrugged. "I felt pretty hopeless last night." She paused… the light, the voice came back to her. Had it only been a dream? "I'm still afraid this morning, but I think we have to try again."

"Really?" Mei's voice sounded a tiny notch happier.

"We have to try," Amy said. Wren hadn't realized she was awake. "I'll die here." Her eyes were puffy and rimmed with red.

The truth of Amy's statement reverberated in Wren.

Amy pushed Damiano, then put her finger to her lips for him to be quiet as soon as he opened his eyes.

What's up? He mouthed.

"We need to try again," Amy whispered. He nodded, but Wren couldn't be certain he'd understood her in his half-asleep state.

"We'll have to make them think we're weak and afraid for as long as it takes for them to trust us." Wren felt this as sure as her own heartbeat. Maybe Sorchae was directing her. She had to believe that and trust that the light would guide her through her own heart.

Another fact resolved within her: she'd have to perform for them—do her job—at least until they could get away.

She gulped down a sob. *Jesus, have mercy on me.*

CHAPTER SIXTEEN

The horror of Wren's life had begun to feel like routine. *Please God, don't let me settle in and accept it,* she'd often pray.

Sometimes they'd be taken out in the dark of night all at once, chained to each other, one wrist cuffed to one person in front, the other cuffed to the next person behind. It reminded Wren of the children's poem about elephants…

Elephants walking along the trails
Are holding hands by holding tails.

Why it came into her mind, she didn't know, but it did—like they were elephants, walking, hand connected to hand, being herded toward the circus to play their roles.

In fact, it wasn't dissimilar.

The nights in Room 17 were gut-wrenching. It took everything Wren had not to throw up on the clients. She learned to swallow it down. Some were kind, others cruel.

Back in the room, she didn't feel like talking to anyone or even looking at them. She didn't feel like eating. Often, she had the urge to rip her own skin off.

It had become difficult to think of words to pray. And the phrases she'd memorized, which had come to her mind in the beginning, had disappeared like sunlight after dusk.

Daddy posted guards at every exit from the property. Romeo gushed over DeeAnn, who must've informed him of their plan to escape. The kidnappers' victory fed their pride.

"You'll never escape," Daddy said during one of his visits to their room. "Just ask Amy. She knows." He winked at her as if they shared a secret. Her head bent toward the floor.

"Where's Liv?" Wren mustered the courage to ask even as she sat cuffed to the radiator, her permanent home when she wasn't being led to a client.

"Now, don't you worry about your pretty little friend. She's being well cared for." He ran his long tongue over his upper lip. "She's living the life of luxury." Daddy cursed under his breath. "Too bad we sent those pictures. We could've used that little filly around here," he muttered.

A shiver ran down her back. What had they done with Liv?

At least his words indicated she was alive. One comfort Wren would cling to.

Daddy's shirt hung open, his hairy chest exposed in the middle. They'd all learned to kiss him on the mouth nearly every day. The gag reflex was easing. Was she getting used to this life? *Oh God.*

Help… was her only prayer.

She looked at Amy up against the other wall

No wonder Amy used to refuse to speak. Speech was one thing a person in their situation could control—a subtle form of rebellion. Wren's respect for Amy had grown over the past few weeks.

"Here, DeeAnn." Daddy handed her a sack. "There's peroxide and cotton balls. Tend to them." His hand swept around the room, indicating all of them. "Or just give them each a saturated cotton ball and they can take care of…" his voice trailed off.

"Of their wounds?" DeeAnn finished for him. Every night at least one or two of them came back with scratches, bruises or wounds of some kind.

"Those are badges of honor," Daddy spoke with what sounded like pride. "They're doing their jobs well."

"Of course," DeeAnn changed her demeanor. Probably hoping to please him.

Lucky for them it was in Daddy's interest to tend to their lesions, or their wounds might get infected and he risked losing money.

He turned and glared at them, one at a time. "Now you know Daddy loves you. No one takes care of you like good old Daddy." He winked at Wren, then turned toward Mei and winked, and went around the circle of the room. "Of course, you, DeeAnn..." He palmed her cheek. "The best of the bunch."

"At least my eyes aren't screwy." DeeAnn laughed and pointed at Wren.

Daddy laughed with her. "But hey, don't you worry, little wren, I'll look after you even if your eyes are screwy. I take care of all my little birds."

His expression changed in a split second from gooey sweet to hard and cold. "Unless they try to fly away." He pushed back his shirttail to show his gun tucked into the front of his pants. "If you do that ever again, I'll shoot each one of you in the face. Then I'll go down the hall and pick one of the little ones to shoot." His cold eyes held Wren's gaze alone. "Then I'll look up your families," he sneered. "And I promise you, every one of them will be sorry you were ever born."

His face turned sweet again. "But we don't need to talk like that, do we now?" He waited for a response. "I said, do we?"

"No, sir, Daddy," they said in unison, even DeeAnn. They had no hope of escaping, did they?

After he left, DeeAnn passed out the peroxide-saturated cotton balls, like Daddy told her to. Well, more like tossed them in their general direction.

Did Wren catch a look of loneliness on DeeAnn's face? Maybe a question about whether what she'd done was right?

Maybe delusion had settled into Wren's mind. She tried asking DeeAnn for a favor. "Would you please bring me the paper and pencils from the bedroom? I could use a distraction. Please, DeeAnn." She tried to put as much kindness and respect into her voice as she could muster.

The girl stood over her, staring at her, considering. "Well, I could, but this is a favor, and I expect something in return."

Oh God, what could that be? "What?"

"I don't know. I think I'll save it." DeeAnn's look of superiority ruffled Wren's composure, but she had to keep the respectful demeanor if she wanted a favor.

"Okay, DeeAnn, but I won't say yes to everything."

"We'll see."

Wren doodled, trying to remember beautiful things and draw them: flowers, bushes, sky and clouds on a sunny day. Her drawing came out with dark clouds and shadowed trees blowing and breaking in violent winds. If only she could see outside during the day. If only she had colored pencils. She always loved charcoal, but now she longed for color.

She shaded black sky around bushes and clouds. *The shadow side defines the subject of the drawing where dark meets the light.* Wren could hear her high school art teacher's voice in her head.

Her thoughts took a sudden turn. She stopped drawing. A scene came to life in her mind of a little brown boy and a larger man standing over him. She felt the boy's fear in her body as he cowered. The boy wanted to hide, but the man stood right in front of him. The man held a rolling pin in his hand, threatening the boy.

Damiano.

She hoped it wasn't him.

Gripping her pencil again, she drew out the scene in loose lines and some deeper shadows for definition.

"I could use another person's story," Amy's voice broke through Wren's concentration as the girl dabbed the cotton ball on the red ring around her wrist. Then touched it to her bruised cheekbone.

"Damiano, why don't you tell us yours?" Mei asked. "How did you end up here?"

He shook his head in a firm no.

"Please," Amy tried.

Show him the picture.

"Maybe it would be good to get it out," Wren began.

"You don't know what you're talking about." The cowering boy looked out at Wren through Damiano's eyes. Why hadn't she seen it before?

"You might be right." Should she show him?

Show him.

"This image came to my mind, and I drew it a few minutes ago." Wren held up the paper so he could see it from his spot cuffed to the pipe across the room. "Then Amy asked someone to tell their story. Is this boy you?"

A night light in the bathroom shone out, but was it enough for him to see anything?

"Is that a...?" He squinted. "Does that man have a rolling pin?"

"Yeah. Do you know what it's about?"

He nodded yes, but his face said the risk of sharing might be too great.

"Don't worry," Wren hoped to encourage him. "We're all in this."

"Okay, I will if you both will." He eyed Mei and Wren.

"We probably won't sleep again tonight anyway. What could it hurt?" Mei answered and Wren nodded.

"I have to go way back to explain." His face twisted, and he went someplace else. "All the way back to that picture." He paused. "When I was six, my uncle raped me."

Wren sucked in air. She hadn't expected that.

"Keep going," Amy urged with a gentle voice.

"He used a rolling pin on my backside if I didn't comply." He turned his face away. "I never thought I was gay, but I guess I got a taste, you know? Like a drug you can't quit even though you hate it."

They nodded. Wren didn't know about any of it, but she had a good imagination… unfortunately.

"At sixteen, I touched a boy at a sleepover. I got arrested and sent to juvenile detention."

"Just for touching?" Mei asked.

"Touching his… you know." His head tipped down, maybe staring toward the floor.

They nodded. Wren tried to pull her cuffed arm toward her to get some relief from the stretching, but it hurt the sores on her wrists.

"The counselors at the detention center told me I was gay. They said that's okay, but I can't do anything like that to a minor. They encouraged me to wait until I was eighteen, then find a boyfriend, eighteen or older. Then we could do whatever." He paused.

"While I was incarcerated, my family disowned me. They never wrote or came to visit, not once." He coughed. Could he have been covering for his wobbly voice? The pain he must've gone through nearly choked Wren. Her heart ached for him.

"After juvie, I was barely seventeen. That was like eight months ago. I had no place to go, no job. My family didn't want me. No one except my uncle, the one who…" he let that thought trail off.

"My uncle said he'd give me a place to stay if I did some odd jobs for him to earn my keep. I had nowhere else to go. Those odd jobs turned out to be sex for money." He turned his head away as if he'd heard something out in the hall, though he couldn't have seen much in the dark apartment.

So, this wasn't the first time Damiano had been in this horrid situation.

"My uncle threatened me. He said if I ever ran away or told someone, he'd grab my sister, rape her and sell her, then he'd kill me. I believed him."

"So, how'd you get here?" Mei asked.

"One man who paid for me—I'd seen him a few times by then. He said he liked me, said I could be a model. He said he'd take me to a modeling audition, and I could get away from my uncle."

Wren knew the rest of this story.

"I guess he got paid well to bring me in. I had hopes of becoming a model, and then an actor. School musicals were my thing in high school, before I got arrested. I thought this would be my chance to get away. Then I'd call my family and warn them about my uncle's threats." He looked away again. "I don't even know if my sister is alive."

Silence filled the room. The tragedy of his story sank in.

"But hey, y'all, let's pep it up a bit." Damiano's voice quickly shifted to his confident, joking side. "Do you want to hear the song I sang in the musical *Beauty and the Beast*?"

Wren loved that Disney movie.

"Yes!" Everyone responded.

"I was the one who had it all… I was the master of my fate…" His voice was fabulous. But the irony of those words hit Wren. "I played the beast," he said.

"That's really cool, Damiano," Mei said. And Amy agreed, wide-eyed, mouth open.

"You're so talented." Wren hoped he knew how serious she was. "I think you will be on the stage one day." She wanted to give him hope… wanted hope for herself. But they were never going to get out of there.

"Yeah, right," he joked. "Whatever." He turned to Mei. "You asked me, so now it's your turn."

She turned her head toward the wall.

"Mei?" Wren asked.

"Okay, then you go, Wren," Damiano said.

"I don't have much to say," Wren said. She'd had a nice life compared to Amy and Damiano. *Thank you, Father—*the first prayer she'd been able to form in days.

"So, Liv told you about my eye. My birth mother's boyfriend beat me up when I was three. The doctors removed my right eye, and my mom lost custody of me. I never saw her again. She didn't even visit me in the hospital. But my adoptive parents picked me up from there. I miss them so much." She sucked in a cry. "Anyway," she swallowed hard. "Liv and I have been best friends for several years. When she said she wanted to do the modeling audition I felt protective and didn't want her to come alone with Cade. How I thought I could protect her, I don't know." Staring at the floor didn't give her any answers. "Why didn't I just fight her on it? Tell her no and tell her mother the plan? That would have been a better friend."

"You didn't know," Amy said.

"Then why did I think I needed to go along? I had a creepy feeling all along."

The room was quiet.

"Okay, I'll go." Mei turned back to her.

Surprised, Wren nodded.

Mei's eyes filled with tears before she even started, the first sign of emotion Wren had seen in her.

But Mei shook her head. "Never mind. I'm not going there." A tear rolled down her face, and she slapped it away.

"Let's all just try to get some sleep. We'll need it," Damiano said.

Talking with the others lifted her spirits a little, but Wren's body ached. She'd never felt this tired and she dreaded another night of fitful sleep in her seated position up against the cold radiator.

Make a plan. Where had that thought come from?

No way. The risk was too great. They'd never make it out alive.

Make a plan.

"Can we try to talk together the first chance we get without DeeAnn in the room?" she whispered to the others before they fell asleep.

She heard sounds of agreement from each of them.

Hauling his overnight bag up the outdoor stairs to his apartment, it felt like an industrial-sized box of copy paper. Jim cursed his own weakness. It had been a long airport day. His flight had been delayed three times, then canceled. They offered him a complimentary hotel stay—the last thing he wanted.

Hotels night after night… He just wanted to be home.

After one more hotel stay, a short flight, and not too long of a drive, he made it to his apartment in Auburn. Fumbling with the key in the lock, Jim dropped his keyring. Setting his duffel down, he finally got the door open, picked up his bag and…

What the heck?

His place was in shambles. Things from every drawer and shelf had been tossed onto the floor, couch cushions sliced open, dishes broken and lying on the kitchen floor.

A knife stood erect in the loaf of sourdough that he'd put in the freezer before he left. Someone had stayed in his place long enough for it to thaw so they could stab the knife into it. A piece of paper stuck to the loaf of bread, held by the knife.

Jim looked around, checking his perimeter. Could they still be here? Like a statue, he stood, listening.

Nothing.

Stepping one toe at a time toward the counter with the bread, he pulled the knife out and took the paper off. It was a message.

Mr. Fielding, your articles and speeches are becoming an irritation.

You don't want to get on our bad side, do you?

We know where your parents live too.

P.S. Your sister was so ugly, her death was no loss to us.

Jim folded the paper and set it on the coffee table next to a chipped clay vase. He picked up the vase, stared at it for a moment, then heaved it across the room into the wall. "Aaaahhhhh!"

With a broom he swept the slashed couch of any items that had fallen there and collapsed onto it, loose stuffing and all. Fatigue and anger gave way to tears. He hadn't cried in years, not even at Stacy's funeral. How had he become so hard?

He hadn't even stayed with his parents for a whole week after they had discovered Stacy's body, planned the funeral, and hosted the reception afterward.

He'd set a course full throttle ahead to stop trafficking in the United States. He'd shifted the focus of his writing, worked himself to the bone, never came home… and for what?

A busted-up apartment and a threat to his parents' lives.

CHAPTER SEVENTEEN

Waking up where he'd fallen, Jim opened his eyes and glanced around his living room. *Dear God,* it hadn't been a nightmare. He turned over and his arm got stuck inside the couch cushion that had been knifed open. He'd managed to call the police and ask for surveillance for himself and his parents before crashing hard. He'd called the Opelika Police Department because they knew him and his situation. Also, they were closest to Mom and Dad.

You're such an idiot! He couldn't help berating himself again this morning.

Jim's stubbornness could cost him everything… absolutely everything. His mom and dad hadn't signed up for this. They hadn't signed up to lose their daughter, and now possibly their son. And they hadn't signed up to be on their daughter's killer's hit list.

What was he going to do?

A picture of his mother, the last time he visited, filled his vision. He saw her sweet hazel eyes now as clearly as if she sat right next to him on the couch. The look of longing, wishing, begging him to be with her a little longer. She had wanted him to stay. He'd known it even then.

She and Dad had lost as much or more than he had, but they didn't run all over the country busying themselves with activity to fool themselves into believing they were making a difference.

No, only Jim was immature enough to do that.

He punched the couch with his fist. One would expect a follower of Jesus to be a better man than that.

Stacy had gone missing and then been found dead while he lived in Washington, DC. His career had been his priority. After college, he moved to where the action was. He'd done well as a news journalist and investigative reporter. In just over two years, he'd become a regular contributor to *The Washington Post, The Washington City Paper*, and an occasional contributor to *The Atlantic*, accomplishments he used to brag about.

His dreams were being realized… until that fateful phone call. He'd been pulling together some notes for a story on a local art crawl for the *City Paper* when he picked up the phone.

His head and his world began a tailspin that hadn't stopped since.

Darkness closed in at the edges of his vision.

You've made everything worse through your prideful actions.

He buried his head, face down in his arms on the shredded couch. He just wanted to sleep for a year and not have to think about all this. The light in the room seemed to dim, darkness crept in around him.

You're no ambassador of God, saving the world from evil people. All you do is spin your wheels and put people in danger.

He couldn't disagree. What argument did he have? And he was no closer to finding Stacy's killers than he was when he started. Neither were the police. Evil people like that usually got away with their actions and continued to harm more people.

His last article had informed the traffickers that the police were gaining ground in finding them. Now they knew Jim's identity and why he was after them. And they knew how much he knew. Well, almost. He had mentioned the modeling auditions, but not what he knew about the motels.

He turned over onto his back, closed his eyes, then opened them again. The room seemed extra dark.

Why?

Sinking down into the darkness he thought, *the world is dark, why shouldn't his apartment be?* He couldn't even make out the ceiling, as if he stared into an abyss.

Then, he noticed a tiny light burning through the abysmal fog. It grew and traveled closer to him.

He kept staring at it, afraid to move or even blink for fear it would disappear. What was it?

A pleasant distraction from his depressing thoughts, that's what.

He watched the light grow in front of him, stopping three or four feet from his face. Peace washed over him. His muscles relaxed.

Light in the darkness? Like Jesus—the light of the world?

"I'm sorry I did all this without asking you," he spoke to it. Maybe he was just dreaming, but he'd go with it. "I'm sorry for my pride in thinking I could do anything without you."

His thoughts shifted to the present circumstances.

He'd been given the opportunity. *The Atlantic, The Post,* and several smaller publications allowed him to submit articles about trafficking and paid him to do it.

That he could pay his bills while getting to research and write what he wanted was a miracle. Right?

On the other hand, what if he'd turned his back on God, missed what he was supposed to do completely and put his parents at risk?

Why don't you ask me?

The thought echoed inside him. Why did it sound so outrageous? To ask the one who knows everything… the one called the Light of the World.

Had he gone off on his own, forgetting to consult the one he claimed to follow?

He knew he had. In fact, he hadn't really had a conversation with the Lord in…? how long? Tired every night when he got back to the hotel or home, he didn't make time to pray. Sometimes he stayed up late into the night researching, writing, or editing, but never praying.

"Okay Jesus," he voiced his prayer into the empty, ransacked apartment, hoping it reached the light. "Did I go off on my own? Or did you give me this opportunity to write, research and track down the perpetrators?"

Yes.

Yes? Both?

Yes.

This had to be the Lord speaking to him. He remembered, as a boy, thinking, why doesn't God answer with more complete explanations?

"Sorry I've been doing all this on my own. I need you. I know that now."

He didn't hear an answer, but Jim felt a presence fill his spirit. His heart rate slowed.

He took a deep breath and let it out slowly.

Do you want me to continue what I've been doing?

Abide in me.

It didn't settle the question he'd asked, but Jim had heard that someplace recently. Oh yes, he'd listened to his home church's Sunday morning service online last week. He'd rarely gone to church or even watched it since Stacy's funeral. He'd been way too busy and figured God understood.

Yes, but what you don't understand is how much you need me.

Right, God understanding wasn't the problem.

How stupid could Jim be? To believe that he could make a difference on his own.

"Stupid"… not my word.

"Sorry, Lord." It wasn't God's character to belittle anyone. God was love, a love that demanded justice but never vindication, never humiliation.

The ball of starlight continued floating in front of him, pulsating as if alive. *My power is made perfect in weakness.*

That had never been one of Jim's favorite verses. But he was weak; he had to admit that. Also, he didn't think like a perpetrator, so how would he ever find these guys?

A new feeling of support and comfort surrounded Jim, like a thick flannel blanket on a Washington winter night.

Your determination and sense of justice are gifts from me, Jim.

The idea thrilled him. That God even thought about him at all was enough to fill him with joy.

Gentleness, however, is a fruit, not a gift. It must be learned and practiced.

Abide in me.

What did it mean to abide in God?

Jim glanced around the messy room. He noticed a Bible underneath the dining room table. He picked it up wondering where it had been that it landed under there. He sat back on the couch.

The starlight had gone, but the apartment seemed brighter.

Flipping through the pages, not sure where to read, he let it land open and started reading in John 15:5.

"I am the vine, you are the branches; he who abides in Me and I in him, he bears much fruit, for apart from Me you can do nothing."

And verse nine, "Just as the Father has loved me, I have also loved you; abide in My love."

God didn't think he was stupid. He loved him. Jim probably needed to soak in that for a while before he'd really get it. If ever.

Yes. Abide.

So abiding was soaking in God's love… all the time. Wow.

He went back to verse five. Without God, Jim would accomplish nothing. But with God… abiding in his love… Jim could bear much fruit.

What would it look like to abide in his love, let God be in control, but still do the work he had been doing for the past year?

How could he keep doing what he'd been doing without being consumed by it?

Set aside time.

That's it! He could set aside time each day—block out half an hour or so on his schedule—and take that time to pray, read the Bible, or just sit and contemplate God's love for him and for the victims, even for the perpetrators.

It couldn't hurt.

And sleep.

Okay, yes. He needed to schedule his sleep. He needed to shut down the driving sirens in his head that demanded he look up one more site, call one more resource, search one more website before going to bed.

He'd have to give all the worry to God so he could sleep.

Yes.

God was kind of practical, wasn't he? Jim smiled. It felt like he shared a secret with him now.

Jim called his mom and dad. They put it on speaker, and he told them about his little talk with God. He left out the part about his apartment being tossed.

They sounded relieved. And he promised to come over for dinner the next night.

After hanging up, he had to call Detective Windly and have him come look at the apartment and the note they left. Then he'd call a cleaning company.

— • ◆ • —

Awake, leaning against the metal radiator as light reached their clouded window, Wren shaded darkness on a page with pencils. It covered the outside of the page, all around the shape of a white star in the center. She used the eraser to make the points trail white away from the center, forming streaks out into the surrounding darkness.

Reminding herself of Sorchae gave her some comfort.

Make a plan.

The words urged Wren's spirit. But terror lurked nearby at the thought. She gazed at the drawing of Sorchae she had just completed.

She set the page down beside her, then thought better and scooted it, with the stack of copy paper and the pencils, underneath the radiator.

The door opened. Cade and Romeo came in with two paper bags. She hadn't seen Cade since the night they tried to escape—the last time she'd seen Liv. Wren guessed it had been several weeks, though days and weeks seemed to run together. She got a clue when she'd seen a tree with almost no leaves around the corner from Room 17 the last time they took her out. Relief washed over her at the sight of Cade. He was alive. She prayed Liv was too.

Romeo gave him a little shove from behind, and he carried in the bags, leaving them on the table. He wasn't free. He was a captive fully now as much as they were.

Cade caught her eye, and she read the sorrow there. Did he know where they had sent Liv? She needed to talk to him.

"Y'all can—" Cade started to say something.

"Uh-uh," Romeo warned and clucked his tongue. "No talking with the help. Remember what Daddy said?" Romeo

188

grinned. He obviously enjoyed rubbing Cade's nose in it. Then Romeo turned to DeeAnn, held out his arm for her, and she nestled into him. "There's my good little bottom girl." He pecked her cheek, and she smiled up at him.

After they left, DeeAnn passed out breakfast sandwiches to everyone. She had a lot more work to do in the apartment since the rest of them were cuffed. And they had to be fed, at least occasionally, or they wouldn't have enough energy to make it down the steps to the motel rooms.

As luck would have it—or a gift from God—Romeo came and took DeeAnn out for a while. Maybe they wanted her to keep feeling special and keep them in the loop. Whatever the reason, this was their chance to talk without her around.

Make a plan. Wren felt the words with such urgency that they drowned out doubt and fear—at least a little.

Wren waited until after Daddy came to escort them one by one to the bathroom—their morning opportunity. When he left, she took a deep breath.

"Y'all, we have to make another plan." She whispered loud enough for them to hear, but not loud enough for anyone who might be outside their door.

"They'll kill us," Amy said.

"It's possible, so we have to be smart about it this time."

"Right," Damiano agreed. "And if even one person gets out, they should run. No looking back. They should keep running until they find a grocery store or some public place to talk to someone—"

"A place they can ask for directions to the nearest police officer or station," Amy added.

"Police?" Damiano questioned.

Wren nodded. "It's smart. They can bring help for everyone else."

"We need to watch for unexpected opportunities." Mei leaned forward. She was in, and she sounded like she knew what she was talking about. "Things like, if Romeo left his phone in here. Or keeping our eyes peeled for anything out of the ordinary.”

“Like what?” Amy asked.

“Like a police car driving in the parking lot when we happen to be walking out there with Romeo or the guards.” Mei folded her sandwich wrapper.

“You can’t trust cops.” Damiano must have experienced more than he shared last night.

They all stared at him.

“My uncle had plenty of friends on the force. I saw things firsthand…” His voice trailed away.

Wren still didn’t understand. And she didn’t really want to, not right now. She needed to believe the police would help them. “We can’t worry about the bad ones right now, Damiano. We just have to trust the ones we find and pray to God, they help us.”

He nodded a reluctant agreement. What choice did they have?

“We need to be creative,” Mei reiterated. “And we won’t know what will work until the opportunity comes.”

“I have some paper if we get a chance to send a message.” Wren offered.

“That’s right.” Amy perked up. No one fought the idea of a second escape attempt, a miracle itself in Wren’s mind. Though she didn’t think DeeAnn would respond well if she knew.

“But how could we get a message out? And who would we get it to?” Damiano asked.

“Maybe if you prayed for us, Wren.” Amy’s voice was so quiet, Wren almost didn’t hear her. She looked up, caught Amy’s eye, and saw the desperation mingling with hope in her face.

Wren nodded. “Okay, but you know, God listens to everyone who talks to him, not just me.”

No one responded.

Wren swallowed and took a deep breath. "Dear God, please help us." Her standard prayer. How often had she begged for his help? Didn't she have anything better? "Give us ideas of how to get out of here safely, and how to free the other innocent people, or kids, who might be here." She hesitated, then continued despite the reaction she might get. "And set Cade free as well. Please don't let him get stuck in his uncle's world of evil."

When Wren glanced up, Mei looked away, but Amy had tears in her eyes.

"It was DeeAnn, not Cade, who told them our plan." Amy locked in on Mei, her voice low but firm.

"Yeah?" Mei challenged. "And how do you know?"

"The next day, DeeAnn was bragging to me about it in the hall when Daddy came to get us. She said Romeo would for sure love her more after what she'd done."

Mei just nodded like she'd heard it all before but seemed convinced.

"What's her story?" Wren wondered out loud. "Why does DeeAnn have a thing for Romeo?"

Amy looked at the door, and Wren listened for footsteps out in the hallway.

"They call her their 'bottom girl,'" Amy said.

"I heard Romeo say that." Wren figured prayer time was over. "What does it mean?"

Amy shrugged. "Like she's part of their kidnapping team, or something. All I know is what DecAnn told me once. She met Romeo at a diner. She'd run away from home, and he offered to help her. He was nice to her, put her up in a hotel room and gave her money for food and spending. They hung out a lot, and DeeAnn says they fell in love. But soon he brought her here." Amy shook her head. "I think it was his plan all along. DeeAnn still thinks Romeo is her boyfriend. He has her convinced that this is their business together and when they have enough money they'll get married, or just be together, or something." Amy shrugged.

"Is she crazy?" Damiano's finger made a circle in the air around his ear.

"She takes a lot of medicine," Amy filled in more details.

"You mean besides whatever they shoot into us before we have a client?" Mei asked.

Amy nodded and looked at the floor.

Wren hated to think about what they'd been giving them. They had less control over their mind and body for several hours after the injection, which could ruin their new plan if it was still in their blood. She never wanted more, so at least her body wasn't getting addicted yet.

They just needed to get out of there, and soon. It was the only answer.

Fear pushed its way into her thoughts. What if they ran? Would they be okay? Out on their own? Would they go through withdrawal?

They might pass out on the street, be discovered and pulled back to the motel by Daddy or one of his goons. They might be separated and shipped off to other pimps. Or they could just pass out, and not be found, and die—especially in their weakened state.

Wren shook her head to free it from the worst-case images. Then Liv came to mind. Where was she? Was she alive? Healthy? Afraid?

Wren pinched the bridge of her nose. She had to give Liv to God. What could she do to help her, anyway?

God, please help Liv, wherever she is. Please keep her safe and help her get free. Us too. Amen.

Wren had found the words to pray again… *Thank you, Lord.*

———•●•———

Wren opened her eyes. It had been another long day sitting in one place, except for bathroom breaks—just a few a day. DeeAnn had come back in the middle of the day yesterday, wearing a necklace, small but pretty. Something she could call her own.

No one brought lunch for them. They'd eaten more consistently when Liv was with them, and Cade had more freedom to buy and bring them things.

For dinner, they received some nuts and dried apricots—giant bags that looked like they came from Costco. At least they had something healthy, but they could only eat so many of those.

Wren dozed off sometime that night, despite the churning in her stomach.

During the night, her eyes opened. It probably wasn't late enough to be awake yet.

Turning her head toward the kitchenette sink and counter, she noticed a light coming from underneath the cabinet door again, like before, in her dream.

Wren pulled but couldn't break the hold the handcuff had on her. Her wrist was sore from constantly rubbing against the metal cuff, and she blew on it, trying to get some relief. But she kept watching the cabinet.

Could the light be Sorchae? How she needed a visit from him. She looked hard, as if she could see through the cabinet door.

Ridiculous.

Staring at the cabinet, the doors seemed suddenly wobbly, like jelly, then they kind of faded and Wren could see things under the sink. It was like having X-ray vision. She noticed the curved drainpipe winding its way up to the faucet underneath the sink.

Behind that, she saw something strange. She hadn't noticed it the other night when she'd been looking under there in her dream. A panel that had been nailed onto the back of the wall.

In that instant, the light was gone.

Wren got no more rest that night. As soon as sunlight peeked through the window, she pulled out a piece of paper and the pencils and drew what she'd seen.

What might be behind that panel? And why would Sorchae, or whatever the light was, point it out?

CHAPTER EIGHTEEN

"What were you drawing this morning?" Mei leaned across the front of their shared radiator to talk to Wren so no one else would hear her.

"Just, um…" Should she share it? Would Mei think she was delusional? "Something I dreamed—or something I saw." Would that satisfy her? The girl was smart. She watched everyone, and when she had an idea, it was usually well-thought-out.

"Did you have another vision?" she asked. Mei would know if Wren lied.

"Maybe you could call it that," Wren admitted.

Are you delusional? Who are you to think you have visions? Like some prophet or something. The thought stabbed.

"I don't know," She adjusted her answer.

"Did you come up with a plan?" Mei's eyes widened and she seemed hopeful.

"Not really." Wren passed her the drawing of the cabinet, which she drew without doors, and the things under the sink, including the panel on the back wall.

Mei took the paper. Her head jerked back, and her eyes shut tight for a moment.

"Are you okay?"

"It like flashed in my eyes."

Did real light shine in Mei's eyes from the drawing? "What did?" Wren asked.

"I don't know." Mei looked at the picture again. "The cabinet under the sink?" Mei looked confused. "Why would you draw that?"

"Look closely." Wren tried to point across the radiator, but Mei held the paper too far from her. "On the back wall, under the sink. Doesn't it look like there's a panel covering an opening behind it?"

Her eyes opened wider still. She saw it.

"There was a bright light under there," Wren tried to explain. "I think the light was trying to show me that panel."

You're delusional. You'll be so embarrassed when everyone sees you're a fraud. The thoughts accused, but she couldn't stop now. "I think there's an answer behind there. Like maybe a passage we could crawl through, or a space we could send a message through to the outside, or—"

"I get it," Mei said. "But we have to get free from these handcuffs." She lifted her arm attached to the radiator.

A bump sounded in the bedroom.

"Good morning, hoes." DeeAnn strutted out of the bedroom, where she'd slept alone all night long. "Y'all rise and shine. Oh, sorry," she laughed. "I guess you can't really rise, can you?" She acted as if she were their captor.

"Hey, Dee," Damiano leaned back, his free arm crossed behind his head against the wall, like he was *chillin'*. "I'll have an order of eggs, bacon and toast." He winked at her. "And you can feed it to me one bite at a time." He spread out each of the last few words, taunting her.

They all knew DeeAnn had had it with waiting on them.

"What are you, crazy?" DeeAnn's face squished up.

"You have to bring us breakfast, and anything else we need." Mei reinforced Damiano's words. Wren began to see their logic. Had he heard Wren and Mei's conversation? "You might be free," Mei continued. "But it means you have to serve us."

Wren wanted to laugh, but she dared not.

"Y'all make me crazy. I am so tired of this crap!" DeeAnn threw her arms up. "I just can't live like this."

Of all the things the girl couldn't take about this life of captivity, to DeeAnn, serving them seemed to be the worst part.

Just then, Daddy waltzed into the room with a large pot. A little steam escaped the top, and Wren's stomach gurgled again. Could it be actual food?

"What'd you bring us, Daddy?" DeeAnn kissed him on the mouth. Luckily, he didn't bother to bend down to the rest of them for a kiss.

"Oatmeal." He paused. "Cade said you might need something healthy to eat if you were going to perform well. That boy might be useful after all. He even did the cooking."

Wren couldn't believe it—healthy and everything. *Thanks, Cade,* she thought to herself.

"Take this and serve it up to the others." Daddy shoved it into DeeAnn's hands.

She walked it to the stove, but Wren noticed how she reacted to the word *serve.*

"I'm sick of serving these guys. I do everything around here." She gestured with her hands as if he were someone to be reasoned with. Wren felt a warning surge through her. "I mean, didn't I help you keep them here? Aren't I one of the team? Why do I have to do all the work?"

Wren watched as Daddy's face changed from cocky and smug to shock, then to rage. The hate in his expression could've killed.

In a split second he backhanded DeeAnn across the face, and she fell to the floor, sprawled out. She put a hand to her face, but Wren had seen blood on her lip.

Daddy bent down and grabbed her arm, jerking her to her feet. He stretched back to hit her again.

Wren couldn't take it. "Hey, you're so tough you can beat up a girl less than half your size."

Oxygen was sucked from the room.

"Maybe I'm picking on the wrong girl." His eyes now gleamed in her direction.

Taking two steps toward her, he stomped a boot into Wren's stomach. Her body lurched. Handcuffed, she couldn't get away, but she blocked her stomach with the other arm. What had she been thinking?

You were thinking of someone else. Someone in your flock.

Stupid thought. She chastised herself as he punched her jaw. Her face and mouth slammed into the radiator.

"Leave her alone," Mei said, not loud, but firm. Though she couldn't have done a thing about it.

He stood and walked out without another word.

Wren moved her jaw around. Not broken. *Thank God.*

"Why…" DeeAnn swallowed. "Why would you do that?" Her bugged-out eyes wide like a grasshopper's, but the rest of her face tensed with emotion. She looked sad, hurt, and confused.

Wren shrugged.

"She's a good person," Amy answered for Wren. "She actually cares about people, even you." Amy squinted at DeeAnn.

Then tears pooled in her eyes. "I—I'm sorry," DeeAnn said to Amy, who tipped her head in Wren's direction. DeeAnn turned to Wren. "I'm sorry, Wren. I'll get you some ice." She ran to the ice machine, wrapped a handful in a towel and brought it to Wren.

"Thank you." Wren noticed the blood on her own lip when DeeAnn handed her a piece of the ice.

Romeo walked right into the room with his keys flipping around his finger. Remembering what Mei had said about being ready for an opportunity, Wren watched. Maybe Romeo would leave his keys in the apartment by accident.

Instead, he went around unlocking their handcuffs. "Daddy says it's been long enough. If y'all behave yourselves, you won't have to be locked up like that again." He kissed DeeAnn on the top of her head. "And she won't have to work so hard from now on."

DeeAnn looked confused, like she wanted the attention she got from Romeo, but still maybe—hopefully—felt bad about how she treated Wren and the others.

Romeo left as soon as he'd come, taking his keys with him.

They served themselves bowls of oatmeal. No sugar, butter or milk, but it tasted amazing.

After eating, they took turns showering. Then DeeAnn suggested they take turns napping on the beds in the other room. Her room. Wren pondered her actions. This was getting close to compassion.

After three hours of good sleep on a full stomach, Wren woke up to the sound of birds.

She lay there listening, forgetting for a moment where she was. They reminded her of wrens, then of Nonna.

Wren had always seen herself as weak and afraid, small like a bird. Her parents thought of her that way too. The way they doted on her and protected her said a lot. But Nonna had never seen her as weak. Nonna saw the strength in those little birds.

Wren had wanted to believe Nonna, but she couldn't. Now however…

Wren had acted with courage on several occasions—a surprise to herself.

Once Nonna had asked her what she liked about *Mona and the Selkie*, which Wren had read many times.

"I like that Mona was brave and strong," Wren had told her. She remembered Mona's lack of fear. "And that Sorchae showed up to help Mona even when she got herself into trouble with bad choices."

"The God that made the birds is the same One who showed up to help Mona defeat her dragon." Wren could see Nonna sitting in her favorite rocker as she spoke. "Our Heavenly Father always watches over the birds of the air, and he watches over you too, Wren." Wren loved hearing Nonna's words, though she struggled to believe them fully. "Just like the birds of the air, you never have to be afraid."

Wren pictured Nonna even now, rocking and knitting, or standing in the kitchen waiting for something to come out of the oven. "You're stronger than anyone believes, my little Wren. The Bible says that when we're weak, God is strong in us. That makes us stronger than the strong people who don't need God." Nonna would smile at Wren and say, "One day, you'll show them all. Sorchae is out there, Wren, and when you need him, he'll find you."

Nonna had been right. In the worst time of Wren's life, Sorchae showed up. When hope nearly died, that light kept her hope alive. She didn't understand why he left her there, but he'd been with her.

Wait...

For a second, Wren had forgotten about the vision of the cabinet. Sorchae had come to bring God's comfort. She felt his presence—God's presence.

Like a wren, you are strong and adaptable. Like a wren, you care not only for yourself, but for the cabinet. And like a wren, you adapt to your surroundings, becoming strong in times of trouble. The words resounded in her spirit, bringing comfort, diminishing her fear, and giving her courage.

Cabinet. Interesting choice of words. Since Wren had made a study of wrens, she knew that a group of wrens could be called a herd, a chime, or a cabinet.

God allowed her to see her moments of strength in this situation all along. And she surprised herself.

This is who you've always been, Wren Marie. Who I made you to be.

She never believed it before. Yes, she'd had many fears over the years, but Sorchae had helped her see that her biggest worries had been for other people.

God saw her.

He knew her.

A thrill shot up through her body at that realization. Wren wasn't weak…

She was strong.

Wren determined that with God's strength, she would be strong for her cabinet of victims in that apartment.

And they were going to get out of here.

In the living room, DeeAnn watched TV, but Mei and Damiano looked at Wren's latest drawing at the kitchen table.

"You're talented," Damiano said and looked up at Wren. "There's a lot of detail here for just using pencils."

"Thanks." Her face warmed.

"It's like this part under the sink is glowing." Damiano pointed to the back wall.

"Huh?" Wren looked at the drawing but didn't see the glow, though she'd seen it in her vision.

"Did you look under the sink yet?" Mei asked.

"I haven't had the chance."

"It looks like there's something in there, right where I saw it glowing." Damiano pointed, but not to the thing she'd been drawing. He pointed to the shadow side of the drawing, to the dark shading she'd made on the opposite side of the panel and drainpipe.

"It looks like a tool," Mei saw it too.

Wren took the paper and stared at it. She hadn't seen that. She looked at them.

They raced to the sink.

"What are y'all doing?" DeeAnn asked, crossed the room to join them.

"What should we do about her?" Mei asked quietly.

Wren shrugged. DeeAnn had burned them before. She loved Romeo's attention too much.

"We can't trust her," Damiano said along with a few other choice words.

"You can. I mean it," DeeAnn said, her tone close to begging.

"You're nuts if you think we're going to trust you," Mei had rolled the drawing up and held it in her fist.

Tears formed in DeeAnn's eyes. Wren wanted to trust her. *Jesus, we can't put the next opportunity to escape at risk. On the other hand, I don't want to leave anyone in the herd behind. Please show us.*

They stopped talking about it and pretended to be interested in whatever was on TV.

———•●•———

Jim sat at his parents' kitchen table, with no light but that from his open laptop, putting the final editing touches on his latest article. He attached it to an email to his editor and hit *send*. He'd been careful not to reveal anything new to the kidnappers in this one. Of course, he didn't have any new information.

The scent of brewing dark-roast drew his attention, and he started to get up when he heard the ding of a new email in his inbox. Might as well have a look.

An email responding to the previous article in which he'd asked readers with information to contact him—the one that had led the traffickers to his apartment. He clicked on it. A reader knew something about a ring of traffickers. He, or she—it was anonymous—gave the name and location of a hotel in New Orleans, *Journey's Inn*. He explained how the operation worked, including the modeling auditions, and named several other hotels and houses across the Southeast United States. The person said he, or she, had seen the girls who went missing from Fairhope, Alabama there.

Jim's heart leaped. Maybe someone on the inside had grown a conscience. Or maybe it was a trap.

Sophie had mentioned New Orleans too. This could be legit. It had to be the ring Jim was looking for. He doubted the traffickers would lead him to the real city of their operation if they meant to trap him. These could be the ones who had trafficked Sophie, who had taken Stacy, and who threatened Jim's parents.

Jim glanced around the quiet house. His parents were still sleeping. This reader must keep hours like he did. It couldn't have been later than four in the morning.

He forwarded the email to Detective Windly before his second cup of coffee. He wanted to call, make sure he got it and opened it right away, but he wouldn't be in his office at this hour.

Jim finally got around to pouring himself that coffee. By the time Mom and Dad got up, he'd have to make a new pot.

He sipped and paced.

Paced and sipped.

"Lord, please let this be a real tip. Help us find these bast—bad guys and rescue these victims." He whispered the words into the dark house.

He sat back down at the computer and typed another quick email to Detective Windly. "Please call when you get this, or I'll call you first thing."

Jim paced and prayed some more.

Trust God. Give it to God and trust him with it, he reminded himself.

He looked at the clock on Mom's oven. 5:12 am. When might the detective get in? Seven sounded reasonable, but how could he wait until seven?

Be still... Abide.

Right. Okay. He could do this. Cup in hand, he walked into the living room and sat in Dad's wide, comfy, leather chair. He set the cup on the table beside him and lifted the footrest.

Jim took a deep, slow breath and let it out. "Jesus, you love better than I do. Your power is greater than mine," he whispered.

Of course, God loved better than Jim. God's love was perfect, and he was all-powerful. But still, Jim could use the reminder.

I Am.

The muscles in Jim's neck relaxed. He dozed off.

At the sound of his cell phone, Jim jumped and spilled a little coffee before catching the mug and setting it right. The phone rang again. He tried to put the footrest back down, fought with it—how did the dang thing work? Then he just jumped over it, tripped and stubbed his toe on the way into the kitchen where he'd left his phone on the table.

"Hello?"

"Hello Jim, it's Paul." Finally, Detective Windly. "I guess you have some details for me. This could be the breakthrough we've been looking for."

Paul promised to relay the email to the Street Task Force he was working with.

"We've been looking at a couple of motels in New Orleans, so this could be the confirmation we've been waiting for."

"Please let me know if you find the motel and if you're going to set something up to go in and take them out." Jim tried to keep the desperation out of his voice. "I'd like to be there."

"Jim," Paul's warning voice came through the line. "I can't have you there. You know that. We don't want to give those creeps any opportunity to wiggle out of their charges after we arrest them. And we don't want them to get away." He paused, then took a breath. "Do you hear me, Jim?"

"I know, but..." But how could he stay away? How could he...?

Abide in me, Jim.

"I mean it, Jimmy." The nickname got Jim's attention.

Right. "Okay but could I see your security footage from that motel. I might see something y'all wouldn't catch."

"I'll run it by the other task force members and get back to you on that. We certainly don't want to miss anything." The detective probably knew he'd better let Jim have something.

"Thank you." Jim paused. Could it be this easy? Might they finally catch these guys? *Please God.* "Hey, what happens to the victims you find in cases like this?"

"There are nonprofit organizations that can help. They are trained and ready to handle the trauma these victims will be experiencing. We'll set them up with local organizations, or one in the area where the victims are from. Can you hang on a moment?" The detective put him on hold, presumably to answer a call.

Jim tapped his pencil on the table.

"Sorry about that. Let's see..."

"You said there are some organizations that can help the victims."

"Yes. There's a wonderful place here in Alabama, *The Haven House.*"

"That sounds hopeful."

"Don't worry, Jim. They will be well cared for. You can check out the website and see what they do."

"Maybe I'll do that."

Jim felt a little better. Still, he wanted to be there when the rescue took place. After all, he was a journalist. He had an excuse to be there, and he had inside information. What better reason than writing a story?

A few high schools and one church in Louisiana had shown interest in him coming as a speaker. He could call them back and see if any had time for him to come in the next week.

Jim popped open his laptop again. He found the *Journey's Inn* motel easy enough. Then, digging through his dad's desk drawer, he found a paper map and plotted out the motel's location.

He cleaned the coffee mess and settled into Dad's chair again.

Glancing out the front bay window, Jim noticed color just appearing in the sky. The sun created gentle pinks and blues in the otherwise dark sky.

I Am.

Jim breathed in and exhaled slowly.

———•●•———

Wren nearly went out of her mind trying to keep herself from looking under the cabinet. Mei and Damiano had also seen something in her drawing. But they waited so they wouldn't tip off DeeAnn. Amy hadn't spoken much and Wren worried she could be losing hope again. Urgency gripped Wren, but she had to wait, be still, bide her time. Oh God, she couldn't do it.

"Amy, are you okay?" Mei asked her.

She nodded but looked away.

Mei glanced at Wren and shrugged.

The next day Romeo came for Amy alone.

"I can go in her place," DeeAnn volunteered to Wren's astonishment. Mei and Damiano stopped mid-action and stared at DeeAnn. Even Amy had her mouth open at this generous offer.

Romeo shoved DeeAnn out of the way. "I said I want Amy."

"But it's that afternoon client that likes her, right?" DeeAnn pressed ahead. "You know how he is, Romeo, and Amy doesn't need that right now."

Her concern for Amy brought a tear to Wren's eye. Had DeeAnn ever sacrifice herself for another person?

"What now, I'm supposed to pamper y'all's emotions?" He turned away from DeeAnn. "Amy, let's go."

"Come on," DeeAnn pulled his wrist gently. "I can make him happy," she turned on the sultry act. "You know I can."

Romeo slapped the side of her head. "Leave me witch, you don't tell me what to do. Who do you think you are?" He took a step toward Amy, and she shuffled to him without a sound.

When they left, Wren realized DeeAnn hadn't moved. Mei splashed some water in her face, and she came to.

"I'm sorry I couldn't go in her place." DeeAnn sat up on the floor where she'd fallen. Was she apologizing to them? "This client is the worst, and he loves Amy." A tear dribbled down her cheek. "I tried."

"We know, DeeAnn." Mei couldn't hide her shock.

"I'll get you some ice for your head," Damiano put some in a towel and brought it to her.

DeeAnn took the offering from him and held it to her head, still sitting on the floor. "Uh, thank you."

Damiano patted her back, then walked away. Wren noticed tears cresting DeeAnn's eyelids, which she quickly wiped away.

When Amy came back later, bruised and bleeding in a few places, they all pitched in to clean her wounds and make her some hot water with honey left from a previous take-out order. DeeAnn gave her the best bed and stayed close to her in case she needed anything.

Wren watched DeeAnn closely. Should they trust her again?

She is one of my wrens, too—part of the cabinet.

Wren left DeeAnn with Amy in the bedroom and crossed the room to Damiano and Mei who sat on the couches. "We need to bring DeeAnn into the plan with us. I think she's changed." She hoped they'd listen. *God, let her be right about DeeAnn.*

"Maybe she's seen enough to realize we're right," Mei said.

"But if not…" Damiano left it out there.

"It's a risk, but we could miss our chance or lose our nerve if we don't act fast," Mei said.

"We need to see what's under the sink." Damiano's gaze moved toward the cabinet. "Let's check now before she comes back in here."

"Amy's sleeping." DeeAnn approached at that very moment. "What are y'all doing?"

"We don't have a choice, Damiano," Wren said. "We may not get a chance if we don't include her. Just check it.

"Do you want me to fill her in?" Mei asked, looking to Wren, then to Damiano.

He grunted and Wren nodded.

They crouched down by the sink while Mei took DeeAnn aside and showed her Wren's drawing, explaining about the light.

When Wren couldn't pull the panel loose, Damiano found a plastic spoon and wedged it behind one side. He pushed until the spoon broke, but there was enough space for his fingers. "I got it. I got it," he said, pulling back with his body as well as his fingers. Then he sat back and pointed for Wren to have a look.

It was dark. She hated to feel around in there. What if she felt a dead rat or, worse, a live one?

"Do you want me to check?" He offered.

"Do you mind?"

He reached in and pulled something out.

A screwdriver.

CHAPTER NINETEEN

Although it was barely December, Mom had filled the house with accents of Christmas as she did every year. Staying with Mom and Dad while his apartment got cleaned and repaired had been kind of nice. Jim definitely ate better. Mom made her famous pancakes with Conecuh sausage. His mouth watered at the scent of the locally produced treat.

At breakfast, Jim told Mom and Dad only that the police had a new, good lead and might make progress on catching the bad guys.

That afternoon, Jim had made half a dozen phone calls and ended up with two bookings in New Orleans. Unfortunately, none could accommodate him in the following week.

An email from Detective Windly came in with an attachment. It read, "Here is surveillance from the hotel you mentioned. There's a lot, so pace yourself."

Scanning the footage, Jim saw an unmarked work van. He remembered a similar vehicle description being mentioned in his sister's case files. Someone had reported seeing one in the area where her body had been discovered.

He couldn't find anything else, so after reporting on that to Detective Windly, he looked up *The Haven House*.

The website described their vision and showed pictures of the building process. Their mission: "…to provide refuge and restoration to minors who are survivors of human trafficking; empowering them through the renewal of spirit, soul, and body."

They offered general education classes and lessons in life skills, cooking, gardening, and even equine therapy. Stacy would've loved that. When she was little, she had always wanted a horse.

If only his sister had been found and taken there. She would've been okay. Maybe she would've even ridden a horse.

A picture of Stacy around five years old filled his mind. He saw her at the fair, sitting on a pony. She had begged him to take her to the ponies. She'd been over the moon to ride that little pony around in a small circle.

He wiped a tear from the corner of his eye, then looked at the drop on his finger. A tear? The second time in less than a week.

Maybe he could help *The Haven House*. He could write an article to raise awareness about what they do.

An art fundraiser.

Yeah, he could organize an art exhibit, with sales of the art going to *The Haven House*. He could also invite wealthy connections and get them to donate even if they didn't buy any art.

Jim put in a call to Brenda Swartz, the founder and director of *The Haven House*. He left her a message and hoped she'd be as excited as he was about the possibilities.

First, he would interview her for an article. It would be nice—no, it would be healing for him to write about something positive for a change. And he'd be supporting local artists. Always a plus.

A little higher now, the sun shone through the trees, forming long shadows on the road. It ushered in the new day and turned the sky to blue.

———•◉•———

The screwdriver was like a priceless treasure to the captives. They kept it where it had been since who knows—maybe when some plumber forgot it there. It could've been ten, twenty, or even fifty years ago. Whoever left it—however long ago it was—Wren knew God had been working in the past on their behalf, watching out for his little cabinet of wrens here and now. This was his light shining into their darkness. It was God answering her prayers.

"Okay. The plan is coming together. We need to be ready." Wren warned the others. "Let's go over it." She sat down at the table by Mei and Damiano.

"I'm so scared." Amy stood near the sink in the kitchen, rubbing her arms like she was cold.

"Me too," Wren said. "We all are. But we've got to be brave now."

"What should we say in the note?" DeeAnn asked. She'd been planning along with them since they found the screwdriver. Even though DeeAnn had changed her attitude toward them considerably, Damiano and Mei still expressed concern. Wren wasn't sure about trusting her either, but they really had no choice. Wren had seen understanding dawn in DeeAnn's eyes and wanted to believe she'd changed.

They all agreed DeeAnn should pretend to be the good little bottom girl Daddy and Romeo believed her to be, so as not to raise suspicion. The rest of them had played the role of weak, scared little chicks, unwilling to risk the wrath of their captors, which wasn't a complete lie.

They planned to get a note to Cade in hopes that he could do something to help them. They only needed him to provide a distraction.

"We shouldn't be too specific in the note, in case someone else finds it," Mei said.

"Right." Damiano nodded. "Who knows if the creep will even help if he reads it."

"Or if he'd be able to help," Amy said.

"There's a million reasons this should never work," Wren admitted. "I've dreamed up at least a dozen worst-case scenarios myself. Don't worry, I won't share them with y'all."

They laughed together, and it felt good for a change.

"So, what do we say in the note to Cade?" Damiano brought them back to the question.

"We'll ask him to create a distraction, something big…"

"Maybe a fire, so the fire department has to come." Damiano raised his eyebrows up and down as if he knew it was a good plan.

"Perfect," Wren agreed.

"It should be when regular motel guests are on the move. The guards will have fewer opportunities to fling their guns around and look suspicious when innocent bystanders are around." Mei sat at the head of the table. "Though I don't know how many real customers stay here. This place is such a dump."

"There are some though, and it should help," Damiano said.

"Okay, let's just ask him to make a disturbance around eleven a.m." That might be a good time. "The people who stay at this hotel are probably not early risers but would have to check out by eleven."

"I hope that's big enough to distract Daddy, Romeo, and the guards." Amy's wide eyes gave away her nervousness, but she bravely agreed to the plan.

"Maybe that's enough," Wren said. "Then we'll put the note to him in a bag for the trash. I'll put something obscure on the outside of the bag to get Cade to open it."

"What?" Amy asked.

"It can't be anything that will trigger the others," Mei said.

"I was thinking, *Page and Palette*."

"What?" Mei adjusted her seat, looking confused.

"What does that even mean?" Damiano asked.

"It's the name of the bookstore, coffee shop and club where Liv and I first met Cade. Plus, if Romeo or anyone else sees it, Cade can just say I was asking for more art supplies."

"If he thinks of that." Mei pointed out the risk.

"So do you think I should write that or not?" Wren needed their input.

"Yes," Amy piped in.

The others agreed.

Wren wrote the note on a piece of copy paper, then wadded it up and put it in the brown paper bag they had saved the other day from the egg sandwiches. Then she wrote *Page and Palette* on the outside of the fast-food bag.

Now, to wait until they allowed Cade to come in. What would they do if Daddy and Romeo didn't let him come back at all?

"Maybe DeeAnn should ask Romeo if Cade could bring the dog up to see us. He might think it will be good for morale," Damiano said.

"I could do that," DeeAnn offered.

Wren inhaled, then exhaled slowly. Their plan was in place.

———— • ◆ • ————

The next day after lunch, Cade and the dog made an appearance, with Romeo, of course.

"Thank you, Cade," Wren said.

"Hi Bobby," Amy was the first to greet the dog. But they all gathered around. Romeo rolled his eyes, like they were such immature children. But they played like it was the best thing they'd seen in weeks. And truthfully, it was.

"All right, that's enough. Let's go, Cade. Get that mutt on his leash."

"Romeo, my love. Will you take the trash out for us?" They'd decided that DeeAnn should ask Romeo to take it first so as not to raise suspicion. But they felt certain he would never do such a menial task.

"Are you kidding me?" Except he didn't say *kidding* and he shoved her, sending her backwards into the table. She'd have a bruise on her hip by this time tomorrow. "I'm not your errand boy. And don't you forget it." The harsh look in his eyes would've been warning enough. Wren knew it had to hurt DeeAnn, but hopefully it convinced her that they were right about him.

"Can Cade do it? It's getting dirty in here." Acting like her hip didn't hurt, she stepped toward him again, pretending to pout.

"Sure." He turned to Cade. "Get their trash errand boy."

Cade offered Romeo the leash while he grabbed the trash, but Romeo blew him off and headed to the door.

Damiano handed Cade a kitchen-sized bag of regular trash. Then Wren picked up the brown bag as a last-minute addition to the trash.

"This one too." She pierced Cade with a look right in the eyes and pointed to the side with *Page and Palette* written on it.

His eyes registered that something was going on, but he was confused. He took both bags in one hand, the dog leash in the other, and headed out. Romeo locked the door behind them.

This was it.

Live or die. Tomorrow they'd run.

---•●•---

"Jim, we've got the place staked out. There've been other reports of suspicious activity at this motel. I've got a good feeling." Detective Windly had called during the few moments he had before they their team rushed in. Jim appreciated the gesture.

"Thanks, Paul. And guess what. I'm actually in New Orleans… if that's where you are, of course."

"Of course, you are," Paul whispered under his breath, but Jim heard him but ignored it.

"I had a couple of speaking engagements out here. If you need anything, or just a pair of extra hands, I'm here. Just a phone call away."

Paul laughed. "All right, Jim. I'll let you know."

Jim couldn't sit still. Pacing the hotel room floor, he tried to pray but couldn't focus. He tried to sleep, but that wasn't happening.

He'd go for a walk. *Café Beignet* was just down the road from his hotel. Couldn't go wrong with a cup of chicory and a beignet. And he'd get some exercise to boot. Always a plus for a writer.

He picked up his pace through the brisk winter wind, praying as he walked. *Father God, please. Let this be the end of the search. Stop these evil men, for Stacy's sake and for the sake of the other victims.*

It felt as if he were begging. Maybe he was.

After his beignet, he walked through a nearby square and sat on a bench. Time passed slowly. He checked his phone—maybe he had missed hearing the ringer. No, if Paul didn't call before Jim spoke at the school tonight, how would he be able to concentrate on his speech?

He made his way back to the hotel and lay on the bed, looking over his speech notes, but he kept rereading the same paragraph.

He decided to grab an early dinner, then head to the school, and go over his notes there.

At a local restaurant, he ordered a bowl of seafood pasta with a baguette and a salad. The waiter brought the food and set it in front of him.

Jim jumped at the sound of his phone and scared the waiter. He waved his apology, and the guy went back to the kitchen.

"Paul?"

"Yes, it's me. Hey. I wanted to fill you in."

"Oh man, it's about time. Did you get them? Please say you did."

"I'm sorry, Jim."

His heart sank, and the rims of his eyes burned. "What…" he cleared a frog from his throat. "What happened?"

"It was the wrong place. But there had been things going on there as well. We caught a group of drug dealers who had been working out of that motel. We got some good leads on the cartel that they were working for as well."

"I'm glad."

"Look, son, I know it's not what you were hoping for, but this is how these things go. We're closing in on them. It won't be long now."

"Yeah?" Jim knew his food must be delicious, but the flavor was lost on him.

He had one more speaking engagement in New Orleans after tonight, so he'd have to stay a few more days.

What had gone wrong? That had been the name of the hotel the informant gave him. What else did the task force know that he didn't?

He picked up his phone and redialed the detective.

"Hello?"

"If your task force is staying on here in New Orleans a few days, can we meet up? I'd like to go over some details with you."

"Do you have anything new?"

"Not really. Just a question about something I saw in the surveillance videos."

"That surveillance might have been of the wrong hotel, you know?"

"Yes, sir, but…"

"Okay, let's talk soon. I have lunch available tomorrow."

"Thanks."

⸻ • ● • ⸻

Wren opened her eyes. Sleeping had been so much easier the last few nights. She'd take the couch over a radiator and a hard floor any night. And to her relief, the number of clients they'd been seeing in the last few days had slowed considerably.

She stretched, trying to release the kink in her side. Thank the Lord her body was feeling better. But her mind swirled with evil presences, fears, nerves, and excitement. *Please give me faith, God.*

All at once a picture came to her mind. An escape route. It had to be. She felt it in her spirit.

Wren reached for the pencils she kept close. She drew a hallway leading to an exit sign—a stairwell door on the left. Three flights of stairs going down to a side door leading outside. Each floor had two flights of stairs with a turn in the middle, but then below the first floor was one more flight of stairs down leading to the outside door at the back of the building.

Shading carefully to form a clear picture, Wren switched pencils to get a better weight. She held the drawing at a distance to look it over. Light burst from the doorway at the bottom of the stairs in her picture out into the room where she sat. Confidence surged through her. This was it.

Outside the door, she saw an open field and some woods behind that. They could run in that direction and hope to get there for cover before someone was looking for them, but they needed to split up so, if followed, at least one of them might get away.

She folded a new piece of copy paper into three sections. Then redrew the vision on every section. Each person would memorize it, then Wren would put them all in the oven against the electric heating coil and burn them.

You know this is crazy. You're trusting your life and everyone else's to the accuracy of something that came from your imagination. You, with no knowledge of this building. You'll get everyone killed.

Her thoughts argued, but there was no stopping now. No matter how the dark words swirled around her mind and pounded in her heart, she'd made her choice.

After the sun came up and they were at the table eating Captain Crunch, Wren showed them the pictures.

"What's this?" Mei set her spoon down to take the paper.

"It came to me this morning. I drew it out. It shows us where to go when we escape."

"Ooo." Damiano wiggled his fingers in the air. "Very mystical." He was in a mood. Then again, they probably all had some nervous energy pent up.

"We've seen this mystical stuff work already," Amy bumped his back. "I don't think we should start doubting now." Then she looked at Wren. "But maybe we should pray before we do this."

"I think you're right. We need all the help we can get." Wren said a quick prayer, asking for God's protection and guidance. She prayed for them to be safe and free... and alive. Then she lifted the page to show them. "Look at this."

Damiano jumped backward. "Whoa. Did you see that burst of light?"

"Yeah," DeeAnn sounded excited. "That's like magic."

"She saw it," Amy said smiling.

Mei and Damiano nodded, each of their faces brighter and hopeful now. They looked to Wren for more instruction.

"In the hallway, we go the opposite direction from how we are taken when we go downstairs."

"I see the exit sign here." Mei pointed to the paper. "Then the stairs."

"They're through a door on the left side of the hallway," Wren explained.

"Then we go down to the first floor?" Mei asked.

"No. We keep going down another half-flight. There's a door to the outside there."

"That's strange," Amy said.

"Are we ready for this?" Wren glanced at each of her roommates, dressed in their street clothes—what each had worn the day they were taken. She took another bite of cereal for strength. "The minute we hear sirens, we need to be ready to move out of here for good." Wren studied their faces, trying to discern their resolve.

"Are you with us on this, DeeAnn?" Wren asked one more time.

Face pale, her petite features tight and eyes wide, she looked like she might throw up. DeeAnn shrugged one shoulder, but nodded her head.

"Well, you better be sure now," Damiano's voice commanded.

"Come on." Wren gave him a warning look. "DeeAnn, what can we do to help you understand this is the right decision?"

She shrugged again. "I don't know. I mean, I saw something in your drawing. And I know it's something we have to do. But what's next? I don't have a family like you. I have nothing to return to. If I leave, I'll end up with someone else like Daddy, and I won't have Romeo. But if I stay, and y'all go…" She paused a long time, then whispered, "They'll kill me."

"Why would you end up with someone else like Daddy?" Amy asked.

"I need the drugs, stupid." Her tone sounded more like her old self.

Wren recognized the signs in that instant. DeeAnn's overly white face, sunken cheeks and dark shadows showed in the circles under her eyes. She probably needed a fix right now.

"There are places to get you clean," Mei said.

"Not when you've been on it as long as I have."

They usually didn't touch each other in that motel room, but Wren put an arm across DeeAnn's shoulders. DeeAnn stiffened. "I've heard of people who got clean after being addicted longer than you've been alive." Wren remembered hearing someone at church talk about their life.

"Do you want to tell your story?" Amy asked DeeAnn so quietly that Wren almost didn't hear her.

"No one's ever asked or listened to my story. I've never told anyone, except a few details to Amy."

"That's why you should," Wren said. "It's healing." She wasn't sure they had time to hear the whole thing, but it seemed important that DeeAnn tell it, and now.

CHAPTER TWENTY

Jim sat at a small table in a little coffee shop within walking distance of the Canopy Hotel—his go-to in New Orleans. He sipped a cappuccino and added notes on his laptop to keep a record of how his talks had gone, while he waited for his breakfast and croissant. Good thing the Bon Ami Café opened early. The clean lines of its I and good lighting were perfect for working.

Jim picked up a third speaking engagement while he was in New Orleans. The first two had gone well. The middle school principal told him that the information had been so helpful she'd like him to send them his outline. She also wanted him to return every year to keep the students aware. The high school principal had been just as enthusiastic.

That was a good start, he smiled, at least for the kids in those two schools. He took a bite of his croissant. Crispy and light on the outside, tender and buttery on the inside, Jim wished for a French bakery near his apartment.

Tonight, he'd speak to a church youth group of junior and senior high school students. He'd modify his own story slightly, but he wouldn't gloss over it. They needed to hear the ugly truth.

Jim picked up his phone on the first ring.

"Jim? Hello, this is Paul."

"Hey, Paul. How's the investigation going?"

"Well, that's why I called." He cleared his throat as if to prepare for a long dissertation. "Our task force is still in New Orleans. We found two more motels to check out, and we think we're onto the traffickers' lair—so to speak." He chuckled a little, but Jim knew Paul didn't take any of this lightly. "Sorry, I didn't mean to trivialize."

"No, I get it. Humor helps, even if it's just a word."

"Thanks."

"You're still here?" If the task force was still working the case in New Orleans, it could be good news. "I'm here too. I have one more talk scheduled for tonight."

"Do you want to join us this morning? We'll get you back in time for the lecture, even if I have to drive you myself."

"Are you messing with me right now?" Jim so wanted to be there so bad he could taste it.

"No kidding, Jim. I told the team that you'd seen photos of the van, and that you had met the two girls who disappeared in Fairhope. And there isn't one of us who doesn't understand how you feel, with all that your family has suffered." He cleared his throat. "Now, I can't promise you that anything will happen today. Sometimes the waiting game gets long, but you might be able to confirm we have the right place, at least."

"I—I don't know what to say, I—yes! Of course, I want to join y'all." He must've just turned into a junior higher, with all those bumbling words.

The detective laughed into the phone. "Okay, but we also know the risks. If you run off with some harebrained idea without my permission, you could ruin our chances forever. I mean it, Jim. There may not be another chance to get these guys."

"Yes, sir, I understand, Captain, sir."

The detective laughed again. "Well, don't promote me before I'm ready, which might be soon if all goes well." Jim heard papers shuffling. "Don't forget my warning, Jim. You can't get in the way. It could be dangerous."

— • ● • —

No clock. How would she know checkout time was approaching? Wren needed to focus on DeeAnn's life story, but she also needed to be sure everyone was ready on time. *Lord God, please work out the timing,* she prayed.

"I don't know if I can talk about it." DeeAnn looked up at them with more vulnerability than Wren had ever seen in her. She recognized the fear in her eyes. How could they make her feel safe?

"Don't worry, DeeAnn. None of us will judge you. We're all in this together, and we're getting out together." Wren got a nod from Amy. She hoped the others felt the same.

"My stepdad raped me when I was eight. It was just once, like to get me into the habit or to know what I was doing or something. Then he started selling me to his friends for sex. He said if I told anyone he'd kill my mom and then me. He showed me his gun too. Said he carried it with him all the time."

My God. Wren tried to imagine being eight years old in that horrid situation.

"At twelve, I finally got up the guts to run away. I didn't know where to go. I thought I would hitch or walk to the nearest town because we lived out in the country. I knew I couldn't even find food or shelter until I got myself to a town." Her eyes looked far away. "I imagined sleeping behind one of those big dumpsters in some city's alley behind a business that had food to throw away."

"You must've thought about it a lot," Damiano said.

"Only every day and night. Sometimes all night." She replied, looking at him squarely, but not in her usual pushy, in-charge jerky way. "I stuck out my thumb, and a car pulled over. The first one that passed. What are the odds? I figured it was fate."

"Was it?" Amy asked.

"Oh yeah." DeeAnn rolled her eyes. "It was Romeo. He was kind, not pushy, you know? And complimented my beauty. He took me to a diner and bought me some supper, then after hearing my story, he put me up in a nice hotel room—"

"Like this one?" Damiano rolled his eyes.

"No." Sarcasm laced her laugh. "It wasn't anything special, I guess, but I'd never even seen a hotel. He didn't have sex with me or try anything dirty. Every night he came back and took me to dinner. He paid for me to have groceries in the room and bought me new clothes. I felt loved for the first time."

"Wow, no wonder you love him." Amy's eyes were wide. "But he isn't like that now."

"Yeah. I know." DeeAnn sounded like she still hated to admit it.

"How long ago was that?" Mei asked.

"Almost four years." DeeAnn paused, swallowing hard.

"What happened?" Wren asked.

"Romeo talked about us getting married. He said he'd help me finish school and then send me to college one day. I started imagining all the good things we could have together."

"Wow," Amy interrupted. "I never realized how similar our stories were… All this time."

DeeAnn pinned her with a look, but it wasn't prideful or hateful this time. "You were right, Amy. It's good to share our stories." DeeAnn slapped at a single tear on her cheek.

"We've been here together for a long time. Others have come and gone to other places, but not us." Another tear got away and trickled down her face.

"We should've helped each other instead of hating each other." Amy opened her arms to DeeAnn. She looked at Amy's outstretched hands for a moment, then leaned into her for a hug, stiff and unsure.

Wren swallowed. It was the most beautiful thing she'd seen since arriving. Still, she hoped DeeAnn would hurry and finish her story. What if they missed the disturbance? What if they couldn't hear it from the apartment?

"So?" Damiano pressed. "When did things change?"

"I wanted to help Romeo pay for all the things he was doing. It was all for me, you know? I wondered if I could get a job or something. Sometimes he said things that let me know it was a burden to pay for it all. But he didn't want me to. He brought me pills to calm my anxiety. I didn't understand they were drugs or how desperately I would need them."

DeeAnn's hands were shaking.

"I started asking him for more, and he brought it. As much as I wanted, he gave me. After a few weeks, I wanted to have sex with him. I mean, he was nicer to me than any of those men my stepdad had me go with. So, we did. We did it a lot." She glanced at the floor, then at the far wall. "We still do."

"Really?" Mei asked.

DeeAnn just closed her eyes, her white face red. "One day he announced he was out of money. He couldn't do it anymore. No more drugs, no more hotel, nothing. It would all go away. He said he lost his job—I never knew what his job was."

"But he had a way for you to earn your keep?" Amy asked.

DeeAnn looked back at her and nodded. "He drove me here, and I've been here ever since. He kept saying it was just until we could earn enough to get married and get out of here, but…"

"The day never came," Amy finished.

———•●•———

Paul picked Jim up from the café to save time. When they arrived at the FBI office, Jim saw at least fifteen armored vehicles parked.

"We call them bearcats." Paul raised his eyebrows as if the name should impress.

Paul made Jim promise to stay in the command vehicle, which had been camouflaged to look like an army vehicle—semi-common in the area. Not as cool as a bearcat, the large van had multiple workstations and monitors inside. The monitors displayed feeds from the surveillance cameras. They'd tapped into a couple of feeds already in place, and they set up their own cameras on telephone poles surrounding the motel, so every angle was covered. Being in the command van, he'd have firsthand knowledge of everything that happened without getting in the way of those on the frontline.

Three camouflaged bearcats moved closer to the motel. The others would stay in an empty lot a few blocks away until they were called in at the critical moment.

The rundown motel felt silent. Jim got the feeling it wasn't just the lack of sound, but a weight in the air that hung over everything, threatening to break the world if a single sound disturbed it.

He watched as the Street Task Force team walk-crawled to their hiding spots like locusts in a field. Then each one stopped when they found a good hiding place. Those guys were patient, ready to go on command, or to stay crouched and hidden as long as it took.

The task force determined late morning to be the optimal timing. The victims would be tucked away together, all in one place.

An FBI agent confided in Jim that their priority was to get the victims out safely, then hopefully they'd be able to get the guards and the lead traffickers, at least the ones working in this location.

"Hopefully get the bad guys?" No, no, no, no. This couldn't continue. They'd just run away and start again with more recruits. Jim rubbed his forehead. *Please Lord,* was about all he could muster in prayer.

"Naw. Don't you worry," a second FBI agent said. "We're good at what we do. And we want these guys." It was the techie guy who remained with Jim in the command van. "I'm Nate." He put his hand out for Jim to shake. Nate had a firm grip.

Jim agreed that all the victims must make it out unharmed, but he also wanted these guys off the street. A tear threatened the corner of his eye.

From his pocket he pulled out two folded news articles he'd printed off. One of Stacy, and one with the picture of the two girls he'd met in Fairhope. He studied their faces. If only he could see them rescued today. What a victory.

Watching the agents wait in vigilant readiness, Jim's mind wandered.

"They that wait upon the Lord will renew their strength." The well-known verse from Isaiah popped into his mind. Waiting and patience—lessons Jim needed.

These agents would not move without the word from their superior. If they did people might die. Trained and ready in every way, they now waited. No matter how long. They waited until the boss said, "Execute".

Jim listened to the still quiet. He buttoned his overcoat against the chill, which seeped into the van. Even the air seemed to know something was coming. The calm before the storm?

What might make those agents move?

He leaned back in the chair in front of a monitor, then forward again. Paul hadn't been kidding—waiting sucked.

"Hey, I see the van." Jim pointed to one of the monitors. It sure looked like the same one he'd seen in the footage he reviewed. Possibly the same one described by the eyewitness in Stacy's case.

"Are you sure?" Nate asked.

He nodded, heart pounding.

Nate whispered the information into his headset. The agents made a slight hand gesture indicating they'd received the information. They couldn't reply with words, of course.

Now they seemed even quieter. Potential energy vibrated the atmosphere waiting for a push.

———•●•———

A dog barked outside. It sounded like—Bobby.

"Hey, wait…" Wren said. "Do y'all hear that?"

"It's Bobby!" Amy said.

"Do you think…?" Wren wondered aloud.

"Maybe Cade let him escape without Daddy or Romeo realizing."

"It's probably close to check-out time." Mei looked at her bare wrist as if she had a watch there. "And people always pay attention to dogs."

"But what about the fire? The fire department?" The dog wouldn't be enough of a distraction.

"Maybe he couldn't get outside alone to set a fire. Let's wait." Damiano put a finger to his lips. "Hear any other commotion?"

At first, they heard nothing at all. Even Bobby had gone quiet. Then more barking.

"Let's look at Wren's drawing again," Mei said. She put it in the middle of the table, and they all stared, as if a few more seconds could seal it in their memory.

Amy flinched her head back. "Did you see that?" She sounded amazed.

"Yeah, I saw it, like a flash," Damiano said.

"Me too," DeeAnn sounded like she couldn't believe it. "What was that?"

"A bright light flashed over the drawing," Amy said. "Then I saw…" She put her face closer to the drawing. "It looks like something's sticking out of the bar that goes across the outside door." Amy pointed to the drawing. On the shadow side of the drawing, at the far right side of the door's security bar, there was a space that Wren missed when shading—a narrow white space right inside the shaded part.

"Was it on the original drawing I made this morning as well?" Wren went over to the couch where she'd slept and then sketched the picture.

"Look, there it is too!" Now DeeAnn pointed with excitement. "What does it mean?"

Wren hadn't noticed it in the dream.

"It's the wire for the alarm." Mei sounded sure.

No one spoke for a moment.

How would they deal with the alarm wire?

"Maybe there's a way to twist it off to disconnect it," Mei said.

"That would probably set it off instantly." Damiano pointed out.

"I know about alarms." Mei seemed confident.

What were they going to do? Why would God show it in Wren's drawing if he didn't have a solution?

The barking started again, then more insistent barking.

Scuffling sounds scurried in the hallway.

"I heard footsteps in the hall," Mei sounded urgent.

A big bang, like a dump truck or something, sounded from outside.

"We've got to move." Damiano grabbed the screwdriver and ran to the door. Slowly, careful not to make much sound, he unscrewed the screws around the old doorknob.

"What about the alarm?" Amy asked.

"I'll pull the wire out before we open the door." If Mei said she knew about alarms, Wren trusted that she knew.

"And if it doesn't work, we'll just run for it," Wren said. "And pray to God that this works. I mean it, y'all. Pray as we run."

They spilled into the hallway, noise everywhere. The guards had gone, but some people were in the hallway already. Wren didn't know if they were guests or what.

"I'll disarm the alarm." Mei started running toward the stairs that they believed to be there ahead of the others.

Damiano still held the screwdriver as he ran. "You don't have the screwdriver."

"I don't need it." Mei's confidence must've convinced him.

Wren heard cries from a room two doors down, along the same hallway. "Damiano, give me the screwdriver," she shouted to him.

"But we've got to run. We have to scatter."

"I know, but…" She took the tool from his hand. "I think there're more in here. You go. Run. Help the others. Don't wait for me or look back."

He didn't have time to argue. He ran.

"I'm here to help," Wren called through the door. "Just a sec." She tried to steady her hands.

One screw fell out.

She swallowed and took a deep breath. *Please God, please.* Come on, hands don't fail me now.

She tried the second screw, but the screwdriver slipped and fell to the floor. Maybe Damiano would have been better at this task. "I'm coming, don't worry," she tried to assure whoever was on the other side.

The second screw fell out.

One more.

"Get whatever you need to run. We're going to find help. Don't worry, just be ready."

"We're ready," she heard a small voice answer from very close on the other side of the door.

Why were her hands so shaky?

Please God, please help these little ones get free, too. We can't leave them here. We just can't.

Time moved in slow motion.

Tears ran down Wren's face. She didn't even realize she was crying.

Finally, the screw fell out, and she shook the doorknob loose.

She wiped the tears from her face with the back of her arm. "Let's go."

There were only two girls and one boy in there—a girl who was older than the other two, and one small boy and a girl. The littlest one clutched a stuffed puppy and sucked her thumb.

Dear God.

"Is anyone else in there?"

The older girl shook her head. "They took Misty away last week."

Wren put a hand on each of their backs. "Go, go, go," she said, pointing them toward the stairs. "It's down three and a half flights of stairs, then run out the door. I'm right behind you."

"That's what you think!" Someone grabbed her shirt from behind.

"Run!" She screamed to the little ones. She should've had Damiano wait and take them with him.

A talon-like hand gripped her arm and nails dug into her muscles. She tried to wriggle out, but it clamped down harder.

She couldn't get away. Now what?

Barking and chaos sounded from outside. The guard flung open the outside door with his free hand and kept his grip on her with the other. Cold air whipped against her face.

Outside the sunshine nearly blinded Wren in spite of the winter air. She was being forced back the way she'd gone most nights since she'd arrived. Down the outdoor set of stairs to the back office where they visited the wardrobe room. A shiver ran across her whole body.

"I got the instigator." The guard said to a few other guards. Daddy and Romeo must've been out looking for the others.

Please God, help the others get away safely.

"Remember these?" The strong, ugly guy held up a pair of handcuffs and smiled, showing a couple of rotting teeth. The gleam in his eye made the picture of an evil character. As if perfectly cast for a movie. A ridiculous thought in such a terrible situation.

He clamped one of her hands in the handcuff and put the other cuff around the leg of the metal desk.

Good, maybe he'd leave and she could lift it and get away.

He closed the door behind him, and she heard it lock from the outside.

She tried to lift the desk, but it was solid metal and weighed a ton. She'd never be able to lift it, much less move it.

Whatever her fate, she prayed the others would get free. Maybe they'd bring someone to get her later.

Though she knew better.

By the time the others got help, the kidnappers would have moved her like they moved Liv on a moment's notice. Or they'd kill her.

CHAPTER TWENTY-ONE

A dog bark split the silence. Jim's body jerked. He saw the mutt on the monitor out in the parking lot, a black terrier mix. The little guy's attention seemed to be focused on the center part of the building.

Where had he come from? What drew its attention? The mutt barked a few times, then got quiet. Nothing else changed.

Jim kept watching the animal. It looked this way and that. Then it sat looking up at the building, its head cocked.

A man walked toward the dog. He looked to be in his thirties, well-built, and probably trained in martial arts or combat. The dog must've seen him coming because it bounced up, away from the guy. Then it started barking like crazy.

When the man lunged for it, that little wiry thing jumped three feet off the ground, avoided the man's grasp, landing the guy on the pavement, and ran from him. Stumbling to his feet, the guy chased it around the parking lot. It ran in circles, barking all the while. The whole thing tickled Jim.

Two other meaty guys joined the one chasing the dog. Maybe the FBI should hire that mutt.

These guys seemed bound and determined to shut that dog up.

Leaving their motel rooms to check out, the hotel guests seemed amused by the dog and its antics. As they rolled their suitcases toward the front office, a few stopped and tried to pet the dog, but it kept running.

One of the big guys tripped and fell into a lady. Her husband seemed quite upset by the whole thing when he suddenly grabbed his wife's elbow and hurried to a car with her. He helped her in and drove up to the front office, presumably to check out.

"Look," Nate pointed to the back corner of the center building on monitor D. Several young people tumbled out of the building. Overly thin with unkempt hair, Jim realized at least some of them didn't wear shoes. They scattered in different directions and ran.

Some looked old enough to be adults, but others were young, some very young.

"Oh, no." Nate started jabbering into his headset. "They're escaping on their own. The hostages are scattering out the back." He paused, but not for long. "Agents at the back, make a perimeter around the kids. Bill and José, you stay hidden back there to keep an eye out for the traffickers."

Jim hadn't realized that Nate was the guy in charge of this entire operation—or at least the coordinator of the other agents.

"Those at the front," Nate fired his words in rapid succession, "Take the guys chasing the dog and any other suspects that come out the front. I'm guessing we're looking at seven to ten perps. Maybe more." He clicked a button and looked up at the monitor overlooking the lot where all the armored vehicles waited. "SWAT… everyone, on my cue." Nate sat silent for several long seconds. It seemed like an eternity to Jim. "Execute! Execute! Execute!" He shouted.

Jim found the monitor showing the back of the building. He scanned the running kids. Could he recognize the two girls from this distance?

"Can we get a closeup on these monitors?" he asked Nate.

"We can, but it may not be as clear a picture." Nate turned a knob.

Jim couldn't tell. He didn't see anyone he recognized. Where were the girls?

"Do you see them?" Nate looked back at him.

Jim shook his head.

The silence of a few moments ago had become all-out chaos. Kids screamed when the agents grabbed them—they must've been so scared—alarms from inside the motel bellowed, traffickers yelled orders to each other into walkie-talkies, and all the while that silly dog barked and ran in circles.

Which monitor should he watch? Something was happening on each one. Jim saw the FBI SWAT bearcats close-in on the motel. Those things could drive over anything. They made their way across the yard without a problem.

Agents in front grabbed two suspicious men dressed in normal street clothes, unlike the all-black-clad thugs chasing the dog. One had long blond hair and looked angry. The other had short wavy hair and looked scared.

FBI agents took the guys who'd been chasing the dog and relieved them of their weapons. They also picked up the dog.

Other agents collected the kids. Some were crying, kicking, but a few just went along with what they were told.

Jim took it all in from the monitors.

The suspect with short hair asked the agents something. He became animated. Then the dog ran to him and jumped into his arms. Jim hadn't seen the screen where the dog got free from the agent who held it.

He looked at the monitor showing the back of the motel as the agents with the kids made their way toward the front.

A few agents held their positions in the woods behind the motel, just in case.

The door to Jim's vehicle opened.

"This guy says he has information for you." The agent addressed Nate and then pushed the short-haired suspect into their van. Cuffed, he stepped up with help from the agents. The officer lifted the dog in with the handcuffed man, so the mutt would stay calm.

He spilled his guts, and Nate tapped in notes faster than Jim ever could, even as a journalist.

"I've been trying to help them, you know? It's just that my uncle… well, he's scary."

"Okay, son, take it slow or you'll hyperventilate," Nate said. "Take a deep breath."

He did.

"I let the dog out to cause a distraction this morning so they could escape. I didn't know you'd be here. How did you know?

"We didn't," Nate said.

"Anyway, I tried before, but I got caught and held inside the hotel after that. Once I hacked into my uncle's computer and emailed a journalist who wrote about the girls from Fairhope—"

"Fairhope?" Jim interrupted.

The guy nodded.

"Now hold on. Let's back up." Nate clicked something on the computer. "First, tell me your name and how you got involved."

"Cade Williams, sir. My uncle—my step uncle—Emil Perez, that's who they call 'Daddy,' he's in charge of all this. He's been my guardian since I was in high school. I didn't know what he did. You have to believe me. And now Liv is gone, and it's my fault, and—"

"Slow down. I want to get this. We can help only if we know all the facts."

Cade nodded and swallowed.

Nate looked at Jim. "Will you get him one of those water bottles over there?" He pointed to the front, behind the driver's seat.

Jim handed Cade the bottle.

"Thanks." The man glanced up at Jim and then took a drink, holding the bottle with both hands, since they were cuffed. "Can you give some to the dog?" Jim complied by pouring some into the mutt's mouth. He licked happily.

Cade slowed down after that.

Jim learned that Olivia, also called Liv, had been moved and wasn't here. But her friend, Wren, was.

"I didn't see her in the group," Jim inserted.

"You're right," Cade said. "I never saw her when they were getting everyone. My uncle and one guard are missing too."

Nate spoke that information through the headset. Jim noticed a few agents move from their positions.

"Where do you think they'd be, Cade?" Nate asked him.

He described the location of the office from which they ran the operation.

What could have happened to Wren?

Cade clearly worried about her too.

———— •●• ————

The door to the office flung open. Daddy stomped in, eyes wild.

Wren swallowed hard. Please help me, Jesus.

"You did this." Daddy's brows narrowed as he got closer to her. "I know it was you. You and Cade. I'll kill him." Wren knew he would. She'd put Cade's life at risk. Daddy might kill her, too.

He got up in her face, held her free hand with one of his and then lifted a blade with his other hand. He leaned his mouth toward her ear. "If you make a peep, I'll cut out your tongue."

He lifted the desk corner just enough to pull the empty handcuff out.

She could only hope the others had made it. Maybe someone would get help and come back for her. *Please, please, please.*

Then Daddy pushed her toward the wardrobe room. If someone didn't know that door was there, looking, as it did, like a regular bookcase from inside the office. Why was he behind her, following her into the room?

She didn't want to be locked in any space with him.

A loud crash sounded behind her before Daddy got the door closed.

"Help!" She yelled.

Daddy backhanded her in the face. Her prosthesis flew out of its socket and onto the floor in front of Daddy.

"What the—?" He jumped back a step.

CHAPTER TWENTY-TWO

"Your eye?" His disgusted look accused Wren. He leaned toward her, his knife pressed to her neck. "Losing you won't hurt me at all."

Jerking backward he dropped the blade. Another arm threaded through his elbow and managed to pull him away from her. A guy dressed in battle gear, like something she'd seen on a police show, held Daddy in place. Even Daddy's goons didn't have that kind of gear.

"You're under arrest," the guy yelled.

Law enforcement! Thank God.

Wren laugh-cried, which turned into all-out crying like a baby. She dropped to the floor, her body releasing all the pent-up energy she'd been carrying. A woman dressed just like the police guy—all black, with pockets and gadgets all over—knelt beside her.

"You're safe now. I'm Patty, and I'm part of an FBI task force sent to find you." She handed Wren a handful of tissues.

"The others?" Wren asked.

"They're safe. Don't worry." Patty pulled some of Wren's hair back. It stuck under her knee. Wren wiggled just enough to release the hair, and Patty pulled it away from her face. She sucked in a breath. "Are you injured?"

"What? Um…" Was she? She couldn't feel anything.

"Your eye, it's… it's…"

"Oh no, it's a prosthetic. It came out when Da—he hit me." Wren reached from her position on the floor.

"Hey," Patty called to the other officer or agent. "Get the handcuff keys from him."

The first officer searched Daddy and tossed Patty the key. She unlocked Wren and removed the cuffs. Wren reached under the desk. Her fingers ran over the plastic bump, and she grabbed her prosthetic eye. Sitting back on her heels, she rubbed the prosthetic between her hands wishing she could wash it first. It took some fiddling, but she got it back in.

———•●•———

Wren and the others were taken to a large red-brick building, where several agents interviewed them separately. They each had an advocate assigned to be with them while they were being interviewed.

It took hours. The officers wanted a complete picture of what happened, but Wren's energy was spent. She could've probably sprawled out on the tile floor and fallen asleep in a second.

Her body shivered. Not from cold… being away from the others affected her. They'd been crammed together for weeks and become each other's safe zone. And now they were safe, but the world felt huge, chaotic and unsafe.

Finally, they all got back together in the lobby area, where there were couches, chairs and large paintings of impressive buildings on the walls. Wren got to see the *little ones* for the first time. They each received a soft blanket and a stuffed animal—even the older ones, even Wren. The little ones clutched those stuffed animals like shields in a battle.

One girl, Charlotte— "…but you can call me Char," she told them—was eleven. Char had been the mother figure in charge of the other motel room. The others were Nancy, age five, and Joey, age seven.

They smiled at Wren, recognizing her from when she took off their doorknob and shooed them out just before the guard grabbed her from behind.

Tears filled Wren's eyes.

"Wren, would you mind coming in here one more time?" The female officer interrupted her thoughts, but with such kindness. "I promise we'll get you to a safe place to rest soon," Patty said. Her gentleness filled Wren with gratitude.

Somehow, Wren stood up on her feet. The eyelid over her prosthetic kept slipping down partway. She pushed it up as she followed the officer. It probably wouldn't fit right again until she saw the ocularist. She might even need a new one.

She walked into a room with one table and two chairs that looked like a place where police would interrogate criminals. Fear shot through her. Then she noticed a stuffed loveseat and a separate chair in the back corner of the room. A man stood from where he'd been sitting. He looked familiar.

It took a moment, but she recognized him. Jim Fielding, the speaker on campus at Coastal who spoke about trafficking. Boy, had he been right. If only she'd known then what she knew now, she would have taken his speech much more seriously.

Patty gestured toward the comfy seats and the man.

He took a couple of steps in her direction, arm extended to shake her hand. "I'm James Fielding. Call me Jim."

"I remember." She shook his hand and was aware of Officer Patty, right beside her.

"I remembered you and your friend, Liv, when I saw the picture in the article. I'm so sorry for you… for what you've been through." Pain registered in his eyes.

She sensed his pain and dropped her gaze. "Thank you." Why hadn't she listened to his warnings? He must think she was so stupid.

"Here, let's all sit down."

"I'm right here," Patty said as she sat beside her on the loveseat. Wren felt sure Jim was a safe person, but she was thankful for Patty's presence.

Jim sat to the side, in a nice chair. "You are so brave." He ran fingers through his hair. He looked almost as tired as she felt. Sitting opposite Jim, she glanced away. Brave? Tears filled her eyes. Yeah right. "A hero, I hear."

She looked up in surprise. Who had he been talking to?

"Damiano explained how escaping was your idea, and the younger kids said you stayed behind to get them out, then you got caught."

"Damiano wanted to stay and help. He's brave too."

"Yes, of course." Jim fiddled with his hands in his lap.

She must look like something the cat dragged in… but she had been beaten and literally dragged. Still, how embarrassing.

"Did you learn anything about Liv?" Wren practically begged. "I've been so worried about her. Have they told where they sent her? I need to find her."

"Cade has been telling everything he knows, but he didn't know where they sent Liv. He seems pretty broken up about it. The police will interrogate the others about it too. I'm sure they'll find out."

Easy to say. "Did they get the ones called Daddy and Romeo?"

"Yes," Patty answered. "They seem to be the major players, at least in the Southeast. Daddy, whose name is Emil Perez, has connections to South America, and I'm sure he's working with a cartel."

Wren nodded. It made sense. She could barely keep her working eye open now.

"Well, I think they're ready to take you all," Patty said.

Wren's stomach cinched. "Wh-where are they taking us?"

"It's called *The Haven House*," Jim said.

"What about my parents?" She missed them so much, but what would she say? How would she even begin?

"The social worker at *Haven House* will call your parents after they've determined the safety of the home situations." Patty said something into her walkie-talkie then returned it to her belt.

"The organization specializes in situations exactly like this," Jim took over for Patty. "They work with minors up to age nineteen, providing debriefing, counseling, life skills, and basically a safe place with all you'll need." Compassion filled his eyes.

"Okay." She had little say in the matter, anyway.

Jim stood. Wren and Patty followed his lead. "You must be tired." He waited. Wren looked up. "I'd like to stay in touch if it's okay with you and the staff at The Haven House."

She nodded.

———— • ● • ————

The seven girls who'd been rescued rode in a van together late into the night, heading to Alabama. The two boys were heading to a related facility, but not in the same city, Wren was told.

The female FBI agent, Patty, rode with them, as did another agent and the driver. Both agents had changed to plain clothes, but Wren knew they had concealed weapons on them.

DeeAnn had been quiet during the drive, a look of uncertainty in her eyes. Wren kept glancing her way.

"Where are we going?" Mei asked Patty.

"It's a place to recover from trauma such as y'all have had. It's a safe, lovely place."

"What's it called?" Amy asked.

"The Haven House: A Place to Call Home." She replied. "That's their tagline."

"I've never had a home, not one that wasn't scary." DeeAnn kept rocking, but at least she was coherent.

"I haven't either, since my parents died," Amy said.

After a long ride, dozing off and on, the van turned right onto a dirt road in a field of weeds. It pulled up to a huge fence, which was really a gate that slid back slowly to allow them to enter.

A large white home with enormous windows and a pink door came into sight, like a lighthouse shining through a storm to shipwrecked fishermen, a warmth from inside reaching out, beckoning them to come in.

Inside, the first thing Wren saw was a delicately painted sign hanging over a comfy couch. The sign read, "HOME is the story of who we are & a collection of all the things we love."

Wren must've read it a dozen times before she could move on. *"The story of who we are..."* How like her favorite author, Samantha O'Connor, would say, "Every life is a story, and every story contains magic." Wren finally remembered the second part of Ms. O'Connor's quote. She wanted to write it and the new quote down where she could remember them.

Glancing around, she realized the others had disappeared down the hallway. Hearing whispers in the night's quiet, she had no trouble finding them.

Gathered with the director, a houseparent, and one administrator of the home, they received a quick introduction. The FBI agents signed a paper for the director and then waved their goodbyes to Wren and the others.

They sat together in an extra-large living room with huge, colorful art on the walls. Calming music played in the background, but it didn't seem to help DeeAnn. Shifting back and forth in her seat, DeeAnn smoothed her hair back on one side repeatedly, her eyes looking wild. She needed medical attention soon.

"…but don't worry, we'll have a full information meeting in the morning after y'all have rested and had some breakfast," said the director, drawing Wren's thoughts in for a moment. They'd eaten dinner at the FBI offices back in New Orleans. Someone had brought in some fried fish, grits, hush puppies, and coleslaw. Wren thought she had never tasted anything so delicious.

They were told they'd have physical exams the next day, since it was so late. Exhausted, Wren couldn't think about anything else. She just wanted to sleep. So much had happened in the last eighteen hours.

"…your own room," the director was explaining. Wren must've missed the first part of what she'd said. Why couldn't she focus?

DeeAnn shrieked, and Wren nearly jumped out of her skin.

The housemother and the administrator came over to DeeAnn, speaking quietly to her. She followed them into another room. Hopefully, they had some kind of remedy to help her.

The director—Wren had missed the introductions, but overheard someone use the name, Brenda—led them down a long hallway. Four open doorways were positioned on each side of the hall. Each doorway led to an alcove with two open doors, each a bedroom. The bedroom doors would be invisible from the hallway. This created privacy without having doors on the bedrooms.

How did they know?

Wren never wanted to be locked inside another space, maybe not even closed in. She never realized that before seeing the layout of the rooms.

Mei would be in the same alcove, the room next to Wren's.

Wren walked into their alcove. Inside her room, she saw a twin bed with a soft floral quilt and a set of new clothes in her size lying on top. Also, a large window, a desk and chair under the window, and a bathroom to herself. A brand-new journal with a pen lay on the desk.

Tears formed in her eyes. Fatigue pulled her body toward the bed, but she wanted to write the quotes in her new journal.

She quickly opened it and wrote:

The Haven House: A Place to Call Home.

"HOME is the story of who we are and a collection of all the things we love."

"Every life is a story, and every story contains magic."

CHAPTER TWENTY-THREE

"Breakfast is in twenty minutes," a voice floated into Wren's mind like a lilting breeze in spring, carrying loose wildflowers in its wake.

Wren opened her eyes a slit. A gentle light crept in through the window around the edges of the curtains.

Curtains? What curtains?

The comfortable bed underneath her cradled her body with soft firmness. She felt rested, as if she had slept for days. Oh no. She tried never to sleep so soundly. Anything could happen.

Wren flew upward to a seated position, her hair splaying around her.

She looked left, then right.

Where was she?

Taking in the neat little room, her own single bed, a closet, a small desk and a private bathroom—so pretty. She must be dreaming.

And she was alone. Where were the others?

Events of the previous twenty-four hours returned.

She let out a sigh. Praise God, they were safe. Moisture welled in her eyelids. They were all at The Haven House. Not the boys, but she'd been told they were taken to the same kind of place for boys—the only one in the U.S. Wren whispered her thanks to God for that one place, so Damiano and the other little boy wouldn't have to go to some detention center or jail just for being a victim.

Thank you, Lord, for this nice place.

Darkness crept into her thoughts—*unless this is a new undercover way to collect girls for the sex trade.*

Wren dropped back to her bed. A gag reflex came up from inside her gut.

"Oh God, no. Please. Please," she whispered into the room.

You're safe, little wren. The words felt fatherly and loving in her spirit. But could she ever feel safe again?

At the scent of bacon in the air, Wren's stomach growled.

What had she heard a moment ago? Twenty minutes until breakfast.

Wren put her feet on the floor and slipped into the new set of clothes she'd found on her bed the night before.

She ripped open the package that contained a new hairbrush in the bathroom and brushed her hair. The action pampered her like a spa. She glanced longingly at the shower, but her stomach spoke louder.

"Hey, Mei." She stepped out of her bedroom door at the same time Mei did. "I'm hungry and I think I smell bacon."

"Me too." Mei gave her a little smile, but Wren got the impression her mind was a million miles away.

"Hello, Mei. Hello, Wren." The house mother directed them to sit at the counter. The table was already full. "We have scrambled eggs, grits, bacon, biscuits, and cereal if you don't like the cooked food."

"I would love the cooked food." Gratitude swelled in Wren's heart and rumbled in her stomach. "Thank you so much." She wiped tears away.

"Me too," Mei said.

Someone was missing. Wren looked all around. "Didn't DeeAnn get up for breakfast?" She had to be as hungry as the rest of them.

"DeeAnn ate before she left." The house mom tapped her wooden spoon on the pot three times. "She had a rough night." She wiped her hands on her apron and then stuck one hand in front of Wren to shake, then Mei. "I don't expect you to remember my name from last night. I'm Shelly, or you can call me Mama Shell."

"Thank you, Shelly," Wren shook her hand.

"She left?" Mei asked without shaking hands.

How could DeeAnn leave? Wren remembered DeeAnn's concerns about where she'd go. She couldn't go back to Romeo even if she wanted to. He'd been arrested. Wren's heart broke for her. "Where?" She couldn't choke out any other words.

"We don't treat drug addiction here." Shelly sounded sad too. "She's going to a rehab facility—but I made sure she had a full tummy, of course." Shelly winked at Wren. "She'll come back here and begin the program at The Haven House when she gets out. Don't worry."

Wren relaxed. "I hope she gets everything she needs."

Mei slid a glance in Wren's direction. "Really?" She rolled her eyes and seemed to go back to the hiding place where she lived, someplace deep inside her. They never did hear Mei's story.

"We set an appointment for you, Wren." Shelly put an oven mitt on her hand, opened the oven door, and took a second batch of biscuits out.

"Appointment?" Wren swallowed a bite of biscuit, stacked with bacon and dipped into buttery grits. Were they sending her away too? She'd had those drugs put in her, but she wasn't an addict, was she?

"Ms. Brenda told me about it this morning. It's with an ocularist to check your prosthesis."

"Oh." Wren relaxed. "Thank you." She hadn't dreamed that she could ask for extras like that, specific to her needs. "I might need a new one." She rubbed her prosthesis around under her eyelid.

"Whatever you need, dear." The woman set her tray on a hot pad. "The Lord will find a way." She walked over to the stove and stirred the pot of grits.

Maybe Wren could learn to cook like this one day. She took another bite. Her whole body relaxed.

"What do you need, Mei?" Shelly addressed her now. "We can go shopping later if there's something we don't have here. Or if you need an appointment of some kind… whatever you need."

"I don't need anything." Mei stiffened, as if Romeo or Daddy were addressing her.

After breakfast, Director Brenda led them to a room of clothes. "Pick out anything you need," she offered. "If you need something we don't have, one of us will take you shopping."

After choosing a few outfits that fit her, Wren finally got that shower. She probably stayed under the warm running water for over twenty minutes.

The residents began the day with devotions together. Everyone reintroduced themselves. Wren met a few other girls who lived at The Haven House before they arrived. They lived on the other hall, since they were further along in their program.

For devotions, they read Ephesians 2:1-10.

> "And you were dead in the trespasses and sins in which you once walked, following the course of this world, following the prince of the power of the air, the spirit that is now at work in the sons of disobedience among whom we all once lived in the passions of our flesh, carrying out the desires of the flesh and the mind, and were by nature children of

wrath, like the rest of mankind. But God, being rich in mercy, because of the great love with which he loved us, even when we were dead in our trespasses, made us alive together with Christ—by grace you have been saved—and raised us up with him and seated us with him in the heavenly places in Christ Jesus, so that in the coming ages he might show the immeasurable riches of his grace in kindness toward us in Christ Jesus. For by grace you have been saved through faith. And this is not your own doing; it is the gift of God, not a result of works, so that no one may boast. For we are his workmanship, created in Christ Jesus for good works, which God prepared beforehand, that we should walk in them."

The woman who had just read aloud laid her Bible on her long lap. She must've been tall for a woman. She was thin, with shoulder-length black wavy hair. "I'm Rita Smith, the spiritual director here at The Haven House."

What did that mean?

She had them each introduce themselves again. Seemed like they'd be doing that for the next several days.

"There's a lot we could talk about in this passage from Ephesians, but what I want you to focus on today, and maybe for the next week, is God's love." She paused, directing her gentle gaze toward each of them. It almost broke Wren's heart when Rita looked at her. Why should that be?

Because she's showing you undeserved love, like my love, Wren felt God say in her spirit.

She glanced around at the others, but not all of them reacted the way Wren had. She could tell.

"'...because of the great love with which he loved us...' That's a line to meditate on." Miss Smith closed her Bible. "Do you know what it means to meditate?"

A girl Wren didn't know—couldn't remember her name—raised her hand. Miss Smith nodded for her to speak. "It's when you think hard about something."

"Exactly. Only it doesn't have to be hard or scary. It's just when you sit and think about it. You can also ask Jesus to help you think about it in the right way. It's kind of a secret way of communicating with him."

Wren liked that idea. She caught Mei rolling her eyes. Maybe Mei didn't know Jesus. Maybe she didn't have a background in the church, which might make this conversation confusing. Then she glanced over at Amy, who sat still and quiet. Wren wondered if fear caused her to be quiet, like before, or if it might be because she felt safe and peaceful?

"That's it. I'm not asking you to do anything else right now," Miss Smith said. "Just take some time alone to sit and think about the great love with which God loves you." She stood from her upholstered chair she'd been sitting on. "And there is a quiet closet, or prayer closet—" she motioned with air quotes "—off the activity room. We call it the Sonshine Room. You can go in there anytime it's available. Just close the door and be alone. You can talk to God in there or just think. It really doesn't matter. But it is a sacred space. That means it's special, and it's a privilege to go in there."

After devotions, they met their new teacher, Betsy Jonas, a retired high school math teacher. The woman seemed very organized and had a love for numbers.

Ms. Brenda, the director, joined them in the afternoon as Betsy explained what afternoon chores and activities they would be involved in.

By the end of the day, Wren's energy had depleted again. Her body had gotten used to being in one place, doing nothing, until they were taken out at night. It would be good to get back into a schedule, but her body would have to work up to it.

Wren glanced over at Mei as Betsy and Ms. Brenda answered questions. Mei sat stone-faced, her usual look looking even harder now, if that made any sense. She seemed uncomfortable or unhappy, almost more than she had at the motel.

Wren would say a prayer for Mei later.

———•●•———

Days passed, and Wren's body adjusted to the schedule. Life started to feel safe. She didn't have to worry, but worry crept in. She'd spoken to Momma on the phone a few times and they talked about a visit. It had been good, scary, and confusing to talk to her. Wren didn't understand any of it but planned to bring it up in her counseling sessions.

Each resident had daily meetings with a counselor. Turns out Mrs. Sherman, Wren's counselor at The Haven House, used to work in a practice in Daphne, where Wren grew up. She even knew Mr. Cho. About a year ago, she got the opportunity to work at The Haven House. She said she couldn't be happier.

"This is such a great place," Mrs. Sherman smiled. "I get to work with girls every day, not just once a month. I see them grow and flourish in a matter of months." Mrs. Sherman's face glowed as she spoke about the passion she had for her work. "You'll see, Wren. If you put in the work, you'll see God's healing flow into you."

Wren hoped so. The initial joy of being rescued and coming to The Haven House had worn off. Lately she'd been having nightmares and dark thoughts in the night hours.

You'll never be the same again. Who could love you now? If they did, it would be pity, not real love. The dark beast hovered near her, accusing and threatening in the nights. *You should just end it now.*

CHAPTER TWENTY-FOUR

Since she had already finished high school, Wren didn't have to attend GED classes during the day. Instead she was doodling with a #2 pencil on a piece of printer paper she got from the woman working the front desk. Ms. Brenda came into the house after everyone started class. "Well hello, Wren." She walked over to the table where Wren sat. "What are you working on?"

"Just doodling." She'd been shading the darkness she battled during the night when she was alone. Still, so oppressive. She planned to shade the whole page.

"Are you an artist?" Ms. Sounded thrilled with the idea.

"No, but I've always liked it." Wren's honest answer weighed on her.

"Miss Rita will be so excited to know we have someone interested in art." Ms. Brenda offered.

"Rita?"

"Yes. Rita Smith, our spiritual director, who's also the director of arts and crafts."

"Right. I forgot her first name." Wren's cheeks warmed.

"What else are you interested in? Anything you'd like to learn or study while you're here?" Ms. Brenda pulled out a chair and sat down with Wren. She leaned forward, eye focused on Wren and so attentive, Wren kind of wanted to hide. "When you're ready, you could even start some college classes."

Wren turned her head and stared through the open door of the project area into the kitchen.

Ms. Brenda waited a moment for Wren to answer. "How about art classes? We could find something… not that you need classes."

"That would be a waste of money, and y'all are already getting a new prosthesis for me." Wren looked in the kitchen again. She looked forward to every meal, not only to eat, but to experience the flavors and to watch Mama Shell mix, chop, roll and bake all those delicious things. "But, maybe cooking. I think I'd like to learn to cook like Mama Shell."

"How wonderful. She needs an apprentice. And you can also take an art class." Her smile lifted her cheeks when she got super happy. It's like Ms. Brenda lived to help the girls become what they wanted to be. Her joy seemed over the top, almost fake, but maybe Wren had been in a place with no joy for so long she'd forgotten what it looked like. She'd talk to Mrs. Sherman about that. "I'll put that on your schedule. Anything else?" Ms. Brenda asked.

Wren said nothing.

"I saw you out in the garden a few times. Do you like plants? Because we could use someone to water them and keep them healthy. Our staff is very busy."

"Uh, yes, ma'am. I'd love to, but I don't know if I can take care of all those." She did love plants, but what if she killed everything and their courtyard became dead and ugly?

"Don't worry. You're not the only one on garden duty. We'll assign you certain plants, then every so often we'll rotate so you learn about all the different varieties."

After the brief encounter with Ms. Brenda, Wren's daily routine included time to learn to cook, time to do art and time for gardening.

Wren could've said she wanted to learn something like bookkeeping that would get her closer to accounting, so she could stay up on it, but she had no desire for it, and no more energy for anything that didn't interest her. Her face warmed. Was she betraying Momma and Daddy's wishes again?

The interests she chose could be done at the house, and they were the hobbies that gave Wren pleasure—energy.

In the quiet times, she fought the negative voices.

You got yourself into this trouble.

You're a disappointment.

You might as well have stayed with your birth mother and her abusive boyfriend. Someone else could have been adopted by Bud and Aria. Someone who wouldn't ruin their lives.

You just threw their money away, since you didn't even finish one semester before you self-destructed.

And now you're learning to cook and do chores. Great, you'll be qualified to be a housewife. Too bad you'll never be able to support yourself.

Sometimes Wren heard God's loving voice too, often on the same day. But somehow the darkness spoke louder, deeper.

"I got this for you." Her counselor's voice broke into her thoughts and brought her back to the therapy room, adorned with soft-colored walls and subtle watercolor paintings, healing tones piped in through a speaker, and calming essential oils diffused into the air. Wren's anxiety relented a bit. She looked up at her counselor, who now stood.

How old was Mrs. Sherman? What was her story? Shoulder-length dishwater brown hair, she wore casual skinny jeans and a loose three-quarter-length sleeved summer shirt. The shirt was pink, never Wren's favorite, but it was soft pink, understated, not the pink that yells at you when you walk in the room. Her whole vibe spoke of calm and confidence. Nothing to show that she was trying to be cool to kids their age. She just was. And Wren was beginning to trust her.

Mrs. Sherman held out a book. Wren recognized the Book of Common Prayer. "Maybe it will help you settle into a rhythm with your Heavenly Father."

Warm moisture formed in Wren's eyes, she recognized it from church and home. "Thank you." She took the thick book with a soft red cover. It would give her a place to start, or maybe words to pray when she didn't have her own. She held it to her chest.

Maybe something in there could help her fight off the negative thoughts.

"Here," Mrs. Sherman directed Wren over to the big round table. "We could do some art. I have charcoals. Miss Smith said they're your favorite. I also have watercolors and oil crayons." She bent slightly, with one hand cupped around her mouth as if she were telling Wren a secret. "I stole them from her cabinet." She winked and Wren offered her a small smile. No way Mrs. Sherman stole anything.

"You've accomplished some amazing things with art, Wren. That's what I've heard. This may be a small selection compared to what an artist like yourself is used to."

"Oh no, ma'am." Wren touched the oil crayons lightly with her fingers. "This is incredible. And I'm not an artist. I'll never be an artist because of my disability."

Mrs. Sherman wrinkled her forehead.

"I have monocular vision—one eye—so I don't perceive depth."

"Does that mean you can't be an artist when you already are one?"

That stumped her. What could Wren say to that? Mrs. Sherman just didn't understand. She wasn't an artist.

She let Wren doodle while they talked. Soon, Wren had shared stories from her past that she didn't realize she remembered. It felt good, and Mrs. Sherman was such a good listener.

"That's it for today." Mrs. Sherman gathered the art supplies, then separated the watercolors and put them, along with a few paint brushes and charcoal pencils, into a shoebox and put the lid on it. She held it out to Wren. "You keep this in your room, then you can create whenever you want."

Wren received the box. An art box for her… to keep in her room. Mrs. Sherman couldn't know how much this meant.

"And take this too." She held out a pad of paper—the kind for drawing, but could hold the paint as well. "There's no use having those if you have nothing to draw or paint on."

"Thank you." Wren swallowed a knot in her throat. She didn't want to cry there, so she said no more.

"You're so welcome, Wren."

In their first session, Mrs. Sherman had asked Wren about her parents, if she wanted to go home to them to stay or for a visit, and if she felt safe with them.

"I miss them so much," Wren had confided. "But I'm not ready to leave The Haven House." It felt safe there, not that she felt unsafe with her parents, but the purpose of The Haven House was to keep girls like her and the others safe. She needed that big fence surrounding her like a cocoon to a not-quite-developed butterfly. And she needed her new family, Amy and Mei. Leaving them now would feel like having a limb pulled out. With Wren's permission, Mrs. Sherman promised to call them and keep them informed about her progress. She had assured Wren that she wouldn't be sent home until they all determined together that she was ready.

In her room, Wren had some time before the others finished class for the day. Soon she'd be needed in the kitchen to help prepare dinner. She put her new art supplies on the bed and sat next to them. She could start on a project. What did she want to draw?

These few quiet moments to herself seemed like treasures after the past weeks living in tight quarters with five and then four other people. Liv's face flashed in her mind.

Liv…

Oh Liv. Where was her friend? Her best friend. Was she okay? Sadness stuck in Wren's throat. She couldn't even cry.

But then tears burst through the dam, and Wren sobbed. She slid to the floor next to her bed, crying so hard it hurt, but she couldn't stop. She cried for Liv, abused and now missing, enduring who knew what. She cried for her own life, which she used to think was damaged, and now it really was. She cried for the younger children who never had a childhood and faced a future having learned it's not safe to trust anyone, especially adults.

Wren reached for the box of tissues on the small ledge next to the bed. Her face a snotty mess, she had to take the time to open the fresh box, and her fingers fumbled, while tears dripped onto the carpet and her new pants.

Finally, she wiped her face and nose. The tidal wave calmed to a hard storm, then to a rain.

The tears might subside, but as long as Liv was out there somewhere, Wren wouldn't be okay. And she would never stop searching for her.

Probably in some other state or country. Pain stabbed Wren's heart.

Poor Liv. What if Wren never found her?

Faith is the promise of things hoped for.

Wren hadn't thought of that verse like that before. What did it usually say? "Faith is the substance of things hoped for..." She never really thought about the word substance before.

God never promised you that Liv would be found, the negative thought countered.

That's true. But it was what Wren was hoping for… so, was it a promise for her to believe in or not?

She squeezed the bridge of her nose. Confusion clouded her mind and gave her a headache.

She glanced at the clock—time for kitchen duty.

———•●•———

Wren replaced her toothbrush in its holder on the wall by the mirror. She flicked the light off in the bathroom. Her stomach growled for breakfast.

In the hallway, she heard someone crying. The sound came from Mei's room, though Mei rarely expressed emotion.

Tiptoeing to her doorway, Wren stood back from the opening and knocked on the wall.

"Yes?"

"Mei, it's Wren. Can I come in?"

Sniffling and scurrying sounds came through the door.

"Yeah. Come on."

"Are you okay? Do you want to talk?"

"I'm fine." Mei's eyes were still a little puffy, but she played it off. "I—I think I have some allergies from all the weeds surrounding this place."

"It's okay to be sad about things, Mei. We've all been through a lot."

"What do you know?" She stood and ran a comb through her hair. "Let's go get some food. I'm starving."

Wren knew better than to force her. That could ruin a friendship, if that's what they had. What did she know about Mei? In all those hours spent together, even handcuffed to the same radiator, she had learned very little about her.

After breakfast, when most of the others went to class, Wren grabbed her Bible, provided by The Haven House for each girl, and the Book of Common Prayer that Mrs. Sherman had given her and went into the prayer closet. She read Luke 15. Then she read it again.

Jesus told three stories about lost things. The shepherd and the one lost sheep, the woman and the one lost coin, and the father whose youngest son took his money and left him. So, the son was lost to the father. In each story, the person who lost something was going out of their mind trying to find the thing that was so valuable to them. And in each story, when the person found what they had lost, they rejoiced, threw a party and celebrated.

You are the lost sheep I found, Wren.

The thought hit her with such force that her heart pounded and hot tears sprang to her eyes. Luckily, someone kept this closet well supplied with tissue. She grabbed a few from the closest box, wiping under her prosthesis first.

You are valuable and precious to me.

The words seeped into her like salve into an open wound. She inhaled and let the breath out slowly, pondering the truth.

She was precious to God. He sent people to go looking for her and the others.

The others? Really? The harsh tone of these thoughts hit into her. *He didn't go looking for and find everyone. God's supposed to love everyone, so why didn't he go looking for Liv and rescue her? And how can he celebrate over you? Doesn't he even care about Liv?*

Tears poured out again. Wren knew the difference between God's voice and the other, but she couldn't deny what it said. Liv was out there somewhere, alone with evil people, maybe hurting. God hadn't rescued Liv.

"Oh God… where is she?" Sobbing took over and Wren couldn't get her mind back to the good feelings she had just moments ago. She pulled three more tissues.

"Take care of Liv, Jesus. You love her, too. Please don't stop looking for her. I want to go looking for her too."

Maybe Jim would find her. He was out there still, helping girls like Wren and Liv.

"God, help Jim help Liv. In Jesus' name, Amen," she added in case that would make her prayer more acceptable.

She used most of the open box of tissues before she finally composed herself enough to leave the closet. She would come back soon and pray more for Liv.

Wren's heavy heart led her to the art supplies. She needed to draw, maybe paint something. Taking the pad of art paper and her box of supplies, she sat outside in the courtyard surrounded by trees and potted plants.

Clouds covered part of the sky, but blue peeked through here and there. The December air had turned cold again, and Wren needed a warm sweater. But the brisk feeling of the northern wind on her face lifted her spirits, that is until the dark thoughts and memories closed in on her again.

When she closed her eyes, images of Room 17 at the motel in New Orleans flashed in her mind. Then memories of the apartment and each person in there, their suffering and struggles. The darkness. The hopelessness. She'd tried to be positive, but hopelessness had gripped her every day.

Such evil existed in the world. The evil had touched her, changed her, and sometimes it threatened to consume her.

Daylight hours were better, but at night…

Each victim had been through so much, even before they were trafficked. They had tried to mask the pain on their faces, but their eyes always told their tragic story. Wren saw the pain in their eyes now.

She needed to draw them. She saw a collage of broken, hurting, gaunt faces with Liv's face right in the center. And that's what she drew, shading darkness around the images and more on the opposite side from the light. Into the background she added a few symbols of their pain: handcuffs, an empty bowl, and a syringe.

How long had she stayed outside? Drawing had helped. As she worked on their faces, shading in the bruises and tousled hair they used to ignore on each other, she prayed. And she felt the Father's heartache over their pain. When Wren drew Mei, confusion filled her. How should she pray for Mei?

Pray that my love will fill her and hold her.

So that's what Wren prayed. Then she prayed it for Liv and each of the others too.

CHAPTER TWENTY-FIVE

At lunch, Wren sat at a round table with Mei, Amy, the two little girls from their motel, and an older girl who'd been there longer.

"I'm Cindy." Her demeanor was brighter than the rest. Happier. Her mid-length layered hair hung simply and gently around her face. She had bluish eyes, maybe hazel with blue, but they were nothing special to look at, and yet they drew Wren in. Liv probably would have liked Cindy.

"So, how are y'all adjusting to The Haven House so far? I love it so much, but I remember the first few weeks were… well, heck isn't the right word."

Nods all around the table, except for Mei, who didn't engage.

"Y'all, I was suicidal," Cindy confessed. "I tried to kill myself. I won't go into detail, but those negative voices sound so true. Don't listen to them." Cindy was chatty, but she was talking real, and Wren could relate.

"How did you get through it?" Wren wanted to know.

"Jesus."

Wren already had Jesus, and she still struggled.

"I know it sounds cliché, but y'all, I never knew Jesus loved me, or that he had the power to change my life. I thought I'd always be the person my worst experience made me."

"I feel that," Amy said in her quiet voice. She'd gotten quieter again since they'd been there, new surroundings, more people and all. Though she had told Wren that she felt safe and happier. They all had a lot to work on.

"Me too," Wren admitted. "And I already knew Jesus. Is there anything we can do?"

"Talk to Jesus, tell him everything," Cindy took a sip of her sweet tea. "It helps to spend time in the Sonshine Room, being quiet with him."

"But the quiet brings back bad images and negative thoughts too." Wren's face burned. She hated to admit it.

"It was like that for me at first too, then Mrs. Sherman said to keep trying. She told me to journal the negative thoughts. That helped, but not 100 percent. However, I don't have negative thoughts nearly as often as I did back then, so I guess it's working."

Journaling… Wren nodded as she considered it.

Or drawing and painting.

Yeah. That was her outlet, and she'd already been doing it. Writing out her feelings in words wouldn't hurt either. She just had to remember that no matter what she tried, it would take time—more time than she wished.

— • ◉ • —

"Jim, I don't know what to tell you," Paul said over the phone. Back to his full load at the precinct, Paul still kept in touch with the task force. The FBI kept him up to date, and he'd be called in if there was any activity near his region. So Jim wanted to know what he knew. "The leader of the cartel has a home in Texas, but he's good at keeping his nose clean. He's got goons who take care of all the business end of the business."

"But you know where the house is, right?"

"Local FBI agents keep tabs on him."

Jim sat in his childhood bedroom again, as the damage to his apartment had been much more serious than he first realized and repairs could take up to two months. He searched the ceiling as if he'd discover some important information up there.

"Do they have surveillance of his house?"

"I'm not sure, but Jim, we can't be sure Romeo told us the truth."

Jim's gaze slipped back down the wall to his poster of Greg Maddux. Jim used to love the Atlanta Braves. "I just have a feeling. Ever since we interviewed him together." Jim paused. Should he tell Paul the rest? "The inside man who helped the victims escape tracked me down, and he—"

"Cade?"

"Yes, we've been in touch twice since the raid." Jim hoped Paul wouldn't be angry. But to be fair, Cade had contacted him through email even before the raid. "He said it made sense that his uncle sent Liv to the leader of the cartel himself. He remembered that someone up the chain of authority didn't allow his uncle to sell her services. Then they shipped her away, alone."

"Is that unusual?"

"Cade said it was. I guess Romeo told him that they sent the girls out in small groups, three to five, to other pimps in the organization across the country, sometimes to other countries."

"Uh-huh." Paul's voice trailed. Maybe he was writing this down. "Okay, it could be, but we don't have a reason to search the place. We can't very well just march in. Guys like these have power and know how to use it."

He knew Paul was right. But there had to be a way. This evil had to stop. They couldn't just leave a girl to her fate, hard or not.

What if someone out there could've helped Stacy, and they didn't because it was hard or dangerous? He glanced at the photo sitting on his dresser of him and Stacy.

"I'll check in with the Task Force and see if their guys in Texas have seen a new, young blond woman in the last couple of months. From what we understand he owns several properties including one in Washington, DC. He could be keeping her there as well, but I'll see if they can check all of his residences."

"Really?" Jim stood from the small, upholstered chair in his old room. "I could kiss you right now."

"Thank God this conversation is over the phone then." Paul laughed.

"Anything would be great, Paul. Thank you. And please get back to me when you hear."

"You know I will, Jim. Have a pleasant evening."

A bit of weight lifted from Jim's shoulders. This could be the break he'd been hoping for.

He should go down and apologize to his mom and dad. They thought he'd be free from his obsession now that they'd shut down the local operation that had taken Stacy. He thought he would too, but this thing just wouldn't let him go. And he didn't want to let it go if he could help save another life.

Still, his parents had a point. He needed some balance. He glanced back at Maddux. Maybe he'd take them to a Braves game next spring.

They need you, not the Braves, and they need you before next spring.

He'd go down and spend some quality time with them right after he made a few calls.

His idea for a fundraiser to help support The Haven House had been a hit with Mrs. Swartz, the director. He'd explained his involvement with the New Orleans case, his current writing and speaking career, and had won her over. When he told what he hoped to do as a fundraiser, she couldn't stop talking about it. He hadn't come up with the idea on his own. The Holy Spirit had dropped that thought in his mind. And if he prayed over each part, it would succeed.

Enlist others to pray too.

He'd call his church, the one he hadn't been to in months. They had a prayer chain, as well as a prayer group—mostly old ladies who knew how to pray.

What he knew about the ministry at The Haven House filled Jim with gratitude. And he felt God's pleasure each time he learned more about them. These places should be built all over the country for girls and for boys, too. And he could help make it happen.

What better way to raise money than an art exhibit and auction?

He'd call his friend, who was a curator at an art museum in Washington, DC. Maybe he would bring a few famous paintings to show at the exhibit and drum up interest.

Jim knew two artists who were making it big in the DC area, and he had a friend who could spread the word to the community of up-and-coming artists. They might give up some art for a fundraiser if it gave them some exposure.

Jim wanted to call Wren.

It was a stupid idea. Besides, she needed to rest and heal. He dialed the number for The Haven House anyway.

The woman on the phone made it clear that no one got to come to the house besides the workers. She told him that he might be able to talk on the phone with Wren if, and when, her therapist approved it. And if Wren agreed as well. The woman impressed upon him that it could take a long time.

At least now he could push that call out of his mind and focus on business.

After making three phone calls and sending about a dozen emails, he went back downstairs. Buttery, flaky goodness hung in the air. Jim inhaled.

"Jimmy, darling, you're just in time for dessert. I made cream cheese maple strudel."

His mouth watered.

"What were you doing up there so long, son?" Dad poured himself some decaf to go along with dessert. "We started to worry."

Jim picked up a dessert plate from the counter containing one square of deliciousness. "I'm okay, Dad, really." He tried to play it off, to assure them he was getting back to a more normal life. "I'm organizing a fundraiser for The Haven House the home that took those girls in. It's a great place. I wish Stacy could've gone—"

"Don't go there, son. You can't. We can't." Sounded like Dad had told himself the same thing many times. "It'll kill ya," Dad added. Jim sighed at the truth of it. He'd almost lost his life a few times in the last year.

Remembering the messed-up apartment and threatening note, he knew he'd come way too close to losing his parents as well. Now he could rest knowing those guys were in jail and couldn't hurt them.

Or could they?

What if the head guy had been the one to do the research and send the local goons to wreck Jim's apartment? What if that cartel leader knew who his parents were and where they lived?

If he didn't know, he could easily find out. And if Jim and Paul started snooping around his personal home...

There is a season for everything, Jim. A season to rest. A season to be with your parents.

He took a bite of strudel and a sip of coffee to mix with it in his mouth.

"Who's playing tonight?" Jim tried to sound lighthearted, talk about something else, anything else. He wasn't even sure what sport was being played until he thought for a minute.

"Alabama and Tennessee." Dad perked up and grabbed the remote. "It should be a good game." He clicked the TV on.

"Their records are tied." Jim had heard someone say that recently, so he lucked out.

"I didn't know you were interested in the SEC." Dad winked and lifted the footrest of his recliner. Then he turned the volume up.

Mom rolled her eyes and focused on her iPad puzzle.

Jim glanced around and smiled. This was their world, and they loved including him in it. He loved it too.

A knot formed in his throat thinking about the blessings he'd been given: loving, godly parents, a good work ethic, honor, and his sense of justice. All of Jim's good character qualities came from these two people.

The phone in his pocket buzzed against his backside. Pulling it out, Jim saw a text from Cade. Thank God Cade didn't have to go to jail. He must've spilled his guts to the police. Paul said Jim's written testimony about Cade's email went a long way too.

Cade: Sorry to bother you in the evening. Call me when you have time. Thanks.

Should he return the call? It didn't sound urgent, but…

No, he'd use discipline and wait until tomorrow. This time was for his parents.

<hr />

Wren had spent several days trying what Cindy had suggested. Mrs. Sherman agreed that more alone time with Jesus would help speed her process of inner healing.

Earlier that morning in the Sonshine Room, Wren had been praying for all her friends again, as well as for herself, of course. She didn't cry at all, an unusual occurrence in that room. Strange that she felt nothing. Maybe she was doing it wrong, or maybe her emotions were broken. But she stayed. She remembered to pray God's love over everyone.

Since she wasn't feeling anything, she stood to leave the prayer closet.

Images of her friends flashed before her face. She plopped back down onto the bench. Close-ups of faces looked back at her one at a time.

Their faces plump, like they'd just eaten three bowls of Mama Shell's stew with her homemade sourdough. They looked healthy, not only physically, but emotionally, and they were smiling. Their eyes even sparkled, so Wren knew they weren't masking their pain.

They looked young, as they truly were, rather than aged with worry.

The individual faces came together, forming a new collage in Wren's mind. Together they looked even healthier... like birds together in a nest, supporting each other, encouraging each other to be their best selves.

My love has the power to heal and set things right again.

So that was it. Their potential in God's love!

Draw this, Wren.

Wren left the Sonshine room on a mission. Her last collage showed the damage their trauma had caused. This time the faces would be full of expectation

Wren shoved the throw rug underneath her bed and laid out a large canvas, which she got from the art room. She arranged the charcoals and oil paints nearby. Like she did with the first one, she would use charcoals first, then add color with oil crayons—or maybe watercolors— sporadically.

Along with the faces she added symbols again, but this time images of their freedom: a cross, of course, symbolizing how Jesus took their suffering on himself, and a star symbolizing God's messenger—his guiding light in the muck of life.

Then, as before, she prayed for each one as she worked on their face. But this time, it was more than just a face. She imagined them involved in some activity, something that thrilled and energized them. Amy wore a stethoscope and had a dog and a cat in her lap. Surrounded by mechanical parts, Mei had a pencil on her ear and wore glasses.

Liv held a microphone to her mouth, a healthy glow shining on her face. As if her face were the sun, beaming over the others. It was like Sorchae inhabited her face.

Why?

Wren didn't understand, but God obviously wanted her to pray for Liv some more. She tossed a piece of plastic wrap over her art things. Her charcoals and paints could wait. She plopped onto her bed, then buried her face in the pillow, bowing her heart to the Lord.

"Is this your will, God?" How silly. "Of course it's your will for Liv to be free, safe and happy, doing and being what you made her to be. That's who you are," Wren adjusted her prayer. "But is this what's going to happen? Please bring her home."

She imagined Liv like a toddler on the back of her heavenly father, cheering with fists raised in the air. "Please carry this lost one home on your shoulders like a shepherd with his lamb. Will you give Liv joy and let her sing, even after all she's been through? Please let it be, Jesus. Please."

Wren lifted her head and opened her eyes. The sun had set by then, but the entire room was filled with bright light.

CHAPTER TWENTY- SIX

Wren sat up. The light didn't hurt her eye, even though it was brighter than any light she'd ever seen. Not a speck of shadow darkened that room.

The light seemed to emanate from one spot in particular—a star ball, hovering right in front of her face.

Sorchae!

It pulsed, and she felt words more than heard them.

I Am.

She slipped down to the floor beside her canvas and bowed her head to the floor. Was this really happening?

I am Love.

I love you, precious Wren Marie.

I love Liv.

Believe. The word kind of vibrated in the room, in Wren.

Suddenly, the room went dark again. Wren realized she was out of breath, like she'd been running. What was that?

A commotion out in the hall stole her attention. Someone called her name.

Wren peeked her head out into the hallway.

"Where've you been?" Amy reached out her hand and grabbed Wren's hand. "I found her," she called down the hall toward the front door.

Ms. Brenda met them in the hallway. "Your visitors are here, Wren."

She followed Ms. Brenda the rest of the way to the front entry. How had she lost so much time? "I'll take you over to the office to meet with them," Ms. Brenda explained. "We don't let anyone come here to the house. Sorry," She apologized. "But this is part of the protocol that keeps everyone safe."

Ms. Brenda drove her to the office building.

"Wren!" Momma screamed when she walked through the office door in front of Ms. Brenda. She and Daddy ran and enfolded Wren in a group hug.

She felt their desperate love and realized for the first time what they must've gone through not knowing where she was or if she'd ever come back and then continuing to be separated from her after they learned what happened.

"I'm so sorry. I thought I needed to help Liv. I thought it was the right thing to—"

"No, no," Daddy said and patted Wren's head as she still leaned into her mother. "Don't worry. You have nothing to apologize for. We love you."

"We love you so much, Wrennie." Momma loosened her grip and wiped tears from her cheeks. She held Wren's face between her hands, studying her. Wren saw the emotion in her mother's deep brown eyes—love, terror, joy, relief. Then Momma wiped the tears from Wren's cheeks.

Wren had thought seeing them for the first time might be overwhelming. She knew they must have a million questions, but Wren wasn't ready to revisit the details, especially not all at once. Momma and Daddy didn't even ask. They showered her with loving support and nothing else. Wren rattled on about the good things happening at The Haven House and they seemed genuinely happy for her.

After a good long visit, they took her and Ms. Brenda to dinner.

The diner had walls that looked like plaster peeled back to expose brick. It looked cool, not like it was falling apart. They sat at a round table toward the back. There were antiques all over the place. Wren guessed their theme was the old days.

"One administrator told us all about The Haven House before you and Mrs. Swartz arrived today," Daddy said after the server took their order.

"Mrs. Swartz?" Wren asked, then realized before she got the answer.

"That's me," Ms. Brenda winked and Wren's face warmed. She should've known Ms. Brenda's last name by now.

"They've made such a good place here." Tears filled Daddy's eyes.

"Yes, they have." Momma reached over and gently pushed the hair back behind Wren's ear. It made her feel like a child. Not patronized, but loved. "But sweetie, you don't have to stay here. You can come home. We can get a counselor, or whatever you want. Or we can—"

"Aria, it's okay." Daddy put his hand on Momma's back. She started crying.

"But, Bud, she needs her family now. We need her to—" Momma wiped her face and eyes with a tissue.

"It's okay, Momma," Wren said. "I love y'all so much. You are my family, always. That will never change, but…" How could she explain it? "I think I need to stay here for a while."

Daddy nodded and dabbed the napkin at his eyes. He swallowed and sniffed. He cleared his throat to say something else as the server came with their order of alligator nuggets.

"Home will always be my home." Wren hoped to assure them, but terror gripped her heart when she thought about leaving The Haven House nest. "I love you so much. And you'll always be my parents. I'm not sure what God wants for me next. I just know I need to heal more, and I can do that here."

The emotion on their faces nearly broke her heart. She hoped they could understand.

"We can take you to your ocularist appointment tomorrow if you want." Momma leaned forward. "We brought the records from the one back home, and we can get a hotel."

"There's no need." Daddy seemed to understand. Relief washed over Wren.

They walked out of the diner together. Wren hated to see them go, but she felt a sense of new beginnings as they drove away.

Okay God, it's just me now. Time for me to be the adult you created me to be.

Her feet moved slowly as she followed Ms. Brenda to the car. They rode back to the house in silence.

———•●•———

Wren made her way down the hallway toward her room, feeling alone in the world. Turning the corner onto her own hall, she heard noises coming from her room or nearby. Who could be in her room without permission?

Fear crept in. Were people stealing her stuff? But all the girls had basically the same stuff.

Except for the art supplies. Oh no. No, no, no. She jogged, slipped around the wall and peeked into her room.

"Miss Smith?" She said and took a step inside. The art teacher and Mei stood in her room looking down on the canvas she'd made. "What are you—"

"What is this, Wren?" Mei pointed, accusing. Why would Mei be mad about this? Wren better not show her the first one stashed in the back of her closet.

"It's a… a painting." Wren didn't understand the question. "If it offends you, or you don't want to be in it, I can paint over it."

"No, Wren," Miss Smith said. "It seemed like your light was left on. Mei and I both noticed light in your room at the same time and came in to turn off the switch."

"We flipped it on, then off, then on… back and forth, but the light never went off," Mei said. "And there was this feeling in here…"

"Then we saw the painting on the floor and couldn't resist looking," Miss Smith pointed to the canvas. "It's beautiful."

"Um, thanks."

"You are an artist, Wren," Miss Smith seemed intent on convincing her.

"I dabble."

Mei stood back, mouth still hanging open as she stared at the canvas.

"No. This is more than someone dabbling." Miss Smith seemed sure, but did she really know art? She was an art teacher, but how much did art teachers study actual artists after all?

"I have monocular vision. I can never be an artist." Wren's vision clouded, and she blinked a few times.

"Who told you that?" Miss Smith stood there, shaking her head back and forth as if already disagreeing with whoever told her.

"My fourth-grade art teacher," Wren said confidently, but even as she said it, the words sounded silly.

"Wren, I'm so sorry that happened, but that teacher didn't know what he was talking about."

"She," Wren corrected her.

"Okay, she didn't know what she was talking about."

"Thanks, Miss Smith, but I don't kn—"

"I do, and y'all can just call me Rita." She put an arm around Wren. "Did you know that Rembrandt is believed to have had monocular vision?"

"What?" Wren sucked in the word. No way. How did she never know that?

"They believe he had a cross-eye that caused him to have monocular vision."

"He's one of the most famous painters in history."

"That's right. And there's a guy now, I think his name is Justin…" Rita took out her phone and scrolled around until she found who she was looking for. She held the phone out to Wren.

"Justin Wadlington," Wren read.

"He lost his left eye in an accident when he was young, kind of like you. But he never stopped doing art. There's even a documentary about him called um…"

"Blind Eye Artist," Wren saw it on Rita's phone and offered the name before she could say it. She'd have to watch that.

"He's famous now, and very important people seek his art for their homes or projects." Rita paused until she had Wren's eyes on her. "Monocular vision should never keep you from what you want to do. You might need to adjust how you do something. Have you ever heard of E. O. Wilson?"

Wren shook her head.

"He is a very famous one-eyed biologist from right over in Mobile. As a boy, he lost one eye in a fishing accident. He wrote about nature and science and made discoveries that no one ever made before. Girl, he even won the Nobel Peace Prize twice!" She waited for Wren to say 'wow.' "Wilson said his lack in vision didn't stop him he just had to change his focus."

If this Wilson and Justin guy could do it, maybe Wren could too. People had always told her that her art was good. Even her fourth-grade teacher said she liked Wren's art, she just didn't think it could be a career. What if that teacher had

had a bad experience? What if she didn't know what she was talking about? All this time, Wren had believed her word over every other person. What if Rita had more knowledge of artists and their careers than that teacher had?

But what if she'd been right, and this was all just wishful thinking?

It would crush you to go after your dream only to see it crumble. You will have made a fool of yourself. You'd have to run to Momma and Daddy for support.

"Mei," Rita's words interrupted Wren's thoughts. "Are you okay?"

Wren looked at Mei, really looked at her, realizing she hadn't said a word. She hadn't stopped staring at the painting either. Her face looked a shade lighter than usual.

"What is it?" Wren asked and looked down at the picture, trying to see what she saw.

Mei looked up quickly and blinked, as if waking from a dream. She glanced at Rita, then Wren. "Oh, it's… um, nothing. I'll see you later." Without looking back, she rushed out.

"I don't want to push her." Rita held up her hands in the sign of surrender after Mei had gone. "Just think about it, Wren. You're great at art. I mean, you really have talent. You obviously think in pictures, and the Lord seems to speak to you in pictures. It's almost prophetic. I believe God will use this in your life…" she paused. "In some way."

Wren stood staring at her own painting, pondering Rita's words.

Go talk to Mei. Wren felt prompted.

She walked to Mei's room and knocked on the doorframe. She didn't presume to go in without an invitation.

"Mei?"

"I'm okay, Wren. Don't worry."

"Can I come in?"

Wren heard scurrying around, sniffling. "Okay. Come in."

"Are you okay?" Stupid way to start, she just said she was.

"Yeah. I mean…"

"What was it? Did I offend you with the picture? I'm so sorry if I did. I—"

"No, it's not like that." Mei wiped a tissue under her eyes. "I… well, I saw something in it."

Wren didn't respond. What could she say? She needed more information.

"Remember how Damiano saw the rolling pin in your drawing of him, and it made him react?"

Wren nodded.

"I saw something that scared me."

"What?" What in the world had she drawn that was scary? This was the picture showing their future filled with hope.

"Come on, I'll show you." Mei grabbed her forearm and led her back to her own room. Mei got down on her knees beside the canvas, so Wren did too. Then Mei pointed at her face in the picture.

"It's you."

"No, look at the glasses. In the corner."

"Oh, that's a little white spot to show the light's reflection."

"No, it's more than that. It's in the shape of a Chinese symbol."

"Really?" Wren examined the little spot. It wasn't a solid square or circle. But. Wait. The longer Wren studied it, the more she could see there was a shape to it. "Kind of like a sliver of a moon with a handle, or some kind of meat tenderizer."

"It's a hammer and sickle," Mei explained. "Not a moon, but a sickle. Can you see the tiny handle at the base of the moon shape?"

Oh yeah. A little circle on the bottom outside of the moon… or sickle. "What does it mean?"

Mei sat back, unfolded her knees from underneath her and crisscrossed them. "It's a symbol of the Chinese secret service."

"Why in the world…?"

Mei got up and looked all around the room. She looked up in the corners, under the bed, in the trash bin, and all around the bathroom.

"I always check for bugs," she said.

"Bugs? This place is spotless."

"No, not crawly bugs, small listening devices," Mei whispered as she sat back down on the other side of the canvas facing Wren. "My mom and I figured out that my dad worked for the Chinese Ministry of Security. That's like the Secret Service. I mean, we knew he worked for the government, but…" Mei lifted her knees and hugged them with her arms. "We had suspicions about him being a spy. Dad was always paranoid, checking every corner and space in every room. He didn't want me to trust strangers. He taught me to pay attention to details and people around me and report back to him. He used to quiz me on who was in a room and what they'd been wearing." Mei's eyes showed that her thoughts had drifted to another time. "One time it was winter like it is here now. Baba wanted to teach me how to stay warm in the wilderness in case I ever got stuck out there. He drove me up a mountain and dropped me off in the forest instructing me to find my way home. Then he left."

"He just left you in the wilderness in the cold?" Wren couldn't believe it. That had to constitute some kind of abuse. "Does it get cold in that area near Beijing?"

"Oh yes. It was snowing. But he'd shown me how to find shelter away from the wind by digging into the snow up against a tree, how to find small animals to eat in the snow. And he gave me a few tricks to get direction, so I'd head in the right direction."

"Wow."

"He taught me lots of tricks."

"Like picking locks?" Wren smiled.

Mei nodded. "He often excused himself in restaurants to go have a private conversation on his phone." Her eyes landed on the small shape again. "After his unexplained death, we found some files that seemed far too confidential. And my mom found a lapel pin with that symbol on it."

"Wow." What else could Wren say? But it was amazing that her shading had left that shape in the bit of white space she'd meant to show the light's reflection.

"After Dad died, they were watching our house… watching us. Everywhere we went, we felt their eyes on us. And I know what you're thinking, that we were paranoid. But we weren't."

"How can you be sure?"

"I turned thirteen a week before he died. A few months after the funeral, someone from the government came up to me after school in Beijing and asked if I wanted to be a secret agent. They knew I was good in math and science, and they said my dad used to work with them too, so I'd be following in his footsteps, and he'd be so proud of me." Mei touched the symbol in the picture lightly. The painting was dry now, so Wren didn't stop her. "I was tempted to think I could do something like that, but I had a creepy feeling the man was manipulating me. Two of my friends had already gone missing, with rumors of government involvement, so I knew they were serious. I wanted to talk it over with my mom, but the guy said it would have to remain a secret."

"Oooh." How awful, Wren thought.

"Yeah, that's what I thought. If I couldn't tell my mother, then it probably wasn't a good idea. There was probably danger involved, which I wouldn't have minded, but I didn't want to risk being killed like my father before I even got to be an adult. On the other hand, it could be just as dangerous to turn them down."

"No kidding!" Wren couldn't imagine having to make that kind of decision at thirteen

"Then Mom found something—she wouldn't tell me what—that made her believe Dad had discovered something he wasn't supposed to know, and they, our own government, killed him for it."

"Your dad worked for them, and they killed him?" How awful!

"We can't prove it, but they don't know how much we know or don't know. Maybe if I'd agreed to work for them, then they'd feel more secure, like they'd have more control over us."

"You don't think this symbol means you should work for them, do you?" Wren got nervous about her picture now.

"No, it's a reflection, like you said. I think it's seeing my past but moving forward in the direction I want to go. I always wanted to be a mechanical engineer."

"Oh, I like that." Wren smiled.

She smiled back at Wren. "But what if it's my past catching up to me while I'm trying to move forward?" Mei's expression changed. "Maybe they're here, and they're following me? Come to think of it… her eyes flew wide open. "The guy who gave me the invitation to the modeling audition wore the same lapel pin my dad had. The one with this insignia."

"That's a crazy coincidence!"

"Is it?" Mei pinned Wren with her black eyes.

"I think they want me out of the picture," Mei said. "My mom, too. What if she's in danger?" Mei's gaze was someplace far outside The Haven House building. "They could've easily kept me in line if I'd agreed to work for them. Instead, my mom arranged a way for me to leave the country and move here. I was going to send for her after I got a green card."

"Have you talked to your mother since you came here?"

"The machine picked up when I tried to call, so I called my aunt and asked her to keep trying my mom. I don't know if she reached her yet. Wren, what if they killed her? What if they were behind the death of my dad? What if they're after me?"

"Mei... I don't know. I mean... it's safe here. We're hidden here."

"Maybe. But they're prepared to protect residents from predators and traffickers, not international spies."

A chill shot through Wren's belly.

CHAPTER TWENTY-SEVEN

"Today's discussion is about creativity and spirituality," Rita announced as she sat in a chair to the side of the TV screen. All the girls had gathered in the living room for this session. Even the littles were there. Nancy sat on Char's lap in a soft, oversized chair. Mei and Amy sat on one cushy couch. Wren and Cindy sat on the other. Wren had a perfect view of the subtle floral watercolor hanging in a thick wooden frame over the other couch.

This session had been added in addition to their daily devotions

Rita had asked Wren to bring her two canvases to show the others during this time, expecting that it would be an encouragement to them. Wren just hoped it wouldn't be like showing off. Rita wanted her to speak—good thing she got her new prosthetic eye two days before. It fit perfectly and looked okay, which helped her confidence, but it didn't eliminate her nerves. The canvases stood at the side of the couch closest to Rita, but out of sight for the moment.

"Genesis chapter one tells us we are all made in God's image." Rita scanned the listeners. "This doesn't mean we look like him, but that we are like him. We think intelligently, we are relational and conversational, and like God we can create."

"Like Frankenstein?" Cindy laughed.

"No," Rita laughed with her. "We can't create people or raise the dead, but using the things God made, we can create what we imagine."

Nancy stood up on Char's lap. "What does 're-lal-shon-el' mean?" she blurted. At five years old, this had to be way over her head.

"It means we all need people in our lives. We have relationships with other people. We can talk to them about things and listen when they talk about things. And we care about them and what they say."

Nancy seemed satisfied with that answer and jumped to a seated position back on Char's lap, which had to hurt. Then she started bouncing.

Rita waved, trying to get Nancy's attention back on her. "So, we are all creative like God, but we all create in different ways. No two painters paint the same way. We each have our own gifts and talents. Even identical twins aren't the same. We are each unique. Isn't God's creation amazing?" She waited for their reactions.

"We still need to work on our creativity. Whatever it is, if we want to improve, we must work at it. We should learn about our craft, watch others, try new things, and practice, practice, practice."

"God made me," Nancy inserted, putting both her hands to her heart.

Rita nodded and smiled. "That's right. Did you talk to Mrs. Sherman about that?"

Nancy made a big show of nodding yes.

"But how many of you—beautiful, unique creations, loved by God—experience negative thoughts about yourselves or your talents?" Rita asked.

Everyone's hand went up, except for Nancy, who might not have understood the question.

"We all fight those negative words, and sometimes we lose the battle. It's easier to listen to the negative voices. It's our attempt at being better. But here's the ugly truth." She paused until she had their attention. "The negative never motivates us to get better. It discourages us and makes us want to quit."

Wren looked around. It was obvious she wasn't the only one who could relate to what Rita said.

"I'm here to say, 'Don't give up.'" Rita pleaded with them, like she wanted them to use their talents more than they did. "You can pay attention to the negative thoughts and work yourself into a depression. You can focus on the bad things you've been through and how much you've suffered, and lead yourself to the point of suicide. I've seen it. Believe me." Moisture filled her eyes. "Ask Mrs. Sherman. She's seen more than her share of tragedies. She's a great therapist, but even she can't make anyone stop focusing on the negative voices if they don't want to." Rita leaned forward. "Or you can choose to focus on the positive." Rita stood up in front of her seat. She looked like a giant, and from this angle, it felt like looking to the top of a tall, thin tree.

"It's hard to think about the positive," Amy said, then dropped her head so she could look at the floor.

"You're right, Amy. This is difficult. The negative thoughts come with no effort on our part. At those times, we must work hard to reprogram our minds to embrace the positive. We can help each other too."

"What are some positive things to remember when we feel hopeless?" Wren asked, knowing how it went when the negative thoughts took over—like a dragon breathing fire down her neck.

"Remember first that God loves you. Remind yourselves and each other of that often. Every day." Rita sat back in the chair and leaned forward on her knees again, looking at them on their level now. "Use truth from the Bible to counter the negative lies. For example, say the thought comes to you that because of your mistakes or the circumstances you've been through, you are no longer valuable to anyone. Counter that thought by repeating 2 Corinthians 5:17, which says, 'If anyone is in Christ, he or she is a new creation. The old has passed away; behold the new has come.' Write down this verse from the Bible and repeat it each time you hear the lie. Also, you can read Ephesians chapter two, repeating the important verses to yourself." Rita paused for them to write down the verse so they could look it up later.

Wren jotted it down and put a star beside it.

Rita cleared her throat. "Another good way to feed the positive is to try different creative outlets. Just let yourself make stuff." She picked up a paper swan from the coffee table. "I folded this paper into a swan. Isn't that cool?" She laughed, giddy over her art project. "I love things like this. I'll go on YouTube and learn how to do things like this. It's called origami—the art of folding paper to make objects. It took weeks of practice before I could make one." She placed the swan on the end table.

"Are there certain things you love doing? Things like dancing, acting, swimming, drawing, playing with clay, organizing a garden and growing plants, building a robot, fixing things, cooking a special dinner for friends, writing a poem or story? These are all forms of creativity, and there are so many more options.

"So, we should just remember God loves us and creative stuff, then we won't be sad and discouraged anymore?" Char pushed Nancy off her lap to have her sit beside her instead.

"Well, that's a little too simplistic," Rita said. "It doesn't happen overnight, but we keep trying, every day, because whatever you give your attention to controls your life."

"What do you mean?" Amy asked.

"If you believe the positive thoughts and ignore the negative, then the negative will become quieter, and the positive louder. You'll start to believe the positive. And when you believe it, you'll live it." Rita took a sip of water, giving Wren and the others a chance to consider what she said.

So, thinking about the positive might help her believe it, live it, and thus make it true?

"Tell me," Rita continued. "What are some things you've been interested in? Maybe you've tried them, and maybe you haven't. It doesn't matter. Now you're going to have the time to try them. If you get started and don't like something you picked, that's okay, try something else."

Rita winked at Wren and nodded her head toward the canvases. Wren stood and walked toward them. Her face warmed as she put the first painting she did in front and showed everyone.

Several people sucked in air. Mei had already seen both her paintings, so it was no surprise to her. They saw their faces, their brokenness, their bruises. Wren's heart ached thinking it might bring back the trauma.

"That reminds me of the motel in New Orleans," Char said. "I don't like it." She made a face and looked away.

"I don't blame you for not wanting to see it. It brings back bad memories," Rita confirmed Wren's fear. "But it's important to look at the bad from outside of it, rather than stuffing it down inside you. Once you're able to look at it and accept that it happened, you'll be able to let it go. You'll probably discuss this kind of thing with Mrs. Sherman in your private sessions."

"Did I look like that?" Amy asked. "So sad, bruised, with messy hair? And did my eyes look so empty?"

Rita waited and looked around the room.

"We all did, Amy," Wren assured her.

Amy nodded.

"Looking at this makes me think about how it felt," Mei said. "It makes me glad we're out of there."

"That's what art can do," Rita said. "It will make you think, or feel, sometimes both." She nodded toward Wren. "Get the next one out. But tell how you came up with it first."

Ack! Wren hated to speak in front of people. But… she took out the second canvas and placed it behind the first. "With both of these, I was praying for you guys, for all of us. I saw our faces this way, in all our brokenness and suffering. Once I saw the picture in my mind, I ran to draw it out. Later I painted over the drawing." She put the second painting in front. "This second one… well, I was praying for y'all again when I saw these images. I saw you happy and successful in the things you were good at. I think, because of The Haven House, and all the help they give us, and because of Jesus giving his life for us, we will have a good future. All of us."

"I've always loved animals." Amy smiled. "Thanks, Wren."

Wren hoped Mei wasn't still worried about the Chinese Secret Service. *Jesus, keep Mei safe from them—her mom too.*

"Mei, do you know what your job is in this picture?" Rita asked her.

"Ask the artist," Mei said with a bit of sarcasm tinging the words.

Wren shrugged, not sure of what job Mei was doing with a lab coat, some mechanical parts, and the funny glasses on her face.

"I think it's for the individual to interpret themselves, Mei," Rita explained. Wen exhaled in relief. "So, Mei, what is it?" Rita asked again.

Mei sat quietly for a moment. She'd told Wren, but that didn't mean Wren understood anything about the job.

"I always wanted to study engineering and go into robotics. I was good at math and science back in school in Beijing."

"Did you come here to study?" Rita asked.

"When things got bad in China, my mom sent me to the States to work with my aunt in a nail salon and finish school. We hoped I could save enough for University, but I barely made enough to buy my food. I lived with my aunt."

"How did you get into… you know, into all this?" Char asked her.

Mei looked uncomfortable. Wren assumed she didn't want to share. "My mom and I always felt like government agents were watching us back home." Mei shot Wren a look. Wren took it to mean she didn't want to talk about all this but she was going there anyway. "We figured out that after my dad died he had been a secret agent for the Chinese government. His job sent us to the States when I was seven, and Baba worked here until I was twelve. When we got back to China, he seemed stressed all the time. Then he was killed in an accident." She glanced away.

"The hammer and sickle," Wren whispered, remembering their previous conversation.

Mei nodded and looked up at her. "We often felt like someone was out there… watching us."

"Creepy," Cindy said.

"A woman approached me after school back in China. She said she worked for the government and they wanted to know if I'd be interested in working for the Ministry of State Security. I told her, no way. She talked to me some more, offered a lot of money, but I could never do that to my mom. After that, I got turned down for every pre-university program. It felt like I was an enemy of the state. Mom acted nervous all the time. She wanted me to have a future. Then one day she said it was time for me to leave."

"So what do you see in this picture of your future?" Rita brought it back around.

"I saw the hammer and sickle in the glasses."

"What?" Rita questioned. "Where?"

Mei pointed it out.

"Strange" was all Rita said.

"But I don't think it means I'm going to work for them." Mei shook her head. "I think maybe I see the symbol in my past. Or maybe I see agents coming after me, but I become a robotics engineer and there's nothing they can do about it."

The room erupted with cheers.

"So, how'd you get caught up in this crap?" Char asked again, referring to the trafficking.

"When I was working for my aunt, a guy always came in with his wife and waited while she had her nails done. He was kind of scary, but he minded his own business. One day, he came up to me and said I had a great sense of style. He didn't seem like the complimenting type. He even asked his wife if she thought I was pretty. His wife agreed. Then he said he knew about a modeling audition that would pay very well. He had a friend in the business, so I could tell them he sent me. I thought it would make more money quicker than the salon and I could get to university faster, so I went."

"Then you got kidnapped."

Mei nodded, then shook her head back and forth. "Baba taught me better than trusting someone like that." Then she looked up at Wren as if talking to her alone. "He was probably sent to get rid of me. And he probably thought he did. The worst part is they might still be looking for me."

CHAPTER TWENTY-EIGHT

After the meeting, Rita carried one canvas back for Wren.

"Thank you."

"Of course." Rita adjusted her hold on the canvas. "Thanks so much for sharing them and talking with the others. I know standing in front isn't your favorite, but it was helpful."

Wren hoped so.

"Listen, Wren, would you consider doing something for The Haven House?"

"What's that?" Wren flipped the light on in her room and set her canvas up against the closet door.

"James, who helped with your rescue, is holding a fundraiser for The Haven House in Washington DC. He has contacts there and believes he could get some wealthy people involved."

"James Fielding?" Wren asked.

Rita nodded and set the second canvas up against the first. "He loved what he discovered about The Haven House and wants to do a fundraiser for us. All kinds of people will come to the event he's organizing. It's going to be an art exhibit and auction, and all the proceeds will go to The Haven House."

"How cool." Wren picked up the art supplies she'd left on the floor and set them on her desk. She'd love to be at that fundraiser. She could see all the great art, and she could see Jim again.

"I'd like you to enter both of these paintings." Rita put one hand on the top edge of the two canvases. "They represent who we help and what we do here better than anything I could think of. Would you mind?"

Wren looked around the room as if the answer were in the wall paint. "Would they be sold?" She hated to give them up. They came from her pain and from her prayers.

"No." Rita's head shook so hard that Wren almost laughed. "We wouldn't allow that with yours. They would just be there to show and give an emotional sense of what we do here."

Wren's heart leaped. It could be powerful. Her art might shape people's mindsets or help The Haven House to continue to do this work. "I'd love that."

"Yay!" Rita did a little clappy thing with her hands. "Now I'm going to see if you and I can get airline tickets to go with the paintings and be at that fundraiser."

"What?" Wren's eyes flew open. Could it be possible? Her heart danced. Flying to another city to have her art featured was a dream come true. "Are you serious?"

"You'd be interested?"

"Absolutely. It's like a dream… a miracle." She actually bounced on her toes.

"Okay." Rita smiled. "I wanted to make sure you're in before I go to Brenda and the board with this. It may take some doing since you're still in the program. I'll probably have to have an official report from Mrs. Sherman on how you're doing."

"Of course, that's fine. I'll give her permission to share whatever."

When Rita left her room, Wren's emotions were in a frenzy. Excitement beat with the rhythm of her heart.

This could mean exposure for her art and for The Haven House. Important people might see it. Maybe she'd get a full scholarship for an art program… or maybe she'd become famous and wouldn't even need to go to school for art.

But what if the board didn't allow Wren to go? She was still in the program… still unstable. She wanted this so much.

You'll never get to go. They wouldn't let a basket case like you out into the world in public. What if you embarrassed them?

Rita had said for them to focus on something positive when negative thoughts came. So, what should she think about? Rita had recently given them some practical advice for this.

I love you. The words flooded her mind so quickly she hadn't had time to remember. *I created you 295niquely. You are special to me.*

God loved her.

God created her to be an artist… at least he gave her the desire for art. And he made her sort of good at it.

I created you to be an artist. Career or not, you are an artist, Wren—made in my creative image.

She would try to remember that. Grabbing her journal, she sat on the bed and wrote those words down so she could remember them when the negative accusations came again.

But should you benefit from the trauma you and others experienced?

The thought stabbed her heart. Thinking of all Rita had shared, she took a deep breath and brushed it out of her mind.

———•●•———

Later that evening, all the girls sat around the largest dining room table having dinner and talking. Mama Shell made lasagna, a vegetable salad featuring garbanzo beans and red bell peppers, and a green salad with fresh kale pieces from the garden mixed in. She offered sourdough bread to go along with it. It wasn't Nonna's lasagna, but it was delicious. Wren and the others were gaining some much-needed weight since Mama Shell started feeding them.

Wren had helped lay the slippery noodles flat for Mama Shell when she was putting it together earlier in the afternoon. She had watched what went into the meat mixture and the cheese mixture and helped stir both.

"Hey everyone," Ms. Brenda walked into the dining room, interrupting their dinner. She rarely came over in the evenings. "I have a surprise for you." She held both arms out to her left side, stepped back from the doorway to the hall, and said, "Ta da!"

In walked DeeAnn, red-faced and wide-eyed.

Quiet swept through the room for an instant.

Wren stood up and crossed the room. "DeeAnn, we're so glad you're back. You're going to love it here." Wren gave her a hug, but DeeAnn stood stiff. After some work with Mrs. Sherman, Wren understood DeeAnn's reactions better. They came from fear. And if she were in DeeAnn's place, coming in alone in front of everyone, she'd be afraid, too, especially if she'd treated people as badly as DeeAnn had. But if Jesus could forgive Wren and heal her, if he could make a way for her to do art, then Wren could forgive DeeAnn.

She'll just spit in your eye and hurt you in return for your good actions. Wren was in such a good mood that she didn't pay attention to the negative voice.

"Uh… thanks." DeeAnn relaxed a bit and gave her a half-hearted hug back. It took Wren by surprise. "Here, sit by us." Wren moved an extra chair between her and Amy.

Amy flashed a face at Wren, then switched it to nice and accommodating for DeeAnn.

"I'll bring you a plate, darlin," Mama Shell said. She'd been eating with them, but she hustled to the kitchen to get a plate and a place setting for DeeAnn.

Wren assumed DeeAnn was clean, or they wouldn't have let her leave the drug rehab. She hated to think about what DeeAnn must've gone through in rehab for so long, and all alone. Now she'd begin the hard work of getting clean in her head—the work the rest of them had been doing for the past few months.

"And I have another surprise." Ms. Brenda reached into her pocket and pulled out a letter. "It's to all of you, from Damiano and Joey." She unfolded the letter.

Wren couldn't believe this day. Could things get any better? Her heart swelled with love for Domiano, and even Joey, whom she didn't really know.

"Joey?" Nancy asked loudly from the other end of the table. She smiled and did a little dance in her chair. Joey had probably become like a brother to her and Char.

"Yes," Char assured the girl in a whisper.

Ms. Brenda began reading. "'Thank you for your letter.'" They'd sent one to Damiano and Joey a few weeks earlier. "'It was so nice to hear news from you all at The Haven House. Joey and I are learning a lot and eating a lot.'"

A laugh circled the room.

Ms. Brenda read the details they gave about their program, similar to her own, with devotions and classes, second grade for Joey. Damiano was learning to sew as a trade, which he hoped to use in theater for making the costumes. And he was looking forward to joining the local community theater in its spring or summer play.

Wren couldn't wait to write him back with her good news. He'd be happy for her.

Or maybe he'll be jealous.

Maybe she shouldn't tell him. Bragging might discourage more than encourage him.

Ms. Brenda sat at the table beside Nancy. "Bring me a plate too, Shelly. You know I can't resist your lasagna."

Mama Shell came back with two plates and forks. "That's what I love to hear." She grinned a big 'ol cheesy grin. "Wren helped me with it this time. I think she'll be the one making it next time."

Wren's face burned. Too much attention. She wondered if she could remember any of Nonna's secrets.

"Good job, Wrennie," Nancy waved Wren's way, her face smeared with sauce. Moisture immediately formed in Wren's eyes. Nancy couldn't have known how that nickname reminded her of home and her childhood when she felt safe and loved. She'd never be able to get those moments back. Wren would never be that same Wrennie again, would she?

— • ● • —

Pencil in hand, Wren sketched a little girl in a hospital bed. She drew a gauze patch over her right eye, then used the watercolors Mrs. Sherman had given her to shine down into the room from a single source of light high in the sky—Sorchae. Maybe she'd make an opening in the hospital ceiling to show the sky.

Wren and Mrs. Sherman had settled into this routine of drawing or painting together while they had their counseling sessions. Wren often drew something from her past that needed to be discussed.

"You've always had a light to guide you through the dark situations you faced." Mrs. Sherman tried to look interested in her own drawing, but Wren knew her focus was more on what Wren was drawing or saying. Talking about hard stuff came easier when the person listening wasn't just staring at Wren. She appreciated Mrs. Sherman's effort.

"Yeah. I guess that's true." Wren stared at her paper.

"It's a gift not everyone has." Mrs. Sherman shaded leaves in the tree she was drawing.

"I feel bad." Wren swallowed as she shaded the dark sky surrounding the light. "Like why were almost all the girls in here raped or molested as children before they suffered being trafficked?"

Mrs. Sherman stopped her attempt at painting. "Statistics tell us that the majority of young people who become victims of trafficking had some form of abuse in their background. Traffickers seem to pick up on their insecurities and target them."

A tear dripped down Wren's cheek. It just wasn't fair.

"Do you feel guilty that you've had less trauma? Or that you've received more blessings?"

Wren couldn't speak the words, so she just nodded.

"Why?"

"Why would God give me those blessings and not everyone else?" She paused. "Why is life so much worse for some people?"

"Do you believe God is good?"

Wren nodded.

"So why do you think a good God would give some people blessings that he didn't give other people?"

"That's what I don't understand."

"Maybe you should ask him."

"Like God would explain his reasons to me." He was God, why should he?

"Maybe not. He doesn't have to. But maybe he wants to help you understand." Mrs. Sherman put the paintbrush and colored the glass of water green. She looked at Wren. "Does anything come to your mind right away?"

Wren stopped the art project. She tried to ask the question to God in her mind. She didn't really hear words, but she got an idea. "Maybe God does give the same blessings to everyone, but they don't have the same support to recognize it."

"What do you mean by that?"

"Like Damiano didn't trust adults, or even police officers, because of what bad ones did to him. Those were the people who were supposed to have cared for him. I had good adoptive parents who protected me, so I could see good in adults and believe there could be good police officers."

"I want you to think about that until next time. Maybe you could journal or paint something about your thoughts." Mrs. Sherman put her crayons in the box and rinsed a few more paint brushes, so Wren did the same with hers. She'd leave this picture to work on it more in her next session. "And Wren, before you go, I wanted to tell you that the board approved your request to go to the fundraiser."

"They did?" Her head swiveled toward Mrs. Sherman so fast, she could've gotten a concussion. She was going to Washington, DC. She was going to have her art displayed in front of lots of important people.

You're no better than anyone else. What makes you think you're so special? This will only hurt the others, your friends, the ones you say you care about.

She didn't know whether to be elated or depressed. Maybe she was schizophrenic.

"Are you excited?"

"I am. And I'm sad that I get all this attention and I get to leave like this in the middle of the program, but the others..." Her feelings were all over the place. Tight stomach, a quickly beating heart, hopefulness, sadness, guilt...

"Wren, you were only involved in a trafficking situation for a matter of weeks, and you had a loving father and mother before that, not to mention your strong faith in Jesus—these are the blessings that have helped you to maintain hope and to heal more quickly." Mrs. Sherman put both of her hands over Wren's hands. "You will not stay here as long as the others."

Fear and sadness cinched her insides as tears filled her eyes. She wiped under the prosthesis, then underneath the good eye.

"Some of the girls won't allow me to put my hands over theirs like this. They don't trust enough yet. They still haven't found the hope that you never lost."

Another tear ran down her face.

"Your guilt won't help the others heal faster. Your love and prayers will. And maybe as they see you succeed, they'll believe they can too."

"What if I never see them again?" The last word caught in her throat.

"You can come back for visits sometimes if you keep healing and being a positive influence on them. And you can write as Damiano did. I'm sure they'll want to write to you."

"What about Liv?" This hurt more than anything. How would she ever find Liv?

"Another one for prayer." Mrs. Sherman squeezed her hand. "Sometimes there's something you can do. Sometimes there's not. Right now, there's nothing you can do to help Liv. When that changes, you'll know it."

So maybe it would change. Maybe one day she'd find Liv and bring her home.

"When you get back from your trip, we'll talk about what's next for you." Wren knew she meant after leaving The Haven House.

"I'm not ready to leave here." Tears filled her eyes. Mrs. Sherman handed her a tissue.

"You will still have things to work through, everyone does. But you'll work through them. You have supportive parents, you have your art, and you have your faith, which gives you hope. That's the most important thing." She squeezed Wren's hand again. "We'll talk about it more when you come back. You'll stay here while we discuss a plan. I'm not saying you have to leave immediately."

But leaving this safe space loomed in the not-so-distant future.

302

CHAPTER TWENTY-NINE

Wren sat next to Rita in coach on a Delta flight to Atlanta. From there, they'd get on a plane to Washington, DC, the seat of political power.

Her emotions had come and gone, but not really changed since her conversation with Mrs. Sherman. Nervous excitement to show her art—and to see Jim, if she were honest—plus sadness and regret that she alone had so many privileges the others didn't. Wren had seen the jealousy in DeeAnn's eyes as she left with her borrowed carry-on.

She'll probably hate you forever. She probably thinks you're the favorite and you're a spoiled witch.

Those thoughts rained ice on Wren's excitement. She would try to ignore that voice, at least while she was at the fundraiser exhibit. She'd have plenty of alone time in which to beat herself up.

Like now, while she was still on the plane.

Her thoughts shifted. What would she do when she left The Haven House? She needed a job or money enough to go to school. And if she went to school, what would she study?

She had no answers.

Ask me. She felt God prompting her.

Okay, Jesus. What should I do when I leave?

Nothing came to mind. Did she not hear him tell her to ask? Maybe it had just been her own voice.

She took out the magazine in the seat pocket in front of her and flipped through the super expensive shopping guide for travel wear, accessories, cars, and homes for sale in other countries. Her eye glazed over.

———•●•———

Rita opened the glass door for Wren to enter the gallery—a beautiful sight.

Large glass windows on the front side were separated by white wall space large enough for vertically shaped pieces of art.

The rest of the space was open with partial walls one could walk around and observe. The works of art hung amidst plenty of white space. With the clean, bright walls and the polished cement floor, the room looked large and open. Pipes ran along the ceiling above the walls, and bright lights hung below the pipes.

"Wren," Rita paused. "Come on in, you're blocking the doorway."

"Sorry."

Rita laughed. "It's okay. I get it. This is amazing."

Wren stepped to the side but continued to stare at all the incredible paintings and drawings. There were two long tables set up with garnet-colored tablecloths. A cashier stood behind one table with information about how to buy or donate. A sandwich board welcomed visitors to the gallery and the fundraiser. Tall, round tables stood throughout the gallery, each covered with the same rich garnet tablecloths, which hung to the ground. Brochures describing The Haven House were scattered on top of every table.

The pictures on the gallery walls ripped at Wren's heart. The art donated for auction represented different genres and subjects, some bold, some beautiful, some finely detailed.

But a number of pieces, in addition to her own, depicted faces with bruises and pain in their eyes. Fear beat its familiar drum inside Wren as she perused them. Her body tensed.

"Maybe you shouldn't stay," Miss Rita said observing her.

"But I don't want to miss it." Even as she said it, Wren's vision blurred a little from tears.

"Wait right here. I'll see if there's another room you can go to until it's time for your presentation."

Wren nodded, looked at the ground and shuffled toward the cashier's table, near the wall.

"Hey, aren't you the star of the show?" A gentle voice spoke near her. She noticed brown loafers under dark jeans, then her eye traveled up toward the face of the one who spoke.

"Jim?" Breath jumped into her lungs. Suddenly she felt lighter. "I—I mean, Mr. Fielding."

"I told you to call me Jim, remember?" He stood so close she could smell him—light cologne mixed with him… Jim.

She smiled. His brown eyes could write a novel. She saw his pain, his trustworthiness, his capacity for love. She swallowed.

"Why are you hiding in the corner? You're a featured artist in this show."

"I…" She hated to admit the reason. "I got a little —"

"Jim, there you are." Rita returned. "I was looking for you. Does the gallery have a private room we could use?"

"No… um, I'll be o—" Wren tried.

"It's okay, Wren, really." Rita probably thought she was reassuring Wren. How could she know Wren might die of embarrassment if Jim knew?

"But—" she tried again.

"Let me check. I think there's a space just back by the restrooms." He rushed off to check before Wren could protest. Luckily, he didn't know why. At least not yet.

Seconds later, Jim returned. "Yes, it's free. We'd been using it to pile the fliers and extra artwork that didn't fit. We can get that cleaned up for you in a few minutes."

"That's unnecessary, Jim," Rita said. "We just need a space to regroup." Wren appreciated her lack of detail.

"Come on." He led them down the back hallway. "Here you go. I can let you know when it's about time for the program, if you'd like."

"That would be nice. Thank you." Rita said.

Wren probably wouldn't get another chance to speak to Jim. He wouldn't want to hang out in a little room with her when all the guests were out in the gallery. Too bad she couldn't handle the displays.

If you were healed enough to move out of The Haven House, this wouldn't be a problem for you.

Maybe she should tell Mrs. Sherman she wasn't ready. Maybe she could stay longer. The Haven House had become her home, her safe place.

But what about Liv? She needed to get out so she could look for Liv.

"I brought some iced tea," Rita walked back into the room. Wren hadn't even noticed that she'd left.

"Thanks."

"Are you okay?"

"Yeah." But Wren couldn't disguise the disappointment in her voice.

"What's the matter?"

"I guess I'm not doing as well as I thought if I can't handle a few pictures in a gallery."

"These are not just any pictures, Wren. What do you expect of yourself? Some of these are very graphic, portraying things you experienced." Rita shook her head, then took a sip of her own iced tea. "I wouldn't be able to do it either. I can barely look at them, and I haven't gone through it personally."

"Really?" It wasn't just Wren being weak?

"When you go out there, keep your eyes on the people in front of you or just an empty spot on the wall. Try not to look at the images."

Wren nodded. But could she pull it off?

— • ● • —

"And lucky for us, we have the artist here tonight. Give a warm welcome to Wren Marie Summerfield." When Jim said her name like that, Wren's heart thrilled, dozens of people would see her work tonight. Suddenly, her stomach clenched.

"Go on, Wren, get up there." Rita gave her a gentle push.

Jim held out his hand to help her up the one step to the small, portable stage near where her two paintings hung side by side on a wall.

Jim handed Wren the mic. It must've weighed fifty pounds. With effort, she held it to her mouth.

"Thank you for the warm reaction to these paintings. Every face in these is of a real person. Each one is recovering from a life no one should ever have to experience." Wren glanced down. Too morbid. She should be chipper at an event like this. "Other survivors and I are making progress at The Haven House. It's a safe place for us to live, learn and grow." She accidentally glanced up, but instead of seeing other paintings, Wren thought she saw… It couldn't be. She must be dreaming—a flash of someone who looked like Liv.

Impossible.

"Now, if you don't mind, I think there are a few questions," Jim said into the mic in her hand, his close presence was not lost on her.

She nodded but hoped they wouldn't ask anything she didn't want to answer.

"I notice the faces are the same in both paintings. What do you see as the difference—what makes the before and after?" a woman in a silky red dress asked.

"In the first painting, these faces are victims. They have no hope and see nothing beyond their daily trauma, not even a way out." Did she see Liv again? She stretched her neck to one side. No. Two men stood together, blocking Wren's view of where she thought Liv had been. One Hispanic and one Asian. Were they a couple?

Jim bumped her just a little sending electrical current through her body. His nearness distracted her as much as her search for Liv in the crowd.

"Sorry. The second painting is an idea of what the future could be for these same women, survivors. Healing isn't easy, but The Haven House is showing us it's possible."

"I saw that girl," one man pointed to Liv in the painting. "Isn't she here tonight?"

"What? She, um…" Wren looked back to the space where she thought she'd seen Liv. Could it be?

The two men watched Wren. They glared at the paintings. Wren had an icky feeling when she looked at them, but she couldn't stop staring. Something about them…

She felt uncomfortable under their gaze. Fear gripped her chest.

After another question, Rita led her back to the room. But she needed to see if Liv was out there.

"Now you just stay here," Rita said.

"But I thought I saw her…"

"Who?"

"Liv. I saw blonde hair, and I thought I saw her. She had a turquoise dress."

"How could Liv possibly be here tonight?" Rita said. "Maybe your nerves caused you to see what you wanted to see."

"No." Wren shook her head. "A guest tonight recognized Liv from the painting. He said he saw her here."

"Really?" Rita's voice lifted. She seemed as surprised as Wren. "If you promise to stay in here, I'll go wander around and see if I see her. Okay?"

"I—I don't want to stay in here alone. What if those men find me?"

"I'll get Jim." A bolt ran through Wren's insides.

Good idea. It may not calm her nerves at all, but at least they'd be set on edge for a nice reason.

Jim sat across the table from her seeming as happy as a clam to sit there with her when so much needed his attention out there. Did he know why? *That she was probably paranoid.* If he didn't, he hadn't embarrassed her by asking. She felt safe with him.

"You saw someone you recognized?" he asked leaning back with one elbow over the corner of the chair back, his body posed to show distance and respect, but his eyes shone dark and warm. Interested. Or maybe she just didn't know how to read those kinds of cues.

"Liv… you know, my friend who got kidnapped with me. The one they sent away."

"That's who you saw?" His eyes grew wide. He stood.

"Please don't leave me."

He sat back down, but his gaze remained on the door. "Are you sure?"

"No. There were two men blocking her from my view. The way they stared was frightening. One Hispanic and one Asian guy. At first, I thought they were a couple, but they had anything but love in their eyes."

"Did you get a good look at them? Do you think you could point them out in a picture if you had to?"

She nodded. She'd been watching them most of the time she was on the stage.

Jim fell silent. She was keeping him from something.

"Do you have to get out and help clean up?"

He laughed. "No. There are volunteers for everything. Don't worry. And I'm not about to leave you alone in here."

She took a deep breath and released it.

He started to reach for her hand, then drew it back and her heart sank. "You know, when I was at your school, I… I mean… you asked about my family." He looked away, then his gaze returned to her.

She nodded.

"Thank you." Jim paused, shifted in his seat. "I haven't forgotten that." His gaze intensified if that were possible.

She smiled, then dropped her head and looked at her heeled sandals. Too fancy for her feet.

"Would you like to go…" his sentence trailed into the abyss. Was he nervous too? "I mean, I've been thinking that when you get out of The Haven House, maybe you can paint more to raise awareness about trafficking."

Help by using art? It sounded wonderful.

"I'm trying." Jim winked. "But I can only write, and as they say… a picture is worth a thousand words. I think we're seeing the truth of that tonight. The sales and donations are going very well."

"I'd like to do more painting and drawing, but I don't know what I'll be doing or how I'll earn money."

"Wren, your paintings are amazing. You could be an artist… I mean, you are an artist, but you could earn a lot of money from your art, for yourself as well as for Haven House."

"Well, I don't know. This show may be great, but it's for a good cause. Hard to tell what people really think… like if they'd buy my stuff if it weren't raising money for something they liked."

"Don't you see how talented you are?" His eyes rounded, and he seemed to look all the way to her spirit.

Cheeks warm, she swallowed and shrugged.

"And beautiful?"

Her eyes flew up to his. Had she heard him right?

"I'm so sorry, Wren. You've been through so much with men. I wouldn't expect you to appreciate a comment like that. I'm sorry, really." His face turned serious, so sincere. "I never want to push you into anything you don't want."

Heat flamed in her cheeks. "Thank you. You're so considerate. I appreciate that." She wasn't ready for a relationship with a man yet. No way. But when she was, he'd be the kind she'd want. Were there any others like him?

"I want to keep raising money for nonprofits like The Haven House," he said. "We'll need to be creative."

"We?" Wren asked before she had time to overthink. Had that been a slip on his part?

Jim cleared his throat. "Well, I just mean me and whoever will help me with administrative tasks and things." Did Jim think about Wren joining him in his work?

How cool would that be? She smiled.

"To be perfectly honest with you," he said. "I have thought about you joining me, traveling together to raise support for these nonprofits. I could write. You could paint and draw. But I realize this probably isn't the right time for you, and you would need to feel perfectly comfortable." He shifted in his seat. "If you're interested…" he let the offer hang in the air. "We'd travel with others as well, of course." He took a breath. "Maybe we could find a singer and someone with marketing experience to join our team."

He'd given this some thought. She couldn't believe the offer he was making—like a dream come true. But fear pounded against her chest.

Pray about it, Wren.

"I, um. It's a great idea," she started. He looked away as if disappointed already. "No. I mean it. It would be like a dream come true for me. But…"

He waited silently for her to finish, vulnerability in his eyes.

"I should pray about it."

His grin grew, defining the dimples in his cheeks.

"I bet you didn't know that Liv is a singer," she added.

"Really?" Jim paused. "And you thought you saw her here tonight?"

"Yes, Rita went to mingle and look around to see if she could see her. But a couple of scary-looking men guarded her."

"How do you know?"

"The way they watched me… I don't know. I just got an icky vibe." Wren had seen the Asian man lean toward the other one, whispering and pointing toward her paintings. "It probably wasn't Liv though." She had to be realistic. "What are the chances?"

"You're remarkable." Jim changed the subject, his eyes gentle and glassy. "Such a strong person."

"Me?" Wren gulped. He must have confused her with someone else.

"You." His voice rang deep and firm. "All you've been through…" he swallowed. "And you still have hope. Hope for yourself and hope you'll find your friend. You helped those little kids escape at the cost of your own freedom, nearly."

"Uh…" She didn't know what to say.

"You are a wren… like the bird, I mean. Did you know they can live in almost any environment?"

"Yes. How did you know?" Nonna would love this guy.

"I used to be a birdwatcher."

"You're not anymore?"

"Well, I've been way too consumed with work to think about hobbies."

"Then, our first date will be birdwatching." Did she just say that out loud?

Jim's eyes lit up, and that enormous grin spread across his face again. "Yes, ma'am." He reached over and put his hand on hers this time. It didn't even feel scary.

CHAPTER THIRTY

Orangy brown pines towered over Mama Shell and Wren as they worked to prepare one of the raised beds out in the courtyard. Spring weather would be in the air before they knew it.

"It's a little late, but better late than never to get these beds cleaned out and ready for planting." Mama Shell sat on a short stool, wearing loose jeans and a comfy floral-patterned cotton T-shirt with her gardening apron tied over the front.

Wren squatted for a while, then sat right on the ground, pulling dead leaves, roots and weeds. She dropped them in a pile behind her.

Mama Shell said they would add more dirt and cover the beds with pine straw for mulch to regulate the temperature and moisture of the "terroir."

"Terroir?" Wren giggled at her bougie word.

"Yeah, you didn't think your Mama Shell knew such words, did ya?" She winked, her round cheeks rising to her eyes. "I know me some *Français*."

They laughed together.

Wren felt a lump in her throat. She would miss Mama Shell. Though the two were different, it felt like having Nonna back in her life.

"I wish I could be here for the spring planting. Who will teach me?" Tears from just below the surface spilled over onto Wren's face.

Mama Shell stood and came over to Wren. She gave her a hug from the back and squeezed so tight.

"When you're ready to learn, you'll find someone to teach you. And if you don't, you just come back here to visit your Mama Shell."

"Really?" Wren tried to take a mental photo of Mama Shell for her memory. Average height, heavy-set, hazel eyes, and gray-blonde hair. A boisterous spirit that would fight anyone who came against her girls. She was beautiful.

Wren stood and hugged her back, holding tight. "Thank you."

"Enough of this mushy stuff. Back to work, little lady. This should've been done back in December."

Wren didn't have a set date to leave, but she felt it looming.

The door opened from the house behind them.

"Hey, Shelly. Hey, Wren," Ms. Brenda said as she stepped into the courtyard. "I got a call. Some FBI agents are coming later this morning. I need you to be ready in about an hour to meet with them."

"Why?" Could Wren be in trouble for something?

"They want to ask you about the men you noticed at the fundraiser in Washington, DC."

A jolt went through her. Fear. Anticipation. Maybe they knew something about Liv. "Sure." She banged her hands together and swept them against each other to clean off the biggest chunks of dirt.

"I'll get that pine straw laid out myself, Wren," Mama Shell assured her. "Just remember when you do it on your own, you'll need to make it about two-to-four inches deep."

"Yes, ma'am," she answered, then turned to Ms. Brenda. "I'll jump in the shower right now."

"Pick you up in an hour."

—•●•—

Wren squeezed around an oblong table in the office building with three officers—or agents—from the FBI, Ms. Brenda, and Mrs. Sherman. They called it a conference room, but it was just a small room with a table. It didn't even have a window, and Wren felt a little claustrophobic.

The officers wanted to know what she'd seen, specifically with the two men. They showed her some photos, and she picked both out, but from different photo books.

"Was Liv with either of them?" she had to ask. "I really thought I saw her near them twice. Or someone who looked like her. Then someone else at the fundraiser asked if that girl in the painting was there. They thought they'd seen her." *Please, Lord. It had to be her.* Wren needed some kind of lead.

The agents looked at each other.

"We should tell her." A woman agent with short straight hair said to the others.

"Maybe that should be up to her therapist." The agent with a dark complexion and dreamy eyes turned to Mrs. Sherman. "What do you think?"

Mrs. Sherman had added a blazer to her usual jeans. Thoughtful, never quick to speak—allowing Wren to come to her own conclusions. This time, however, she jumped in with authority. "Absolutely. Wren's progressing well. And since she's still here, if she needs to process anything that happens today, we can work through it."

Thank you, Mrs. Sherman, Wren wanted to shout.

"We believe the Hispanic man you saw is the leader of the cartel over the trafficking ring. It's likely he took Liv to live with him at one of his homes."

"Like his girlfriend," the woman agent added.

Wren couldn't believe it. She never expected them to know so much. "Will… I mean… Are you going to arrest him?"

"We have people watching him," said the third agent, a man with short blond curly hair. "They're gathering evidence for that purpose. However, he's careful and has other people do his dirty work."

"Why would they come to the fundraiser? And how'd they even know about it?" Wren had as many questions as the FBI.

"We think the cartel has been watching James Fielding, hoping he'd lead them to you and the others. He gave too much information in one of his articles."

Jim? Oh no.

"What about the other guy I saw?"

"That is an interesting connection," the woman said. "A team from the CIA had been following him. Our two teams ran into each other at the fundraiser. The two men met there, and we don't understand how they know each other or what brought them together."

"It makes us think this cartel may have business on a much larger scale," the blond guy inserted.

"Where is the Asian guy from?" Why did Wren ask that? It had nothing to do with her or Liv.

"He's from China. We think he has ties to the Chinese Ministry of State Security."

Wren sucked in. Mei… this was about her.

"Do you know anything about that agency?" the blond guy asked.

"Mei," Wren said. "She was with us and she's at The Haven House."

"What about her?" the woman asked.

"She said her dad used to work for the China State Security of…"

"China Ministry of State Security?"

"Yeah, that."

"Do you know more than that? This could explain the connection."

Something stopped her. Mei might not want this shared. "Um, maybe you should talk to Mei."

"What's her full name?"

"Yang Mei."

"And she's at The Haven House right now?"

Wren nodded.

"I'd like to talk with Mei about this before y'all speak with her." Mrs. Sherman was protective of all her cubs.

"Well, this has been helpful." Dreamy Eyes paused, then elbowed the woman in the side.

"Okay," she said, then faced Wren again. "We'd like to set up a sting and trap the cartel leader—"

"And we could rescue Liv, if she's with him when we go in." Dreamy Eyes added, hope in his expression.

"We don't know what will happen, you understand" The woman side-glanced a warning at the other agent. "But we could use your help, Wren."

The blond guy sat up straighter like he'd become more interested. "These guys know your face. They know you knew Liv, so they might expect you to come see her if you knew where she was. They might even want to get you back. They take it personally when someone escapes."

"You don't have to do this," the woman said. "It's extremely dangerous. Things can go wrong out in the field, and they do, all the time. You're safe now, and you should stay that way."

"But I could help get Liv out?" Wren glanced at Mrs. Sherman, whose face she couldn't read, but she could guess. Then she looked at the agent telling her about the opportunity.

"It's a possibility," he said.

"It's just as possible that you'd get killed or kidnapped," Ms. Brenda inserted for the first time. "We can't allow it. I can't believe you even brought it up to her." Wren had never seen Ms. Brenda mad before, but her momma tiger appeared now.

"If we were going to do this, we would surround the place with agents. We'd put a vest on her…"

"A vest? You mean, in case someone shoots at her with a gun?" Ms. Brenda would never allow Wren to do it.

"I want to do it." Wren tried to pour all her pleading into her one good eye. "Please. I told myself I'd find Liv. And if I don't do it with the FBI, I'll go looking myself. Jim and I already talked about it."

"You did what?" Mrs. Sherman questioned.

"We would work together with the CIA on this." The blond agent took a sip of water from his paper cup. There was a stack of them next to a pitcher of water—conference room accommodations. "We'd plan it out carefully. You can be sure that Wren's safety would be our priority."

"If that were true, you'd never ask her to do this." Ms. Brenda stood and started pacing. "You know good and well your priority is getting those guys with enough evidence to convict. Wren is not your priority, and neither is Liv." She sounded like she was scolding children.

Ms. Brenda and Mrs. Sherman would not allow her to decide then and there. They knew she wanted this. They also knew she could wait until she left The Haven House.

If she did this, she'd probably stay at The Haven House until the sting. Or maybe she'd be home, living with her parents again. Either way, her plans with Jim would be on hold until the FBI decided it was the right time for the sting.

She wished she could talk to Jim.

"Prayer is the most important thing. You want God's will in this, right?" Mrs. Sherman encouraged.

"Of course." But why wouldn't God want Wren to help rescue Liv?

———•●•———

Wren prayed about it in the Sonshine Room. Did God want her to help the FBI get Liv free? He must.

He wanted Liv to be free; that was his character. And Wren was a person who cared for her flock. That's the way God made her, right?

So, of course, he'd want her to help. And he'd protect her for doing the right thing.

People doing the right thing aren't always protected.

Okay, but in Wren's case…

And people who do the wrong thing for the right reasons aren't always protected either.

But she was doing the right thing. Wasn't she?

Every day that week, she knelt to pray—it helped her focus. And every day that week she got up from prayer more confused than when she went in.

Why couldn't she hear an answer from God? Why didn't he send Sorchae to reveal it to her?

But she already knew his answer. Didn't she?

When she opened the door and stepped out, she bumped into Rita, who was coming to get her.

"I'm sorry, are you hurt?"

"I'm fine." Rita rubbed her shoulder. "I was just looking for you. You have a phone call. I'm having the office transfer it over here to the front desk."

"Who is it?"

"James Fielding." Rita winked at her.

Her face warmed. "I needed to talk to him."

"And he has something to talk to you about too, I guess." Did she know something Wren didn't?

Anyway, she couldn't wait to hear his voice. They'd made an exception in approving her use of the phone.

Rita led her back to the front entrance, where the desk sat behind a glass. She opened the door for Wren to go in. "I'll be nearby if you need me."

"Thanks, Rita," Wren called back as Rita closed the door behind her.

"Hey, Wren." Jim's voice sounded like music, calming and exciting all at the same time.

"I'm so glad you called—and that they let me talk to you. I needed to talk about the timing of our tour."

"No need." He cut her off. "I already know."

"You do?"

"I know the FBI wants you to take part in a sting to get the head of the cartel."

"It will delay our tour. If you still want me to join you." Wren twisted in the desk chair as she twirled her finger in the old-fashioned phone cord. They must have installed it intentionally to keep the only phone right there at the front desk.

"Of course I do. But Wren, I don't want you to do the sting. It's too dangerous."

"But Jim… it's Liv. What if it's her way out, and I said no?" She twisted back untangling herself from the spirally cord and faced the desk.

"But you're not trained to go undercover."

"I wouldn't have to be. They know who I am, which is why they might let me in."

He sighed, as if trying to decide how to talk her out of it.

"What if it were Stacy?" Wren said. "What would you do?"

"That's not the point."

"Maybe it is."

"If you're going to do this, then I am too," he said. "They asked if I'd set up another art gallery event with you answering questions live. They think it will draw them out again."

"The FBI said the cartel knows who you are, and they keep tabs on you." Wren fiddled nervously with the cord again, pulling it straight then letting it loose to spiral again. What if something happened to Jim?

"That's why they think my fundraiser will get their attention."

"But Jim, they might try to harm you." This suddenly felt real.

"And they could kidnap or kill you." He paused. "I want to be at the gallery with you and anywhere you might have to go after that. I want to know what's happening every minute."

"I guess that's up to the FBI team." But she'd feel safer with Jim there.

"If they don't let me, you have to refuse to do the sting."

"I'm not making that promise."

CHAPTER THIRTY-ONE

Ms. Brenda and Mrs. Sherman decided it would be best for Wren to stay at The Haven House until after the sting. Designed to be well-hidden, its address wasn't even public. No one came in except the staff.

Mrs. Sherman had approved Mei to be part of the whole sting operation. She said it would be safer for Mei if the Chinese agent were caught and off the street. Afterall, she couldn't stay at The Haven House forever. One day, she'd be out, and she'd still be a target.

"I can talk about my hopes of education and becoming an engineer," Mei said about her role at the fundraiser. "It's no secret. And they already know I'm in the States, so I won't be giving anything away."

After the decision had been settled, Wren and Mei were together a lot. They'd stayed up late talking three nights in a row.

"Those who come to the fundraiser can ask questions of either of us," Wren said, "It'll give them a better understanding of The Haven House." She only hoped she'd be able to focus on answering questions while looking for Liv.

———•●•———

Rita traveled with them back to Washington, DC, just as she had with Wren before.

The gallery looked beautiful, though not decorated as it had been for the first fundraiser. This would be a more intimate night, a smaller group of people interested in knowing more about The Haven House and possibly becoming regular supporters.

The exhibit was still about trafficking. Wren had already warned Mei about the pictures on the walls. She seemed to handle it much better than Wren had.

This time Wren kept her eye on the ground as much as she could.

Jim brought them each some iced tea. Then went about setting up.

"You like him," Mei said—a statement, not a question. Wren smiled and turned away. "Okay. I get it. He's *smokin'*," Mei teased.

"Are you nervous?" Wren changed the subject.

"I'm chill."

That girl was always chill. Nothing rattled her. Wren was going out of her mind. Why did she feel like she'd be on a TV screen with everyone watching?

People trickled in, nibbled on the meat and cheese trays, took some champagne, and stood at the tables. Mei, Rita and Wren stood at one tall table near the stage, engaging anyone who came over. They got to brag about The Haven House and how much it had done for them.

When the program began, Jim explained the purpose of The Haven House. "And we have two survivors who have gleaned the benefits of The Haven House here tonight. The first is our featured artist. The second is one subject of her paintings. Wren Summerfield and Yang Mei. Let's give them a warm welcome."

The cheering support nearly overwhelmed Wren—so many people encouraging her, hoping the best for her, Mei, and the others. She felt their welcome and relaxed.

Wren gave a brief introduction to her paintings and told a short version of her story. Then the questions began.

As Jim introduced Mei, Wren thought she saw the Asian man in the crowd. She glanced that way again, but didn't want to stare.

Mei summarized her story. No details about China, its government, or her suspicion that they might've been involved in her abduction. She spoke matter-of-factly as always, but the crowd followed her every word.

Wren didn't see the Chinese man again. At the end, while people wandered around looking at the art, Jim and Wren cleared the plastic plates and forks. Mei, Rita, and the others hired to work started breaking down the stage.

"Wren." The voice came quietly, almost crying.

Wren spun around. "Liv? Oh my God, Liv, it's really you." She threw her arms around Liv. "You're alive!" She noticed Liv's face had rounded a little and her stomach pooched a little.

"Yeah," Eyes watery, Liv made a short laughing sound and placed a hand on her belly. "And I'm pregnant."

"Oh, my gosh. You're going to be a mom." How far along was she? She'd probably be twenty by the time of the birth. Wren read a kind of fear in Liv's eyes she'd never seen before, not even when they were captives together in that horrid apartment. "What is it, Liv? Are you free?"

She made a slight no movement with her head. And glanced out of the corner of her eye. "I came to say, 'Go away,'" she whispered. "This is too dangerous, and I don't want to get you into anything else."

"Why would they let you come?"

"Hey, Liv!" Mei's voice registered her surprise. "It's so great to see you. We didn't know if you were even alive."

"Hi, Mei," Liv's face blushed and her lip twitched.

"I'm Jim." Coming up from behind Wren, he put out his hand for Liv to shake. Wren felt his nearness and his need to be protective. "We met once, at my lecture at Coastal."

Liv nodded absently and shook his hand. She looked at Wren. "I'm supposed to get you and you, Mei, to come see me at the condo where we're staying in Washington, but really…" She looked to the side from the corner of her eye again. "Don't come. Don't come looking for me. They'll take you both, and you'll be worse off than before. Believe me." Liv straightened then pasted on a smile. "I'd love to have y'all come and see our Washington condo." Her voice was loud and cheerful. "It's the best." She laughed, then leaned close. "Now run and don't come, please," she whispered urgently. Then she held out a piece of paper. "Here's our address." The fake bubbliness returned. "I'm having a few friends over for tea and sandwiches Wednesday afternoon. I hope you'll still be in town." Her cheery, fake voice again.

"We want to help you, Liv. Please." Wren's voice low, she couldn't keep the tears from her eyes, though she tried to play the role Liv wanted her to.

"We'd love to come, Liv," Mei said, overloud. "We're so glad you're happy. Congrats on the baby too!" Mei made a big display of shaking Liv's hand up and down to show her excitement—great spy material. Hopefully, they bought it.

"Just call the cops," Liv whispered. "Let them take care of it."

"The cartel would have you out of that place so quick the police would never catch you," Mei whispered the obvious. "And then we won't be able to help you."

"It doesn't matter what happens to me now. I have a baby to think about. And you, I don't want you to get into something horrible…" She pinned Wren with a blue stare. "Not this time, Wren."

Wren reached for her hand, but Liv was already heading out the door.

What if she never saw her friend again? A cry choked in Wren's throat.

"They want you too?" Rita asked Mei.

"I guess if they deliver me to the Chinese agent, they'll build up a lot of goodwill with the Chinese," Mei said. "Makes sense."

"Why would they want me, though?" Wren didn't have any ties to the government. She wasn't the prettiest to look at, especially in the eyes.

"You're a loose end." Mei's frankness sent a shiver down Wren's spine. "Also, your art is gaining recognition, and they want it to stop."

They wanted her dead. A chill shivered back up.

Rita and Mei went to talk to the officers and agents who'd been undercover at the gallery event.

"I don't like this, Wren." Jim rubbed his chin, then dropped his hands at his side.

"You said that." Wren smiled. "It's noted."

He started pacing. "Noting is not enough." He stopped in front of her, his face inches from hers. "I need you with me. We're going on tour together. Like Mei said, your art will make a difference. And we… I mean, we haven't even had that date yet. Come on, Wren." His deep brown eyes pleaded.

Wren's heart wobbled. Dangers on every side, but Liv had to get free. "We will. I promise."

"That's not in your control." His nearness threw her off guard. She steeled herself.

"It's in God's," Wren reminded him. "We must trust that he'll protect me." Even as she said it, she realized she hadn't gotten a clear answer from the Lord. But she had to do this. And God loved for people to take care of each other, so she would take care of Liv.

———— • ● • ————

Wren got to call her parents from the hotel to update them. Like Jim, Momma and Daddy had opposed her decision to help the FBI, but she and Mei were both in. After all, they would both be looking over their shoulders until these guys were caught and locked up.

And there was Liv to consider. Liv and her baby needed a safe place to live and safe people to support her.

Wren's parents had been in touch with Liv's mother, as had the FBI. Momma had mentioned that she started coming to church with them.

Wren imagined Liv's mother's expression when she got Liv back.

— • ● • —

All the girls at The Haven House and at the supporting churches, as well as Wren's church back home, were praying for Wren and Mei.

They'd stayed in Washington, DC, until the day of Liv's luncheon at the condo. Wren tossed and turned in the hotel bed the night before. She got up to use the restroom and get a sip of water, then lay down again, forcing herself to be still and breathe deeply.

Sleep wouldn't come. Why? Nerves? Fear?

Probably both.

You'll be a living target out there. All your brave actions to care for your flock will come to nothing, and you'll look like the fool you are.

The dark presence slithered through the air in Wren's room.

"Jesus, please have mercy on me and Mei, and on Liv. Please keep us safe," she whispered to herself.

He never promised you safety, only tribulation. He's sending you to the slaughter.

It felt so real. A tear slid down her face and into her ear. She wiped it with a corner of the sheet.

"Jesus, Son of God, have mercy on us," she called out into the darkness. Not even the moon or a star shone through her curtains. The blackness of that night seemed never-ending.

Pray.

She tried, but no other words came to her. She couldn't even think about what to pray.

No one will hear your prayer, anyway. There's no one watching over you. No one to save you, just like no one prevented you from being taken and trafficked like a slave.

Wren swallowed hard. She wanted a tissue, but the box was across the room. Fear pinned her to the bed. She wiped her eyes with the sheet corner again.

Father God, help me. Please.

A star flickered in the sky between the edges of the curtains. She saw it clearly between clouds in the night sky.

"Look down, O Lord, from your heavenly throne, illumine this night with your celestial brightness, and from the children of light banish the deeds of darkness; through Jesus Christ our Lord. Amen." The words from the Book of Common Prayer had dropped into her spirit at once, comforting and giving her the words to pray.

———— • ◉ • ————

Liv stood on a hill with snow-topped mountains behind her. She held a baby wrapped in a knitted blanket in her arms. Her blonde hair blew toward her face, and she her eyelids gently closed.

Peaceful, Wren thought. Liv seemed happy and relaxed. Why was she in the mountains? What mountains were they? They looked too big to be Blue Ridge. Maybe she was in a different country.

But she was safe. Wren felt that clearly in her spirit.

On waking, Wren realized she'd gone to sleep, and she had dreamed about Liv. In the morning light, Wren felt confident that she and Mei were doing the right thing and that Liv and the baby were going to be okay.

What do your feelings have to do with reality? The dark thought countered.

Okay, so fearful, accusing thoughts remained, but she felt better than she had during the night.

Happy she'd packed the half-size paint pad and her charcoals, Wren sketched Liv with her baby on the mountain—a beautiful sight, even in black and white. The contrast made the wind blowing through her hair look real. Wren almost felt it on her face. She shaded the shadows into the picture, creating more depth before meeting Rita and Mei for breakfast.

———•●•———

Mei, Wren, and Rita sat together in the hotel conference room in Washington, DC, joined by half a dozen FBI agents, two CIA officers, Jim's friend, Officer Windly, and Jim, who'd somehow wormed his way into it, which made Wren smile. Mrs. Sherman and Ms. Brenda joined the meeting by video conference from The Haven House's offices. They discussed how it would play out.

Those undercover would surround the condo building, blending in as casual passersby. They couldn't surround the place with their SWAT trucks as they had in New Orleans. The FBI assumed the cartel had trained militia watching the place.

They believed the cartel was hosting this gathering intentionally to show the agents they had nothing to hide, that Liv was happy and willingly dating their leader.

"And they might want an opportunity to take you out, Wren." The same female agent warned.

"What about Mei?" Wren asked, glancing sideways at her friend.

"We're not sure what they want with you, Mei," the agent addressed Mei directly. "But with what you've told us about your father, they must think you have information they need, or that they could use you in dealing with the Chinese. Either way, you won't be safe until that Chinese agent is behind bars."

"I just want to go on record that I don't like this." Rita viciously chewed her gum and popped it between her teeth.

"Your concern is noted," one of them said.

Wren and Mei held each other's gaze, realization of the danger settling in. Without words they agreed to see this through.

CHAPTER THIRTY-TWO

Wren wore linen, flowy pants, and a blouse picked out by an FBI agent. Mei wore a tight faux-leather mini skirt and sequined blouse with a stylish, waist-length jacket. Dressed in party attire, they stood in front of a modern condo building. The daunting building covered in glass reflected the afternoon sun. Wren shaded her eye to look to the top where the penthouse and Liv would be.

She swallowed hard. The clearing of a voice sounded in the tiny microphone in her ear. She glanced at Mei, who nodded.

"We read you," Mei answered the sound.

"Now, no more talking to us. It's all undercover from here on out."

"Yes, ma'am," Wren answered for both of them.

They walked in together, with wrapped gifts for their host, a high society expectation. Wren realized she had forgotten to ask what the gifts were. What if they asked?

She'd have to play it off somehow. Father, help me think on the fly.

They stepped into the glass elevator alone and watched as the floors passed them by one at a time. When the doors opened again, Liv stood right in front of the elevator.

"Y'all made it? I'm so thrilled to see you. You can't imagine how I've missed you." Liv gave them each a kiss on the cheek. She was still a brilliant actress. Maybe even better than before.

"Are you okay, Liv?" Wren asked honestly. The agents said the men around Liv would expect Wren to be suspicious of her health and happiness.

"Yes, that's why I wanted you to come, Wren. I have to show you this fabulous place. And we have three other homes around the world. We can live in any of them any time we want." Liv flashed her fake smile.

"We brought you and your boyfriend some gifts." Mei held hers out to Liv.

"That is so thoughtful." Liv motioned to a Hispanic guy who seemed close to their age. "Can you take these? Just set them on the dining room table." He did.

The condo was huge. It took Wren a moment to find the dining table amid the huge open-concept room. The kitchen, dining room and living room faced floor-to-ceiling windows, which encased doors opening out onto a wide balcony with a spectacular view of downtown Washington, DC.

This guy did all right for himself. To say the least.

They followed Liv out onto the balcony where a man stood enjoying the view. His pressed pants and soft-looking V-neck sweater screamed wealth. "Manny, this is one of my best friends in the world, Wren. And this is Mei, another friend trapped in that terrible situation I was in until you saved me." She leaned her head against his chest.

So, that was the narrative he wanted them to believe.

He tossed his long black bangs away from his eyes and held out his hand to shake theirs. "Nice to meet you both." The man must've been close to forty. "I'm glad to hear you're both safe now. Liv talks about you all the time." The hint of an accent added to his smooth persona.

"Nice to meet you too," Mei said with ease, but Wren's voice caught in her throat.

"No need to be intimidated by the condo, Wren," Manny said. "It's just a place to live. Go on inside with Liv and get a drink."

"Thank you," Wren managed.

Inside, Wren pulled out the paper picture she'd drawn of Liv. She pressed it into Liv's hand.

Liv unrolled the small scroll and stared at the picture. "What's this?"

"It's you, Liv. It's the future. You're happy and safe. You're away—"

Liv put up her hand to stop Wren from speaking. "I told y'all not to come here. Why did you?" Liv's words were so quiet, it was more like she mouthed them. Then Liv motioned to the leafy plant on the kitchen counter and then to her ear. Manny must have the place bugged. They'd have to be careful.

"Would you like a white wine spritzer? It's so refreshing, especially when you drink it out on the balcony." She took a pitcher of lemonade and poured a glass. "I'll stick to lemonade." She blushed and rubbed her belly.

"Sounds wonderful," Mei answered.

Wren noticed people shuffling around. Also, only men had come to this party other than Mei and Wren. She glanced around, and her stomach cooled. Fear threatened to crumble her resolve.

———•●•———

Jim waited with Paul and Rita at the FBI offices, far from where the action would go down. He paced.

They watched camera feeds from around the building. Not their own, but they'd tapped into city feeds. The agents on the scene wore cameras on their clothing.

"Don't worry, Jim, these guys are professionals." Paul sounded way too cheery. "They're ready for anything."

"Anything?" Jim knew better. No one could anticipate everything.

"Well, pretty close." One look at Paul's face and Jim knew he didn't believe it himself.

"Thanks for trying."

He glanced at Rita, who sat in a wide chair biting her nails and staring out a window. Jim could tell Rita was praying. She had the right idea.

Jim excused himself to the bathroom. He just needed to get away from the cameras for a bit, maybe a few moments alone, in the presence of the One who could do something.

He laid out his concerns to the Father, who cared about Wren more than he did. "Please bring her back to me, Lord Jesus. Please protect all three girls. And please put an end to the evil these guys create every day. Amen."

Taking a deep breath, he headed back to the camera room.

"Looks like the energy on the street has gone up a notch."

Paul was right. The agents didn't look different, but they seemed more focused, like a cat still before the pounce. But what did it mean?

All at once, guys were running on the street, running into the building from every entrance.

"Rita, you'd better come over and watch this," Paul advised her.

They'd talked about what would happen, so Jim knew what was going on. They'd posted agents inside those entrances. Those would stay at their posts. Others rushed to every elevator to await any guest who exited on each floor. Still others were to take the stairwells.

The agents wore protective vests under their street clothes. Only Mei and Wren were unprotected. Jim's stomach cramped at the thought. The cartel guys would've recognized bulletproof vests immediately.

It seemed safer when they'd explained it. Now he wasn't so sure.

"Was that the sound of a gun?" Jim shouted at Paul, who stood right next to him.

"I think so," Paul looked worried.

"Oh, my Lord Jesus," Rita said, and put a hand over her eyes. Then watched again.

"I've got to get out there." Desperation blurted from Jim's mouth.

"Jim, you don't know where you're going. Stay here, or you'll ruin everything."

"Ruin? This sting might kill my girlfriend!" he yelled.

Paul smiled then. "Girlfriend, is it now? I had a feeling you were extra invested."

"Well, she's not really… I mean… ugh." His stupid mouth. "We talked about going on a date."

"Right." Paul nodded enthusiastically. "Girlfriend sounds better." He winked in Jim's direction.

Rita had a cheesy grin on her face for a moment too.

Then it dawned on Jim that Paul had used this opening to distract him and Rita from the chaos on the screens.

His attention whipped back and a rock lodged in his gut.

Noise.

Commotion.

Gunfire!

Sirens…

Jim felt sick. These cameras weren't enough. Where was Wren?

He heard radio chatter. On screen, people streamed out of the ground floor of the building. Several men were being led out in handcuffs. Agents swarmed from everywhere. Some directed crowds inside and outside of the building. They stopped traffic to allow emergency vehicles close access to the door and directed the ambulance workers into the building.

"Ambulance?"

"Remember, Jim, they planned to have an ambulance standing nearby no matter what happened. It's just a precaution."

Yes, but now it seemed the precaution had become necessary.

What was happening?

"What's going on?" Rita spoke his thought aloud.

Jim paced. Stopped. Looked at the screens one by one. Paced. Stopped. Looked again. Then he paced some more.

Paul's phone rang.

"Yes?" He paused, muttered an uh-huh, and hung up.

"What? What did they say?" Jim might have a heart attack before Paul got the words out.

"She's alive, Jim. They're all alive."

"Praise God," Rita exclaimed.

"And unharmed?" Jim asked.

"They're taking Wren to the emergency room. She was shot."

CHAPTER THIRTY-THREE

"My God!" Jim grabbed his leather jacket and swung it around his shoulders as he spoke. "But she's alive, right? She's going to be okay?"

"She's alive. I know that." Paul picked up the keys to his rental car. "Come on, I'll drive. You'd kill yourself."

"You know what hospital?"

"Yes."

Rita ran with them to the car. Rain started before they found a space in the hospital parking lot. Jim barely noticed getting wet as he all but ran to the ER doors.

"Wren Summerfield?" They asked at the emergency room desk.

"Right. FBI case." The man scrolled through something on his computer. "She's in surgery. It could be a while, and I'm not sure who has clearance to be up on the floor with her. You'll have to wait here." He pointed to the crowded waiting area. "There's a smaller room down the hall if you'd like a quieter place."

"Thank you."

They waited four hours, which seemed to Jim like four days.

A thirty-something man in green scrubs and a notebook entered, "The approval came through. You can go up to Miss Summerfield's room now," he said. "The nurses will bring her there when she wakes up from the anesthetic."

———— • ● • ————

"Wrennie?" Wren's mother's voice came to her from far away. Like she was in a cloud that muffled her words. Wren tried to answer, but nothing came out.

She tried to open her eyes but couldn't. Then, a small slit of light pierced her left eyelid.

"Wren…Princess?" Daddy's voice sounded closer.

She opened her eyes. Daddy. She smiled, then moved her head and found Momma too. Where was she?

"You got shot, Wrennie." Momma's tears spilled over her eyelids as if they'd been held there until she spoke.

"But you're okay," Daddy rushed to assure her. "You had the best surgeon in the state, maybe many states. We heard he did a great job, and you should regain full use of your arm."

Arm? Which arm? What about her hand? Where had she been shot? Could she still draw?

"It's okay, my sweet," Momma said, pushing back the hair from Wren's forehead. "You'll see. Everything will be fine."

"But… art…" her voice came out groggy.

They nodded, seeming to understand her concern.

"We know you love it, Wrennie," Daddy said. "The bullet got you in the right shoulder. But you'll get back to art soon. I promise. We'll do anything to get you the therapy you might need."

"And you can go to school for art if that's what you want," Momma quickly assured her. "We've heard so much about your art. I'm so sorry I didn't believe in you."

"Thanks, Momma," Wren said as Momma kissed her on the forehead.

"Have some ice chips." Momma got a spoonful of crushed ice from a cup and fed it to her. It felt amazing.

Someone cleared their throat at the doorway. Wren couldn't see who it was.

"I think someone would like to see you now." Daddy winked at her, and both her parents backed away, then turned and walked out the door.

As they did, she caught sight of Jim.

Her heart pounded and swelled inside her. He'd come.

Pain drew itself in the lines of his face. He said nothing, just looked at her with shiny eyes. How long would he wait to speak?

"Did you think I died?" Wren finally broke the silence.

He laughed and nodded. "Yes," he said, wiping a tear from his eye.

"What happened?" she asked. "I don't remember."

"They wouldn't let me anywhere near the sting. I'm sorry. I'm so sorry I wasn't there." Maybe she meant more to him than just a business partner.

"It's okay. What could you have done?"

"I could've—"

"And if you had tried, you might've gotten shot or even killed."

"But I needed to be there." He leaned his head down near hers. Feeling his breath on her face, her heart raced.

"Thank you," she whispered in his ear, so close to her. "How long have I been here?"

Jim stood and sniffled. "You came in yesterday and they rushed you into surgery. These FBI—or maybe it was the CIA guys—they have pull around here. They flew your parents in on their private jet."

"So, I slept last night and most of today?"

He nodded.

"Where's Liv? Is she okay? What happened to the guys who kept her? And what about Mei?"

He laughed. "Liv's fine, Wren. She's confused and scared, of course, but she's safe at The Haven House now. Mei's okay, too. No one else got injured."

"Will they allow Liv to stay with her baby and everything?"

He shrugged. "She has five or six months before she's due."

"Can we barge in now?" Momma asked from the doorway.

"Of course," she and Jim said at the same time. But Wren sort of wished she had more time alone with Jim.

"The doctor just said you can leave tomorrow if you promise to follow your instructions," Momma said. "You'll have to keep the arm still for a while, but then you can start therapy in a week."

"We have arranged a flight for the three of us back to Alabama. You'll stay at home with us now. I hope that's okay," Daddy said with hesitation.

"Of course it is." But she wanted to see Liv… and how would she see Jim? "How is Mei getting back?"

"She and Rita caught a flight back yesterday as soon as your parents got in," Jim said.

"And what about you?" Wren looked at Jim. "Where will you go?"

"I've canceled my next two lectures so I can come with you. I'll stay at a nearby hotel. We'll all head back to your home, but next week we have to drive to The Haven House office for interviews with the FBI."

"Good." She sat herself up in the bed, and Jim adjusted it so that the top came up to meet her back. "I want to see Liv, Mei and the others one more time before I move home for good."

"We know, dear." Momma stroked her forehead again. "We'll all go." She paused, gazing at Wren the whole time.

"You really are, a little wren taking care of everyone in your nest, like Nonna used to say."

Wren swallowed hard. How often Nonna's words, Nonna's faith in her, came back. "Nonna used to say that when I'm weak, then I'm strong because Jesus is strong in me."

"She was so right." Daddy squeezed her hand.

"I wish I had seen it long ago," Momma said. "Moms like to protect their little chicks, keep them from danger. But you showed me I don't need to protect you. The Lord will give you all you need when you need it. And he's given you so much strength."

Wren nodded. She knew it, now more than ever. "God sent Sorchae to guide me, Momma."

"Sorchae?" Momma looked confused. "Like from the storybook?"

"Yes, God's light fairy—his word of truth. He guided me..." she paused. "So many times he guided me." Wren glanced at Jim to see if he thought she was crazy. He looked a little confused but not like he was ready to send her to an asylum. She smiled at him.

He winked back.

Pain seared her upper arm, and she sucked in a breath.

"They need to get her some pain medicine." Jim headed for the hallway, presumably to track down a nurse.

"You need to rest, sweetie," Momma said, squeezing her other hand. "The airplane ride won't be easy for you tomorrow."

"Yes, lots of sleep, baby girl," Daddy said and kissed her forehead.

A nurse came and put something into her IV with a syringe. Wren relaxed and dozed off.

———•●•———

Wren sat on a plane, going home.

Her home.

What might that be like now? She'd been through so much. Her stomach cinched when she thought about being in her childhood bedroom and house. Would she be different? Would her parents be disappointed? What if they imagined what she went through over and over in their minds? What if they looked at her differently?

Resting on the plane turned out to be difficult. Sharp pains pierced Wren's upper right arm, which was harnessed to her body at a stiff angle. And her mind wouldn't rest.

She thought of Liv, of her parents, of Jim… that last one captured more than just her mind.

Too bad he couldn't have gotten the same flight. She'd love to rest her head on his shoulder or in his lap. She remembered the way he smiled at her, or got that worried look in his eyes when she might be in danger.

Could he be in love with her? They'd only seen each other a few times. But she'd felt drawn to him from the start, before she ever met him. And he seemed so caring and gentle when he was around her. Maybe it was just his way.

Like laundry in a rinse cycle, her thoughts of Jim came round and round again. The way his bangs hung down below his eyes on either side of his face, his dark, gentle eyes, the creases and dimples at either side of his generous smile. Most of all, his heart for the hurting. He cared so deeply.

Maybe he cared for her in a different way.

There must be some attraction…

Don't get your hopes up. They'll just get dashed to shreds.

———•●•———

Wren got settled into her room. Sleep called to her. She hadn't slept in her own bed since before… she couldn't let her mind go there, not yet. Maybe never. She refused to relive that experience.

She'd have to retrieve her things from The Haven House when they went down next week.

———•●•———

After a long nap in her bed—her own bed from before… nope, she couldn't let her mind go there—Jim arrived for dinner.

How unusual to have a guy over for dinner with your parents before they'd even gone on a date? Wren laughed to herself.

After dinner, she and Jim sat outside on the front porch swing. Momma and Daddy didn't even invite themselves to join them. Was this a setup? Did they want Wren and Jim together? Wren had never seen this side of them before.

"So did you like dinner?"

"Your mother's an excellent cook," he said with a tiny touch of tiramisu on his cheek. Wren didn't tell him, though. "I've never had anything as good as that bolognese. And then I tasted the tiramisu. My gosh. If I grew up eating like this, I'd be as wide as a cargo ship."

Wren enjoyed the easy feeling of conversation with Jim. She'd never had that kind of connection with someone other than Liv. It felt even better than that.

"Let's talk about what happens after you complete your therapy." Jim had a get-down-to-business tone. "I want you with me on tour."

"What if I can't draw?" Fear stuck in her throat.

"Even if you can't, your testimony will be powerful."

"I don't know, Jim." She glanced off into the darkening sky.

"What do you mean? Don't you want to join me?"

"Yes." She swallowed again. "I always wanted to use my art. But… I mean… what if it's too hard to talk about it… relive it?"

Jim sat quietly for a moment. "I'm sorry, Wren, I wasn't thinking. I never want you to experience that trauma again."

"I know. Your heart has always been to help victims and to keep others from becoming victims. And I see how my story might help, so—"

"No," he interrupted. "I was wrong. You can't go through that again. It's time for me to stop this." He took a deep breath. "My parents have been saying it for over a year now. This is insanity. I've been obsessed, and it's not healthy for me. And it's definitely not healthy for you."

"I'm not saying you should stop your crusade. It's a good thing, Jim. I just don't know if I can be there by your side."

"If you don't go, I don't go. I want to be with you."

"What are you saying?" She smiled. "Why should I keep you from your work?"

Now it was his turn to look off into the dark sky. "You don't even know, do you, Wren?" He looked back. "I care for you… so much."

She sucked in a breath.

"I know. It's crazy, but I've thought about you since I first met you and Liv. When you asked about my family. Since that moment, I haven't been able to get you out of my thoughts."

Was she dreaming?

"Then when I read the article about you and Liv being kidnapped, I knew there was nothing I could do to stop it. My heart broke, knowing what you were going to experience. I couldn't stand it. I didn't even know you and I was dying inside." He paused. "I'm sorry. That's too much to put on you right now. Forget I said anything… Please." He looked so pitiful.

A brief laugh escaped.

"Don't laugh at me." He flicked her arm, a smile in his eyes.

"I'm not laughing at you. It's just… well, I might feel the same way. I know we have to get to know each other better, but—"

He leaned over and kissed her, his lips gently touching her cheek, resting there for a moment. She hesitated, wondering if she'd associate it with her experience, but she felt safe, as if swaddled in a weighted blanket.

"Was… Was that okay?" Hope and fear mingled in his eyes.

"Yes." She smiled, gazing into those deep pools of brown, then at the dimples that formed when he smiled.

Looking back at her, vulnerability in his face, Jim swept a stray hair from her forehead, then kissed where his finer hand touched her head. "You are so beautiful."

He didn't seem to notice her odd eyeball or the fact that light freckles scattered her face.

They sat for a long time in comfortable silence together. She enjoyed the feeling, but how long could it last? How could they work out the logistics?

CHAPTER THIRTY-FOUR

Jim used the Summerfields' Suburban to drive Wren and her parents down to The Haven House offices in a town near Montgomery. He'd offered to rent one, but they wouldn't hear of it. They didn't argue over his offer to drive, though. It would take about three hours to get there.

The sun moved from the horizon up into the clouds and began its display of color as they got onto Highway 65. Quiet reigned in the car as he shook off sleep and enjoyed the beautiful view.

The FBI had arranged their hotel rooms and paid for them. That seemed like the least they could do after all Wren had been through.

Wren sat in the front with Jim, the conversation sparse. Later, she'd switch with her dad and sit in the back with her mother. Jim just wanted her to be comfortable. She would begin therapy on her arm the day after they got back to Daphne.

May she recover quickly and completely, he prayed often. Not drawing had already rattled Wren. She needed that outlet. It seemed to help her process the stresses of life, and she had endured plenty.

On the drive, they listened to a couple of podcasts, then a digital recording that Wren had of Liv singing. She had a beautiful voice.

Arriving at the hotel, they unloaded the car and checked in. Haven House director, Brenda Swartz, picked Wren up an hour later and took her over to the home. Jim and Wren's folks couldn't go or even see where it was. Understandable. And Wren needed to visit the other girls and gather her belongings.

As they watched Mrs. Swartz's car pull away, Mr. Summerfield clapped a large hand around Jim's shoulders. "So, tell me more about yourself, son."

This could be a long morning.

— • ● • —

Strange to be back, but not living at The Haven House. Wren had missed it. She missed the girls. They'd gone through so much together. At the same time, she no longer belonged. In some ways, they treated her like a guest, which she was, technically.

Where did she belong now?

She looked for Liv and found her out in the courtyard. "Liv!" She rushed up behind the back of her chair and wrapped an arm around her friend from behind.

Liv jumped, then turned. "Wren?" She had a frightened, distant look in her eyes. Was she really there? Did she feel the same about Wren as she had before? Were they still friends?

"I'm so glad you're safe and here at The Haven House. Do you like it?"

Liv shrugged. Her eyes slanted a gaze out into the trees beyond the boundary of The Haven House.

"Liv?"

"I don't know what to think, Wren. You weren't there. No one was there. Manny treated me well… at least, most of the time." Wren noticed the remains of a bruise on the top of her cheekbone. "The baby is his, you know?"

Wren nodded, moisture forming in her eyes.

"My baby's father is in prison." The pain in Liv's eyes broke Wren's heart. "He might never get out. The baby might never know his father." A single tear dripped down her face.

"I'm sorry, Liv. I'm so…"

"Are you?" Was Liv mad at her?

"Liv, he was bad. He hurt you and a lot of people. He would've hurt the baby one day—"

"No! He would never hurt his own child."

"Really? I—"

"Just stop. You don't know him."

"Would you want to be back in that situation with him right now?" Wren couldn't believe this whole conversation.

Don't push her, my child. She needs time.

Wren took a deep breath.

Liv shrugged, but her eyes told Wren that deep down she understood there wasn't a better way.

But how long would it take for her to admit that? How long before she and Liv would be best friends again? She wanted to catch up, tell each other everything that had happened since they took Liv from her. She wanted to tell her about her budding relationship with Jim, but all that would have to wait, possibly for a very long time.

"Maybe you should go get your things together," Liv said after a long moment of awkward silence. "I'll see you before you leave."

Wren walked back to her old room, then allowed herself to cry it out into the mattress.

"Knock. Knock." Mei's voice came through the door. "Can I come in?"

"Sure." Wren sat up on her bed and blew her nose.

"You talked to Liv?" Mei seemed to know exactly what had upset Wren. She nodded.

"Yeah. She's going through a lot, plus hormones, you know." Wren never knew Mei to be so sensitive. But she was right. "How are you? I hated that Rita made us leave before your surgery was over."

"It's okay, Mei. I'll recover, I think." Wren touched her right arm. "I start therapy when we get back. They say I should get full use back, but no one is saying how long it might take."

"It must be tough for you, not drawing."

"It is." Wren felt seen. Mei surprised her. She'd always been observant but never talkative. She was almost chatty today. "How are things around here?"

"They're good. We got a new girl two days ago. I don't really know her yet. And DeeAnn is becoming an actual person."

Wren laughed. "That's progress. Where is she? I'd love to say Hi."

"I'll make sure you see her before you leave." Mei paused. "I saw him."

"You saw him? Who?"

"Sorchae."

"You saw Sorchae?" Wren couldn't believe her ears. She'd never met anyone who'd seen him—the light fairy— like she had. She often wondered if the author of *Mona and the Selkie* had or if it had just been a story to her. Her description was so close to what Wren had seen, even as a child, years before she'd read the book.

She wanted to believe it had been real, but sometimes her rational brain told her it was just her imagination or dreams after reading Samantha O'Connor's description. "What did he look like?"

"Well, I was worrying about you and about the Chinese government coming after me again, which made me worry about my mother, who's still over there. It felt like all the worries were strangling me."

"When was this?"

"The night after we got back from Washington. The night of your surgery."

Wren nodded, following her timeline.

"I seriously had the feeling that I might suffocate, like something was choking me. The room sort of went dark, as if I was blacking out. I tried to scream, but no sound came out of my mouth." Mei had both hands around her neck as if she were strangling herself as she recalled what happened. Wren could feel the fear Mei must've felt. She knew the feeling too well.

"Then I saw a small light in the middle of the haze. I thought I was dying… you know, 'Go toward the light,' they say."

They both kind of laughed, breaking the intensity of the story.

"The light was like a ball of fire, burning brighter and brighter from within itself. Like a—"

"A sun?"

"Yes." Mei's eyes lit with recognition. "It came toward me, growing bigger and brighter. I didn't feel afraid, and it never burned me."

Wren nodded, remembering.

"It seemed to stop and hover right over the picture of my mother on my desk."

"I didn't know you had a picture here."

"My aunt sent it after she found out where I was." Mei brushed her hair back over her ear, and Wren noticed that she'd gotten a haircut. Her style had grown a little shaggy over the weeks they spent in New Orleans. "Sorchae said nothing, but in the bright light I saw my mother working with my aunt in her nail salon. She was safe, and she was here, in the United States." Mei had tears in her eyes. One escaped, and she pushed it away.

"That's amazing, Mei."

"I don't know how it can be true. Do you think it could really happen?"

"I know it. If the Lord—"

"The Lord?" Mei looked confused. "Is this a religious thing to you?"

"Well, yeah. I mean…" How could Wren explain it? "I see Sorchae as God's words, or his comforting presence, and his direction. Like the light fairy represents God's presence in our situations."

"Oh," Mei sounded a little annoyed, or just skeptical. "But you think my mom will come to this country?"

"I don't know for sure, Mei. But I think so."

"I wish you could draw me a picture to keep that hope alive."

"Maybe I will."

"The girls are waiting for you, Wren," Mama Shell said from the hallway. "And dinner is almost ready."

"Okay," Wren called back. She'd better get her stuff together. After dinner, she had to get back to the hotel.

"I'll help you." Mei started putting all of Wren's belongings on the bed.

"Let me help." Amy popped inside the room. Wren hurried to her and they embraced in a tight hug.

"It's good to see you." Wren would've been crushed had she missed seeing Amy. Her bright spirit gave Wren hope, hope that Amy was healing and hope for Liv's healing in the future.

— • ● • —

The next morning, Wren, Jim, and her parents met Rita and Mei at a local diner for breakfast. Wren ordered eggs, grits, bacon, and biscuits—southern comfort food to ease her into a stressful day ahead. After breakfast, Momma and Daddy went back to the hotel since they couldn't be in the meetings. Jim and Wren rode with Rita and Mei to the offices.

Wren sat beside Mei in the back of the car. She had an unsettled feeling. Something like danger. But why? They were just going to answer questions. Looking at Mei, Wren thought she might have the same feeling. She glanced out of the car.

A car followed close behind them.

Naw. She'd seen too many movies.

But she could've sworn she saw that car on the highway yesterday when they drove up from Daphne. Weird.

"Um, y'all… is someone following us?" Better to say something and let everyone think she was crazy, just in case.

"No, I'm sure it's nothing, Wren." Rita glanced in the rearview mirror. "I'll just drive around another way. I know how to wind through the country roads around here."

"Thanks. Sorry if I'm just paranoid."

"You have every reason to be," Jim said, looking back at her over the front seat of Rita's old Ford.

She mouthed a thank you to him as Mei looked out the back.

"He's following us every place you turn," Mei said. Then she got up on her knees for a better look. "And he's Chinese," she shouted and slumped to the floor.

"Are you kidding me?" Rita screamed.

"Just stay calm, Rita," Jim suggested with a firm tone. "You'll be fine. They don't know we're onto them yet." He picked up his cell. "I'm going to call Detective Windly." He punched some numbers into his phone. "Paul, this is Jim. We're taking the scenic route. It seems there's a Chinese man following us. He's been following us since…" He looked at Wren.

"Since the diner, I think," Wren said. "And I think I saw the same car on the drive from Daphne."

"Since the diner. And Wren thinks she recognizes the car from our drive up yesterday." He paused while Paul talked. "Well, Rita's taken us all over creation on backcountry roads and he's still there," Jim said uh-huh twice, then clicked off.

"What did he say?" Rita's voice shook.

"He said to drive to the offices. They have enough backup there to take the guy down. Drive us right to the front door. We'll all get out and run inside while they surround his car with theirs. He won't have a chance."

"Are you sure?" Rita's voice wobbled again. Wren's heart did the same.

"Stay down, Mei," Wren said. "He's after you."

"He's after all of us if we saw him at the fundraiser. We're all loose ends," Jim pointed out.

"That's not reassuring, Jim," Rita said.

"It'll be okay, though, trust me." Confidence saturated his voice. "I know Paul, the detective. And I've seen these guys in action."

"Here goes nothing." Rita squealed into the parking lot with the car behind them squealing on their tail, pretense out the window.

"On the count of three. Open the doors and run," Jim ordered. "One. Two. Three."

Chapter Thirty-Five

When Jim yelled, "three," Wren ran. Ms. Brenda and Paul held the office doors open. They made it inside as gunshots sounded. One shot hit the glass door right behind Wren.

The agents inside showed them into the windowless conference room. Wren glanced around to be sure everyone had made it.

Pain seared her arm. She must've bumped it on the way in, but everyone was accounted for.

CIA officers took the guy out with little effort. He obviously hadn't expected to run into the CIA or FBI on this trip.

Thankfully, something had made Wren notice that car on the highway as they drove the day before. A reflection of light had caught her attention, and she had simply noticed the car.

The rest of the day went as planned. The other agents brought in a picture of the man they just cuffed. He was the same one she'd seen at the fundraiser with the cartel guy.

"He's the man who told me about the modeling audition and even drove me there," Mei said. "He must be with the Chinese government."

"He is, Mei," the CIA officer said. "We've been after him for a long time. This is the breakthrough we needed." The guy smiled and winked at Mei. "And he started talking as soon as we offered not to send him back to China, where they'd kill him for sure."

"You mean I'm safe now?" Mei asked.

"As far as we know, he was the only undercover agent assigned to your case."

"What about my mother?" Fear filled Mei's eyes. "She's a sitting duck now. They'll come after her. They'll arrest her and kill her."

"We'll get her and bring her here, Mei. She'll have asylum."

"She can stay here forever, with me?"

"She sure can."

The rest of the day, they gave eyewitness accounts of everything they'd seen while in Washington DC.

———— • ● • ————

Eight weeks later

Wren had never been to The Hope Farm restaurant in Fairhope. The heels she borrowed from Momma clacked on the rich wood flooring. Wren admired the crisp white walls and round chandeliers. She wore a cream-colored dress, lace over a built-in slip with lacy straps over the shoulders. Jim took the sage-colored sweater from her hand and draped it over the back of a chair. He pulled the chair out for her like the gentleman he was. She'd need to put the sweater back on soon. By mid-June, restaurants blasted the air-conditioning.

How did the cream-colored dress reflect the coloring of her face? Hopefully, Jim would find it attractive in this light. The whole ensemble made her feel pretty without feeling exposed. Still, her stomach jiggled with nervous energy.

Thank goodness she'd been able to lose the sling before he returned from his travels. She still had physical therapy twice a month, but she'd made progress—so much healing in just weeks' time. Twelve weeks since she'd been shot, and the cartel members had been arrested, and eight weeks since the Chinese agent had been arrested. Wren had had to practically force Jim, but Jim had resumed his previously scheduled speaking engagements.

For the 4th of July weekend, she and Jim planned to drive up to Opelika and spend it with his mom and dad. Momma and Daddy encouraged them to go.

They were seated at a round table so they could both face the windows. The sun's descent poured light into the spacious restaurant. The colors of the sky changed from orange to red and pink, then purple streaks as the sun set— an incredible display of color by the original Artist.

Everything was perfect. Could this be a dream, or were she and Jim finally on their first date? They'd been talking on the phone every night for hours while he'd been traveling. During their long conversations, Wren and Jim had talked about their future together. Now, finally, they were able to sit down at the same table and eat a meal together.

Wren ordered ravioli, and Jim chose the Gulf catch. They held hands, watching the sunset as they waited for their food to arrive.

"Your arm is so much better. I know you've been drawing some. How's that going?"

"I feel like my confidence is coming back." She smiled, squeezed her hand into a fist then released to show her strength.

"That's fantastic!"

She glanced around to see if others in the restaurant had reacted to his outburst. No one seemed to notice.

"I can't wait to see your recent work." He smiled, then his face turned somber. "Have you heard from Liv or any of the others this week?" He seemed to understand what those girls meant to her.

"I talked to Liv for a few minutes the other day. I wish she could stay at The Haven House longer. She's finally settling in and being open to what they have to offer."

"Yeah." He took a sip of water. "When's the baby due?"

"Less than two months. Too bad they don't have the facilities to care for an infant."

"At least she'll be with a supportive family, and you'll be able to visit her often."

"Her mother and I are very excited." Wren smiled imagining what Liv's baby might look like.

The server brought out their plates. How did the woman hold them both on one arm?

The scent of ravioli made Wren's mouth water.

"Can I get you anything else right now?" she asked them.

"Some Parmesan?" Wren said.

"Of course." The server shredded a hunk of real Parmesan onto Wren's pasta. Still nineteen for a few more weeks, Wren ordered a mineral water, and Jim had a glass of wine.

She'd never felt so grown up.

"It'll be great for Liv to have you close by, too." Jim got quiet, his deep brown eyes far away.

"What are you thinking about?" she asked between bites.

"Do you still want to go on tour? Maybe you'd rather stay here so you can help Liv." He took her hand in his.

"I want to go, Jim. I think we should. There are so many who need to hear. I think the art and fundraisers will raise awareness so The Haven House can help more survivors."

"Really?" His wide smile lit up the restaurant. "I don't want to put you through any trauma—"

"I've had as much mental therapy as I've had physical therapy. Also, I've been meeting with a pastor at our church for spiritual direction, and I feel strong. The tour of fundraisers will give me a chance to use art to make a difference. And if there's a time when I don't feel like talking about the trauma, I trust you to allow me that freedom."

"That's not a problem at all," he said with complete assurance. "Then we can plan a tour over the summer and stay home the rest of the year."

"Where's home?" She knew he had lived in Auburn until recently, and his parents lived in Opelika.

"Home is wherever we find a place."

"We?" Her heart pounded.

"Well, I mean, me… somewhere close to you. That is until you're ready for it to be *we*."

She blushed and smiled. "But why only tour in the summer?"

"I found this great art program I thought you might be interested in. And there's a grant you would qualify for." He pulled a folded flyer from his pocket and passed it to her.

When her fingers touched it, a spark of light flashed on the paper. Had it been the setting sun catching the gloss on the brochure?

"I can write from anywhere, and you can go to art school." He winked. "We can live anywhere you want, so pick the best art school in the country."

"What about my parents? And Liv?"

"We can always come back for visits or come back and live here after you finish. I want you to have every chance to succeed as an artist."

Wren gazed at Jim. A tiny star, bright and beckoning reflected in the rich brown of his eyes. A glimmer of that one true Source.

EPILOGUE

Eight years later…

Wren had been planning for weeks. Why did five seem like such an important birthday? Jim wanted pony rides for Maria Wren Fielding's fifth birthday. They lived on a few acres outside of Fairhope, so they had plenty of space at the house.

Spoiled much? That little girl loved her Daddy for good reason.

Maria had invited nine friends, kids from church, and her preschool, which meant their families as well. Wren made sandwich squares and a deli tray for the adults and ordered a cake for the kids. She had looked forward to it as much as Maria.

"Hey, Wren," Liv waved, holding Cadence, her toddler son, as Heather, her eight-year-old, ran ahead, yelling for Maria.

Cade followed close behind with the cake Wren had ordered. They'd picked it up from the bakery on the way from Liv's mom's house.

Cade and Liv had met up again at a fundraiser during the years Jim and Wren were touring. Liv's mom used to keep Heather from time to time so Liv could help them raise money and awareness by singing at their fundraisers. And it gave her an outlet she needed.

Cade had never gotten over Liv. Whenever they had an event in Alabama at which Liv sang, he always showed up. They started talking on the phone a lot. He drove over from Mobile and attended church with Liv, her mother and her daughter. At the age of five, Heather couldn't contain her excitement when she got to be the flower girl at their wedding.

Liv and Cade had a son not long after the wedding. Cadence was three now, and Cade loved both kids like crazy.

Wren and Jim weren't far behind. Their Maria was already five years old. Where had the time gone? And Anthony would be two on his next birthday. Unreal.

"We got here a little early, so I could tell you our news first," Liv said, clasping Wren's hand in both of hers.

"What news?" Wren wouldn't mind if they had another baby.

"Cade got a job in Breckenridge, Colorado, so we'll be moving." Wren saw excitement and sadness on Liv's face, and she felt both with her.

She threw her arms around Liv and squeezed. "You'll love the mountains, Liv." A mental picture of Liv in the mountains holding a baby flashed in Wren's mind. Maybe Liv and Cade would have another baby. "I'm going to miss you so much."

"Promise y'all will come visit," Liv said. "We'll make sure we have a place with at least one guestroom just for you."

"We will."

"Hello. Are we too early?" Samantha called out. She and Bae clasped hands as they came from around the house into the backyard.

"No, come on in," Jim called back, then gave Bae a hug. "Just family here so far, so you'll fit right in." He flashed one of those welcoming smiles, and Wren thought he had a lot in common with her old teacher. She smiled.

"Hey, Samantha." Wren hugged her friend. "How's the writing coming?"

"I just finished a new story." Samantha's green eyes sparked as her Irish-red hair fluttered in the breeze. "Between visits from Aisling and our sweet grandson, and marketing, it was quite a feat."

"I can't imagine." Wren shook her head. "Art is more immediate. I'm not sure I have the patience for a novel."

"Speaking of art," Bae winked at his wife. "We brought you something."

"I'm not the birthday girl," Wren said, glancing over at the girls running around the circle of ponies who'd been tied to a single post. She hoped the kids didn't get too close, but the owner who brought the ponies stood nearby.

"It's not a birthday present, just some news," Samantha said without giving away the surprise.

"I've nominated three of your paintings for the Creativity for Social Change Award," Bae said, a burst of energy nearly lifting him from the ground.

"Oh, my gosh." Could it be real? Wren had been admiring those award winners for years. "Do you think I have a shot?"

"Of course." Bae's face held complete confidence. "Your art has made a difference to more victims-turned-survivors than you'll ever know in this life. Not to mention the lives of those who experienced the trauma with you."

"Are you still in touch with them?" Samantha asked.

"Of course." Their friendships motivated Wren to push ahead to greater greatness every time she thought of them.

"You'd be a shoo-in!" Momma picked up Anthony and took a few steps closer to their little gathering.

"Thank you, Momma."

"My princess, an award-winning artist," Daddy added, not far behind her.

"Let's not get ahead of things," Wren said.

"Are the others from Haven House doing well, Wren?" Samantha asked. She'd mailed Christmas presents to the residents there every year since Liv and Wren had lived there.

"Yes," Wren could happily report. "You know Liv, so I don't have to tell you how well she's doing." Wren turned to glance at her friend frolicking with the kids in the yard. "Mei is an engineer, like she always dreamed. She lives with her husband and her mother, who now has full citizen status in the U.S."

"That's wonderful. And what about DeeAnn and Amy? I always pray for them." How many survivors owed their success to Samantha's prayers? The woman inspired Wren.

"DeeAnn has grown such a tender heart. She's working with the elderly now and loves it. Amy. It took Amy a while to finish high school, then college. She told me that she loved studying. Now she's in veterinarian school." Wren paused, remembering. "I always pictured her with small cuddly animals."

"That's wonderful."

"Wasn't there a boy with you?" Bae asked. "Do you hear from him?"

She smiled. She'd just received an email from Damiano. "Yes. I just got a note from him. He's doing well too. You know he's married to a sweet lady and has twin girls. He manages a department store and in his free time, volunteers at an inner-city boys after-school program. He hopes to keep others from the kind of abuse he suffered." Wren thought about the staff at Haven House. "Oh, and I still exchange Christmas cards with Rita, Ms. Brenda, Mama Shell and Mrs. Sherman. I go up to Haven House a couple of times a year to meet the girls and give a talk about art and journaling during healing."

"It's just wonderful, Wren. Really," Samantha choked up a little.

Wren took a deep breath, looking over their yard full of friends and family.

Light always dispels darkness.

She saw it clearly now.

Jesus sent his light when Wren needed it most. She'd learned to trust God's strength when she was weak, and like a wren, she'd always take care of her flock, which included anyone in need around her.

She squinted up at the sky—sun on her face, and light in her heart. Darkness had not been able to steal the light from their lives.

Light shines the brightest in the shadow side of life.

AFTERWORD

The Shadow Side is a fictional story. None of the characters or plot is based on a specific real-life person or story.

That said, I did a lot of reading and listening to firsthand accounts of trafficking survivors. I talked with people who work in nonprofits that help survivors, and a former police officer who now works with the victims during court appearances. I also spoke with an FBI agent who has been part of these task forces.

My overall impression is that being kidnapped at a modeling audition is not common. By far, the majority of victims enter the trade when a family member, or some other person they trust, gets them involved.

Another common scenario is with people hoping to immigrate to the US. They get stuck in trafficking situations when they ask for help to get to the US, then are expected to work for the one who helped them. Because of a lack of support system and poor language skills, they can be easily manipulated and led to believe that if they go to authorities for help, they will be deported, which, for some, is a fate worse than working as a sex-slave.

The Haven House is a fictional representation of a real place, which I discovered through our family's charitable trust, *H. G. Clay Foundation*. We had the privilege of learning about and supporting *Camille Place* as it was being built. Their director is full of knowledge about, and passion for, this ministry. Last time we spoke, a boys' home was being built and set to open in the first quarter of 2026. This will be the first place of its kind for boys in the nation. According to the UNODC's Global Report on Trafficking in Persons, released in January 2023, males account for 40 percent of all identified victims of human trafficking.

RESOURCES

Camille Place (the real Haven House), also **Samuel's Place** (for boys, coming in 2026)
>Corporate Office 251-302-2022; info@camilleplace.com
>For emergency placements, contact director@camilleplace.com

U.S. National Human Trafficking Hotline: 1-888-373-7888.
>**Global Human Trafficking Hotline**: 1-844-888-FREE (3733)
>**National Center for Missing and Exploited Children Cyber Tip Line**: https://www.missingkids.org/gethelpnow/cybertipline

988 Suicide & Crisis Lifeline: Call 988

Jim's notes for speaking engagements: Although Jim is a fictional character, the points he makes in his lectures could be helpful to someone facing circumstances like those Wren and Liv face. Following are Jim's lecture notes. (The following notes were gleaned using ChatGPT)

Prevention: Avoid Being Trafficked

1. Be skeptical of opportunities that seem "too good to be true." Offers to make a lot of money with little effort. If you need love, success, money, provision, or need to escape the situation you're in now, you could be targeted.

2. Always tell a trusted adult where you're going. Don't go to interviews, parties, or travel with people you don't know well.

3. Be careful about what you share online. Traffickers scan social media for vulnerable people. Avoid posting

about loneliness, running away, or financial desperation. Set profiles to private and don't accept friend requests from strangers.

4. <u>Signs of grooming</u>:

-Showering you with attention, gifts, or affection too quickly

-Then trying to isolate you

-Asking for secrecy

5. <u>Trust your gut</u>. If something feels off, even if you can't explain it, leave. Your intuition is a survival tool. Don't worry about being rude or overreacting.

Jim wished to heaven that Stacy had known about these tips before she was taken.

If Being Trafficked: Protect Your Mind

1. <u>Remember who you are</u>. Traffickers try to erase your identity and self-worth.

-Hold on to your memories—your family, friends, dreams, faith.

-Silently repeat truths to yourself: "This is not my fault. I am still me."

-Be positive: "I will get out."

2. <u>Don't believe the lies</u>. Traffickers often say things like, "No one's looking for you," "You're worthless," or "This is your choice." These are manipulations, not facts. Remind yourself that they are liars.

3. <u>Force yourself to be aware</u>. Notice patterns:

-Start mentally tracking locations, routines, names, accents, or schedules.

-Even minor details can help you escape or aid police later.

4. <u>Keep your mind active</u>.

-Count things.

-Make mental maps.

-Recite favorite books or prayers.

-Draw images in your head.

-Do anything that strengthens your mind and builds resistance.

5. <u>Watch for small windows of escape</u>. Traffickers try to convince victims there's no way out.

-Keep your mind from accepting this.

-Stay alert and aware.

-Wait until the right moment. It might be best to pretend to be weaker than you are, either mentally, physically or both, so they're not concerned about you trying to escape.

-Waiting for the best time is not weakness.

-Staying mentally ready is survival.

OTHER RESOURCES USED

Creativity for Social Change Award - https://www.creativityforsocialchangeaward.org Learn about this award and/or nominate someone to receive it here.

Information on **E. O. Wilson**: **https://en.wikipedia.org/wiki/E. O. Wilson**

Movie: **Blind Eye Artist,** the story of Justin Wadlington - https://blindeyeartist.com

Poem: ***"Holding Hands,"*** by Lenore M. Link (partial poem used)

Song: **"Come to me," by Wendell Kimbrough -** https://youtu.be/uEzY-nvwtig?si=KjAn9ViYun4jM15K

ACKNOWLEDGEMENTS

To Jesus, light of my life, my comforter and guide—my true life Sorchae. Thank you.

Thank you, Dan Thompson, for encouraging me to write, for reading women's fiction when you don't have to, and for loving me all these years.

Thank you, Larkin Peters and Nancy Raia, for your expert advice in areas related to art. My art is writing; I know very little about drawing, shading, or painting. You gave me a glimpse into that world and I'm thankful. And Nancy, I'm so grateful for the brilliant line you contributed: "You only need one eye if your whole soul sees the world." ~Spoken by Bae to Wren.

Many thanks to you, Emmanuel Sealls, for taking the time to meet with me, more than once, and answering my emails and texts. Your work is important, and I appreciate all you do for our community. (Former special victims detective, police trainer, member of Baldwin County Critical Incident Stress Management Team, mental health and first aid instructor for state and federal agencies, Field Force Operation coordinator and instructor for local and state agencies. Currently: Baldwin County Juvenile court-appointed multi-systemic mental health therapist, and Christian counselor).

Thanks also to the super FBI agent who talked with me, helped me get a feel for what you guys do, and gave me feedback on the scenes that involved FBI and CIA. I am thankful for the work you do and have done for victims. You're not anonymous to me.

Thank you, Chris Ziebach, and all your staff at *Camille Place*—the real-life Haven House—for your prayers and hard work on behalf of minors in the sex trade. You help victims become survivors and thrive. I can't express my gratitude for all you do. Y'all are superheroes! And thank you for seeing the need for a place like this for male victims, and for working to open *Samuel's Place* very soon—the first like it in the country!

Thanks to *Write Minds*, my local writers group, for the accountability, encouragement, friendship, and tea that it takes to pull something like this off.

Thank you, Lauren Whiteurst, my crazy, hippie, workout, health-nut, brainstorming buddy. Without you, I'd be fat, hunched back, and stiff from sitting at a computer all day without exercise. Thanks for challenging me to be strong in body, mind, and spirit.

Thank you to the new Alabama chapter of *American Christian Fiction Writers*. I'm so happy you're here.

Many, many thanks to my beta readers: Mollie Bond, Bruce Russell, Kai Young, Lauren Whiteurst, Linda Tyler, and Anna Rose. Y'all endured reading this manuscript when it looked much worse than it does now. Thank you for your honest feedback. You'll never know how important that is.

Special thanks to Megan Schaulis, developmental editor extraordinaire! I'm so grateful for your encouragement as well as helpful suggestions to improve this novel.

Thank you, Cynthia Hickey, *Take Me Away Books*, and *Winged Publications* for cover development and publishing of the *Nonprofit Series,* including book two: *The Shadow Side*. Also, thanks to Alice Shepherd with *Winged Publications* for doing the final edit.

Last, but certainly not least, I am so thankful to the staff and volunteers who work long hours helping people in need through nonprofit organizations all over the world. May the Lord protect and provide for each of you and your organizations. And thanks to the *H. G. Clay Foundation* for introducing me to some of them.